D1516883

THE BARROWFIELDS

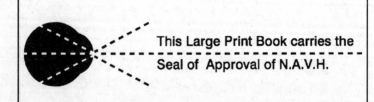

This Large Print Book carries the
Seal of Approval of N.A.V.H.

THE BARROWFIELDS

PHILLIP LEWIS

THORNDIKE PRESS
A part of Gale, Cengage Learning

GALE
CENGAGE Learning·

Farmington Hills, Mich • San Francisco • New York • Waterville, Maine
Meriden, Conn • Mason, Ohio • Chicago

GALE
CENGAGE Learning®

Copyright © 2017 by Phillip Lewis.
Grateful acknowledgement is made to McIntosh & Otis, Inc. for permission to reprint an excerpt from *You Can't Go Home Again*, copyright © 1940 by Thomas Wolfe, copyright renewed 1968 by Paul Gatlin, C.T.A., administrator of the Estate of Thomas Wolfe. All rights reserved. Reprinted by permission of McIntosh & Otis.

Thorndike Press, a part of Gale, Cengage Learning.

ALL RIGHTS RESERVED
This is a work of fiction. Names, characters, places, and incidents either are the product of the author's imagination or used fictitiously. Any resemblance to actual persons, living or dead, events, or locales is entirely coincidental.

Thorndike Press® Large Print Bill's Bookshelf.
The text of this Large Print edition is unabridged.
Other aspects of the book may vary from the original edition.
Set in 16 pt. Plantin.

LIBRARY OF CONGRESS CATALOGING-IN-PUBLICATION DATA

Names: Lewis, Phillip (Phillip E.), author.
Title: The Barrowfields / by Phillip Lewis.
Description: Large print edition. | Waterville, Maine : Thorndike Press, a part of Gale, Cengage Learning, 2017. | Series: Thorndike Press large print Bill's bookshelf
Identifiers: LCCN 2017009859| ISBN 9781410499271 (hardcover) | ISBN 1410499278 (hardcover)
Subjects: LCSH: Fathers and sons—Fiction. | Fathers—Death—Fiction. | Homecoming—Fiction. | North Carolina—Fiction. | Appalachian Mountains—Fiction. | Psychological fiction. | Large type books. | GSAFD: Bildungsromans.
Classification: LCC PS3612.E976 B37 2017b | DDC 813/.6—dc23
LC record available at https://lccn.loc.gov/2017009859

Published in 2017 by arrangement with Hogarth, an imprint of Crown Publishing Group, a division of Penguin Random House, LLC

Printed in the United States of America
1 2 3 4 5 6 7 21 20 19 18 17

FOR ASHLEY

O brothers, like our fathers in their time, we are burning, burning, burning in the night.

— Thomas Wolfe
You Can't Go Home Again

PROLOGUE

The desk is the same as he left it. The raven or whatever it is on the wall. Wolfe. Poe. Chopin. A first-edition copy of *The Stranger*, price-clipped, chipped, and cocked. A signed first edition of *Look Homeward, Angel* that he prized more than any other book. A first edition of *Tales of Mystery and Imagination* signed by Harry Clarke in blood-red ink. A Bible, King James, black leather cover. Three candles; copious spent wax. A bottle of Hill's Absinth, empty. Two bottles of vodka, empty. A bottle of Spanish wine, also empty. A book of matches. A lamp, no bulb. Fifty-one journals, handwritten. The title page of an unpublished novel with an annotation in Latin. Nine years of collected dust and a handful of pictures that must have meant something to him. I open *The Stranger* to read the inscription in my own hand. I turn the page and see the first

line of the book: "Mother died today." I am
beginning to understand.

■ ■ ■ ■

PART I

■ ■ ■ ■

1

My father was one of only two children born in Old Buckram's cinderblock hospital in the cold and bitter autumn of 1939. The other child, a young boy who didn't live long enough to get a name or a soul to be saved, was buried by his mother on a hillside near town when the ground warmed enough to dig him a proper grave. There was no service and no one sang any hymns. The boy's headstone, if you could call it that, was a large smooth rock from the creek. He was laid to rest with only his mother's voiceless prayer to an absent God. She asked that he be forgiven the original sin and kindly allowed into heaven to await the others when, in the Lord's wisdom, their day should come.

Old Buckram, where this story begins, is an achromatic town high in the belly of the Appalachian Mountains. It's situated uneasily about as far north and west as you can go and still be inside the surveyed boundaries of North Carolina. In 1799 the population there was 125, and by 1939 this number had swelled to 400. It's a town where the streets and sidewalks are lonely and seldom traveled. Where the few paltry shops — an aging hardware store, a feed store, a cobbler, a discount clothier, a café, and a headstone maker — scarcely see enough business for a living and close early in the dark days of winter before the snow falls. It's an old railroad town, but the train hasn't gone there in years. It's a town with one-room red-brick churches on the hillsides and in the hollows, a town that believes in a God living but remote, and a town with one funeral home that buries almost all the dead. It's a town of ghosts and superstitions. It has the Devil's Stairs and Serpent's Tongue Rock and Abbadon Creek, which carried an entire family into oblivion in the flood of 1916. Up behind the creek at the edge of town lay the Barrowfields, where by some mystery nothing of natural origin will grow except a creeping gray moss which climbs over mounds of rock and petrified stumps that the more credulous locals believe are grave markers from an age before time. Others say a great wind-blow came up over the mountains a thousand years ago and ripped out the trees and carried away all the goodness in the soil so that nothing could ever grow there again. Nearly everyone thinks it's haunted ground. There's never been a picnic on the Barrowfields, of that you can be sure.

If anyone ever knew how my father's family found themselves there, in Old Buckram, their stories have long since been silenced by many steady turns of the imperturbable clock and no record of that enigmatic journey has been left behind. My grandfather, whose given name was Helton, told me once that the family might have migrated there from the far north sometime in the 1700s, down the Great Wagon Road that ran from Pennsylvania to the North Carolina Piedmont. He said our ancestors were probably some of the first settlers on this rugged and unforgiving land. "Goes to show," he told me, "that my and your daddy's folks were none too smart."

The family was damn poor, impossibly poor, like almost everyone else in the mountains, but over time through hard work and determination they managed to cultivate a fairly dignified existence. The children were well cared for even if food and clothes were hard to come by. Helton was a laborer who would take whatever work there was and do it honestly and diligently without complaint except for whatever he might have said to God on Sunday mornings during prayer. He worked for several years on the Blue Ridge Parkway as a dynamiter for the WPA and after some time had lost his hearing in one ear and was immune to most conversation that was conducted in his presence. He became somewhat like an old dog that sits quietly in the corner of the room, oblivious to all the goings-on around him.

I know of nothing extraordinary that he did in his life, except that he worked five days a week and remained married to my grandmother, Madeline, despite uncountable bitter winters and unrelenting poverty. He accumulated no money and no property of consequence. On the date of his death, he owned nothing of real value other than a middling farmhouse that leaned when the wind blew and a plot of fit-for-nothing land he'd purchased at auction for five dollars an acre. The only book he ever owned or read was the Holy Bible, which came to me when he passed away. On the first blank page of parchment, there is a note from his father — my great-grandfather, William — that says in barely legible scrawl: "Read this Bible and govern yourself accordingly." The next page contains a faded reproduction of

Christ in the garden of Gethsemane by Heinrich Hofmann. My grandfather signed the Bible and over time wrote into its pages several annotations of unknown provenance, the first of which appears at the beginning of the Book of Genesis. It reads simply "4004 B.C." For him, this is when time began.

Despite living in Old Buckram his entire life, my grandfather appeared in the local newspaper only once. Against his better judgment, he ran for office after being encouraged to do so by the pastor of his church, who regarded Helton as a quiet man with common sense and decency. Confusingly, after a brief political campaign during a frigid autumn, he wound up with only two votes out of the twenty-five that were cast. The newspaper reported only a sentence:

T. VANHOY OF VELLUM'S CASKE DEFEATED H. L. ASTER FOR THE OPEN SEAT OF COUNTY COMMISSIONER BY A WIDE MARGIN.

Knowing that he'd voted for himself, he'd only say later that it made him trust both his wife and his preacher a good deal less.

The next day, before he went into town, he took great pains to clean and ready his gun — a fact that was observed with silent concern by everyone in the family. To hear Maddy tell it, he stood from the table and inserted the pistol with significant gravity of movement into his belt. At long last, she said, "Helton, where in tarnation are you going with that gun?" He said, "I figure a man that's got no more friends than I do would be wise to protect himself." Whereupon he closed the door behind him and walked the long road into town. He never ran for another office, and no one ever suggested to him that he should.

As a boy I used to ride with my grandfather in his rusted Ford pickup truck to the Buckram Abattoir north of town some days after school and on some weekends. On the main level, the store sold bacon, sausage, vegetables, and various other subsistence items. Out behind the store was a large cement slab with four crudely cut channels running to a black drain. On the sign in the front was a black-and-white hog.

At the Buckram Abattoir, everybody knew everybody. My grandfather and I went in one Friday afternoon to buy milk, and a giant man in overalls approached my grandfather and slapped him on the back.

He said, "Helton, what do you know?"

My grandfather said, "What do *I* know?

Hell, I don't even *suspect* anything."

The man in the overalls smiled and winked at me kindly. Outside, men with no work to do sat on benches for hours and told jokes and picked at their teeth with toothpicks and watched people come and go. Inside, men idled on straight-backed chairs with seats of woven hickory slats and leaned openmouthed over checkerboards, lifting their heads occasionally to look around or spit. They poured plastic sleeves of peanuts into bottles of Coke and drank them, and talked about the weather and how things were changing so fast, even though they weren't. Rows of red and yellow tomatoes with bulging excrescences sat on a display next to wicker baskets of green beans needing to be snapped, and potatoes caked in dusty brown earth rested in paper bags borrowed from the town's grocery store. An antique drink machine with glass bottles of soda you'd pull out horizontally hummed in the corner. The uneven wooden floor creaked as people walked up and down the aisles.

A black man nobody knew came in to pay for a gallon of gas. A quiet came in with him, and left when he left. When he was out the door and headed up the street, one or two old men shook their thick-jowled heads

19

in disbelief. There were few black families in Old Buckram, and with rare exception they lived together in one linear and well-kept neighborhood behind the car lot in town. It was a common, unseemly joke among locals that there were exactly one hundred black people in the whole county — no more, no less. With a lopsided grin, they'd look askance and say that if one more came into town, another one would be politely asked to leave. This usually produced some knee-slapping and guffawing, and pearls of slick mucous getting dislodged from old throats long coated with the fuliginous stains of cigarette tar.

Less than a thousand people, whites and blacks, lived in the town limits during my years there. Nearly everyone else lived in the hills beyond, on dirt and gravel roads that wound endlessly back into the mountains until finally dwindling into nothing. People on these old roads lived in rusted single-wide trailers with slick tires on top to guard against high mountain winds, or in small wooden shacks with wood-burning stoves and asbestos roofing shingles that just barely kept out the rain. Lots of families lived in hollows that would run up a hillside off the public road. In the hollow there'd be a creek, an old house, a few leaning, dilapidated barns where things of no value were stored, and trash.

My grandfather and I left the Buckram Abattoir and headed back into town and then, leaving again, drove out Larvatis Road all the way to his and Maddy's house. Maddy was outside hanging clothes on a line in an increasing wind.

"Y'all are just in time for dinner," she said. "I was fixin' to eat without you."

"You wouldn't have done that," said my grandfather. The heavy truck door, rusted in the hinges, complained loudly as he opened it and shut it again.

"I would have, too," Maddy said. She gave me a suffocating hug in the folds of her apron. "Oh, I have a surprise for you!"

"You do?"

"I sure do. Let's get in out of this wind. It's gettin' cold out here and you don't have a coat on."

"It was warm earlier," I said. An unusually mild October was quickly moving on toward winter. A kaleidoscope of leaves lay in the tall yellowing grass of the yard.

"Son, in the mountains, it *always* gets cold when the sun goes down. It don't matter whether it's spring, summer, or fall. I know your daddy knows that, too." Maddy always had wisdom for the weather and the seasons. She could tell you better than any meteorologist if it was going to rain or snow, and she knew it before anyone when the winter was going to be especially hard. I don't know how she knew, but she always did.

Helton and Maddy lived at the end of a dirt road about four miles out from town in a sharp-cut valley hidden from the sun. A stream ran down the mountainside behind the house and followed a deep weedy gulch all the way out to the highway where there was a one-lane bridge made out of cut logs. A weeping willow drank from the stream, and in its shadow Maddy had put a wooden bench that no one ever sat on. A crab-apple tree stood in the side yard opposite, and rotted apples lay shriveled in piles on the ground beneath it. Inside, there was a wood-stove in the kitchen and another one occupied a corner of the living room. When both stoves were going, you almost couldn't stand to be in there. On cold winter days Maddy would get up early and start them roaring and this would drive my grandfather out of bed. He'd go around opening windows and get scolded for it. "You're letting all my heat out," she'd say. And he'd say, "I'm just trying to keep everything in here from melting."

Maddy made cider with the crab apples she picked up out of the yard. She cooked it on the stove in the kitchen where it would simmer and steam all day long. I could smell it as soon as I got out of the truck. We went in and Maddy poured me a mug to warm me up.

In high school Maddy was a fair student who joined the few clubs that were offered, but otherwise she had an unremarkable academic career. She didn't go to college, so after high school she got a job working as an assistant to the minister at one of Old Buckram's few Baptist churches and kept the job for almost her entire life through more preachers than you could count.

When she wasn't working, she liked to sit quietly and paint ceramics. She'd filled the entire back porch of the house with porcelain coffee cups, pumpkins, plates, and jars that she had decorated and proudly signed with her initials. She had all kinds of odd, worthless trinkets. There was a fossil of a flower in a wedge of limestone that she'd bought for fifty cents at a street market in Ohio. It sat on the windowsill year after year. It was brown and the petals of the flower had become invisible with time, but of this curiosity she was mighty proud.

She'd pick it up, look at it, and put it back down.

She liked to cook but by most sources was not as good at it as you might think. My grandfather used to say it wasn't natural to her. Her mainstays were the cider and a nearly inedible cornbread reminiscent of masonry that had to be dissolved in milk to be eaten. After she got sick and couldn't work anymore, their finances dwindled, and it was rare that they could afford a meal out of the house. They acquired no luxuries in their lifetimes and they expected none. They only spent what limited money they earned on what they truly needed. They learned to get by and be content with very little.

I sat holding the cider to warm my hands and Maddy stood in the doorway of the kitchen smoking a cigarette. She cracked the door and blew the smoke outside, but the wind brought it right back in again. She coughed until my grandfather took the cigarette from her and helped her into a chair.

"I'm sorry, honey," she said to me. "How's the cider? Is it good?"

"It's good," I said, but it wasn't. It was horribly tart. It drew my eyes in together so much I thought they would touch.

"Do you notice anything different about it?"

I did not, but I didn't say so.

"I put cinnamon in it this time as a special treat." This was my surprise.

"It's delicious," I said.

"Well, drink it before you have to go home."

"I will. Are you taking me home?"

My grandfather sometimes took me, but Maddy never would.

"No, sir," she said. "I've been there one time and that was enough. That house reminds me of a mean old *vulture* just sitting up on the side of that mountain." I had heard this sentiment before.

"That's where I live," I protested.

"I know it is, and better you than me," said Maddy.

My grandfather put his large hands over my ears. I looked up at him and thought his head might touch the ceiling. Maddy got up and threw another piece of wood into the stove, and I sat there stinging from her words and drinking my awful cider that now tasted even worse.

"It wouldn't burn so fast if you didn't get the stove so hot," said my grandfather.

"It's freezing cold in here," said Maddy.

"Do you want to put on your coat? I'll get it."

"So now I have to wear a coat in my own

house? I think not." Maddy smiled at me. Her hair, a mixture of gray and black, was held back on the sides by an array of bobby pins. She put on a smear of orange lipstick to replace what she had left on her last cigarette. "If you keep this up," said Helton, pointing to the stove, "there won't be a tree left in any forest in America."

Maddy took out her checkbook and did some figuring. She sat at the small square table in the kitchen where they ate all their meals. The vinyl tablecloth stuck to her elbows and cracked when she lifted them. About ninety percent of the counter space in the kitchen was covered in jars and containers of one sort or another. A clock on the wall showed the same time it had on my last four visits there. I watched it to see if it would move, but it didn't.

"Helton, did you hear that little Ola Hamilton is sick?" Viola Hamilton was, at fifty-two, a young widow whose husband had been killed when a row-crop tractor he was driving rolled over on him several years prior. She hadn't remarried and it was unusual to see her in town anymore.

"No, I sure didn't. What's happened?"

"She can't get out of bed, for one. They say she's got arthritis real bad, and her joints are in flames. It may be time to send

26

in the Balm Squad." This is what they called the group of elderly church ladies who would descend on a sick person's home like a muster of peacocks, carrying food and bread and more pies than one person could eat in a lifetime. A splinter group, the Psalm Squad, would be brought in later if the patient was also ailing in the ways of the Lord.

"Can you take her something for me?"

"I sure will," said Helton.

My grandparents were good, kind people. They picked at each other like folks will do, but they loved each other dearly. And despite a lack of hanging diplomas, they were plenty smart. You'd never catch either one reading for pleasure, but they were clever in the way that all mountain people are, which comes from learning how to survive unending winters of ice and falling snow, and wind that could take the roof off your house. They started having children as soon as they were married and didn't stop until they'd had five and knew beyond any doubt that a sixth one would starve. With one part self-sacrifice and several parts plain good fortune, they managed to rear all of the children, with some fits and starts, into adulthood. The youngest of the children was my father.

2

It was common for children of families in Old Buckram to start school but not finish it, and not surprisingly none of my father's predecessors in lineage had received much voluntary education beyond high school. I recall once naively asking my grandfather if he'd been to college. He replied wryly, "No, son, but I've been *by* a few colleges. I didn't stop, though." And indeed I'm sad to report that until my father was born, not one person in my family on that side could be accused of anything approaching real intellectual curiosity. This meant that my father's older brother and sisters did not aspire to attend college, and if they did, this aspiration lay dormant and was not acted upon. If there were things they wished to know, you couldn't tell it from outward appearances.

Yet my father, among all these children, was different. Completely and bafflingly different. This became apparent early in his life. In a family for which proficiency in reading was deemed a bare necessity and not by any means a virtue, he learned to read almost without tutelage. He was always with a book, even before he knew what he was supposed to do with it. People'd say, "That boy *always* has a book with him," or "Where'd he get that?" He spoke in complete sentences with advanced grammar despite growing up in the midst of a casual mountain dialect. No one knew where this strange ability had come from and guests of the family would measure his head for normality and marvel at the boy as if he were a singing frog. His aunt George (long story) explained the mystery by saying with conviction to anyone who would listen that he was the reincarnated Mark Twain — even though they looked nothing whatever alike.

In his elementary-school years he wasn't well accepted by the boys his age, and many were the days he'd come running home down the dirt road in the cool heat of the mountain summer to thrust his sobbing head into Maddy's waiting lap. She'd take him into the living room and they'd sit for a while, him on the couch next to her, a cigarette in her left hand, a book in his, the two of them planted there like two stone golems in the colorless light of a Saturday morning, the sound of the creek and all the morning birds coming through the open windows from the outside. "There's nothing in the world wrong with you," she'd tell him, his eyes wide and impressionable. "Henry, if you'd rather read, you just keep right on doing what you're doing. Don't you let anybody tell you not to."

In truth, the whole idea of his exceptional literacy was an affront to her common sense, and it gave her no end of trouble. If she were honest with herself, she'd say he was wasting his time — he should've been outside with the other boys — and that he was going to be cross-eyed before he reached adulthood. Each time she'd reluctantly give him an assurance that all that reading he was doing was just fine, it went right up against her better judgment and was like a hot smack to her forehead. So after comforting him thusly and holding it in as long as she could stand, invariably she'd be unable to resist appending this indelicate caveat (or one similar): "But if you keep it up, at some point there ain't gonna be nothing left for you to read. As long as you know that."

By the time this precocious child was eight years old, he'd become sufficiently self-aware to surmise that he'd been born into a caste of lower dignity than he thought was fit for himself. While there was never a haughtiness or condescension to his demeanor, he always believed to his fretting core that he would transcend his given lot in life and rise above his rank. And so in time he became an outsider, and would remain so, as are all great men and women of their day among their contemporaries.

He devoured every book he could find. The family had no money to buy books, so he spent hours at the county library, one time even staying so late that he got locked in there overnight. By midnight, every person in town was looking for him. Some mused darkly that even though he was only a boy of twelve, he'd likely just "outgrown" Old Buckram and run off to a big, bustling city — maybe Charlotte or even Raleigh. Raccoon-like and strangely ebullient, he reappeared at home early the next morning carrying a hardback book no one in the household had ever seen and recalled his nocturnal literary adventure to an astonished family. By some odd chance, he said, a Thomas Wolfe novel in the "to be discarded" pile had caught his eye and he'd stayed up all night reading it by the light of a street lamp. Leaving them all speechless, he then went in and went to bed and didn't get up until it was time for dinner. It wasn't long after that that he got his first pair of glasses.

A year later his library privileges were permanently revoked when it was discovered that he had, over the course of several months, removed more than a hundred books from the school library's repository of reading material. The heist was revealed when Maddy went in one day to change his sheets and nearly fractured her left foot on the spine of *Brideshead Revisited.* She threw back the bedclothes at once and discovered his literary plunder. The books were stacked in neat, alphabetical rows under the bed he shared with his brother, who had said nothing of the enterprise. And he had done all this without raising a modicum of suspicion from anyone, including the waspish librarian, Mrs. Tichborne, who preferred that no one check out books in the first place. An interrogation followed in the school's tiny detention room, where a large wooden paddle, pockmarked with holes, hung ominously on the wall.

"What were you going to do with all those books?" asked Bent Smeth, the school principal, who had threatened to expel the chronically bibliophilic boy. Mr. Smeth was tall and thin, like a young birch tree, but he had an awful curvature to his spine that made him half as tall as he might have been otherwise. As a boy he'd been scalded with boiling water from a kettle that held the family's clothes he'd been assigned to wash (a wooden leg of the pot rotted and gave out), so he was spotted like a cow and part of his face was sallow and one half of his mouth was turned down, giving him a look of permanent and aggravated dyspepsia. Mr. Smeth was conducting the examination. Mrs. Tichborne, who by all reports was blind as a cave fish from staring so many years at Melvil Dewey's damnable taxonomic invention, stood anxiously at Mr. Smeth's shoulder. She had a long history of discouraging students from reading, particularly with respect to books of more prurient interest, like fiction, and had it been up to her she would have summoned the State Bureau of Investigation and asked them to issue warrants. Unable to control herself any longer, she demanded to know what he was going to do with her books under his bed, and the very question implied an indecency about the whole affair.

"I planned to read them," said my father, who'd been positioned in a fraying caneback chair in the middle of the room with his inquisitors circling like a couple of buzzards. "In fact, I've already read most of them." He began to explicate a detailed and heretofore unformulated hypothesis about the human mind's psychological readiness to read a given book at a given moment, and how important, nay, critical, it was to have the book one wanted to read at the absolute ready when the inspiration struck. The gist was that when you decide you want to read something, you want it handy so you can dive right in. His argument was not persuasive.

"He was just gonna read 'em." Helton came to his son's defense, and just in time. "It's not like he was gonna sell 'em. Not exactly a market up here for books, you'll admit. You can't punish the boy for wantin' to read."

"Yes, that's true," said Mr. Smeth, "but he could of read them just the same by checking them out *one at a time.*"

"Well," said my grandfather, "I can't argue with you about that."

"I didn't steal them," said my father. "I planned to return each and every one. And I have returned them, as you well know, and they're all accounted for. It's fair to say I took a rather liberal construction of the library's checkout policy, but that does not constitute larceny in the state of North Carolina."

Later, after finding it in his heart to grant clemency for the infraction, Mr. Smeth said to my grandfather, "That boy is *awful* queer — you know that."

"Oh, do we know it."

At age fourteen my father wrote a few short plays but kept them to himself. Everybody began to notice him in class, writing all the time. In study hall, he was writing. After the bell rang, he sat at his desk and wrote more. When he was sixteen he got a job at the town newspaper, the *Old Buckram Echo,* first delivering papers by bicycle and then quickly moving up to writing copy. In a matter of months he was the de facto editor in chief. He wrote nine out of every ten articles, brought in a syndicated crossword puzzle, reformatted the front page, and changed the name of the paper to the *Old Buckram Meteor,* which was met with some resistance among the locals. The year was 1955. Tennessee Williams had just won the Pulitzer Prize for *Cat on a Hot Tin Roof* and Nabokov had published *Lolita* in Paris. It was the year of Claudette Colvin and Rosa Parks. It was a time of change everywhere in the world except Old Buckram, which plodded heedlessly along with its one-lane roads and unoccupied front porches, with nobody taking much notice of the affairs of the wide world beyond — except for my father, who singularly burned for escape.

The owner of the paper sent him to a journalists' conference in Charlottesville, Virginia, and this was the first time he'd ever been out of the state. He became enamored with the university there, and its book collection was unlike anything he had ever imagined. Like-minded people, the first he'd met, engaged him and embraced him without the weary sidelong and dubious glances he'd grown accustomed to in Old Buckram. It's a wonder he ever came home.

By this time he was handsome as hell, with black hair pushed back over a high forehead and the physique of a long-distance runner. He had been gifted with a strong, lean body and an assured gait that suggested purpose and confidence. He had a broad but self-conscious smile that contracted around two pronounced eyeteeth, which, in the right light, made him look unsettlingly vampiric. He kept these hidden most of the time. Looking at the few photographs of him from that year, he had the aura of a veritable time traveler, standing apart from his friends and family and looking like he belonged to a bright golden era yet to come.

Maddy had been telling him since he was old enough to listen that, given his obvious intelligence, he could surely get a job with the local savings and loan were he to want it, with or without college. "It's a *good* job," she said. "You've got a good head on your shoulders, and it'd be a shame to waste it." A selling point she returned to often was: "Your daddy's second cousin Bishop Stone-cipher has been there, at the bank, twenty years this October, and he's nearly ready to retire. We'd never thought he'd amount to much, but he's made a *good* livin'. I'm happy to call down there and talk to him for you if you want. I bet I could get you in." You can imagine how this was received.

In the month before he graduated from high school, and knowing full well of his intention to leave the morose mountain town for college come hell or high water, Maddy sat him down on the couch in the living room and said, "Son, you are such a bright boy. And we're glad you're goin' to college, if that's what you wish to do. I sure wish we could do something to help you pay for it. We just don't —"

Henry knew they didn't.

"Okay, so listen to me for a minute," said Maddy, there on the couch. "Eventually you're gonna need to find some way to

37

make money, and I tell you I'd be awful surprised . . . Well, how do I say this?" She
reached over and deposited her ash into a
paper cup: two quick muffled taps, a familiar sound, a fingertip's friction on the yellowed paper of a cheap cigarette. He heard
the irritation in it; sensed it arose from her
being inarticulate as to her own thoughts.
"Let me just say I've never truly understood
this fascination you have with books. Lord
knows we've tried. Books ain't everthing,
honey. Writin's not everthing. The truth is,
and you're not gonna want to hear this, but
you can't make a living that way. You just
can't. You need to take my word for it. I was
talkin' to your daddy the other night and he
said — and what he said was true — he
said, 'I've never known of a single writer in
the history of the language except for Jesus H. Christ who was worth a damn.'
Honey, he's got a point. And look what happened to Jesus." She eyed him slantwise
through the tobacco smoke and just shook
her head. "There's just so much more that
you could do with all the bounteous gifts
the Lord has seen fit to bestow upon you."

This was not helpful advice, principally
because it was inaccurate in almost every
sense, and so it went unheard and un-
heeded. He had his mind made up. He ap-

plied to and was accepted by the University of Virginia and no other colleges. He didn't have a car and knew no one else who was going, so he hitchhiked to Charlottesville, where he studied American literature and fell deeply in love with Wolfe and Poe and Faulkner. It was here that, notwithstanding Maddy's loving but misguided counsel, he decided in earnest that he wanted to write for a living, although he was unsure what his subject matter would be.

After graduating in three and a half years, he sent out résumés and interest letters to several major universities hoping to land a teaching job. His plan was to be a professor during the day and spend his mornings and evenings writing. This was a wonderfully romantic notion to him. I don't know that he ever set out to pen the "great American novel," whatever the hell that is, but he felt that inside him was something magnificent. He had a way of looking at the world and wanted to tell everyone who was interested what he observed and knew to be true, and find someone, somewhere, who would understand him for who he was.

He got some offers from colleges in the upper Midwest but turned them down. Another offer came in, this one from Appalachian State, and it got him thinking about

Old Buckram and the mountains and Helton and Maddy, but he wasn't interested in being so close to home. Another came from the University of Baltimore and there were to be no more. This was the best offer he got, so he took it.

In his first year of teaching he found he didn't have as much time to write as he had hoped and this caused him great frustration. He managed to complete a succinct southern novella but felt it was too similar to the previous artistic achievements of others, so it went into a drawer and he tried again. In a burst of inspiration he wrote an avant-garde quintet of short stories with a fugue of interwoven themes and characters, and this he got published as a short serial in a prominent literary magazine of the day, bringing him brief but select notoriety among the postmodern literary set. He experimented with and combined forms to produce several more short works, a few of which were printed by lesser journals and which generated some interest but mostly confusion among critics. One review said simply, "Aster's work, for all its brilliance, is impenetrable." Having learned important lessons, he started work on a novel.

After another year of teaching during the day and writing into all hours of the night and slowly taking on the pallor and visage of an apparition, he had fifty thousand well-ordered words. This time, he was writing the story of his life. He was writing about his mother and his father, and the mountains of North Carolina, and a bright young man who had been born there out of place and out of time.

Somewhere just beneath the view of his awareness, purposely hidden, pushed down by him among all those acrid and forgotten memories of home, there lurked a self-poisoning notion that when he had written his book and it had been published to acclaim, he would return to Old Buckram and present it to Maddy as conclusive evidence of his worth. In moments of quiet, when he allowed himself to bring this demon into focus and considered his unconscious desire for this future reckoning, he would drive it back down again and tell himself that her opinion didn't matter and that he wasn't doing it for her. He knew, without knowing, that she'd never read a word he'd written, and this should have been enough to save him. But in fact her doubt would be a distant yet implacable weight upon his shoulders that would not abate. It diminished him. It drew away from his power.

And still he worked. Day after day, night

after night, he worked. He wrote hundreds of pages but wasn't satisfied with what he saw on the paper before him. Critical to him was to develop and hone a truly unique style of his own. He sought, in essence, a new way of writing, of storytelling — but it proved elusive. The thought occurred to him that perhaps he should spend less time writing and more time reading until he found this new voice. He revisited all the classics, studied them in microscopic detail, and kept journals of his thoughts about them. He read every book on the *New York Times* best-seller list to see what people were writing, but thought most of them largely homogeneous and consequently not worthwhile. Disturbed by a growing listlessness in his pursuit, he turned to and explored the full Roman index of expurgatories and enjoyed these a great deal more, but they lent little to his endeavor. Something told him he had more figuring to do; that the book he would write was inchoate in his mind; that it needed to cook awhile longer. So he set aside what he had written of the novel and the tide of his life carried him on. On a whim, he enrolled in the University of Baltimore law-school night program, expecting only to take a few classes and learn something new and challenging. On a Saturday he went to the library to pick up a Latin to English dictionary.

He'd been to this library almost daily since his arrival in Baltimore, and more than once a student assumed he was employed there because he was so frequently seen toting heaps of books up and down the stairs. It wasn't uncommon, too, for paid library personnel to ask him for help in locating materials or making recommendations. He went in through the heavy wood-and-glass doors and the smell of all those books came to him and gave him the sense that wherever he'd been, he had just arrived home. The whole of the library was etched in his memory and he knew right where he was going. People came and went carrying books. A group of his students walked by, nodded with respect, and said, "Professor." This pleased him. Then a young lady he didn't know walked out of the library office in front of him. He watched as she pulled on a pair of white gloves and mounted the steps to the rare-book room, where she retrieved an antiquarian tome and returned with it to the library desk. He'd never seen anyone so beautiful. He forgot where he was going and why he was there. She walked past him and said hello, and he became instantly incapacitated (ponytail — legs — in-

43

timate familiarity with rare books). Every neuron in his capacious brain misfired all at once and went rocketing off in new and unfamiliar directions.

While her account of this encounter (reserved and understated) and his account (*soaring* hyperbole) differ in the telling, there are a few salient details the stories have in common. For example, they agree (more or less) on her attire and general appearance: her hair was blond, and she was wearing green clamdiggers. He described them as "viridescent capris"; she referred to them more modestly as "light green pedal pushers I'd borrowed from my roommate." On top she wore a simple white blouse. This he said was "décolleté" and "years ahead of its time." He offered an affidavit to this effect. She said it was conservative work attire, and more believably so, but in any event close enough.

It is undisputed, though, that he was unable to speak for several minutes. He eventually had to walk outside and come back in before he regained his composure. They agree he'd forgotten what book he came to the library for, and that when he recalled what it was and learned that the library's only copy was checked out, she offered to call him when it was available. The phone number he left, however, was inadvertently in error by several digits. He said it was similar to when you begin a flourish of words on the typewriter but your fingers are all on the wrong keys.

She asked his name. He responded: "I'm Henry Aster. I'm a writer. May I ask yours?" She blushed and said her name was Eleonore.

3

He forgot about everything else and spent his days dreaming about her. He wrote her love letters filled with verse, but she was immune to his poesy, or nearly so. He had read of men who would recite Byron and Keats and (lesser) women would swoon as if in the hands of a conjurer, but Eleonore was far too pragmatic for this type of elevated approach. On their first date he took her to a production of *Waiting for Godot* and wasn't allowed into her apartment later that evening. On the second date, he wised up and took her ice-skating.

She wasn't much interested in academics or scholarly pursuits in the traditional sense, but make no mistake: She was *far* from being a dimwit. He readily conceded in the end that she outranked him in terms of native intelligence, but hers was applied to markedly different enterprises. She loved the outdoors and flowers and birds and cool spring mornings and warm summer nights. By her own training, and with only the close tutelage of Mother Nature, she was an equestrian, a botanist, and an ornithologist. She could tell you the name of every plant, flower, tree, and weed on the Atlantic Seaboard. She had learned, and if asked would recite, every known species of eastern bird, migratory or otherwise.

Her childhood memories were made in Canonsburg, Pennsylvania, south of Pittsburgh, one block away from Chartiers Cemetery, where she played as a child and learned not to be afraid of ghosts. She got her first horse, an indomitable Arabian named Kashmir, when she was twelve years old, and there was no looking back. She trained Kashmir herself after reading books on the subject, and he behaved with the dignity of a Roman horse of war. A girl of that age who learns to train and care for a majestic animal of such grace and stature all on her own without guidance of any kind (save her own instinct and initiative) has intelligence of a different kind than what is often brought about with a typical schoolhouse education.

She had three sharp-looking older brothers known for their academic pursuits. They each attended an Ivy League school — two at Harvard, one in a master's program at Yale — and due to absurd, unstated chauvinism, no one in the family entertained the notion that she might have done the same. With her soaring siblings at institutes of higher learning in the northeast, the time came for her to move on from high school and determine the altitude her life's trajectory would achieve. Her parents had not spoken to her of college and whenever she brought it up, her father pretended not to hear and her mother walked quickly into the kitchen. One night she sat down with them at the dinner table and told them she wished to go to college, and that she had a few good ones picked out that she thought would be affordable. Her father responded with an acidic laugh and commenced a fusillade of biting, unrestrained sarcasm. What would *she* do with a college degree? he asked. Did they have classes on horseback riding? Had she called the local community college? *They* had horses, he thought. Anyway, there was no money for this frolic. Every dollar for years to come had been pledged to pay for the boys' educations, and they had scholarships. Did she think money grew on trees? It certainly did not.

Evenly, she said, "So you're not going to help me?"

Her answer — the upturned palms of her father, which supplied the response: "See? We have nothing." A year earlier their neighbors across the hill had been murdered by their own son. He was Eleonore's age — the boy who did it — and until that one bright August morning after breakfast when he went to the barn to get the ax, he had been an exemplary child. After killing them, he sat for a while in the new-found peace and quiet and then called the police to report the crime. When asked why he did it, he replied, "I'd had about all the sarcasm I could take."

Eleonore got up to leave.

"Where are you going?" said her father.

"To the barn."

"To get the ax?"

"No — to tell the horses goodbye."

That fall, she took her own money and her broken heart and enrolled in California University of Pennsylvania. In two years she had earned a teaching certificate and was ready for anything that life could offer. Knowing the time had come to strike out into the world, she headed south to Baltimore where she would begin her new life. She chose this destination for no particular reason other than the desire to go somewhere away from home and to show herself

49

that she was brave enough to do it. She'd been working at the library for three weeks when Henry walked in and everything changed.

I am, I suppose, fortunate my parents met and were sufficiently attracted to each other to bear children. I realize now, though, that they would have been better off if this had never happened.

My father had come out of Old Buckram with grand plans. He believed he had the raw materials — the intellect, the instincts, the ear — to become, over time, a beloved American writer. By reading and truly understanding all that had come before, by advancing the craft in a way that only he could, he might one day ascend to the ranks of Wolfe, Faulkner, Fitzgerald. He would produce an unparalleled work of fiction that would attempt to redefine the very nature of language. Yet at last, he was only a man, who, like so many of us, had dreams that exceeded him.

And this man thus described met the shining soul of a woman who was to become my mother. Years would pass and life would be visited upon them, and its toll would be great. His unquenchable thirst for all things would deliquesce like phantom smoke; her indomitable spirit would resurrect itself only in isolation, only as she galloped fiercely through the fields, a solitary knight in battle, with only herself to witness the courage. They were indeed doomed. But this eventual destruction was foreseen by no one at the time.

In 1967, upon my father's graduation from law school, they were married by the magistrate and moved into a second-floor apartment on West Fairmont Avenue in Baltimore in close proximity to and roughly equidistant from the Edgar Allan Poe house on the east and the H. L. Mencken house on the west. My mother had come to love him and couldn't have been happier. I can see it in the photographs. There is a patient and sweet contentment in her smile.

And he began again to write in earnest. He wrote of Maddy. He wrote of Old Buckram. He wrote of the white mist rising and churning in the valleys, and the once-green mountains in the foreground fading to shades of magnificent blue in the distance. He wrote of wood-smoke from distant fires on early autumn nights as the Milky Way rolled into view. He could remember every detail. He told her time moved more slowly there, but not for him. For him, it was different. For him, Old Buckram carried a sadness that he didn't think he'd ever get over and he didn't know why. He called it a "stillness of disquiet." At night, anguished, he would read to her what he had written and she would lie at the foot of the bed with eyes full of wonder.

He moved his typewriter a dozen times, trying to find the perfect place to write. The apartment they shared had a Juliet balcony in the main bedroom overlooking the street, and in the early evenings with some lingering light of day he would push his desk to the open doors and work, looking up from time to time to watch people moving up and down the lonely corridor. He was easily distracted and would become fiercely perturbed at just about anything that drew his attention away from writing. "Shostakovich wrote his music out in the hall," he once said, "not to protect his family from the terror of the KGB when they came to take him at last, but because he was trying to concentrate."

He lovingly called his new wife all sorts of oddly sweet names — "sonnet" and "rabbit" were two that I have heard (the latter taken from *For Whom the Bell Tolls,* no doubt) — and after a few fits and starts she allowed him to write and took good care of him while he was doing so. He would call to her from the balcony and she would take him another beer in a glass or a vodka tonic or some of whatever bottle they happened to have at the moment. When it began to get dark, or when the cold began to come in through the balcony doors, she would bring this fact to his attention. She would make simple dinners for the two of them, and on those nights when he couldn't be bothered, she would set his plate on the desk next to him and eventually he would find it and eat.

One night two cars collided in the street immediately below the balcony, and when asked to recount the event to the police officer who arrived on the scene, he confessed that he had seen none of it. Another night a man walking by spotted him and, standing on the street below, called up and asked if the man at the typewriter could spare a cigarette and a drink, both of which it was apparent were being conspicuously consumed. So he took a break from writing and rubberbanded an opened pack of cigarettes to a half-empty bottle of vodka and tossed them over the railing to the man, who said he'd never forget it. Perhaps he never did.

On a Friday in the spring of 1968 he started writing early and drinking even earlier, and by late afternoon he'd become cataleptic with gin and the words were not coming. He drove Eleonore out of the apartment with his frustration, and she was just outside when she heard his typewriter crash like an airliner in the middle of the street. So it went. For a while, then, he just wrote by hand.

Soon thereafter he received a terse letter from Helton on a scrap of unlined paper. Helton had never gained a reputation as an epistolary, so just receiving an envelope in his father's rarely seen hand suggested ill tidings from Old Buckram. "Your mother is not feeling well," Helton wrote, "but I'm sure it will pass. I just wanted you to know." On the back of the letter was this afterthought: "No reason for you to come home unless coming home anyway. Will manage." Helton didn't want to impose, but the implication was clear enough.

The thought of Maddy's declining health began to weigh on his mind like an anchor. He hated to be so far from home, leaving everything to Helton, who could barely care for himself. A few weeks later he got another letter from Helton. This one said, "I'm starting to get worried."

The night of the second letter the young couple sat in bed together with legs entangled. A string of Christmas lights ran high around the perimeter of the room, and the balcony doors were open to the warm outside. He drank wine and read Updike by the room's one lamp and tried to fool himself into thinking there was nothing he could do about Maddy. Unprompted, he said to Eleonore, "I don't want to go back."

She had seen the letters. "I know you don't," she said, "but maybe we should."

He got up and retrieved the wine bottle from their small kitchen, and then returned to bed. "It doesn't feel like home to me. It never did."

"It doesn't have to be home," she said, taking his hand. "If we don't like it, we can leave as soon as —"

"As soon as what? We no longer need to be there?" As soon as Maddy dies is what she meant but didn't mean to say, and he knew it.

"If I go," he said, "will you go with me?"

"Of course I will. You know that."

The act of saying the words, of imagining it as real, made it suddenly seem possible. In her mind, a move to the mountains of North Carolina in high summer seemed a happy and adventurous prospect. She had heard it described, and she longed for the simplicity and beauty it offered. A brief vision of Old Buckram's green hills and upland fields washed over her, and what she saw was lush and eternal. A beguiling optimism is often the first step toward folly.

"If we decide to go," she said, excited now and feeling the momentary enchantment, "do you think we could —"

"Get a horse? There are lots of horses in Old Buckram."

"Are there any Arabians? You wouldn't know. I'd be surprised if there were. We'd need a house with a fenced pasture beside it or somewhere near it, and a barn. I'd take care of the rest."

"If we get a horse," he said, "I want to be the one who names it."

"Henry," said Eleonore, resting her hands on her stomach, "there's something else I've been thinking about. I don't want to raise a child in the city."

Before leaving for Old Buckram, my father visited the Poe house a final time to say goodbye to so many things. Eleonore found him there, sitting on the front steps, loudly and drunkenly reciting poetry she had never heard before. " 'Now, to me the elm-leaves whisper / Mad, discordant melodies, / And keen melodies like shadows / Haunt the moaning willow trees . . .' " He was three-quarters of the way into a bottle of vodka.

This was not an auspicious beginning, but it was a suitable end. The next morning, after studying maps of three states while he slept, she loaded him into the car and they made their way to the misty mountains of North Carolina. He was going home.

4

In my father's childhood, during the emerging spring when the dogwoods were blooming white and gold in the long blue mountains, his father would drive the family down a meager dirt road over and around the wooded hills to the farmers market and back. At the apex of one of the hills, the woods cleared away to the west and the hillside fell into a great valley and climbed steeply up again to reveal the stone-gray face of Ben Hennom, an ancient mountain worn smooth and dark by the weathers of time. On a high shoulder of the mountain, half hidden by a row of wraithlike trees as old as time itself, sat an immense house of black iron and glass. During the day, it was an odd architectural curiosity. Due to a subtle trick of the mountain's folding ridges, it seemed always to be in shadow, even when the sun blazed in a cloudless sky above it. From morning to night, it was cloaked in a slowly swirling mist as thick as smoke from a fire. At night, it brooded in darkness like an ember-eyed bird of prey on the edge of the mountain. Never before had a house been built like it, and never would another be built. The children would scramble to the windows of the car to marvel in awed silence at the great and mysterious structure.

It was brought into existence in 1918 by a vice president of the R. J. Reynolds Tobacco Company in Winston-Salem who no doubt wanted to escape the oppressive summer heat of the Piedmont and found relief in the high elevations of Old Buckram. He bought the hundred acres surrounding the house for next to nothing — at that time land was inexpensive and plentiful — but on the structure he spared no expense and gave little regard to prevailing attitudes on architectural taste. The house was designed floor to ceiling by the man's brother-in-law, who was a full architect and half an occultist. To say he had a penchant for the macabre is an understatement. As a younger man, not more than a year out of Princeton, he had traveled to Palenque by virtue of the generosity of his wealthy father. The purpose of the trip was to derive inspiration for his nascent career, for he was far from satisfied with the unimaginative state of American design in the south. After a frightful encounter with a large black bird that pecked at him viciously and tried to take his eyes, he came down with a horrid fever that shook his body for weeks. He nearly died before leaving Mexico and was never the same thereafter. A dark cast had taken his soul. Upon returning home, he commenced work on what would simultaneously be his first and last creation and his magnum opus: the great house on the hill. The fever returned and his last breath turned to vapor in the cold mountain air before he could see his drawings brought to life — but yet it would be built.

The house saw little use or occupation for decades, and in 1963 it was sold in a dilapidated state to an eccentric hotelier named Kaeron who envisioned it as a recherché bed-and-breakfast that would give his wife something to do to pass the time other than wait for him to come home in the evenings. When that went the way of all bad ideas, he and his wife moved in and lived there with their three children, Mary, Tebah, and Abigail. They built a gate at the bottom of the hill and slowly disappeared from public life. Later the house and grounds fell back into disrepair, and it was whispered in town that the hotelier had an exotic disease for which there was no cure. Then someone noticed that all the lights in the house had been turned on and were never turned off, day or night. As the weeks passed, the lights went out one by one. Eventually someone called the police, the gate was scaled, and the premises were searched. No one appeared to be home. When the fifth mortgage payment didn't arrive, the bank sent someone out to inquire. After knocking and looking in all the windows, the man who lost the bet kicked through a pane of glass and went inside. The house was completely furnished and in order, as if company were expected. He called out, but no one answered. After a terrifying exploration through the cold and darkling fortress, he ran out of the house and called the police.

The detective assigned to the case wrote in his initial report: "Something horrible has happened here. I can't tell exactly what. It's strange. Two adults are dead. The three children are missing. No indication of their whereabouts. Cause of death for the parents is undetermined (analysis pending), but could have been self-inflicted, either voluntarily or involuntarily (under duress). Excavation of the grounds to begin this week." And then three weeks later: "Children found today. Buried face-up in a pit in the woods behind the house. Lined up (not piled in). Multiple broken bones apparent." A supplemental report indicated the cause of death for the children was drowning. The police were never able to put together a coherent explanation of how or why the killings occurred.

Five years later the bank still owned the house and no prospects for its sale had materialized. That was the state of things when my parents returned to Old Buckram, Eleonore now with child, and moved into the cramped little farmhouse at the end of the dirt road with Helton and Maddy. They took up residence in a room that was just large enough for a sagging twin bed and a small desk, upon which my father placed his typewriter. Before six months had passed, the desk was removed and replaced with a mildewing hand-me-down crib from the attic that was vigorously cleaned, painted, and structurally reinforced. My parents named me Henry, after my father.

Because there wasn't room elsewhere, my father's desk and typewriter were both unceremoniously relegated to the back porch, where all of Maddy's painted ceramics were stockpiled on dusty shelves. For hours, then, in the lowering night while the house slept, my father would sit outside by lamplight, surrounded and besieged by fluttering white moths and what might have been items for sale at a roadside flea market, and try to write.

Upon their arrival in North Carolina, after finding no teaching jobs within a hundred miles that were of interest to him, my father commenced a brief legal career with one of the two law offices in town. A lawyer's salary is rarely as exorbitant as many people think it is, and this is especially true for lawyers whose practice consists in part of "dirt law," particularly in the more rural parts of the state. There were months when it seemed he was barely breaking even. Most of the work he did was for folks who couldn't pay. So in order to augment the income he was making from mundane real-estate closings and simple criminal matters, he used his crushing intellect and took a few complex malpractice cases on a contingent-fee basis, pursuant to which he was entitled by agreement to receive a third of any recovery. The first three cases cost him money and nearly got him fired. The fourth one settled before trial for just over three million dollars. His first thought was, *Now we can get Eleonore a horse.*

Shortly after collecting his hard-earned

fee, he reluctantly accepted a position on the board of the Old Buckram Bank to serve as an adviser. It was in this latter capacity that he learned the great house on the hill was for sale and could be acquired for far less than market value. He ascended the steep gravel driveway for the first time exactly four and a half hours after this propitious discovery and beheld in proximity what he had hitherto only seen from a distance. He was amazed at what he saw. The house towered black and malefic into the gray of the cindered sky and it terrified him. It was a monstrous gothic skeleton. From the courtyard looking to the east he could see the few town lights of Old Buckram, and to the southwest the aged mountains of the Blue Ridge could be seen blue and distant. He pushed open the leaden front doors and wandered wide-eyed into a mausoleum of a foyer that greeted him with curtains of cobwebs and a cadre of scurrying mice. Slowly he was drawn into the core of the house, where he discovered a great wood-paneled library on the second floor with high windows and endless shelves running up to the vaulted ceilings above. Books lined the walls and were piled in every corner. He was instantly determined to make the house his own, no matter the cost. *Here, I can write,* he thought.

Far below the crags and a vertiginous decline, the property accompanying the house leveled as it neared the road, and a black barn as old as the mountain hid in a grove of birch and black oak. At least thirty acres of this lowland area had been cleared and fenced, although the fence was down in more places than it was up. That night Henry went home to Helton and Maddy's and said to Eleonore, "We're moving, and we're getting a horse. I want to name it Annabel Lee." It took them less than a day to move in and the rest of their lives to leave.

5

If all the wood had been stained and polished to a high, elegant gloss, the interior of the house would have been opulent beyond imagining. With eyes half-closed, you could look and see what the maddened architect had intended, although the structure could bear that likeness no more.

The scowling face of the house looked east toward the rising sun. The first room entered from the front through a massive oaken door was the aforementioned foyer, tiled in somber slate and more than twice the size of the Baltimore apartment. Arched hallways ran off in all directions, and a sweeping staircase with steps the color of venous blood curled asymmetrically up and out of sight. To the right, through a succession of doorways, was at first a dour sitting room (forever unused), a dining room with space enough for fifty people, and a smoking room, drab and drear. We didn't use it in this way, but plainly this was its purpose in the former life of the house, as evidenced by two waist-high granite obelisks, the pyramidic tops of which could be removed so that spent cigars and cigarettes could be placed in the canisters inside.

The exterior walls of this room were floor-to-ceiling glass, matching a similar room on the southeastern corner of the house. From this point of vantage looking toward town, the old dirt Avernus Road was intermittently visible, winding over the hillside opposite — the same road my father's family traveled on the way to the farmer's market so many years before.

Behind the smoking room was an open chamber we called the Painted Parlour. In a well-intentioned yet futile attempt to bring some much-needed cheer to the otherwise cadaverous ambience, one wall had been painted olive green; the second wall, paprika; the third, canary; and the fourth, lavender. The mixture of colors was arresting. Eggshell picture-frame molding ran high along the top of the walls and tried without success to tie the room together. Bleak pictures depicting despairing winter scenes in the mountains hung on the walls in bizarre contrast to the tsunamis of color. In each corner was a high-backed armchair, colored and striped vertically in opposition to the walls joining behind it. Father continually threatened to whitewash the whole affair, but Mother found it charming, and so it remained.

A small door in the southern wall of the Painted Parlour gave entrance to a corridor which, at its end, climbed three steps and opened at last into a sprawling room in the exact geometric center of the house. This was the Great Room. It was half the size of a modern gymnasium and, with its dark woods and baroque carvings, instantly gave the impression of an old English cathedral. Along one wall was a burnished oak bar with a set of six silver stools. Behind the bar were dozens of bottles of every kind of consumable spirit you can imagine, along with tumblers, wine glasses, mixers, and the like. Next to the bar on a recessed surface sat a glittering phonograph with a speaker of the cornucopia variety. Opposite were four arabesque planters the size of Volkswagens and painted Aztec oranges and blues. The room was heated by four stone fireplaces with mantels of carved wood.

At one end of the Great Room sat a goliath of a square grand piano. Originally built in 1889 by Henry F. Miller and J. H. Gibson of Boston, it was later painstakingly restored piece by delicate piece by Fendom Bower, the eccentric owner of Old Buckram's one music store who made a living selling rebuilt instruments and tuning the few local pianos. Whether by design or by happenstance, the piano, when played, would fill every room in the never-ending house with sound.

A most remarkable feature of the house was a giant elliptical opening in the ceiling of the Great Room that spanned thirty feet by the major axis, twenty by the minor. Through this vast portal the room was open from the ground floor all the way to the ornate iron-and-glass roof three stories above — similar in some manner to a rotunda except that instead of a pleasing parabolic dome on top, it was all oblique angles and irregular vertices. Thus, one could stand at the bar and, while waiting for a drink, look up and watch a waxing crescent moon in a field of stars pass by far overhead.

Immediately above the Great Room and orbiting the elliptical aperture was the famous library. It was this room that my father had seen on his first visit to the house, and that which had brought him there. It was indeed the dark heart of the dwelling. One could reach the library by a spare spiral staircase that climbed up from the Great

Room, as well as by the Dali-esque stairway from the foyer.

The walls of the library were bookshelves twelve feet high, with gothic windows of stained glass and wide-set ledges in each wall of shelves. Between the windows were four doors standing alone, one in each of the four bookshelfed walls, and positioned at the four points of a cross. Each door opened to a hallway that led down to a series of bedrooms. At the southern end of the library was an apsis containing a simple sitting area with leather chairs and a small rolling bookcase that had at one time belonged to a clergyman. A door at the base of the apsis led to my parents' room.

An iron railing with patterns of irreducible complexity ran unbroken around the oblong chasm in the floor. If you were to get lost in a book whilst strolling about, this barrier would keep you from accidentally plunging headlong and surprised into the Great Room below.

On the third floor of the house, more modest in dimension than the floors below, were several smaller rooms of cold, creaking wood connected by narrow passages and hidden stairways that ran arterially about in an altogether mystifying fashion. Offset among these was a simple glass observatory facing east, with a small reflecting telescope mounted on a brass swivel in the floor. After being sent to bed on the rare nights my parents had company, I often made my way from my bedroom up the back staircase to the observatory, where for a time I would lie on the floor, unseen, peering down through the library into the Great Room, as my parents entertained and bright voices and laughter drifted up and played auditory tricks with the ornamental glass architecture. Then I would turn to the telescope and spend hours on end searching with amazement all the illimitable wonders of the night sky. Fond memories, indeed.

And yet despite all the foolhardy extravagance and excess, there was inescapably an emptiness, a bleak chill, and a hostility to the house that could never be ignored or forgotten. No matter what efforts were undertaken in the way of decoration and the quaint placing of personal effects, the house had a way of communicating its chronic malaise. There were far corners and hallways that refused to be illuminated. There were rooms that couldn't be heated, and wintry drafts from no identifiable source that numbed your feet and breathed a cold and unwelcome omen down your neck. There were closets the tops of which always harbored imperturbable spiders with thick irrational webs, and in all seasons chittering black bats, excited by the tethered moon, circled high on the chimney spires at twilight.

In the full context of this haunted estate, let's go back now to the second floor and walk around the library together. You hold on to the railing and let it slide through your fingers, a faint trace of rust accreting on your fingertips and in the palm of your hand. Looking at the towering shelves, you think, *How many books can this hold? Could I read that many books in a lifetime?* As we walk around, we come to a small hallway in the corner of the room that breaks off into darkness. You didn't see it at first; it's almost hidden from sight. When I show it to you, you see that it leads to a small cubical chamber, a prison almost, inside of which is a desk, a chair, and a lamp. This was my father's space. It was here that he would sit and write, and where all his hours vanished.

6

Father picked me up from Helton and Maddy's an hour after dark. Maddy met him at the door and gave him a nice long hug and he kissed her sweetly on the cheek. Pulling back, he examined her face, her posture, for signs of change. Maddy turned away from the scrutiny and brought Father inside.

"Is my son here somewhere?"

"We haven't seen him," said my grandfather.

"I'm right here," I said, but they all pretended I was invisible. This was a game we played. "I'm right here!" I pulled at Father's coat.

"Thanks for looking after him. I know he's a handful."

"He's no problem at all. We have fun."

Maddy began to cough into the crook of her arm and this went on for more than half a minute. After waiting a time to be sure the coughing would not return, she deposited some nacreous spit into a tissue, wadded it up, and threw it into the stove. Father asked if she was okay.

"I'm just fine. I just had a little tickle in my throat. Can you stay for dinner?"

"No, I've got to get home. I've got some work to do tonight. But thank you."

"You're always rushing around, aren't you?" said Maddy.

"I am. I don't have much time, I'm afraid."

"I don't know why time moves so fast for you but so slow for me."

"It's a curse on us both," said Father. Turning to me, he said, "Son, where's your coat?"

"I don't have one," I said.

"It's cold outside."

"I still don't have one."

"Well, I'll tell you what your grandmother said to me once when I was about your age: If you're going to be dumb, you've got to be tough. Let's go. You'll likely survive." When we were outside, he took off his coat and put it around my shoulders.

The next morning, a Saturday, I came out of my room into the library to find Father still working at his desk, his head bent down and his face and hair almost touching an open notebook. He was writing but languorously so, and what he wrote was not legible to me. Papers and open books stacked one on the other covered the desk and the floor. An empty bottle of wine lay on its side like a placeholder in the crease of his immense dictionary. I must have startled him, because when I touched his arm he slammed the pen on the desk and shot out of his seat like he'd heard a trumpet. I'd come to expect this wild-eyed frenzy from him after long nights of writing.

"Did you go to bed last night?" I asked.

"I have no idea. What time is it now?" He looked around for an indication of the time and saw the morning had come. "Damn it," he said. "I'm going blind."

"I'm hungry. Can we go get some breakfast?"

"Can you drive us?"

"I'm ten."

"So, no?"

"Do you want to live?"

"Where's Threnody? Do we need to take her with us?"

Threnody was my sister. She was born when I was nine, on the twenty-seventh of June. Mother named her after a poem Father had written, which I've looked for but never found. When people asked how to pronounce her name, Father would bristle and say, "It almost rhymes with trinity."

"No," I said. "Mother has her. They went to Blowing Rock to shop for the morning."

We drove into town and stopped at Dick Swift's Diner on the backstreet. It was a hole in the wall, but it was the only place in town that offered breakfast. The usual fare consisted of watery scrambled eggs, biscuits, country ham salted to the point of mummification, bacon, and fried potato polyhedrons that were usually more grease than potato. Thin black coffee was served in paper cups. Every table had one or two plastic ashtrays next to fluted salt and pepper shakers and thimbles of creamer. Usually the ashtrays were full of spent, twisted cigarettes. A woman with hair from a bygone era greeted us at the door.

"Y'all sit anywhere you can find. We're awful busy this morning, and we're out of the country ham." Bright light from the morning streamed in through the front windows, making it warm inside. The small dining area was nearly full, but it was quiet as a church except for the noise from the kitchen. Weaving through the tables, we came across Charles Young, who my father practiced law with just down the street.

"Good morning, Charlie."

"Good morning, Henry. Good morning,

young man. Is your father treating you to breakfast?"

Charlie had a good-natured, lively face that resembled nothing so much as a bright full moon. His eyes were those of an old, sweet dog. They just spoke kindness to you. He was there with his wife, Sarah, who was equally kind. I never met two people who I thought were more sincere.

"I hope so," I said. "Hello, Mrs. Young."

She said hello and turned her head to the side and smiled. "Your father says you've become quite a little whiz at the piano. Is that true?"

"I don't know. I like to play."

"Well, I'd like to hear you play sometime."

I said thank you and drew a circle on the ground with the toe of my shoe. Charlie looked my father in the eye and said, "Henry, I thought what you did for those folks was mighty kind. I think they got some measure of justice — if justice can be had when somebody loses a child like that. I still can't believe it."

"It's what you would've done," said Father. "It's what anybody would've done."

"No, not anybody," said Charlie. "Sit down and eat with us." He split a biscuit in half with his fork and loaded it up with eggs and bacon. In two bites, he just about polished it off.

"You folks go ahead and eat," said Father. "We don't want to interrupt. Charlie, I'll see you on Monday if not before."

We found an empty table along the wall. Father sat down and took the ashtray and placed it on the floor. He was unshaven, unshowered, and looked like a man from an asylum. His hair went a thousand different directions and his glasses were chipped on one corner, which was a new development. He was still wearing his work clothes from the day before, but his white Oxford shirt now had charcoal stains on both elbows. A man in overalls and muddied work boots sat at a table next to us and smoked, exhaling directionally toward the ceiling.

"Do you care what people think of you?" I asked Father.

"Why do you ask me that?" He took off his glasses and squinted down at me. In the light, I noticed a red stain on his lower lip and a matching one on his shirt that I surmised must have been from the wine.

"You don't look like you're from around here," I said.

"That's not something I do on purpose."

"I don't think I want to be from here, either," I said, misjudging his attitude about the matter.

"You're from here," he said, "and so am I. Even if we wanted to, there's nothing either one of us can do about it."

Our waitress ambled up to our table and stopped there as if she were out of breath. I noticed that the sole of one shoe, her right, was much thicker than the other by a matter of inches. Leaning on Father's chair, she said, "How're y'all doin' this mornin'?" This was said in the same slow, deliberate way that she moved about the diner. Age spots covered her hands, and her arms resembled old tree roots, dug up and left to dry in the sun. Still a little winded, she brought a notepad out of her apron, wet her thumb and two fingers with her tongue, and peeled back an earlier order and its carbon to get a fresh page. "Can I get y'all somethin' to drink? We got Pepsi products." Father ordered two coffees, black, and I asked for orange juice.

She scratched a quick note on the pad and shuffled away. As soon as she was gone, a local man walked up and put his hand on Father's shoulder. Fixing his eye on me but intending the question for Father, he said, "D'you finish that book yet? The one you's reading here the other day?"

Father said, "Not quite. I'm getting close, though," and patted the man's hand.

"Thank you for asking."

Just like when he was a boy, Father developed a reputation around town as the man who always carried a book with him wherever he went. At lunchtime during the work week when the weather cooperated, he'd take a sandwich from home and sit on a stump at the edge of the Barrowfields and read by himself. Other times, he'd do his reading at an empty table in the corner of one of Old Buckram's few restaurants, like this one. Every week or two he had a different book. He'd read and take notes in a series of thin blue journals that he'd carry just inside the book's cover. When people would ask him what he was reading, I'm sure he resisted the temptation to say, "You've probably never heard of it." Almost every time he and I were out together on a Saturday or a Sunday, I'd hear people ask him, "Did you finish that book you were reading?" He'd usually say "Not yet," or "Just about," or "I sure did," smiling politely, even folksily.

After the man had retreated, I asked Father why he spent so much time reading. He laughed and cleaned his glasses with his shirttail, and I judged from his expression that he had just noticed the new chip on his lens for the first time. "I love to read," he said. "I love words and language. I always have. There's nothing I enjoy more."

"And why do you spend so much time writing?" I asked.

I could see him thinking about it. I could see I'd asked him something which he didn't know the answer to but had spent his whole life trying to figure out.

"I write," he said, looking me in the eyes, which he rarely did, "because it's one of the only things that seems real to me." He then thought for another moment and said, "It's the only way short of death to make time stop." This was not a simplified explanation for a ten-year-old. This was his truth.

We finished our breakfast and drove across town with the windows down — the work truck Father used for miscellaneous errands had no air conditioning and the heat barely worked. We stopped at Baldwin's Sunoco station on old Highway 820 for gas. After pulling up to the pump, two young men came out and one pumped the gas while the other started washing the windshield. It was always the same fellas who worked there, year after year. Arnie Baldwin was the owner. He had two enormous front teeth, sharp as scissors, that gave him a rabbit-like appearance. Seeing Father, he came out of the garage and leaned way into the driver's side window of the truck for conversation. His hair was white and pushed back like my grandfather's. While they were talking, I jumped out of the truck and ran into the gas station to get a Mountain Dew, the cost of which one of the attendants helpfully added to the gas bill with a quick mental calculation. While inside, I heard screeching tires and the horrible sound of one vehicle slamming into another. I ran out to find a large black Buick with its front solidly in contact with the back of our truck. Steaming green fluid was spilling out onto the ground.

The lady who had hit us was notorious in the county for being a horrendous driver. Her name was Dorthea Graybeal. By one account, Ms. Graybeal had caused hundreds of accidents, thankfully all of them very minor. Everyone in town knew Ms. Graybeal and her car all too well. If you saw her coming, you were smart to pull off the road and get out of the way.

I came out of the station in time to see a dazed Ms. Graybeal trying unsuccessfully to get out of her car. She seemed unable to locate the door handle. Father was the first person who made it over to her to be sure she wasn't hurt, followed by every gas-station employee, and shortly thereafter by the folks who lived across the street. Seeing that she was not injured, they helped her out of the car and Father walked her over to a bench where she could sit down.

"Was that your truck? I just feel terrible about hittin' it. I thought there was a hummingbird in my car," she said, looking over at Father, who was sitting there next to her with half a smile on his lips.

"That's all right, Dorthea," Father said. "It was my fault. Don't you worry a thing about it."

"Oh, thank goodness," said Ms. Graybeal.

A few minutes later, after her car had been separated from the back of the truck, Arnie and the attendants walked over to Father and said, "It weren't your fault. How could it be? You were sittin' completely still."

Father said, "Well, it was my fault. I'd heard that Dorthea was going to be out driving today, but I decided to come to town anyway." All the men roared with laughter.

He put on a fairly good showing, but the truth was that here, in Old Buckram, he was indeed out of place and out of time. His body carried his brain to and from work each day, to the grocery store, and back to the house on the top of the hill. And his brain, looking out into the world with the benefit of his eyes and his connected optical nerve, uprighting images and extrapolating multidimensional surfaces, observed his knowable universe and looked upon it as a stranger. He must have seen it all as would a man from a faraway land and time, sent here to live among other men. The men here, the ones he left behind when he went to college and the ones he returned home to afterward, were not like him. They didn't think like he did. In any conversation he might *think of,* but not make reference to, a parallel from Whitman or Coleridge or Proust that occurred to him as particularly apposite to a situation. The thought would remain inside him; it would die within him, and no one would ever hear it. He knew how to talk like them, though. He knew how to cock his head just right, and hold his mouth open, and say "You don't say" and "Damn," when he heard a remarkable story, and "Yep" and "Naw" and always "Come with us," at the end of any conversation with an acquaintance met in an unexpected place. He'd run into someone he knew at the grocery store and listen intently as the man talked. He'd listen with a kind of deep focus, looking dead into the man's eyes, almost unblinking and without saying much of anything, hunched slightly to be more or less on the same level with the man, without anything much beyond an anthropological interest in the story and the man telling it, and at the end of it he'd offer amusement and say something like, "Well, all right, Junior. I hope you have a good night. I reckon I better get on home."

That was how the discourse was carried on. And Father could do it, and he could do it well, while in his mind he must have been smack-dab in the middle of Yoknapatawpha County, even though it and Old Buckram are separated by a good six hundred miles and probably four thousand feet of elevation.

We got home and I ran in to tell Mother about Ms. Graybeal hitting the truck. She said, "Oh my lord. Was anybody hurt?"

"Father was badly injured," I said, as he had instructed me to do. "He's in the hospital awaiting a transplant."

"He'll wish he were," said Mother.

Father came into the kitchen and kissed her on the cheek.

"I need to sleep for a while," he said.

"I thought you might. Are you going to want to eat soon?"

He didn't answer. He walked out of the room and climbed the staircase to the library and slept until dinner.

7

When it was time to eat, I woke Father with a sharp knock on his door, and soon he came down from upstairs carrying a microphone and a tape recorder, both attached by a cord to an analog gauge of some sort that was in turn tied to a small printing device the size of a desk calculator. He went into the dining room and arranged them on a half-moon buffet table along the wall and left again. In a few minutes he returned with a long boom stand like you might see on a movie set. Once we started with dinner, he got up and fiddled with the controls of the recorder for a while. We were so used to odd behavior by then that no one said a word or questioned what he was doing. Dinner went on as usual, with Threnody singing away nonsense sounds in her own little universe of happiness. Father attached the microphone to the boom stand and walked it up to within about two inches of Mother's face.

She sat very still.

"Just do what you normally do," he said. "Pretend there's no microphone next to your cheek."

Mother carefully lifted a bite of food to her mouth. Father pressed some buttons and returned to his seat at the head of the table. Every so often, the little printing device would clack out a few inches of paper.

"Don't mind me," he said. "Carry on."

We carried on until Mother needed to return to the kitchen for a refill of asparagus. Grown in our garden and fertilized with horse manure, a single asparagus shaft would be the size and density of a broom handle. It became the subject of legend in Old Buckram.

"Can I get up now?"

Father inspected the readout and said, "Yes, that's enough." She returned from the kitchen with her asparagus and asked if we needed anything.

"No, thank you," I said.

"Coo," said Threnody.

After a moment, Father looked up from the readout and saw us all staring at him. "Yes?"

"Suffice it to say," said Mother, "we're just a *little* curious about whatever *this* is." She drew a circle in the air around Father and his devices.

"Right. Fair enough. It's an experiment. You're going to think this is crazy, but — okay — just hear me out. Don't take offense. I have always suspected that, for whatever reason — perhaps due to a congenital deficiency in the amount of cheek . . . padding you have —"

"Cheek padding?" said Mother.

"Cheek thickness," said Father.

"Hmmm," said Mother.

"Perhaps due to a congenital deficiency in cheek thickness, I have suspected for some time —"

"How long?" said Mother.

"A while," said Father. "— that the noise level generated by your mastication —"

"My *mastication*?" said Mother.

"Your chewing, as it were," said Father. "— that the noise level generated by your *chewing* was louder than, say, what might be normal or typical or customary for a person of your age and size of mandible. So naturally it occurs that this is an empirical question —"

Mother got up and walked into the kitchen.

"You're an idiot," I told him.

From that night forward, we always had

music playing in the house when dinner was served.

After dinner I helped Mother get Threnody to bed by reading her picture books and singing her the little songs I knew. This was our nightly ritual. It's what we did to find happiness in the lonely old house, which so often fell deathly quiet in the nighttime hours when Father was writing. After Threnody succumbed to sleep, I went to my room to retrieve my book and, desperate for Father's company, dared to disturb him at his writing desk. There was only one chair at the desk, and a second was never provided, so I sat down on the floor, my back against one of the room's bookcases, and began to read.

"What are you doing?" he asked with annoyance, my presence in the room already straining his patience.

"I thought I'd read in here with you for a little while," I said carefully. "I'll be quiet, I promise."

The momentary absence of a pen scrawling on paper showed he was considering it, and I awaited his decision with shallow breath. At last, he said, "That's fine, *but* —" I knew the warning; it could remain unsaid.

He went back to writing and I went back

to reading. After a few minutes more, he handed me a folded note under the desk. It said: "Please try to turn your pages just a fraction less dramatically. Thank you."

And then an hour, at least, passed without another word between us — but the room was not silent. As he worked he'd read his new sentences aloud time and again to gauge their rhythm and meter, revising them further with every pass, until a paragraph could be recited in its entirety to his satisfaction. Forgetting I was there, as I sat hidden from him on the other side of the desk, expletives, both foreign and domestic, would boil up out of him into the air. Having reached a point of frustration, he stood to take a break and only then remembered I was in the room with him. "I thought you'd gone," he said, coming to sit beside me on the floor. I stayed quiet and stared at my open book without reading the words, only pretending now to read. I'd come to learn that he'd need a few minutes to decompress.

"What do you have there?"

"*Flatland,*" I said eagerly, showing him the book.

"By Edwin Abbott. Do you like it?"

"It's cool."

"Have you seen the one I've got?" He got

up and went out and walked down the bookshelf on the eastern wall with me close behind him. Finding the A's in fiction, he scaled up the ladder to get the book. He handled it as if it were a magnificent antiquity. We took it back to his desk and studied it under the light.

"Is it a first edition?"

"First edition, first printing," he said.

"Is it signed?"

"Unfortunately not."

The book was indeed a thing of beauty. Like most of Father's rare books, it was wrapped in a chemically inert, pH-neutral, clear polyester cover that went around the dust jacket like a glove. The brown cover of the book looked like an old treasure map and suggested infinite mysteries inside. "FLATLAND: A Romance of Many Dimensions. By A Square. Price Half-a-crown." At the very top, in italic type, was printed *O day and night, but this is wondrous strange,* and at the bottom *And therefore as a stranger give it welcome.* Responding to my enfilade of questions, Father carefully explained the idea behind Abbott's clever pseudonym ("A Square") and the quotations from Hamlet. Transported and bewitched by the elegance of it all, I begged him to let me keep his copy, and he said,

"Not on your life."

"Did you steal this one?"

"Pardon me?"

"Where did you get it?" I asked.

"In an old bookstore outside Baltimore about ten years ago. I don't think they knew they had it. It was one of those great old bookstores with books piled to the ceiling in no particular order. I remember it looked like it might catch fire any minute. It smelled like old, wet laundry that's been allowed to sit in the hamper awhile. I went in and asked the owner how the books were organized, and he said, 'They're in alphabetical order, except where they're not.' So it was basically a scavenger hunt. Half the books were still in boxes. A third of the books were behind pieces of furniture — old turntables, dressers, chairs. And there was no air conditioning. The owner just had fans sitting here and there. With the two of us in the store at the same time, he couldn't have taken delivery of a butter knife. So I rolled up my sleeves and started looking. After four hours I was covered in sweat and I had found this book and five others that I'll show you sometime, all first editions in one form or another."

"How did they not know they had it?"

"My basic theory is that it's best to look

for rare books in bookstores that are in areas of comparatively low literacy per capita. In Manhattan, say, this book would have been picked up in an instant. In rural Kentucky, however, different story."

"That's brilliant," I said.

"I've found a lot of books that way," he said. "Fewer and fewer, though."

"Can I please take this to school to show everyone?"

"Let's discuss that in the morning. Just leave it here on the desk for now." This was his polite way of saying no way in hell. "More importantly," he said, "will you go downstairs and ask your mother to make me a drink?"

I jumped up and ran down the front stairway, through the foyer, through the sitting room and the smoking room, and finally into the Painted Parlour, where Mother was sitting reading a book of her own.

"Father wants to know if you'll make him a drink."

"Ask him if he's forgotten where the bar is." The bar, of course, lay along one wall of the Great Room, which was below and visible from the railing that ran around the inside perimeter of the library.

I bounded back up the staircase, ran the length of the library, and, turning down his hallway, slid to a stop in my socked feet by Father's desk.

"She wants to know if you've forgotten where the bar is."

"Tell her if I get up and walk twenty feet I can see the bar, but that I'd like her to make the drink so I can walk to the railing and look down to see her beautiful face." I flew back downstairs with this message.

"He says he wants you to make it so he can look down and see your beautiful face."

"Ask him what kind of drink he would like."

I charged back upstairs, now completely out of breath.

"She wants to know what you want to drink."

"Tell her vodka tonic, neat, hold the tonic."

Mother and I followed the corridor into the Great Room and she poured the drink as requested. As promised, Father came to the railing and called down to her.

"Thank you, my darling."

"Perhaps we should put in a dumbwaiter or an intercom."

"Why would we do that when we have this energetic boy to carry messages back and forth?" I walked back upstairs holding the glass of vodka very carefully and thinking it smelled like some type of combustible fuel.

"Thank you, my boy, for procuring this delicious restorative. Now your father needs to get back to his writing."

Long after I'd gone to bed, I heard music coming from downstairs. Father was at the piano, playing softly by candlelight. On many nights after we'd all turned in and he'd given up on writing for the evening, he'd quietly play a handful of dulcet, melancholy pieces that would wake us but then soothe us sweetly back to sleep. This was especially common on the weekends — at least until, as he would say, the earth had swallowed all his hopes.

Father had taken up the piano shortly after coming to occupy the vulture house, and why not? The piano was a masterpiece of engineering and seemed to sulk like a retired racehorse at the edge of the pasture when it wasn't being played. He never had lessons, but after hearing a particular Chopin nocturne on the radio one afternoon he became inspired and just decided he would learn how to play it, technical obstacles and lack of training be damned. One nocturne led to another, the next more difficult than the last. He furrowed his brow and bought arcane books on technique and read the first few chapters. He sat many an hour, head cocked like a fox terrier, listening to recordings of the piano masters with his determined eyes trailing along in a book of sheet music.

His ear was decent but untrained and it usually took him a few weeks to learn one entire piece. He'd play it again and again — one slow, methodical section at a time, rehearsing the runs up and down the keyboard ad nauseam, slowly at first and then eventually to tempo, until finally he had the whole thing more or less correct. He was hampered by an inability to read music proficiently, so he'd go through his music books and painstakingly write all the notes in with a pencil, eventually learning the pieces such that he could play them only from memory. All the music he loved was slow and bittersweet. I really didn't know what any of the pieces were until years later. After he left I carried those melodies around in my head like a name I'd forgotten. They would move in and out of my consciousness, lingering just out of reach like a star you can only see when you're not looking directly at it.

This night when I awoke he was playing a piece I didn't know, but of course then I knew none of them. It began with three notes within a chord played so softly 1-2-3 1-2-3 1-2, and then a rest, and then an exquisite melody commencing with the right hand — delicately, slowly, played with more sadness than the music required. I got out of bed and went up the back stairway to the darkened observatory and lay on the planked wooden floor with my face pressed cold against the iron railing. From above I looked down upon his back. He wore a white shirt, his large cuffs rolled back loosely onto his forearms. Even from so far away I could see that his hair had become wildly disheveled, no doubt from having his hands thrust into it time and again as his frantic mind searched for words and crafted sentences hour after hour. If he had even a modest ability at the piano, he would have appeared to the world like a virtuoso sitting down to a concert performance. In my imagination I accounted for this discrepancy by pretending I was observing him in the act of composition.

He began again: 1-2-3 1-2-3 1-2, the three notes within a chord played so softly. At once the fingers of his left hand fell upon the wrong notes and he stopped abruptly. He sighed, took a long, patient drink from his glass, and then started once more — and this went on for hours until I was fast asleep.

8

That Sunday morning we got up and Father was already up writing and everybody put on nice clothes and we went to church. I was in something like a Lord Fauntleroy suit and Threnody was in a lace dress that, from a distance, brought to mind a Fabergé egg with auburn hair. We attended a Baptist church about a mile outside of town, but we did so with no real regularity. The church itself was a quaint wooden structure with a white and gray exterior, a green-shingled roof, and narrow stained-glass windows, eight on a side. It was a small church, with only one primary chamber on the main level and ten wooden pews on each side of the aisle. An elevated and creaking organ sat at the back. Stairs ran from the foyer under the organ down to a concrete basement, where children were given Sunday-school lessons and taught in ominous tones about the realities of heaven and hell.

On cold days it felt as if the church didn't have heat. It did not, in fact, have air conditioning — a luxury that was extraordinarily rare for Old Buckram residences and businesses alike. In the summer, the weekly service was held an hour earlier and the windows were rolled open to allow air to circulate among the perspiring bodies. In the winter, people dressed warmly, sat close together, and shivered.

The church sat right next to the road, with a white picket fence providing its only protection from passing cars. Behind the church was a field that sloped gently down to a tributary of Abbadon Creek, a narrow ribbon of mountain water that was home to tadpoles and crawfish, both of which boys and girls who escaped the torturous confines of Sunday school loved to fish out and hold in Styrofoam cups as up the hill their parents sat in solemn contemplation of the holy scripture.

Maynard Houck, the preacher and walking registrar of attendance, was omnipresent on the steps of the church before services. For years Maynard served dutifully as the church organist, but at an opportunistic moment upon the nearly simultaneous death of the church's now-late pastor and his second in line, a man named Council

Ward, the former having gone the old-fashioned way via sudden cardiac arrest, the latter from a well-placed bee sting on the temple, Maynard was vaulted into the open pulpit and he never looked back.

For a man who had purposefully eluded enlightenment's pursuit, he was a master of linguistic nuance. He had a hundred different ways of suggesting, without saying, that this church member or that had been derelict in the ways of the Lord. He could say "Good to see you" in a way that meant it was genuinely good to see someone (reserved for well-attended parishioners), and then he could say precisely the same words again to the next parishioners in a way that meant "It's certainly been a while since you've been to our house of worship." Perhaps moral opprobrium is more easily heard by one with a guilty conscience.

Of his entire congregation, which seldom exceeded a hundred people, there was no one Maynard targeted more than my father. He had my father's number, to be sure. He never missed a chance to pick at him; to take some kind of well-calculated shot. The source of the antipathy, from what I could tell, was Father's barely concealed disdain for the local, rather unacademic interpretation of the holy scripture. His very real indifference to Maynard's religious exhortations caused the poor man an ongoing paroxysm of grief, and Maynard took any opportunity, however small, to volley subtle antagonism back at Father. Generally we just pushed on through and ignored any mordant remarks from Maynard. However, on this particular morning he took special care.

Catching us on the steps of the church, he said (through badly divided teeth), "Welcome, folks! Glad to have you today. We *missed* you last week." Then almost inaudibly: "And the week before that, I believe." He feigned a smile and showed two rows of Indian corn. His thin, pale tongue emerged like a snake from a hole and switched back and forth across his translucent lips. This was an absurd affectation he had developed; apparently he thought it charming. "I can't recall the last time I saw the whole family here. I'm so glad y'all saw fit to come down this morning." He sidled up to Father and walked along beside us as we entered the sanctuary.

"I almost forgot to ask. Are you still working on that book of yours?" Always clever, this was how Maynard would needle Father today.

"I am," Father said.

"That's good. I thought it would be con- siderate of me to ask. Do you plan to finish it one day?" Maynard laughed; Father did not.

"I do."

"What's this one about?"

"My life, I suppose. My father, my mother. But I'm not going about it in the usual way —"

"— Your mother!" interjected Maynard. "That precious woman. How's she doing? I've heard not all that well." He gave an obligatory solemn shake of the head. "Bless her heart. Time goes so fast for all of us."

"Indeed," said Father. I could almost hear him grinding his teeth.

"You know, Henry, I wish I'd written something," said Maynard, modulating to counterfeit sincerity. "I guess we all want to be writers. We do, don't we? And here you already are. But — you're also a lawyer. Are you a writer or a lawyer? You can't be both, I wouldn't think."

"I'm both, although at times it seems I don't do either particularly well," said Father.

"Common sentiment," said Maynard, who rushed right into: "Still! It's good when y'all make it. I was honestly beginning to won- der if y'all'd changed churches on me."

"Maynard," said Father, his patience in meteoric decline, "on a beautiful day like this one, I often prefer to observe the Sabbath by staying at home — with a cardinal for a chorister, and an orchard for a dome." This last little ornamentation about the cardinal and the orchard was a bit of Emily Dickinson. I'd heard my father invoke this reasoning on prior occasions to avoid attending church with Mother. At once she seized Father's arm and encouraged him into a pew ahead of her and away from Maynard. I heard Father whisper, "Has a murder ever been committed in a church?"

Mother said, "Maybe. Why?"

"Because I was about ten seconds away from killing that mephitic little charlatan." At the time I didn't know what this meant, but context suggested it wasn't a compliment.

My father's attitude toward religion was complex and seldom articulated in my presence. Many of his relatives were so-called Primitive Baptist, and it would be fair to say by most reasonable standards that they were *excessively* spiritual. Treated as a group, they fell somewhere between fundamentalist and fanatical in the continuum of religiosity, with some of them approaching a wild zealotry usually reserved for the clinically insane or those malingerers exploiting religion for personal gain. His parents, while God-fearing and in regular attendance at their church, were not overly devout, so it was a mystery to me why so many of the children and cousins turned out to have such fervor.

Mother's religious beliefs were much simpler. She believed that people could be good just by virtue of being good, notwithstanding any religious affiliation or devotion one might have had. You did what you believed was right, and that was the whole analysis. She believed it was possible to be a good, honest person just for goodness's sake, whether in the presence or the absence of God. She was known for helping others in the community, and she did these things without any expectation of reward — on earth or elsewhere. She just thought it was the right thing to do.

She sometimes delivered food to a local home for troubled youths called the Copper Kettle. During one visit, one of the young men snuck out a window, set the house on fire, stole her car, and promptly rolled it three times into a cow pasture two miles away. Thankfully, no one was seriously hurt. Mother was called to testify at his criminal trial. He was seventeen years old and had no living parents, having been abandoned early in life. After testifying under oath as to the facts, Mother offered her unsolicited non-expert opinion to the jury that the young man, with whom she had endured a great deal of contact over the years, needed a hug and someone to take him into a permanent home and love him and look after him far more than he needed any type of extended punitive confinement. Upon leaving the stand, Mother walked to the defense table and gave the poor boy a hug. For several minutes afterward, he just sat there and cried. At the end of the trial and after no more than five minutes of deliberation, the jury returned with a verdict of not guilty. The jury foreman asked the judge from the jury box what the prospects were of getting the defendant into a good foster home.

Mother enjoyed going to church, but it was not because she felt the need to seek forgiveness for her sins or because she was interested in the content of the day's sermon. It was more that she enjoyed the fellowship of her neighbors and she loved to sing hymns. When it came time to sing, Mother would be first up from the pew with her hymnal open, singing triumphantly and gaily, unself-consciously, like a songbird. All of which explains, or helps explain, why we attended church in the first place despite Father's distaste for most brands of mountain religion.

After the service, we filed outside to the northern end of the church where our car was parked. Here, in the cold shadow of a giant blue spruce, the church elders were buried. Their once-white headstones, now covered in black moss, protruded from the earth at odd angles, suggesting the entombing soil had moved glacially through time like glass in a cathedral window. The names were still legible, but no one ever read them anymore. Just beyond the creek and the next valley the Barrowfields lay brown and desolate.

Before we reached the car, we were collared by the always shrewd Rancy Grubb, who was a member of our congregation and several others. She was an incorrigible and corrupt town gossip who'd made a mostly dishonest living buying and selling county real estate from people who were easily duped, and this she did happily and without remorse. Part of her trade was knowing everyone's business, an endeavor she undertook tirelessly as both a habit and an occupation. She seemed to delight in (and often profited from) the misfortune of others, which made her particularly unsavory. The fulcrum of her power was to know the bad news about people before they knew it themselves and use it against them.

Standing at Father's driver's side door to prevent our escape, she said, "How have y'all been?" in a delectable, unctuous drawl. She held a plastic drinking cup with only her fingernails, like a claw, and set it on top of the car.

"Just fine," said Father.

"I tell you, Henry," said Rancy, her long, venal fingers closing around Father's hand, "I've been busier than hell on judgment day. You'd think at my age I'd slow down a little." Father looked down at me and shook his head.

"Look, Henry — I've been meaning to ask you: Do y'all have any interest in selling some of that land? I'm not talking about the house. I don't want that. I'm talkin' about the bottom land down there where those horses are kept."

"I don't think so," said Father. "Not anytime soon."

"That house now — that's something different," said Rancy, with bulging eyes and a look of mystification. "That's your problem. You'll never sell it if you were to ever move."

"It's nice inside," said Mother. "And we

107

can see everything from up there." The last of her words dissolved out of hearing as a tractortrailer carrying crates of chickens in low cages rumbled by on the narrow road a few feet away, leaving dirty floating feathers and a putrid smell that soured everyone's faces.

"Is it true that something awful happened to a whole family of people in that house?" Rancy stared up at Father, mouth agog, waiting for a response. I'm certain she already knew the answer but just wanted to hear it firsthand. It'd give her more credibility when she retold the story later on.

"That's what we understand," said Father. "But it was a long time ago and it never crosses our minds."

"What happened exactly?"

"No one really knows," said Father.

"But it was a murder, right?"

"It appears so."

"Did you know about it when you bought the house? It's a material fact, you know. It has to be disclosed. You could sue."

"I'm not sure that's true," said Father.

"It *is* true," said Rancy, still holding Father's hand like a supplicant.

"Is it?" said Father.

"Well, you're the lawyer," said Rancy, finally releasing her grip.

"It doesn't bother us," said Father. "Everyone who's had a house that's more than fifty years old has lived in a house that someone's died in. It's not all that uncommon. In another twenty years, no one will even remember."

"That's right," said Mother, ushering Threnody and me to the other side of the car. "It's not out of the ordinary. And we try not to talk about it in front of the children."

Before we left, Father, with his long black rider's coat streaming out behind him like a pennant, moved with his customary long strides over to Maynard outside the church and said, "See you in a few weeks." Maynard was unable to formulate a reply, but I know now that he vowed then, as he always did, to one day repay Father's irreverence. And this he would do in time.

When we got into the car, I asked what had happened to the family who had lived in the house before us. Mother and Father looked at each other. "That's a story for another time, young man," said Father. "Don't ask about it again." And that was that.

9

A mile from home we drove by Violet Clay-bank's house. She lived on the side of a hill just above the road in a white and blue single-wide trailer. The front yard featured a few scraggly trees and an old metal bed-frame, inside of which Violet had planted rows of flowers.

Looking alarmed, Violet was out by the road in her pajamas and she flagged us down as we went by. The only thing I knew about Violet was that she did strange things to her cat, which was named Princess Mary Love. She had caught it somewhere, prob-ably in a trap. Violet was never blessed with a husband or a child, but once she got ahold of this poor lost cat, she never let it out of her sight again. She would sometimes set it outside, but only if it was affixed in some manner to a large red brick. Violet would attach the cat to the brick (or vice versa) with a long piece of baling twine, and then she'd set the cat and the brick on her little front porch together, both of which were entirely out of place in the company of the other. At first, the cat would merely venture just far enough off the porch to use the bathroom. Later, the cat grew more daring. It would drag the brick off the porch and pull it with obvious strain all over the front of the hill. When you drove by, you'd sometimes see the cat sitting there looking out over the valley, but the brick was never far away. Occasionally you'd be lucky enough to see the poor thing climbing back up the grassy hill very slowly, one grueling step at a time like a rock climber, trying to make it back to the trailer with the brick in tow.

I heard someone ask Violet once, "Ain't you afraid a dog or a mountain lion is gonna come along and get that cat? It can't run when it's tied up to that brick."

"No, I watch her from the winda in yonder," Violet had said. "I'd just like to see 'em try. I got a buckshot rifle I've been itchin' to use."

Out the window of the car, Mother called over, "Violet — is everything okay?"

"No," cried Violet. "It's not. It's not okay at all." She was white as biscuit flour.

"Honey, what's wrong?" said Mother, getting out of the car.

"It's Princess Mary Love."

Mother and Violet huddled in the yard briefly and then Mother solemnly returned to the vehicle. She looked at me and said, "Violet needs your help for a little bit."

"What's she need help with?"

"Her cat."

"The one she ties to a brick in the front yard?"

"Yes."

"Well —"

"The cat's no longer with us," said Mother.

"I was afraid of that," said Father.

"Did it run away?" I said. "Does she need help finding it?" This seemed like an interesting conquest to me.

"No — it died. She thought you could help her dig a small grave and bury it. I told her I would do it, but she said she didn't think she'd need a very big hole and that you were more fit for the job."

"Did it strangle on the rope?"

Mother disclosed that the beloved cat-child had come to the end of its days in the clutches of a hawk that came down out of the woods and killed it before Violet, ever vigilant, could get out the door to save it. The hawk tore the cat apart with Violet right there swatting at it maniacally with a broom.

She had already put a homemade wreath on her front door.

"Do I have to?"

"Yes, son, you do."

I got out of the car and watched with despondency as it moved slowly up the road and away from me behind faint nebulas of trailing dust. Reluctantly, I was set into the involuntary servitude of the crazy cat lady. She took me around to her backyard, where a box made out of discarded fence board sat on the ground under a dogwood tree. I gathered that this was the coffin that she or someone had made for the cat. The box was easily large enough to accommodate a child.

"Where would you like me to dig the hole?"

"Right ch'here, under the shade of the tree." Violet's pendulous breasts swung loosely under the fabric of her nightshirt.

"Do you have a shovel?"

"Yes, I've got a shovel. I'll go get it."

I started digging vigorously and soon needed to take a break. Violet said, "Have you used a shovel before? You have? Well, look. You don't have to go at this like you're killin' snakes. That hole's not goin' anywhere."

It took me a solid hour of hard shoveling to produce a hole of sufficient size to fit the box and I wound up with a large, painful blister on my right hand. I could hear Father telling me that I should have asked for a pair of gloves.

Finally the time came to lower the box into the hole, which required more effort than I expected. Violet then disappeared into the house and came back out in a black dress suitable for a funeral with a Bible and some flowers that I surmised had come from the flower bed in the front yard.

"I want to see her one more time before I bury her," she said, crying all the while. She knelt down beside the cat grave, muddying her knees, and removed the lid of the coffin, which had not been affixed with nails as I had assumed. I edged closer to the grave and peered into the freshly dug hole, morbidly curious to see the dead cat and the damage done to it by the hawk. To my horror, I saw that the cat had been dressed like a doll, in a doll's dress and white lace hat, like a dead child. It lay there on its side, its calico legs sticking straight out, its tongue protruding oddly from the side of its mouth. The dress had been cut down the front to allow for the legs to escape and then refastened under the cat's chin. It appeared to be missing an eye.

I remembered myself and looked over at

Violet, who was silently weeping as one hand stroked the stiff deceased animal. After what seemed to me an interminable period of time, she closed the coffin, placed the flowers she had picked on top, and stood to commence the eulogy.

Putting the dirt back in the hole did not prove nearly as hard as getting it out, and by the end of another hour I had produced a nice, smooth mound of dirt under the tree.

"Now we'll need some rock," she said. "You'll find plenty out there in the field."

I walked home after sitting with Violet in her kitchen for a suitable time to drink a glass of milk and reflect on what had transpired. She gave me a hug and said she'd drive me home, but I said I preferred to walk.

I hiked up and over the side of the hill through the tall grass to the near side of the woods, and then followed the line of woods around to where the hill came back down to meet the gravel road. Through a clearing off to the west I could see the black face of Ben Hennom and our house planted on the weathered rock like a tree without soil, and I thought about the people who had lived there before and wondered what had happened to them and if I was sleeping in one of the rooms where someone had died.

10

I looked for Father when I got home to re-
lay my adventures with the dead cat, and
was not surprised to find him in his office
writing. Hoping to gain entry on the basis
of the permission I'd received the previous
evening, I grabbed *Flatland* out of my room
and quietly resumed my place on the floor
next to his desk. Finally taking notice of
me, he looked up a bit dazed as if he might
have just awakened. He laid down his pen
and pulled me into his arms.

"How was it?"

"Worst experience of my life," I said,
plucking absently at the whorling cowlick
on the top of his head.

"Really? That bad?"

"Pretty bad."

"Did you get the cat buried?"

"We sure did. It was wearing a dress."

"The cat was?"

"Yep." Father showed genuine astonishment, and I was glad to have impressed him with that bit of grotesquerie. He picked up a pen and wrote *dead cat / cerement: child's dress* in one of his notebooks.

"If she gets another one," I said, "I'm not helping her bury it. I don't care if she files adoption papers for it at the courthouse." Father said he thought that was reasonable.

I asked him if he would take me on an adventure into the woods behind the house, which ran up the mountain for hundreds of acres over boulder and crag and had never been sufficiently explored by anyone, so far as I knew. Father called the woods the Gnarled Forest, and the name was apt. I had made several timid forays along the edge, but I'd never had the courage to go far enough to get lost. He said, "I really need to work, son. Let's do it some other time." I pleaded with him and did a little dance and he reluctantly buckled. Closing his notebook, he brightened considerably.

"I'll tell you what. I'll go if your mother will pack us something to eat. We obviously don't want to die out there." And then brighter still: "Have you heard of Magellan? Ponce de León? Cavendish? Alexander Gordon Laing? George Drouillard?" These he compiled into a space of about five seconds and my head spun around.

"I've heard of Magellan," I said. "What do you smell like?"

"God knows."

"Are you trying not to breathe?"

"No — of course not." He was, though.

"It smells like licorice."

"It's not, I can assure you."

On the wall in front of his desk was a framed photograph of Thomas Wolfe, standing desolate in a greatcoat and vest in the corner of a room with his shadow cast in triplicate upon the closed door next to him. To the right of the desk was a ghoulish daguerreotype of Poe in a black leather frame with a copper inlay of asterisks (* * * *) that ran around it. A simple painting-lamp illuminated it from the top, day and night. On one of the arms of the lamp Father had positioned a shiny black facsimile of a bird that contributed to the absurdity. From any distance, to see the man hunched over his desk with the bird above him on the wall made you think of madness. In the day, the scene was a caricature. At night, it was ghastly and haunted my dreams.

"What kind of bird is that?"

"I don't know exactly," said Father, examining it from below. "It might be a blackbird. Or a crow, possibly. Maybe a grackle. It's supposed to be a raven, but it's not. You can tell from the beak."

"Where'd you get it?"

"I found it."

"Impossible."

"No, I did."

"Where?"

"You're going to find this hard to believe, my beamish boy, but I swear to you this is the truth: I found it in a cornfield."

"This bird."

"Yes, this very one."

"What was it doing in a cornfield?"

"I have no idea."

Mother packed us ham sandwiches and wrapped them in wax paper with tape. With a roll of her eyes, she crossed herself as we were heading out of the driveway into the woods. Father and I set out up the hill like desert cartographers. He told me that at the top of the mountain the woods ended and there was a clearing from which we could see the whole county and probably Tennessee and Virginia. He said he'd never been up there, but that he could see the bald of the mountain from town.

Walking into the woods was like entering a cave. The trees were obsidian, timeless, and immense. Rotted limbs lay on the ground amidst blankets of decaying leaves, and heavy, writhing vines hung down to the

119

ground in places, but these unfortunately were not vines that one could swing on, as I discovered time and again. Laurel bushes and rhododendron fought for an existence under the forest ceiling and often appeared frail and in need of sunlight. Gargantuan rock slabs jutted sharply out of the earth at angles, making broad shelters and hollows.

Some of the going was very steep, requiring both of us to grab hold of vines and trees to propel us up the hill. For the second time that day, I regretted not having gloves. The roughness of the locust trunks was wearing my hands raw and tearing at the weeping blister.

"Did you bring any gloves?" I asked Father as he pulled himself up on a rock ledge just ahead of me.

"Yes." He had them in his back pocket. "Did you bring yours?"

"No," I said sullenly.

Father sat down on the mossy platform onto which he had just ascended and waited for me to catch up. "Well," he said, "we've got four hands, but only two gloves. Any ideas?"

"No," I said. "You could give me yours."

I joined him on the ledge and we took turns drinking water from the thermos Mother had sent with us. His glasses fogged and he cleaned them with his shirt, only to have them fog up again. He took off one shoe and shook a rock out of it.

"Son, who is tougher? You or me?"

Not thinking this through, I said, "I am."

"I expect you're right. By that measure, then, I need the gloves worse than you do."

Having delivered some enigmatic lesson, he tossed me the gloves and we resumed our trek up the mountain. Our trip recalled to his voracious mind every forest and tree poem he had ever read. This began with our encounter with a birch tree. He broke off a twig and gave it to me to chew on, and then came the Robert Frost. "Birches" — he knew one or two complete stanzas from that one, and then there were others. He taught me "Nothing Gold Can Stay" and made me recite it over and over again until I had committed it to memory. We climbed on. The beauty of wild growth prompted a few lines of Coleridge's poem about a lime-tree bower. " 'Well, they are gone, and here I must remain . . . / On springy heath, along the hill-top edge, / Wander in gladness, and wind down, perchance, / To that still roaring dell, of which I told . . .' " As the forest grew deep and dark in our ascent, he resorted to Poe, which seemed more apt then: " 'Dim vales — and shadowy floods — /

121

And cloudy-looking woods, / Whose forms we can't discover / For the tears that drip all over.' "

"The cloudy-looking woods," I sang. "The cloudy-looking woods!"

It took us two good hours of diligent and steady climbing to reach the top of the mountain. Nearing the peak, the trees and undergrowth became sparser, and short clumps of fragrant heather grew in peculiar patterns. As we continued to climb, a few bedraggled trees remained but the vegetation thinned, for underneath our feet was not soil but white, ageless stone with nothing around it but the blue summer sky. Remnants of fallen trees lay about in places, turned bone-white like skeletons of ancestral forgotten beasts by the unrelenting eye of the sun. At the top of the mountain, on this broad stone face, we stood and looked out over an immeasurable swath of green hills, forests, and pastures, all rolling imperturbably into the Blue Ridge Mountains lying to the west and north. The effect was dizzying.

Just below the top of the hill looking south was a magnificent tree. It stood absolutely alone at the edge of the mountain — there were no other trees around it — and below it the elevation fell sharply away five hundred feet. At first I thought it was dead; most of its limbs were bare and it had been stripped of its bark. But then I noticed a single green and yellow leaf waving in the sun at the utmost top. And then I noticed more; one here, and another there.

"What on earth happened to it?" I asked.

"It looks like it's been struck by lightning a few times. Yes — see how the trunk is black here all the way up? It looks like it's been burned, maybe on more than one occasion. I guess that's not surprising. The poor tree is out here all by itself." Father put his hands on the trunk as if he were saying goodbye to a dear friend.

Over time I developed a well-trodden path up through the Gnarled Forest to the top of the mountain where the venerable old tree stood. It became a place to escape to; a place to go to read, or to think, or to absorb oneself in the ocean of inconsequence that could be delivered upon contemplation of one's place in the universe from the top of that lonely hill. It would be six years before I would stand beneath the tree with my father again, and that would be the last time.

11

Maddy had been in a slow but measurable decline since my parents had moved back to Old Buckram, but it seemed now that the pace of her deterioration had quickened. Her fits of coughing had grown worse and her legs and feet swelled even more. She couldn't go anywhere without a walker, and even then it was with great difficulty. She left her work at the church and stopped meeting her friends for lunch and stayed closed up indoors all day, not even venturing out to sit on the front porch when the weather was nice. Gradually, the smell of cinnamon and cider faded from the house and apples piled up and rotted in the uncut grass. Another autumn came, and then winter, and with the winter came heavy snow, frozen ground, and cracked earth. I sensed that death would arrive that year uninvited.

Father was the only one of the five children who returned to Old Buckram after moving away, so he was the only one of them who saw Maddy regularly. Going into Helton and Maddy's house in the fall and winter was always like walking into the mouth of a furnace, and this phenomenon had only become more pronounced. Maddy had grown colder with the earth, and she seemed determined to heat the world from the inside out. On this February night there was a good six inches of hard-packed snow on the ground and the wind continued to blow long after the sun had gone down. Earlier in the week, the drugstore on Main Street had caught on fire due to an electrical short and burned to the ground because the municipal water supply was frozen. Firemen opened up the hydrants and hours later there were just billowing plumes of ice on the sidewalk as tall as a man.

Father and I came inside after stomping the snow out of our boots and shaking it off our coats. My grandfather was standing in the kitchen in a pair of shorts and a short-sleeved shirt.

"How are you doing?" said my father. The men shook hands. My grandfather was at the age that questions of this sort were no longer rhetorical. "Pretty good, I reckon," he said, feeling absently at his chest. "How are you?"

"Fair to middlin'," said my father, playing the part. "I can't complain."

"Wouldn't do any good," said my grandfather.

"Did anybody tell you that it's winter outside?" said Father, observing the summer shirt. The men laughed and Father started unbagging the vegetables he had brought from the store.

"God almighty, it's hot in here."

"Obviously, I'm not in charge," said my grandfather.

"I got you some things. A couple sweet potatoes —"

"I don't really care for sweet potatoes," said my grandfather.

"I know. And I got you some butternut squash. I thought they looked good for this time of the year. And I brought you a zucchini."

"That looks an awful lot like a cucumber."

"It's not a cucumber. It's a zucchini. They're related, but only distantly."

Winking at me, my grandfather said, "I'll pass on the zucchini. It looks like it comes from the cucumber family, and I liked to be killed by one of those one time."

"Your grandfather discovered that he has an allergy to cucumbers," Father explained, looking first in the refrigerator for a beer and then in the cabinets for something stronger.

"Listen," said my grandfather, "imagine you've got two hogs. If you feed one of them nothing but cucumbers, and the other nothing at all, the one that eats the cucumbers will starve to death first." He aspirated a winded laugh and Father just shook his head. You can't teach an old dog new tricks.

Maddy came in from the living room one slow step at a time using her walker and we were all in the small kitchen together, the ceiling low over our heads. She was wearing heavy fire-retardant pajamas made of oven-mitt material, and on her feet she wore socks with rubber treading that she'd brought home from the hospital. A cheap cigarette case with a twist clasp sat alone in the basket of her walker, and when she finally came to a shuffling stop, she fumbled with it and shook out a cigarette. Holding it between two fingers, she said, "Hello, son," to Father and kissed me on the cheek, leaving a trace of orange lipstick and a fragrance like the smell of a wetland bog. All at once she was hit by one of her hacking coughs and, knocking over her walker, desperately sought a hold on the back of a chair that was just out of her reach. The cigarette fell to the floor and rolled under the table where the linoleum had come loose and was curling up. Father and Helton each caught an arm and held her while she convulsed. When the coughing relented, Father helped her back into the living room to sit down.

"I'd like to watch the television," she said, so Father turned on the small black-and-white TV and adjusted the antenna wrapped in foil until the picture was clear. The news came on and we were silent as we learned that a husband and wife had been shot and killed in Charlotte during a robbery, and that four people had died in a traffic accident with a tractor-trailer on the interstate near Statesville. Helton and Maddy just shook their heads in disbelief. "What's the world coming to?" said Maddy. "It's not safe to be anywhere."

After the news a short-lived variety show came on and a fellow doing a comedy routine told a joke about a man who got to drive the family car while his wife had to walk everywhere she needed to go. This reminded my grandfather of a story, as almost everything did. All his stories began with "It's like the man said —" This was his introduction to every dispensation of wisdom or humor. "It's like the man said," he began. "He saw an Injun riding a horse one day, with his squaw walking along behind him. The man said to the Injun, 'Why is she walking when you're riding?' The Injun replied, 'She ain't got a horse.' " I laughed because I hadn't heard that one before, and Father pretended to be wryly amused. Maddy just made a sour face and lit another cigarette, no doubt having heard it all before. I believe by then she had pretty well given up. She was tired of living.

My grandfather sat in a La-Z-Boy recliner in one corner of the room wearing fabric deck shoes that his toenails had made holes in the tops of. Maddy was at one end of the couch and was spitting into a cup with a paper towel crushed up in the bottom. Father was at the other end of the couch and I sat on a chair brought in from the dining room. It was strange to go from the house on the hill with books in every room to this house, which had no books at all.

"How are you feeling, Mother?"

"I'm good. I'm tired."

"She's good," said my grandfather. "She's just tired."

"Is there anything I can do for you?" asked Father.

"I don't think so, unless you want to shovel out the walk sometime this week. If we had an emergency, Helton might break his neck trying to get me to the car."

"We'll do that," said Father, giving me a nod, which meant I needed to be the one to remember this. "I brought you over some things to eat —"

"I heard you saying that," said Maddy. "Helton, please turn that fan off me. It's givin' me a sore throat." My grandfather got up and adjusted a small oscillating fan that was blowing heat from the kitchen's woodstove into the room. He stopped the fan from turning and rotated it thirty degrees so that it was aimed toward the wall, where it now rattled a picture frame hanging beside the window. I was anxious that it might fall but no one else seemed to notice.

Maddy said, "How're you comin' with your book?"

Father sighed and thought about what to say; then said, "I've made good progress, I really have. I think I'm finally getting close."

"You've been workin' on that book a long time," said Maddy. "A *long* time. As long as I can remember."

"I know," said Father, "but I'm nearly to a point where I can —"

"You've been saying that for a long time, too."

"Well, damn it, it's hard work."

Maddy looked aghast at the vulgarity.

"People're writing books all the time. Your cousin Eddie just wrote a book that they're selling at the gas station. He wrote that in less than a year from what he told me."

"He and I are not writing the same kind of book. His book is about waterfalls. He printed it on a copy machine at the school."

"Still. Maybe you should talk to him." Maddy wiped at the corners of her mouth with a folded tissue and returned her attention to the television.

"And I'm actually finished, to tell you the truth," said Father to the center of the room; to no one. "I'm just working on a few revisions now." I tried to meet his eyes to show him I was listening and that I understood, but he didn't see me.

"That doesn't sound like you're finished, then," said my grandfather, laughing. It was the most important thing in the world to my father, and they acted as though this was just one of a dozen foolish hobbies he'd soon forget, like he was collecting postage stamps as a child.

"Helton," said Maddy, "I've got to get to bed. Will you help me in there? Boys, thank you for coming over. I wish I was feeling better and could talk more."

We walked Maddy into the bedroom and Father helped her to the bed, where, before lying down, she lit another cigarette. The room, painted gray or colored that way from years of exhaled smoke, had blinds over the windows and valances but no curtains, and the walls showed nothing except nail holes in the plaster — a faint reminder of facsimile paintings once hung, now taken down for reasons unknown. A dresser sat against one wall, and on the dresser in a thicket of unmatching frames were pictures of family, all long out-of-date. The wooden floor next to the bed on Maddy's side showed a cluster of burn marks where she'd fallen asleep with her cigarette lit and it had dropped to the floor to burn itself out, miraculously not burning the house down with it. Father sat down on the bed beside Maddy and she took his hand and held it. A mother — her son. There was nothing else to say.

Father and I left them there in the bedroom as if we had never been there; as if we had walked into and out of a scene from a play in which we were not actors and which didn't realize our presence. On the way home, Father said, "Son, if I ever catch you with a cigarette or any other kind of tobacco, you can rest assured that you won't live long enough to have to worry about cancer." Light from the few streetside lamps moved in and out of the truck as we passed.

I could see the pain on his face.

"Can't you just *make* her quit? Just take the cigarettes whenever she buys them."

"I wish I could. I have certainly tried. And she's not buying them. Your grandfather is."

"Doesn't he know they're bad for her?"

"He does. He doesn't want her to smoke. It's complicated."

"He shouldn't buy them for her. You should tell him. Do you want me to tell him?"

"I learned a long time ago that you can't make a grown person do something they don't want to do. You just can't. That's the way the world works."

The snow began to fall again, as it had for days. The wind stopped and the snow fell slowly, serenely, in large flakes that were made bright by the headlights of the truck with nothing but an impenetrable black sky and black world just beyond, and it no longer felt as cold. When we got to the top of Ben Hennom, Father turned off the truck but just sat and stared out into the darkness. "I just realized," he said, "that I've run out of time."

The next night he asked that we say grace before dinner. Saying grace was something we almost never did. The one or two exceptions I can recall occurred when Maddy was dying.

And then Father stopped going to work. He stopped eating, as far as I could tell. He stopped doing anything that occurred in an expanse of time — except writing. I think he was trying to finish his book before Maddy died, or trying to keep her alive somehow by not finishing it. His purgatory would continue as long as she lived, and this he would do for her if it would save her.

His hair grew long; he stopped shaving and sprouted an unkempt beard. Day and night he sat at his desk. Because my room was next to his writing room, I could hear him in the middle of the night. The sounds I remember: his chair sliding on the floor away from his desk; his footsteps going quietly down the stairs to get another drink; a tipped bottle, caught at the last second, followed by a vacuum of silence; wine being poured into a glass from a great height; his excited walks along the shelves; the muted creaking of the rolling ladder, and his weight on it as he climbed to get a book. In the mornings, he would be gone.

12

In the hours before dawn on a moonless night in September 1981, my grandfather awoke with a start. He no longer heard Maddy breathing next to him. She had died quietly in the night. He held her in his arms and wept, and whispered in her ear that her suffering had finally come to an end. When I heard the phone ring, I knew what had happened.

Maddy had made it known that she wanted to be buried in the old family cemetery plot in Avernus. That was where the funeral service was to be held. There was a flurry of discussion that morning about what I was to wear, and whether Threnody would attend. She had been sick and Mother thought she ought to stay at home.

Father and I drove to Helton and Maddy's house where we met the family. The driveway was full of unfamiliar cars, and people I didn't know were standing on the porch in suits and dresses of mourning. People from all over had brought enough homemade food to feed us all for a month, and the containers covered the kitchen counter and the small dining table and even the coffee table in the living room. Father's sisters were up from Hickory and Lenoir with their husbands, and his brother had driven up from Elizabethtown. We went inside and everyone held hands and cried and laughed and told stories to relieve some of the pain.

I didn't know what to think or how to feel about Maddy's passing. I walked around in the shadow of everyone else's sorrow. The new and unfamiliar sense of loss I felt was, I think, somehow secondary; somehow subordinate to the feelings of Father and my grandfather, who were so much more acutely affected by her death. The immediacy of their suffering was apparent. The sadness I thought I felt on that morning and in the coming days was not, of course, the isolated sense of grief that eventually settles on you and clings to you like a heavy coat in the many quiet days after a funeral when, intellectually, you come to understand that the person who has died will never return and the world is now permanently altered from how it once was. It was more the very real pain that comes when a loved one is hurting and nothing can be done to help it.

We drove out to Avernus and followed a dirt road up to the top of a broad, flat hill that had been cleared of trees. On the hill were dozens of old grave markers that were scattered about and clustered here and there in groups. It was evident that interments here did not occur in any organized way. Many of the tombstones were of a sufficient age that the engraved lettering, if there had ever been any, was so eroded by time and weather that it was no longer visible. In the farthest corner of the cemetery a makeshift tent had been set up next to a large pile of red-clay mud. Beside the tent was an aged gray hearse, and in front of the hearse were two folding tables on which someone had arranged four half-gallon containers of sweet tea and a few plates of thin store-bought butter cookies. A dozen metal chairs leaned against the tent. There were no table-cloths or linens. Paper cups had been set out for the tea and a small pile of paper nap-kins sat on the edge of the table, held down by a stone.

A gaunt man in polyester slacks and a wide-collared shirt stood near the table clutching a Bible to his chest and chewing on a stick of slippery elm. His name was

Harold Specks. He had recently taken over as interim pastor at Helton and Maddy's church. He had no formal theological training, but none of the other Old Buckram preachers did either. He had never read a book other than the Bible except the ones he read in the first few years of his schooling. He had no special insight into the machinations of God or Jesus or the Holy Spirit or the flights of the angels or the schemes of the demons that populate and blacken the air, but the certitude with which he condemned sinners to hell elevated him to the head of his church at a young age and he preached for his entire life. On this day, Pastor Specks would deliver the sermon.

We arrived early. Over time, more and more cars came up the hill and parked in rows next to the cemetery. Most of the men and women who got out of the cars were elderly. They trudged slowly up the hill to the faded green canvas tent standing over the grave. Women who needed to sit were given chairs while the men stood. Quiet greetings were exchanged here and there, but solemnity reigned and no laughter was heard. The September sky was monochrome from horizon to overhead.

By 1:30, the last of the cars had come up

the road and a group of about sixty people stood in a wide arc around the gravesite. Wind whipped at the fabric of the tent, but the few trees on the hill behind the cemetery were unmoved.

Pastor Specks stepped forward into the circle, gripping the book in his left hand in that peculiar way that mountain preachers hold a Bible. He would not read from it. This was not to be a eulogy for the departed. This was to be a sermon, and the people would listen.

He preached for an hour. It was all hellfire and brimstone, every word. He hardly paused to breathe. In the punctuated cadence of a diabolical auctioneer, the preacher's voice rang out in the hills. He spat as he called out the message. A sticky white froth formed in the corners of his mouth and drew up between his lips. He held the Bible high over his head and shook it at the heavens as his increasingly hysterical oratory rained down upon the people. They watched him without expression. They had all heard this before and they believed. Oh, they believed. This message, they knew, was not for them. It was for a nonbeliever among them. The preacher knew that a man in his presence harbored doubt in his black heart, and the doubt had to be torn out like a cancer. The preacher knew there were doubts, because in moments of dark and shadow, he knew what it was to doubt. He comprehended not the enigmatic Trinity; he had not wrought a true miracle of his own. There were books of the Old Testament he had never read, and some he had read and not understood. Only by raising his exultant voice and filling the air with the sound of the Word of God would the demons be run from the sacred temple.

At long last, he exhausted himself and returned to the quiet and shadow of the burial tent to sit in vacant contemplation of nothing.

The time had come to return sweet Maddy to the earth. My father and the other pallbearers removed her austere wooden casket from the hearse and carried it with great difficulty to the grave. Father closed his eyes and wept when she was lowered into the ground.

13

He became a ghost, my father. In the days and weeks after Maddy's funeral, he sat at his desk but no longer wrote and seldom read. Our house, at night, was quiet but for the saturnine sound of the piano coming from downstairs, but it was I who played, and not my father. As my artistic endeavors increased, his declined precipitously, as though in our house there was not room for both. This went on for months, with no end in sight.

Later that year when winter returned to Old Buckram and the anemic sky was invisible day and night, it seemed my father's depression only deepened. One arctic morning while Father and Threnody slept, Mother and I got up before the sun to attend to the horses. The wind that had circled the house and cried at the windows all the previous night had gone elsewhere. Now the black-white winter world was still.

In the barn at the bottom of the hill I scooped the sweet feed with a discarded coffee can and smelled the black pelleted grains and molasses. A cold steam rose from the watering trough. As the horses worked their buckets, I climbed the ladder into the loft and threw down two bales of hay that bounced and cartwheeled to a stop at Mother's waiting feet. With a hoof knife, she cut the twine and tore out a fistful of hay from the middle of the first bale, held it to her face, and breathed it into her lungs. "That smells so good I could eat it," she said. Alfalfa was a delicacy to her.

"I'd like to see that," I said, laughing.

"You don't think I'll do it?" She pulled down her scarf and put an alfalfa stem in her mouth, Huck Finn–style, and chewed on it. "Oh, that's so good," she said. "I should make myself a sandwich." She saw me looking down skeptically from the loft. "You don't believe me? You want to try a piece?" I climbed down and tried one. It was as advertised. Sweet and dusty and floral. "I can see why the horses like this stuff," I said.

Father was at the piano when we came back inside, but he wasn't playing. He was just sitting there upright, his hands folded in his lap. There was no decaying sound in the air and no lingering hint of a last-played chord. The piano was dormant. Mother and I, giddy and excited from our time outdoors, quickly realized from the abyssal silence that we had intruded upon Father's realm of purgatorial quiet. He cocked his head to signify that we'd been observed and then returned his chin to his chest.

I walked quickly by and whispered an inaudible apology for our intrusion. On the steps I turned and looked upon him again. He was unmoved. Quietly, I said, "Good morning." My voice broke and what emerged was surely unheard by him because he didn't respond, so I repeated my greeting. He nodded without looking at me and tried to smile. "My ears are ringing a little," he said. "I've noticed it happens when I play. It's distracting me." I looked and saw a tuft of white cotton protruding from one of his ears.

Mother drove me to school that morning. I walked in through the gymnasium and down the hallway to my first class. Ms. Williams, who taught English, caught me by the sleeve. She was a friend, or perhaps an ally, of my father. She seemed to understand him better than most people in Old Buckram did, which in general was not at all, and this understanding was rooted in their shared love for books and literature. She'd even come by the house a few times to peruse what she called his "staggering collection of books," and usually when she spoke to me, it had something to do with Father. I'd never seen him say much to her and he'd never so far as I knew engaged her in any conversations that one might have with a close friend, but he clearly appreciated her interest in his books. I hadn't yet had her for a class, but she'd always been very kind to me and so I was very fond of her in return.

Looking excited, her nose still red from the cold, she said, "I just found out — can you believe it? What did your father say?" I didn't know what she was talking about, which she deduced from my baffled expression. "About the book! What'd your father say about it? Is he furious?" I was at a loss. At first I thought she was talking about Father's book. "He hasn't said anything," I said. "What book are you —"

"Oh, you don't know. Okay, well, then, I don't feel so terrible for not knowing. The library — Mrs. Ester" — she indicated down the hall and mouthed the name with a scowl — "they're trying to outlaw another book. In fact, they've done it already. This all happened last week."

"I didn't hear," I said.

"Somehow I didn't either," she said. "I'm sure someone made a calculated decision to keep me uninformed as long as possible because they knew I'd raise hell about it. Do me a favor, please. When you see your dad today, tell him to call me. This time it's Faulkner, of all people."

On two earlier occasions, well prior to the point I attained meaningful literacy, the school had banned books from its library and the commissioners had followed suit, removing the same books from the county library as well. The books were, predictably enough, *Lolita* and *Tropic of Cancer.* (The school and county systems apparently did not have a copy of *Tropic of Capricorn* or know it existed, or that one doubtless would have been prohibited as well.) Father had appeared in a public forum and made a subtle and eloquent plea for an abrogation of the decrees on both occasions, and somehow won over a sufficient number of townspeople that the prohibitions were reluctantly reversed upon his recommendation — although, as an inevitable concession, certain age limitations were placed on the books that remain in effect to this day. He was the only one of them, naturally, who had read the books and therefore knew the contents and whether they were as irredeemably salacious as popularly claimed. I knew of these prior battles only because I had been so informed by the dear Ms. Williams, who spun these legendary tales of battle for me in fantastical, even improbable, terms, and regrettably I was too young and foolish then to doubt the veracity of the stories or to know that tales where good triumphs over evil become more fantastical and improbable over time.

Faulkner's trouble in Old Buckram came at the behest of Mrs. Ephegene Ester, a prudish cousin of the aforementioned Mrs. Tichborne, maniacal librarian of note. Mrs. Ester, more formidable even than Mrs. Tichborne, wielded significant political clout with the board of education due to her family's long tradition of service in the Old Buckram school system and their rigidly upright standing in the community (dare not describe it as *erect*). Upon hearing of the "unflattering discourse about the Holy Father" in *As I Lay Dying,* Mrs. Ester made the decision to interdict this masterpiece from the school library and all school reading lists. This was done with the full support of a coalition of local churches, including our occasional church. When the county commissioners were told what Mrs.

Ester had done, they couldn't get a quorum together fast enough to remove the offending book from the (rather paltry) county library as well. Disappointingly, the literary embargo barely made news in Old Buckram.

I daydreamed through my classes and fancied how Father would receive the news and fly into action. I foolishly saw this as an opportunity to return him to his previous vigor. At school I raised the issue with several teachers and classmates and proudly announced to anyone who would listen, "Believe me — my father is going to set these people straight." I said things like "Oh yes, he's a *lawyer*. I fully expect he'll bring a lawsuit against the county if he has to," and "There's no way in creation he's going to let this stand. Mrs. Ester is going to rue the day she pulled that book off the shelf!" I even lied once and said I'd talked to him and that he was livid.

When I got home that afternoon I went straight to Father's library, where I found three copies of the book and promptly started reading the one that appeared to be the least expensive. It wasn't as prurient as I had hoped, or prurient at all, for that matter. The part I read didn't make a great deal of sense to me. Still, I couldn't wait to tell

Father. I knew he'd be furious and would rush to mount a spirited public defense. I waited that night bundled up and shivering on the terrace to see his headlights coming over the distant hill and caught him in the driveway.

"You're not going to believe this," I said, my teeth chattering out of my head. "Mrs. Ester and the commissioners banned Faulkner!" He walked by me in the dark.

"So I heard."

"Can you believe it?"

The response he gave was the merest shrugging of his shoulders. His indifference went through me like a spear.

Dismayed, I trotted along after him and followed him inside. He took off his coat and laid it over a chair in the foyer. I sensed an unspoken irritation; an unidentified source of frustration. Hearing Mother coming down the stairs, he picked up his coat and quickly cut into the parlor and then down the corridor to the Great Room. When he entered the room he dimmed the lights with an abrupt *thwack* of the switch and, with visible impatience, began straightening a few items he perceived as being in a state of disorder, such as a pillow that had fallen forward in its chair and a stack of books that had been pushed aslant. He then ducked down behind the bar and reappeared with a dark liquor of some kind that was made no less opaque by the addition of water or mixer or ice. He glared at me with exasperation.

"Do you want one?"

He was destroying me, one word at a time.

I said nothing, so he talked to his glass: "An old client gave me a bottle of moonshine the other day as payment."

"Did you try it?"

"Not yet. I'm saving it for a superior occasion."

Drink consumed. Another poured. This one took ice. He looked around the room where evidence of passed time had begun to accumulate. A forlorn vase of forgotten spring flowers and a scattering of dried petals. Stacks of unread newspapers. A room redolent of promises made and unfulfilled.

"The book," I said.

"Yes, the book. Tell me about it." He was hardly paying me the slightest attention. I could have said "I'm going to set this house on fire," and he would have said "Superb." My enthusiasm routed, I said, "You honestly don't care?" He said, "Tell me why I should."

"It's Faulkner," I said. "They're banning Faulkner. They're banning *As I Lay Dying,* for god's sake. You have three copies of it. Three hardcover copies. How can you not care?"

While Father and I talked, Old Buckram was abuzz with activity. Word of my boastings at school had gotten around. With all my talk I had unintentionally caused an escalation in the Faulkner affair. In response to my intimations of a swift and devastating reprisal by my father, literary hero to the masses, there had been a meeting of the church coalition, led by none other than Maynard Houck. In this case, after being notified by someone at the school that I had (unwittingly) issued a challenge on Father's behalf, Maynard wasted no time in calling together his like-minded clergy to discuss strategy. Word was disseminated along the usual channels, and within a couple of hours an impromptu bonfire was organized at the Barrowfields, where copies of the offending text would be brought and returned to ashes and dust.

Our phone rang at eight thirty, well after dark, and long enough after Father's arrival that he'd finished one bottle of spirits and started another. I could tell from Mother's voice that the caller was not a stranger but also not a close friend, and that the news was something disconcerting.

150

"Where is this happening?" I thought I heard her say. "And why are they doing this? Yes, I'll tell him, but —" I ran into the room and found her standing, hands on hips, in a posture of indecision.

"Where's your father?"

"He's at his desk. Why? Did something happen?"

"I don't even know if I should say anything. Come with me so I only have to say this once."

We went upstairs and Mother spoke to Father's back. He was not working or reading. A closed book sat on the desk to his right under the lamp, but I could tell from how it lay there that it wasn't being read and would never be read. A serpentine trail of faded condensation rings, lately stained into the wood, made a loose spirograph on the desk, the last one partially occluded by the tumbler now resting in Father's right hand.

"Henry," said Mother, "that was Catherine Williams on the phone. She wants you to know that they're going to . . . they're going to *burn* the books tonight at the Barrowfields. She said she knew you'd want to know. She hopes there's something you can do, but —" This dispatch was delivered with all the gusto of an executioner relaying a death sentence to a man on the gallows. Father turned to look at me but said nothing to Mother. "What books?"

"*As I Lay Dying!*" I shouted. "I told you earlier!" To Mother, I said, "They're going to burn them?"

"Your mother said *books*, plural."

"All the copies of *As I Lay Dying*," I said in disbelief. "They're all going to be burned."

The news of the burning sent me into a wild delirium. In my adolescent paranoia, I interpreted the burning as a direct affront to my father in response to my boasting — an affront intended for our whole family. They were thumbing their noses at us. The open defiance was sickening to me.

My father stared into the well of his glass. Its contents snaked their way into his mouth and disappeared down his throat.

"It doesn't matter," said Mother. "There's nothing that can be done."

"We have to do something," I said to Father. "How — how can they do this? We have to go down there and stop them." He remained unmoved.

"You're not going anywhere," said Mother. "Think about it. Would you have your father ride in there on horseback and fire pistols into the air? And what do you think would happen if he did?"

I screamed "How can you not care?" at Father and went out to his library and brought back a book. "You don't care that they're going to take those books and set them on fire?" I opened the book and tore out a handful of pages and threw them on the ground.

"Stop it," said Mother.

I went back to the bookshelf and came back with another book.

"Don't you dare," said Mother.

"You're telling me you don't care. Fine. If you don't care — then I don't care." I ripped out another handful of pages and this time threw them on the desk in front of him.

"That's enough!" said Mother.

"We have to stop them!" I cried. "We can't let this happen!"

"Quiet," said Mother sharply. "You're going to wake Threnody."

"What can we do to stop them?" said Father at last, his sudden words startling Mother.

"We have to go down there!"

"That's *not* a good idea," said Mother. "Someone could get hurt."

"No one's going to get hurt," said Father, his tongue thick with brown liquor. "But,

153

for god's sake, as you say, there's really nothing that can be done. We're not vigilantes. There's nothing strictly illegal about what they're doing. If they want to burn the library of Alexandria, they can bloody well do it."

Seizing on what I thought to be a clever technicality, I said, "They're going to burn books that belong to the county. Tax dollars paid for those books. They're public property!" Like a spoiled child, I pulled at Father's arm to bring him to his feet.

He resisted and said again, "Son, there's nothing to be done."

"Then I'll go," I shouted. "I'll go and handle it myself!"

I stormed out of the room and ran outside to the balcony of the porch. Through my heaving breath, I stared into the dark and looked across the valley for a glow from the Barrowfields. There wasn't one — they hadn't started yet. A dryness began to form in my mouth and in my throat. I thought for the first time about going down there alone — of going without him — and a crushing, overwhelming sadness moved through me. I was scared half to death. What would I say? Would I say anything? I knew I wouldn't say a word.

The door opened quietly behind me. It

was Father. I dried my tears with my shirt-sleeve and turned to face him, trying to re-assemble my courage and defiance. Before I could speak, he said, "Let's go."

Relief flooded through me and the feeling of deliverance was so great that I almost fell to my knees. Before I could reach him, he said, "Son, this is a mistake."

"Why's it a mistake?"

"Because no good will come from it."

"I don't understand. We have to do some-thing. I said you'd —"

"I know," he said. "I know."

We loaded up with warm clothes and got out to the driveway. Mother came outside with a blanket wrapped around her shoul-ders and a muted but insistent colloquy en-sued between my parents. Father's head dropped in resignation and then Mother's did the same. She came over to talk to me.

She said, "You don't have to do this," but I couldn't be persuaded. My passion had somehow become tied to an irrational belief that, with the gentle tug of my insistence, Father would rise up out of the ashes and find himself again. I started pleading my case to Mother, but she cut me off. "You don't have to tell me," she said. "Believe me, I know how you feel. You are, after all, your father's son."

"We need to go," I said. "We're going to miss it!"

"I wish you wouldn't go."

"I'll be fine," I said.

"It's not you I'm worried about."

We parked on Main Street about three hundred yards from the edge of the Barrowfields. There were more cars in town than I ever remembered seeing and people were standing about in small, frigid clusters, breathing into their hands and rocking on their feet to stay warm.

I was ready to leap out of the car and storm the Barrowfields, but Father didn't move. He just sat there staring into nothing as the wheels turned in his mind. This went on for at least two full minutes. His mouth moved, but I couldn't hear what he was saying. I imagined that he was recalling the entirety of the text of the forbidden book. Somewhere in his brain he knew every word of it. He could do that. I'd seen him do it. I was sure he was envisioning what was going to happen; what his strategy was going to be; how he was going to convince the huddled masses. I was thinking, *There he is. There's my father. He's got this.*

He closed his eyes and said, "You're not going with me. Do you understand? Stay here and don't get out of this car. Stay here

156

or there's going to be hell to pay." Maybe this was the deal he'd made with Mother. The finality with which this message was delivered made it clear that arguing would be of no benefit. "Do you understand?" he asked again. I told him I understood. He buttoned his coat up to his neck and went off into the night.

I watched as he walked out of the streetlights and in the unlit direction of the Barrowfields. When he was a good distance away, I made my way after him. Unsure of which way to go, I walked instinctively toward the faint sound of voices and the suffused glow that lay almost beyond the limits of my vision. The black moss covering the ground which looked so smooth and even from a distance was actually coarse and tangled and unyielding. I stumbled and went down hard on the frostbitten ground. I knew a seldom-used path wound through the Barrowfields, but I'd not managed to find it.

I finally came upon a wide circle of people, men and women, orbiting a hidden nucleus of activity. An unhelpful luminescence resulted from the interplay of a few flashlights. I couldn't find Father so I pushed my way through the crowd until I could see what all the people had come to see: a pyre of sticks and branches constructed around a great wooden spool used to hold telephone wire. Atop the pyre was a makeshift platform, and propped upright on the platform as high as a man's head was a single hardcover copy of *As I Lay Dying.*

The onlookers surrounding this meager assemblage of wood were hardly festive. The mood was more akin to what you'd see at an Old Buckram funeral. The people gathered there were solemn and unsure and I saw eyes skeptical and afraid. Father had told me about the hangings in Old Buckram, and how the last man hanged in front of the courthouse was in 1907 — "not all that long ago," as Father put it. I sensed that this morbidly inquisitive crowd would be of the same state of mind if, instead of a book burning, someone was going to be hanged on this night.

Maynard and another man arrived out of the darkness with two more armloads of wood. A thin, deliberate man in gas-station overalls came in just behind them. He was carrying a large red container of fuel, its sides gummed with oil and sawdust. Someone called out, "Put the light over here," and then Maynard began dousing the pyre with fuel as though dispensing holy water onto an unwilling congregation. I frantically scanned the faces but couldn't find Father.

Maynard straightened his frock and shouted to the crowd. "Quiet down, now! Quiet down. Can y'all hear me back there? Quiet down, now." His worm of a tongue was flicking around the corners of his open mouth. It was his moment. "Okay, okay. Listen up —" Here in the now-quiet space he allowed the time and the quiet just to sit for a minute. Then he said, "Y'all all know why we're here."

Someone called out, "Why *are* we here, Maynard?" and a few people laughed. The man who had carried the fuel lit an oil-soaked rag affixed to the end of a metal pole. He stabbed the pole into the ground and wisps of burning fabric left the torch and floated down and around the mossy stump where Maynard's foot was habitually, metronomically, pumping away at an imaginary pedalboard. In this new light I saw the pastors of Old Buckram's several churches standing gloomily in a line. If Maynard was the judge, this was the jury.

Maynard resumed: "This is not a joke, y'all. This is serious. Now I know there're two sides to this" — a pause, and then with the spurious crescendo well known to, and perhaps invented by, religious orators — "but I know what side I'm on!"

"Amen," said someone standing beside me. Another hearty amen came from the far side of the circle. Another voice said, "Tell it, brother." Two ladies near me began to whisper their own disparate prayers that crisscrossed and wound around each other like two snakes climbing the same tree.

"Now, I haven't read this book," said Maynard.

"You haven't read it?" Father said incredulously. He had appeared out of nowhere next to Maynard, whose expression of surprise was so great that I thought his eyeballs might tumble out of his head.

"You haven't read it?" Father said again, this time with a little more effort. He was still feeling the effects of his alcohol and was having trouble getting his words out.

"No," said Maynard through his parted teeth. "I haven't read it, and I'm not goin' to." Then to the assembly, he called out, "But I know what's in it!"

If the crowd had been ambivalent before, it had now chosen a side. At Maynard's words a cheer went up, and as the cheer subsided a lady's voice was heard saying, "Ain't no point in reading that nonsense!"

Father cleared his throat and said, "If I may, if I may," and turned now to address the gathering. His first words took a long time to come to him. At the end of an age, he said, "Listen, folks. It just doesn't make any sense to do what Mr. Houck is proposing." His words were uncertain and I could hear the slightest tremor in his voice. "This book," he continued, "the one you're all here to see burned, it's not a bad book. It's really not. It was written by a man you're all familiar with and for good reason. He's a great writer. He's one of the most important American writers who's ever lived, and we should all be proud of that in the same way that we're proud of Mark Twain, and John Steinbeck, and Emily Dickinson." You could see his eyes searching the faces in the crowd and trying to come up with names they might have heard of, and finding very few. Sensing he was gaining little traction, he buried his hands in his coat pockets and began again. "In 1949, the man who wrote this book was given the Nobel Prize for literature, and that's an extraordinary honor, I can assure you." No one appeared to be impressed by this fact. Someone directed a flashlight at his face and held it there, and Father blinked and looked away. "Look — I'm not asking you to take my word for it, and, in fact, you shouldn't take somebody else's word for it. That's the whole point of this. You shouldn't let someone else tell you

161

what you can and cannot read."

A man from the crowd called out, "Well that's exactly what you're doin'."

"No, no it's not," said Father. "I'm not telling you that you *have* to read this book — that I'm going to *make* you read it. I'm saying *you* ought to be the one to decide whether you're going to read it. Not Maynard Houck. Not Ephegene Ester. Maynard says he hasn't even read this book, and I wonder how many of you who are here to condemn it have read it." I was glad he didn't ask for a show of hands. "I'll tell you that I've read it," he said, "and I'll admit it's not my favorite book, but before you go to setting books on fire, you should at least open them and see for yourselves —"

The onlookers had begun to stir and murmur and it gave the appearance that Father was rambling. His alcohol was more visible now in his speech and I think to them he had the persuasiveness of the town drunk. A dirt clod was launched and it struck Father hard in the middle of his chest, sending dirt flying up into his face. Another one passed through the air like a bat but missed its mark. Someone called out, "Henry, go home." This was said with sympathy, but not with hate.

After getting the dirt out of his eyes, Father turned toward the woodpile for the first time and saw the book sitting there, waiting patiently to be consumed. He began to smile. Another clod hit him hard on the back and disintegrated. A horrible anger was settling on me, and I was at that very moment plotting to find and kill the people who were launching these attacks. My hands were shaking and I couldn't have spit if my life depended on it.

"Wait," Father said, "hold on. Hold on, people. Maynard, I have a question."

"What is it, Henry."

"You've only got one copy?" Father tried hard to conceal his amusement. He wasn't laughing, but I could tell from his expression that, for some reason, he found this to be of unparalleled hilarity. "In this whole county, there's only one copy of this book?" No one else thought this was funny and people shifted about uncomfortably.

"Get out of here, Henry," said Maynard, having lost all patience. He didn't enjoy being ridiculed. "You're not going to stop us."

"Yes, I am, Maynard," said Father, and just like that, on his prodigiously long legs he scrambled unevenly to the top of the un-lit pyre. Having seized the book, he steadied himself on the makeshift platform as if he were a drunken sailor manning a masthead and looking for the North Star. People gasped and someone said, "What in the world?"

"Get down from there, Henry," said Maynard, clicking his teeth. "There's an ordinance in place now. That book's illegal here."

"There's no ordinance and it's not illegal," said Father.

"You wait and see." Maynard was pacing now and slavering from the sides of his mouth with increasing agitation. "And after I burn this one," he said, "I'm going to come to your house and get *yourn.*"

My father sparked into a rage like I'd never seen before. His black coat moved on the wind like a storm cloud, and he rose up and shouted, "If you want to see something burn, Maynard, you come to my house and *try* to take my books!"

Maynard upended the torch and threw it onto the pyre, and an explosion of fire lit the heavens. I screamed and charged into the fray but was trampled to the ground by the stampede that followed. For a moment, all I could see was Father in the center of this empyreal furnace, still clutching the book, shielding his face from the flames. I had the sensation that I was suffocating.

And then it was over. Father jumped from

the pyre and landed a few feet away, mostly unscathed, the forbidden book still in his hand. A fire truck had been positioned in town at the ready, and as soon as its emergency lights were turned on in response to the inferno, the witnesses to the burning, not wanting to be implicated, dissipated into the darkness. I don't know what happened to Maynard, but he and the other pastors were nowhere to be seen.

When I got to Father, he was on his hands and knees, trying to breathe. I fell down beside him in a fit of uncontrolled hysterics and tried to drag him away from the fire, now already dwindling and smoking heavily on account of the wet, green wood that had been improvidently used as fuel. I pulled him up onto a stump and held him under his arms until his coughing stopped. I was crying and the two of us were alone together, sorrowfully, on the Barrowfields.

14

As you might expect, this misadventure did little to resolve my father's melancholia. He felt a great humiliation because of it, and his sense of isolation only increased. Our dinners in the following weeks were perfunctory and silent. Afterward I would read and sing in whispers to Threnody until sleep came and charioted her away. I would then venture downstairs to sit at the piano and play in the encircling dark by flickering candle while Father drank himself into oblivion. We did this night after night, waiting for the spell to break; waiting for the pall of depression to lift with the coming of a bright new morning.

But the bright new morning never came. Instead, nature, so often cruel or damnably indifferent, brought my parents a new child. Mother had been pregnant at Maddy's funeral but told no one, not even Father. The news, when it came, was bittersweet.

After Threnody was born, they had not intended to have more children, so the pregnancy was something of a surprise. Indeed, the baby was a shock to both of them. Father pretended, very briefly, to be overjoyed. Then their new daughter came prematurely and was as pale blue as an early morning sky. After a time in the hospital she was diagnosed with a form of cancer that even the strongest of children rarely survive. The expression I heard my parents say with hollowed black eyes and clenched teeth was "sooner than later."

Yet defying all grim statistics and expectations, she lived to see her first birthday and then her second — an emaciated, frail little girl, but darling, with a ponytail tied in daffodil ribbons that she loved. We began to allow ourselves a vagrant hope that, despite what we'd been told, one day she'd grow up and be fine. We said, "She's tough. She's going to surprise us all. Watch — she'll outlive every one of us."

When she was home from the hospital, Father sat with her in her room day and night and held her, and rocked her in his arms, and told her silly animal stories that made her laugh — a sprinting giraffe with legs of different lengths that, at the start of each race, would go off in every direction at once; a daddy longlegs that would ride about on the head of his companion, a talking golden retriever, the two of them finding unlikely adventures together. There is nothing in this life more extraordinary or more precious than a laughing child.

On nice mornings Mother carried her down to the barn and out into the field through the buttercups and dandelions so she could see the horses and pet their cold noses through the fence. After a few precarious trips around the pasture in front of Mother on the saddle (never faster than a walk), she came to love the horses as much as Mother did. We bought her every toy horse we could find in three counties, and in no time at all she had accumulated at least a hundred of all shapes and sizes. Some were little and would fit in the palm of her hand or in the pocket of her dress. Others were larger, with manes and tails that she would brush until the hair fell out. Her love of horses was, I think, just something in life she could cling to. Something tangible in the realm of the living that would lend meaning to an otherwise inexplicable existence. That was the part of her that was fighting to hang on. It was an expression of her courage.

On the floor in her room she had a little

barn of her own, and a little fence meticulously laid out with all her horses inside it. She and Mother painted a set of green wooden triangles to serve as the trees in the pasture, and she insisted on having real hay from the barn for her horses to eat, which Mother would cut with a knife and bind with rubberbands to make play-size haystacks. She'd whinny and then tip and clack the horses along the ground to make them gallop. Threnody, at that time six years old and in the first grade, helped her name them and wrote the names in a notebook that became covered with stickers and contained rudimentary equine drawings of black and brown.

One night I read a picture book to her as she sat on my lap. She was as light as a feather. I noticed that, as we read along, she began to move her face closer and closer to the book — almost as if she were trying to peer into a nonexistent keyhole in the middle of the page. Becoming concerned, I pointed to a picture and said, "What do you see here?" She pressed her face close to the page and looked with only one eye, then the other. "A butterfly?" There was no butterfly. She was almost blind, or had become so.

That night I was relieved to hear that Mother and Father had become aware of her vision problems long before I did. For her third birthday that year in April she got a pair of glasses, but they were of little practical help. They were heavy and awkward, and came with a little hook that wrapped around each ear that was supposed to keep them from falling off when she walked or looked down. Because they so often fell forward, the oversize lenses were always smudged with her fingerprints. She hated to wear them and I didn't blame her, but without them she could only pretend to see.

And being unable to see well made everything more complicated. She stumbled often, and her arms and legs were always covered with dark bruises. Over the summer of her third year, however, she seemed to grow stronger and more confident. By the time autumn arrived, she was moving well on her own and had discovered how much fun it was to climb up and down the many staircases in the house.

One rainy morning she awoke before the rest of us. After putting on her glasses and finding that no one else in the house was awake, she made her way out the door and down the hill to the barn. No one saw her go out. No one heard the door close behind her. I imagine she was looking for one of us, but I prefer to think she had just found within herself the stoutheartedness to go visit the horses on her own. Mother was the first to notice she was gone. I walked out to the terrace and looked down far below through the moving fog and saw her at the edge of the pasture. She was balanced on the second board of the fence, a trick she'd learned from Threnody. The horses were gathered around her, nipping lazily at her fingers and hoping for a treat. Relieved, I climbed the stone steps back to the house and yelled to Mother that I'd found her. When a moment later I looked back to where she'd been standing, she was no longer there. Her glasses had fallen, and, unable to see, she had crawled on her hands and knees under the fence to retrieve them. For her, that was when time stopped. Death's empty consolation was that the fatal act — a careless misstep by a horse; the breaking of her delicate spinal vertebrae as soft as paper — was sudden and without lasting pain.

Two days before the service Father and I went for a drive, and for reasons unstated he wanted to go to Avernus to see how many gravesites were left next to Maddy. He seemed to be thinking all the time like he was trying to solve some puzzle that none of the rest of us could see. When we got there we saw a rusted blue Chevrolet pickup truck parked on the hill near the cemetery. A skeletal man with a Habsburg jaw and mossy red hair was there digging in the rain as if he'd been sentenced to do the work. We pulled in at the bottom of the hill where we'd parked for Maddy and walked the dirt road to the cemetery without either of us saying a word, except Father said, "He must be getting ready for another funeral." We got out to the center of all the graves, old and new, and Father asked me if I knew where we'd buried Maddy because he couldn't remember. He hadn't been there since she died. I don't think he could bear to do it. Distantly I recalled where it was and headed that way, toward a feeling more than a precise location; toward the man throwing dirt, and Father followed me. It was getting dark and we had to lean down and squint to read the headstones and there were more than we thought. We couldn't find Maddy's grave anywhere and finally Father asked the man digging if he knew where it was and through a toothless mouth the man said, "Yep — I just saw it. It's right here." He slapped a muddied hand on the top of it to indicate. Mother had already called the funeral home and I guess they had sent someone out to go ahead and dig the grave while the weather allowed but Father didn't know it and we just stood there looking once we realized what we were looking at.

15

On a quiet November day after the funeral, Father left and did not return.

Summer in Old Buckram the year of his leaving had been biblically dry. The mountain wells had gone empty and the flat black stones in the bottom of Abbadon Creek had become like bone, but the fall had come with a steady pouring rain that, day after day, refused to end. Abbadon Creek again overflowed its banks with cold, turbid water, and fog lay heavy in every dark corner of the hills. The tops of the mountains were hidden behind clouds that never moved.

The day: November 16, 1985. A Saturday. Rain-sodden, black, with night coming early. Mother had gone to Asheville to visit an ailing friend, leaving Father and me at home to look after Threnody. She and I had spent the morning at the far end of the library telling stories and reading a Tolkien book we'd begun the night before. Growing tired, she went into her room for a nap and I left the house and drove out to the Blue Ridge Parkway to destroy or embrace an expanding sense of anxiety that had begun to work at the edges of my brain like a stitching awl.

When I turned sixteen I'd been given an old Scout 800A to use as an automobile. The Scout, which by literary cross reference my father referred to as the Arthur Radley, was kind of like a dog you love dearly that is mean to everyone else. It was the greatest car in the world, but it sounded and smelled like a badly maintained biplane using the wrong kind of fuel. I drove with the heat on and the windows down, and Zeppelin's *Presence* album at auditory levels considered dangerous by most god-fearing people.

As a rule, after the leaves change colors in October and fall from the trees, tourists no longer see any beauty in the parkway and the road is deserted to a point that is surprising. You can drive to an overlook and have it all to yourself. This day was to be just such a day. The world belonged to me — at least this isolated part of it.

The road was wet and clouds the color of coal smoke were set low against the sky. The absence of other vehicles on the road gave me comfort and aching distress. I stopped at the overlook for Elk Mountain but couldn't see ten feet out into the fog, so I tried another one with the same results. Being utterly alone, I sat on the tailgate and read for a while and took furtive sips from Father's flask that I'd stolen from his desk that morning. After two hours of this and having become exhausted by my loneliness, I roared home in the gloom to old Ben Hennom.

I could see as I drove across the ridge opposite the house that no lights were on. It appeared that no one was home. I looked back at the road and Threnody came into my headlights and I had to slam on the brakes and slide into the ditch not to run her over. She was pale white with dark circles under her eyes as if she had died that day. She was walking down the road in the falling rain. I got out of the car and she fell sobbing into my arms.

"Did you see him?" she cried, her whole body shaking with the cold. "Did you see him?"

"Did I see who?"

"Father! Did you see him?" She was hysterical.

"No, I didn't see him. Was I supposed to? Where is he?"

Her shirt was wet and covered in dirt. The

palms of her hands and her elbows were dirty and bleeding.

"I fell coming down the hill," she said through her sobs. Her jeans were torn and her knees were bleeding through the fabric. "I was looking for him and I fell. He said he was going for a walk, but he never came back. That was hours ago."

"We'll find him," I said. "I promise we'll find him."

I carried her around and put her in the car and sped the rest of the way home and up the hill between the sickly trees that lined the long driveway.

"Is Mother home yet? Threnody, what happened with Father?" She buried her face in her hands and wept.

I told her to wait in the car and ran into the house. The front door was standing open, but there was nothing but emptiness inside. I ran through the house and up the staircase to Father's study, screaming his name until I began to suffocate with terror. His desk when I came upon it — was different. I stopped and stared, trying to understand what it was that had changed. I could think of nothing other than my unmistakable sense that he no longer occupied that place and had no intention of coming back. A single sheet of paper lay upon the floor: the title page from his book. It contained handwritten words in Latin I did not know, god damn him. Some part of me knew he was gone and that he would never come back.

■ ■■■

PART II

■ ■■■

16

One year and nine months later. Mother stood looking out the kitchen window and watched me walk to the car. It was packed for my trip to college. I kept my back to her so she couldn't see me crying. Upstairs, Threnody lay face-down on her bed and refused to turn on the light or open the curtains. She wouldn't tell me goodbye. I told her I'd come back often to see her and she said, "No, you won't. You'll never come back."

"You'll see me all the time," I said. "And when I can't see you, I'll write to you and I'll call you every single day. I'll probably come home at least once a month. And when I can't come home, if I've got an exam or something, I'll fly you up to see me and you can walk around campus and go to all my classes with me, if you want to." I knew every word of this was an improbability but hoped it wasn't. "This won't change anything," I said.

Without turning over, she said into her pillow: "Who's going to read to me now, and who's going to sing me to sleep? And who's going to play the piano so I can sing? Mother can't play the piano." The last book we had been reading — *The Witch of Blackbird Pond* — sat on her night table. We had tried to finish it before I had to leave, but several chapters remained.

"I'll still do all that," I said. "It'll just have to be over the phone for a while."

"That makes a lot of sense. Our phone bill would be ten thousand dollars a month. You'd never be able to afford that."

"No, I probably won't," I said. I rubbed her back, but she shook one good time like a horse trying to free itself of flies, so I stopped. She started to cry, and I cried, too.

"I'm going to be scared here without you," she said, and how could she not be? The house and all its emptiness were frightening to us both, but for so long we had each other and that was our guard against the baleful maledictions whispered by the vulture house against us in the darkness. Threnody often used pencil and graph paper to design new houses where she and I would live one day, and she had a whole collection of them. We always said that soon we'd be able to leave Old Buckram and get a little house of our own at the beach, one with just a couple of rooms, and we'd sleep in sleeping bags on the floor or string up hammocks on the porch, and we'd find her a school nearby that we could walk to. I told her that's why I was going away: so I could get a job in order to make money, so that one day we'd be able to get our little house together. I said she could start thinking about what kind of house we'd buy and where it would be and how the house would be arranged. She drew so many little houses. She made so many lists.

The fallacy to this shared delusion, of course, was time. This fantasy we constructed over a period of years with blocks and timbers of increasing legitimacy assumed no passage of time between my departure and my return at the end of my schooling, such that we would pick right back up where we'd left off and move into the little beach house and she'd still be a child of nine years old, which she would not. The reality I recognized but didn't say was that by the time I'd graduated and made enough money to buy any kind of house, she'd no longer be a child, and the childhood she was going to spend in our house at the beach would have ended. I knew this, and yet I left all the same.

I told her I loved her and gave her a big hug and I could see her turning inward from the world. I pushed away all the tears, but they came back and I couldn't stop them. She said nothing and I needed to go. I'd put it off too long already. I walked downstairs with my insides torn out.

"It will go by faster than you think." This was the advice of a family friend. "Enjoy it as much as you can. It'll be over before you know it, and then you'll be right back home." *I'm not coming back here,* I thought, but this I did not say. *This place, with all its bleakness and sorrow, is not for me.*

That morning before having the abortive talk with Threnody I'd gotten up early because I couldn't make myself sleep. It was still dark when I got out of bed. I finished packing a few things and because no one was awake I went outside and walked down in the cool morning to the edge of the terrace to be alone and to think about what the hell I was doing. There'd been no rain, but the long grass was wet and bent over, and the leaves were heavy with dew. I pulled myself up on the rock wall and looked out over the valley to think about what I was leaving and maybe come to terms with all that had happened there. As I sat waiting for the sun to rise and prove to me that another day would in fact arrive, I felt a lonely sense of unpassing time that one can sometimes find in the mountains of Old Buckram. This was an intimation of the peacefulness I hoped one day I might find — but after a moment the emptiness of the forested hills and the seldom-used road winding through them and the barren lay of the Barrowfields crawling west out of the distant town was audible and consuming and left me stricken with grief.

Mother came walking up the hill from the barn and saw me sitting there. A bird feeder that she had hung on the near side of the terrace hadn't been filled in weeks. When she walked by it she touched its wooden post with a quick expression of remembrance and regret, as if to say, "I know. I haven't forgotten about you."

She climbed up on the wall next to me and, sensing my unhappiness with her presence, put her arm around me. "Are you all right?"

"I'm fine," I said, not wanting to talk.

Respecting my silence, she lowered her voice to a whisper. "I saw a downy woodpecker this morning. Cutest thing you've ever seen. Have you ever seen one?" Then noticing that a lilac tree she'd planted near the terrace wall had died, she said, "Oh, shoot. I don't think it was getting enough sunlight. I thought if it can just get tall enough, it will be as happy as it can be. Dang it." She hopped down from the wall and inspected it for signs of life. "There may be some green in there," she said. "You just never know. I'll give it a little more time."

"You never know," I said. She came back and leaned against the wall. She had hay in her hair.

"It should be a good day for your drive."

"I hope so."

"I don't want you to worry about us," she said. "I know that among the many things you're thinking about, you're thinking about us and what we're going to do when you're gone. We're going to be fine. We've gotten accustomed to it just being us here. Threnody has made some friends at school, and that'll be good for her. I'll get her out of the house more. And I've decided that I'm going to read all those books I've always wanted to read. We've got a whole library upstairs —" Her voice broke. She swallowed and began again. "And don't put too much pressure on yourself. I know how you can be."

I lied and said, "I won't. I promise."

"And promise me you'll keep playing the

piano. You've worked too hard to give up on that."

"I'm going to college — not into the army," I said.

"Do you know when you'll come home?"

"I don't know yet. It'll be soon. I don't know how long it's going to take me to drive it. I may have to fly back."

"Are you nervous?"

"About what? No. Not even a little. I'm excited."

Mother appraised my expression and sagely determined that I was terrified by the uncertainty. "I've got a little something for you. Stay right here. Do you want some coffee?"

I told her I'd love some coffee and off she went up to the house and was gone for several minutes. She came back outside with a book and an envelope but no coffee, and climbed back up on the wall and handed me the envelope and told me to open it. It had four hundred and sixty dollars in it, with the last ten dollars consisting of one-dollar bills. "I'm hoping that will cover your gas money going up there, and your books for your first semester, and maybe there'll be a little left over for a few fun things."

"Thanks, Mom."

"Are you taking your heavy coat?"

"Of course."

"It's going to be cold up there."

"Could it be colder than it is here? I'd be surprised," I said.

"Did you say goodbye to your sister?"

"I will."

"She's going to be fine," Mother said. Her turn to lie to me.

We sat for a moment in silence and evaluated our respective situations. I'd become restless and wanted to get on the road, no matter what uncertainties it might hold. Mother said, "Look at me for a minute." I looked at her and saw a resolute determination in her face. As if the words had been carefully rehearsed many times, she said, "I know if your father were here, he'd get a book off the shelf and read you something profound for the occasion, or else he'd just conjure up something from T. S. Eliot out of memory, and it would be perfect."

"But he's not here."

"I know he's not here. Still, I've been trying for two months to find something like that to tell you before you left because that's what he would do and everything I've read just reminds me of him."

"I'm sorry."

She held up a book with a tattered travelogue cover and black lettering against the backdrop of an African sky. It was *West with the Night* by Beryl Markham. "You haven't read this, have you?" I told her I hadn't.

"This is one of my all-time favorite books," she said. "I was reading this when your father and I moved here from Baltimore. At the time, it gave me the courage to come here and the hope to believe that it would be an extraordinary adventure. And after all this it still gives me hope. And I want you to have hope, too, although I can see why you might not."

"I have hope."

"If you don't, it's okay."

She opened the book to a place she had marked with a single blade of grass. Inside was a paragraph she'd underlined, probably years before. "Yes," she said, reading it again before handing me the book, "this is what I wanted you to see."

The worn pages were dry to my fingers, and delicate like flowers that had been pressed. In the margin next to the underlined passage were the words *Remember this* written in Mother's hand. The passage spoke about how to leave a place you have lived all your life, a place where your soul resides and where all your ghosts and demons still persist and will remain for all the years of your life no matter how far away you travel, or how long you are gone. Leave it quickly, was Markham's counsel. Reading over my shoulder, Mother pointed to these lines: *Passed years seem safe ones . . . while the future lives in a cloud, formidable from a distance. The cloud clears as you enter it.*

Closing the book with my hands, Mother said, "Go — this is what you should be doing. We'll be just fine until you get back."

My life, and our life together as parent and child, had not been as perhaps she had wanted it to be. And now I would leave this place — these lonely mountains she had come to with a man who had now left her here — and she would remain. And yet she was to begin a new journey of her own. It would not be a journey of distance, but it was nevertheless a leaving and a starting over. For now, on the hill, it would just be the two of them. Life had been rearranged. The quiet of the house would be a different quiet, and the dark of the night more dark, now that the house was more lonely by three.

17

With a stack of maps on the seat beside me, I set out for Connecticut, to college at Wesleyan, where I'd been fortunate enough to receive a music scholarship. At the beginning of my reluctant journey north, I didn't even harbor a remote expectation that I'd arrive at my destination. I had no idea what to expect, or even if my laboring mule of an automobile would make it out of the state. Father, despite his perpetual close curiosity of all things minute and mechanical, never demonstrated much proficiency at vehicular maintenance, and it was long odds that my car's engine, choking and straining under the hood like a piece of rusted farm equipment, had received much competent scrutiny in recent years. Still, I desperately needed to get away. Remembering Mother's words — clinging to them with a preposterous and ill-founded faith — I told myself the cloud would part as I entered it, but this was not great solace. The whole arcing world on my horizon seemed vast and empty.

Just getting out of the mountains of North Carolina and southern Virginia on narrow ribbons of highway laid over what were once truly wagon and horse trails seemed interminable. I was being gravitationally dragged back into the pit that was Old Buckram. The Arthur Radley, myopically unequipped by the engineers at International Harvester to cope with the up-and-down-again changes in elevation, started to run a little warm, so I stopped to get gas and let it cool somewhere south of Roanoke. While the car was fueling I got out my maps for the tenth time and traced the long route up through Pennsylvania and New York, and honestly to my watering eyes it looked impossible. It had taken me three good hours to get as far as I had. I assumed it would take me twelve more to get to Middletown if my car cooperated, and that wasn't happening.

When I started the car again, the temperature gauge shot straight back into the red. In a state of mortal despair I drove around until I found an abandoned bank and parked in the shade of the drive-through to let the engine cool some more. *At least I made it this far,* I thought. *I can probably catch a bus from here if I have to.* I wondered what I could get for the car. More than once I looked back down the road toward home and wondered how Mother would take it if I just went back. I figured she'd understand, at least eventually. She'd be badly disappointed, but I could live with her disappointment. What kept me going was Threnody. I could half close my eyes and see her there in her room, her door locked, her small body curled up facing the wall, a stuffed animal she'd outgrown held close for empty comfort, and rain moving in over the mountains and darkening her room with artificial sadness. I could see her there without even trying, and I knew if I lost my courage and went back and reappeared at the top of that hill having been defeated by the prospect of the unknown, somehow I'd be letting her down the most.

I had seen Wesleyan once on a brief weekend tour the preceding year, but my memories of it were kaleidoscopic and distant. I had arrived by airplane. Mother had sent me alone to save on airfare and because there was no one to watch Threnody. I was to view the campus with an orientation group and then later play two pieces of music (selected by the college) as part of the scholarship process. The whole trip was terrifying, and my premonitory sense of doom was made worse by weather that could fairly be described as borderline apocalyptic. I'd brought it with me. There was Old Buckram fog on the ground and rain from an upside-down ocean of a sky that tumbled about and swirled galactically in ways I'd never seen a sky behave, and at that impressionable age it's easy for a young man to conceive that he's seeing the beginning of the end of the world and then maybe even hope for it a little bit. *These are the signs,* I thought. On top of all this there were menacing-looking black squirrels (one showed its teeth to me) and inverted umbrellas and droves of wet falling leaves that were sparrowed suddenly up, back, and around by winds that got inside your coat and under your shirt.

The one bright spot of this adventure was a lovely brown-haired girl from Austin, Texas, named Ashley Taylor. She was part of the tour group. She was the one student with the kindness to introduce herself as I awkwardly fumbled my way into the room, rain-soaked and frenzied, unsure if I was in the right place. While arresting my boyish stumble over my own feet, she caught my right hand and, pulling me up straight, introduced herself just like a good Texan would ("I'm Ashley Taylor"). Then turning away from me, she made a quick, deliberate pivot to the side, set her chin a little forward (I thought valiantly), and returned her attention to our tour guide, who'd been waiting on my arrival to begin.

As an Old Buckram boy, I'd never seen anything quite like Ms. Taylor before. Erubescent nail polish; spangled bracelets; rings that until then I imagined were only worn by Mesopotamian kings and queens at their own burial; and shoes that reflected every surface in the room. She had on a short dress of fine cloth and the confidence of an oil baroness. We set about on our drenching walk across the Hitchcockian terrain with Ms. Taylor happily a few steps ahead of me. It was not difficult to find her the most compelling aspect of the scenery notwithstanding the beauty and endless green that is Wesleyan, although not on that day.

She and I were the only two students on the tour without their parents in tow, and naturally after a while we figured this out and migrated like butterflies (a little haphazardly) to each other and spent the day trying to appear intelligent and worldly to the other. Intelligent I could manage; worldly I had to bluff. During the lunch break at Memorial Chapel we sat together in a small window-lit room apart from the other kids and picked at our stale boxed lunches as the hard rain fell. Ms. Taylor was perched deliciously in a chair next to me with her legs crossed in the traditional manner at first and then later in the more informal Indian style (with her pocketbook in her lap). She was staying that night with some family friends who lived in a neighboring town and had to be on a bus by three o'clock, a fact that, once disclosed, pulled loose the arteries from my heart and emptied all my febrile blood out on the floor at her reflective feet. At the end of our short time together, despite my unanswered pleas to the various deities of antiquity, I found myself standing in the windy street holding my coat around me, despairingly watching her walk up the steps of an aging municipal bus. She turned to say something, but the bus doors closed between us. After a moment they opened again and she smiled down at me. She said, "Today was fun." I've long been plagued by an inability to say the right thing at the right time, particularly in romantic contexts, and this bright occasion, sadly, was no exception. As an unfortunate consequence, those three words marked the end of our short but delightful time together.

The musical performance later that day was not my best, but it was apparently good enough to do the job. I sat for a while on the steps of the music building feeling relieved and then, during a brief respite in the weather, I walked to McDonald's to eat and then to a convenience store to buy provisions sufficient for the evening. Well stocked, I boarded a bus to my lodgings at the edge of town. Ms. Taylor and her impeccable everything had left me in quite a state. I hoped by some twist of fate I'd find her at my motel or otherwise come across another girl to spend the evening with, and I was positively ashiver with a combination of anxiety, dread, and excitement. The one elevator wasn't operational, so I hiked up a dank stairwell that smelled of urine and locked myself in my room on the second floor. Envisioning the teeming bacteria of a thousand previous tenants, I stripped the comforter off the bed and propped myself up to read and settle in for the night. Thinking of Ms. Taylor at length made it hard for me to concentrate, so after a few hours of reading and masturbating to the point of needing an IV, I ate again and at last found glorious but fitful sleep. It was Ms. Ashley Taylor from Austin, Texas, I was thinking of as I began to put more slow miles between myself and home, but the truth is that she didn't enroll in Wesleyan and I never saw her again.

It ended up taking me two full days to get to Middletown. The driving was much easier at night when there were fewer cars on the road and the sun had redirected her glinting antagonism to the other side of the earth. I stopped twice at pay phones and called in to report my progress to Threnody, but no one answered when I called.

At Wesleyan when I wasn't studying, I spent hours on end with my hands on the piano, which was one of the few activities that kept my half memories, half nightmares of home just outside the firelight of my imagination. I made a few good friends, but none of them were from anywhere near where I'd grown up. In fact, in my four years there, I never met anyone from the North Carolina mountains. And, perhaps not surprisingly, no one from Wesleyan had ever heard of Old Buckram or even Blowing Rock. I routinely resorted to saying I was from "somewhere north of Charlotte." Most people found this a satisfactory reply.

Eight weeks into my first semester, my

roommate, a tadpole-faced boy from Albany who looked like he'd spent a good deal of time as an infant sleeping on his stomach, was expelled. He had succumbed to a severe drug and alcohol addiction that by all rights should have killed him half a dozen times. He would often stumble into the room at two in the morning and throw up unchewed food into our shared trash can, which I would be forced to wash out in the shower. Several times I came in from class to find him sitting by the partially opened window smoking pot or doing lines of cocaine off his dresser. The room would reek of incense and a wet towel would be on the floor by the door to prevent smoke from escaping into the hallway. He'd yell at me to come in and not let the smoke out. I'd usually gather my things and head right back to the library or the music department. One Saturday night during exams he overdosed on god knows what and had a Woodstock-grade brown-acid seizure. I held him while he rattled and choked, and his mouth foamed all over my bare leg while I waited for the paramedics to arrive. Having him gone was a tremendous relief, but I didn't get another roommate until the beginning of my sophomore year and the room got damn lonely at times.

And after all, Threnody was right. I did not go home. I don't know why; I just couldn't bring myself to do it. Sometimes I'd walk down to the post office at Silver and Elm and mail Threnody a letter or a book. I called occasionally and had distant conversations, but certainly I didn't do this often enough. Each time I called, it was as if I knew them less and less. I'd promise to come home at the next holiday, but I never did. I told myself going home would just open old wounds that we all had tried so hard to heal. The longer I stayed away, the harder it was to return.

Christmas break my second year: I got back to my dorm after my last exam and wandered through the emptying parking lot where the remaining cars were being loaded and families were picking up their kids for the holidays. I checked my mailbox even though I'd only received two letters since the beginning of the semester. In the narrow aluminum slot was a letter from Old Buckram. It was from Mother. It said only that I needed to come home for the holidays, if not to see her, to see Threnody. It said if I would call her, she would send me airfare so I wouldn't have to drive through all the snow. *She really would like to see you,* she wrote. *She misses you a lot. And I do, too. She got you something for Christmas that she's excited about. You should see the job she did wrapping it. It took her a solid hour, she was being so careful. The paper has pictures of books on it.*

It'd been a year and a half since I had left my life and my family behind in the mountains of North Carolina. It had been that long since I'd seen Threnody and Mother. Weeks had passed since I'd talked to either of them, but I didn't go home that year for Christmas. I didn't call and I didn't write and I didn't answer the phone, and I'd listen to messages left for me with a pain I had never felt before and I have no idea why. I'd make myself be alone. I'd wake in the early morning with a shudder and a trembling, and a feeling that the night's sleep had been a traumatic event. When the sun came up low in the east and brought light through the cracks in the blinds and illuminated my cloistered existence and my eyes opened wide upon the white block walls and white ceiling of my room, I was struck instantly by an unspecified dread in the very pit of my stomach and an omnipresent chill in my bones, and the dread would stay with me all day as I read my books and shivered alone in my room, not eating and not drinking until night came and it would be time at last to ease the dread and bleed out all of my pain and angst and loneliness with cheap light beer and my acoustic guitar, which I played nightly for hours until I was too stupidly drunk to play anymore, and then I slept only to repeat the cycle all over again with the new day.

During the semester I had a job at the campus bookstore, but when the semester ended my hours dried up and I began to run low on money. At the end of December, in optimistic anticipation of the arrival of spring, I sold my heavy coat for fifteen dollars. On the fourth of January I took a bus to Hartford and sold a watch I'd been given for graduation to a pawn shop for thirty dollars. Later, I sold a pen set for five dollars, a stack of my used CDs for twenty dollars, and my leather gloves to a guy on the street for two dollars. I didn't eat anything but white bread dipped in noodle soup for two consecutive weeks and lost weight I didn't have to lose.

Mother wrote to me again at the end of the spring semester and sent me a new address in Charlotte along with five hundred dollars and a handwritten note:

I hadn't heard from you in a while but

I was able to confirm with the university that you're still alive, so I thought you might need some money. What I really want you to do with this is buy a plane ticket home and stay with us for the summer. It's up to you, though. We really miss you a lot and we talk about you a lot and wonder how you're doing. Bird has grown about two feet since you left. You won't believe it. She's taller than me now. She looks a lot like you.

The big news is that we left the old house on the hill. We're living in Charlotte — it's a long story. It was hard to leave but we didn't really have much of a choice I don't think. As to the horses . . . I didn't want to tell you like this . . . I just couldn't do anything with them . . . Not too long after you went away to school I gave them to the lady who used to come and ride — the one with the pastureland up in the northern part of the county. I think she's taking good care of them and will give them back to me if something happens and I can ever take them back. And something else . . . I broke my leg last year (again, long story) and it's taken a while to heal and I was having a hard time taking care of the house and the hill and everything all by myself. There was just too much to do. All our furniture is still there because I don't have anywhere to put it for now. I didn't touch anything in your room, although I threw away the beer I found in your closet. I've got the house for sale but who knows if we'll ever sell it. So far no one has come to look at it except people who are just curious about seeing it on the inside. I might turn it into a museum — who knows! One guy who looked at it with the realtor wanted to buy some of the books, but I said no for now until you have a chance to pick out the ones you want.

Please write or call and let me know that you're okay. Just hearing from you would mean a lot to me. us.

Mom

I used some of the flight money to buy a twelve-pack of Heineken — an indulgence — and to put a deposit on a one-bedroom apartment I would rent for the summer. When I got back to my dorm, I threw away everything that wouldn't fit in my car and took all that remained and dumped it in a heap in the new apartment. It had been furnished when I had seen it; now it was empty and looked like absolute hell. It needed paint. There were holes in the walls, including one the size of a fist. The carpet was thin and stained, and the kitchen needed to be cleaned or napalmed. I put my beer in the fridge and went out to pick up a large pizza — another indulgence. When I got back to the apartment I found out that the refrigerator wasn't working and my beer was half-warm, so I went back out and bought a cheap cooler and a bag of ice. After I ate the pizza, I played guitar until my fingers were raw. I didn't have a bed, so I slept on the floor with my sweatshirt for a pillow. In the early morning dark I started the long drive back home. I thought about Threnody the whole way.

18

I called her Bird. I don't know when this began, or why — but to me, she was always Bird. I called her Bird and, for reasons even more inscrutable, she called me Henry lion.

An early memory: she was three; I found her outside on the terrace with her hands in a little triangle around an unseen object in her lap. It was an inchworm, green and yellow, that she had befriended and was protecting. Her pink nose and a child's furrowed brow pointed downward in an attitude of investigation. I said, "Bird, what do you have there?" She said, "This is Mister Worm. He's lost. I'm helping him get back home."

She was so kind to all living things, a gift she inherited from our mother. Sitting in the tall grass, she'd position her hand to allow a beetle or an ant to crawl across it, and after inspecting it like a young Charles Darwin, she'd daintily set it down again with an encouraging word.

In the mornings, she'd often save part of an apple from breakfast to share with one of the horses. We'd walk down the hill together and deliver the apple slice through the boards of the fence, with Threnody saying politely, "Here you go. Please don't eat my fingers. Thank you." Before walking back up the hill, she'd put her ear against the boards to listen for carpenter bees, so careful not to disturb them.

At four she contracted chicken pox. I'd wager that the body of medical literature on the subject doesn't contain details of a more prolific case. She was covered head to toe, and despite being quarantined on the third floor of the house lest the pathogen spread to our sister, she was admirably resilient. One night before bed I was putting an oatmeal paste on her back so she could try to sleep. She'd put her long brown hair up in one of my baseball caps so it wouldn't be in the way. Fanning the sticky concoction to make it dry, I said, "There you go. That should help."

"That does feel a lot better," she said, even though I'm sure it wasn't true. "And maybe one day," she whispered to herself, "they might even go away."

"Oh, Bird," I said, "they're not going to

last forever. Just a few more days and you'll be as good as new."

"Really?"

"Yes, sweetheart."

"That's good news." She was so relieved.

In the summer, we put on towel capes and masks made of string and papier-mâché, and went on ridiculous exploits into the Gnarled Forest, where we hunted for caves and filled our stomachs with giant blackberries, and I had her stand as lookout as I tried to swing from rock outcroppings on immobile vines that hung down from the tops of trees. The door to her bedroom was visible from mine on the second floor, and because we were continually getting in trouble following our ill-planned and ill-fated adventures in the woods, we were just as frequently being placed under temporary house arrest in our rooms until such time that Father got home to hear our arguments for innocence (or, more often, our pleas for leniency) and thereafter handed down his judgment — which was almost always just, in light of our transgressions. During periods of confinement, we would open our doors and sit in our doorways so we could see and talk to each other across the chasm of the great library.

And this wonderful child, more than any-

thing else in the world, loved books and stories. It didn't matter what time it was or
what the circumstances were. Her most-
asked questions, day or night, were "Will
you tell me a story?" and "Will you read me
a book?" I don't remember ever telling her
no. The best part of any night was finishing
one book and then excitedly going through
the library to find the next one that we
would start that evening. Once we had a
new book picked out, we'd reconvene in her
room and she would fidget with excitement
and listen for as long as I was willing to read
or until she fell asleep. Some families play
croquet; some play cards. Some sit down by
the lake and fish for trout. We did none of
these things. Our principal pastimes were
reading and telling stories.

On the day in November before Father
left, I was downstairs playing the piano and
Threnody called me from upstairs.

"Henry!"

I kept playing.

"Henry lion!"

I found her waiting at the top of the iron
staircase that led to the library. She was
dressed like a sleuth, with a magnifying glass
and a trench coat too big for her that hit
the floor around her feet, artifacts left over
from our reading of all the Sherlock Holmes

stories. It was a disguise for her mourning. We were dealing with the death of our sister in different ways.

"Hello, Bird."

"It's time for a new book, isn't it?"

"It *is* time for a new book," I said. "Want to pick one out?"

Threnody climbed on the ladder and upon the impetus of a well-practiced push, she shot away from me down the wall and the ladder scraped noisily along its rails before clattering to a stop.

"You're not supposed to do that," I said. "My god, if something were to happen to you —"

"All the good books are down here." By "all the good books" she meant Father's collection of literary fiction. By that point he had at least as many books as the public library, and certainly his varied assortment was worth far more. Many of them were signed first editions, and all the books he had read through the years contained loose pages of his notes tucked inside the front jackets. He always looked up and wrote down the definitions to all the words he didn't know, and he would consult these lists from time to time as an aid to his writing. As long as we handled the books carefully (certain books required supervision and gloves) and they didn't leave the premises except under careful guard, we were encouraged to read anything we could find.

"Do you think I'll ever be as tall as you?" We stood eye to eye, with Threnody on the third step of the ladder.

"You'll be taller," I said.

"You and I look a lot alike, don't we?"

"Yes we do, Bird."

"I wish my hair was blond like yours."

"I know," I said. "I wish my hair was brown like yours."

"Maybe it will turn brown."

"I'm sure it will. If it doesn't, I'll color it brown."

"I like that idea." She began randomly pulling out books and inspecting the covers.

"I know you're going to veto whatever I pick out," she said.

"No, I won't. Okay, maybe I will."

"You always do," she said.

"Because I know the really good ones. Have I ever let you down?"

I was surprised to see that Threnody gave this question some real thought.

"So there have been a couple," I said.

She first selected *The Mists of Avalon* because she liked the cover, and with some reluctance I wielded my veto power as she predicted and found *The Hobbit* for us to

211

read instead. "This is a real adventure," I told her, thinking it would be good for us both to spend some time in the Shire instead of in rainy Old Buckram.

"Is it really?"

"It is, really. I promise. You'll love this."

She said, "Let me see it," but her red, sticky fingertips suggested otherwise.

"Father will kill us both," I said. "Look at your hands." She instinctively licked at a shiny thumb to salvage whatever was left of a lollipop or jawbreaker that apparently had to be removed from her mouth several times before it could be consumed entirely. In the interest of our mutual survival, I gently replaced the early-edition, archivally wrapped copy of the book with a dog-eared paperback version that sat on the shelf beside it (73rd printing; August 1979) and handed it over to Threnody for a close-eyed inspection. She scrutinized the cover — Tolkien's painting of Bilbo coming to the huts of the Raft-elves — with a sour face. I told her to trust me and she said, "You always say that."

"One chapter and you'll be hooked," I said. "Look at these maps!" I showed her Thror's Map and the map of Wilderland, with the spiders, and the dark forest, and the dragon, and the mysterious runes. Threnody was always a sucker for maps. We both were. There was little that would entice us into a good book more than an ancient-looking map.

"You've got my attention," she said, which was one of Father's famous lines. I followed her in the wide arc around the library railing and turned down the hall and into her bedroom. She climbed into her bed and I sat in the chair beside it. We had spent many an hour reading in these respective spots.

"Are you okay, Bird?"

"I think so."

She closed her eyes and said, "Read to me, please."

I read until I thought she was asleep.

"Bird," I whispered. "Are you still awake?"

"Yes," she said without opening her eyes. "Keep reading, please."

"I think you just fell asleep."

"No, I didn't. I just have my eyes closed."

"Then what just happened?"

"Gollum just asked Bilbo what he has in his pocket."

"Well, what does Bilbo have in his pocket?"

"The ring, of course. Please read."

She was innocent like children are, and full of wonder. In the winter, she was an observant downy bird on a frozen branch waiting eagerly for spring. In the spring, she was an early flower straining skyward beneath a cold and hopeful sun. And we all left her — every one of us but Mother. We left her there, in her encroaching world, where her magnificent heart diminished. I crossed the land between us with a sad and heavy heart.

19

A lonely twilight lay upon the city when I arrived in Charlotte. I had told no one I was coming, and a dull, persistent ache turned my stomach inside out. Still, Mother's "just in case you decide to come visit" directions were good, and I found where I was going without a lot of trouble.

The house was situated just off Sharon Road in Myers Park. This, I discovered, was (and still is) a very nice part of Charlotte. The kind of place where you drive by a stately brick manor that spans half a block and say, "Is that one house or two?" Every yard I drove past was manicured with organized, expensive landscaping, and all the houses had hand-washed, glinting German automobiles parked out front. There were wooden jungle gyms built by licensed general contractors, and archways, and trellises, and green-tiled roofs, and perfectly cultivated ivy covering entire walls of stucco.

Mother's new house was no exception, but nothing in the world felt right about it. I rang the bell and then knocked but no one came to the door, so I walked around the yard and found Threnody sitting on the back porch reading a book. I stepped through an imposing hedge of Leyland cypress and startled her violently, but she didn't get up. She just looked at me and I looked at her. I said, "It's okay. It's me." Had it been so long that she no longer recognized me? "Go back around," she said. "You can't get in this way." She met me at the front door and gave me a halfhearted hug and immediately returned to the back porch where she resumed reading. I followed her out there.

"Is Mother here?"

"No — she went to dinner and the movies. She won't be back until late." The porch was partially enclosed and a trio of white wicker chairs with red-striped comfy cushions sat at 9:00, 12:00, and 3:00 with a glass table between them. The house backed up to a golf course and the voices of four Scottishly attired men purled through the interstitial trees and reached us as indistinguishable murmurs. I asked Threnody what she was reading because otherwise it seemed she was content not to speak to me.

"Ender's Game," she said without looking up. "You've probably never heard of it." With the feigned indolence of a teenage girl, she languidly turned the cover of the book for me to see. "It's good. I'm almost finished with it if you want it. I'd say I'd let you borrow it, but it's not mine." She went back to reading.

She had grown so much — had changed so much — since I had last seen her. Her hair, a soft chestnut brown, fell just at her shoulders. It was no longer a child's haircut and made her look prematurely grown up. Her knobby knees and elbows and coltish legs that used to go in six different directions were still coltish but now appeared strong and lean. Her movements, though, were abrupt and unsure. When she stood and walked, she took on the slightly stooped posture of a girl who's not yet accustomed to her new height.

I stared at her and tried to figure out who she looked like. I finally realized with a mild shock that she had our mother's face but our father's expressions. Her eyes went back to her book and began to scan the page with a look of profound concentration. I tried again.

"Do you want to go for a walk? It's a nice night," I said. "You can show me around the neighborhood —"

"No," she interrupted, and turned a page. It was clear she was pissed at me and I deserved it. I had it coming and there was nothing I could do but take my lumps.

"Are you hungry? Do you want to go get some dinner somewhere? I haven't eaten anything —"

"No, I ate already."

"Oh, really. What did you eat?"

"Chicken something something with asparagus and holiday sauce." This was an old shared joke delivered without mirth. With an exasperated sigh, she closed her book and put it neatly on the seat between us.

"I'm embarrassed that I don't even know whose house this is," I said. "It's nice."

"You should be. It's Mother's boyfriend's. Isn't it lovely? I don't really have my own room here. I mean, I have a room, but it has someone else's things in it."

"She has a boyfriend?"

"Why else do you think we'd be staying here? You'd know if you ever called. They've been dating for a while."

"Interesting. Where'd they meet?"

"You'll have to ask her. It's gross. His name is Hurricane."

"Hurricane? You're shitting me."

"Nope — it's on his birth certificate and

his nine million diplomas. I'll show you."

"Wow."

"Could be worse. He could be named Threnody."

"How does one —"

"I have no idea." She pretended to examine her fingernails and I admired the carpeted golf course gleaming away behind huddling poplars and pines that clustered self-consciously in the backyard.

"Do you like him?"

"He's all right. Mostly harmless, I guess. He doesn't really like to drink, which bothers Mother. When he does drink, he only drinks expensive beer he gets from Germany or somewhere. This also bothers Mother. Something about pretention."

"You'd think she'd be thrilled with a little moderation."

"I know. She can't have it both ways."

"What does he do?"

"Not much of anything. He's a lawyer, but he doesn't go to court. He wrote a book once."

"Yeah? Did you read it?"

"I did. It was beyond terrible. Here's terrible, and here's the book." She held out her hands like she was measuring for a couch.

"What was it about?"

"It was about a lawyer — who . . . wrote a book." We laughed and I remembered how we always had exactly the same sense of humor and how we'd always simultaneously die laughing at things no one else found funny.

The mosquitoes got the best of us, so we went inside and Threnody showed me perfunctorily around the sprawling house before sliding onto a velvety, decorative chaise longue stuck in one corner of the living room. Overhead, a lighted paper globe hung from the ceiling like a minor planet. Even though we'd been apart for so long and so much had happened in the temporal and spatial gulf between our increasingly divergent lives, for a moment neither of us could think of anything pertinent or appropriate to say. Threnody got up and put on some music and then resumed her position cross-legged on the chaise. Again, certain cuticles and then the fabric of her skirt became of momentary interest. Remembering her manners, she said, "Do you want something to drink?"

"No, thank you."

"Help yourself."

"I will, thanks."

"Make yourself at home. Fridge is in there." Pointing.

And then: "I've really missed you, Bird."
She held herself and began to cry.

On Saturday morning, Mother was waiting
for me in the kitchen when I got up. Apri-
cot pajamas, lemon designs. Soft-soled slip-
pers with pretend leather laces. She was
drinking coffee and had Leonard Cohen
playing somewhere in the sun-drowned
house. "Hallelujah" ended and "So Long,
Marianne" began discordantly and waltzed
and chugged away in the void and moved in
and out of my awareness. She ran to hug
me as I walked down the wide hallway from
the guest bedroom dressed in my clothes
from the previous day.

"I couldn't believe it when I saw your car
in the driveway last night. It was everything
I could do not to go in and wake you up.
Why didn't you tell me you were coming? I
would've been here."

"I didn't know for sure I was coming," I
said, not intending to be cryptic, but not
correcting myself when I realized it was. She
looked me up and down; synclinal eyebrows
told me she was not altogether pleased with
my appearance.

"I think you might've grown," she said.
"You seem taller than you were before. Or
else you lost weight. . . . Can I make you

some breakfast?"

"I'm not really hungry yet. I don't really eat breakfast," I said. "I'd love some coffee, though."

"Let's go in and sit down. I want to hear about everything."

I followed her into the living room. I passed a couch upholstered in what looked like rhinoceros skin and sat on Threnody's chaise. Mother sat in the chair opposite. Our usual places, but this time in someone else's house. Between us, a vase of flowers sat on a coffee table, white and cornflower blue.

And so it began:

"How are you? How are things up north? School is good? I'm *so* happy that you came down. Are you here for the summer? Do you know what you're going to do yet? Threnody is so happy you're here. You guys will have lots of time to reconnect."

I've always felt uncomfortable talking about myself. It feels like interrogation, and this time it made me surly and recalcitrant for no good reason. "School is good," I said, fielding the one question I could safely answer. "I'm learning a lot." My coffee was too hot to drink, so I set it on the table. A band of sunlight caught the rising steam, and my eyes burned from lack of sleep.

"Yeah?"

"Yeah. I'm taking a lot of cool classes."

"What are you taking?"

"Is this where you're going to live now?"

Mother looked around for Hurricane. Listened for him. Evidently he wasn't there.

"There's no piano," I said. "There's not much in the way of books."

"I don't know where we'd put it," she said, fielding the one question she could safely answer. "This isn't my house. But I miss hearing you play. Are you playing a lot?"

"Yes — I'm playing some, and the guitar, too. Believe it or not, I can actually play some of those pieces that used to give me so much trouble."

"Are you doing any concerts?"

"No — I could have, but I didn't sign up for them."

She held her coffee in both hands as if to warm them. I looked around the room at nothing in particular. In the time I was away, we had become strangers. She took another drink of coffee and pulled her legs into the chair.

"I know I've told you I want you to play that one Liszt piece at my funeral. I just love that." Whenever Mother heard a piece of music she thought lovely or sublime,

223

she'd ask me to make sure to play it at her funeral. It wasn't as dreadful a sentiment as it sounds. It was more of a way to poke fun at death; to say she wasn't scared of it.

"Which Liszt piece?"

"The really beautiful, slow one you used to play. The one that twinkles like the stars."

"I didn't play that. Father played it."

"Are you sure you didn't play it?"

"I'm sure. It's one of the Consolations. Father played that one."

"I'll have to make a note," she said. "Still, can you learn that one to play at my funeral, and then also play 'Greensleeves'? That's my other favorite."

"I'll have to make a note," I said. Silence flowed into the space between us and then Leonard Cohen returned and "Bird on the Wire" emanated nasally from the ether.

"Are you getting along okay down here?" I asked, finally getting over myself; finally remembering that it wasn't all about me.

"It's a lot different. The hardest part, and maybe you wouldn't guess it, was letting go of the horses, even after everything that happened. Maybe *because* of everything that happened, I don't know. There's a horse place north of here that I've heard about — it's at some kind of plantation, with nice rock walls running along the road and some nice trails along the Catawba River — but we'll just have to see."

"Any Arabians?"

"No — mostly quarter horses. Which I don't mind. But it's something to think about for now."

"Something to think about," I agreed.

"Your sister's struggling a little bit in her new school."

"What do you mean?"

"She doesn't have many friends."

"I'm not surprised by that."

"Why do you say that?"

"Because she's like me. The things she's interested in, other kids her age are not interested in. How many kids do you think she's going to school with have already read *Crime and Punishment*? I'll tell you. Probably zero."

"I'm so worried about her."

"Why? She seems fine."

"She's not. You were her best friend. You've disappeared from her life. She's had too much of that already."

"Thanks," I said. "That makes me feel good."

"Where are all your things?"

Mother could tell from my look that I wasn't staying. She got up and walked out of the room. Leonard was singing *I have tried in my way to be free.*

20

On Saturday night Threnody and I stayed up after Mother went to bed. As it turned out, Hurricane, or Cane, as he preferred to be called (unsurprisingly), had some good beer in his garage refrigerator and I decided to drink it. Threnody was lying in bed listening to me in the half-dark. I was sitting in a chair I'd pulled in from the living room.

"You might not remember this," I said, "but Father used to tell us stories that he made up about our distant relatives in the mountains."

"I kind of remember."

"They were actually pretty good. He had a whole cast of ridiculous characters, half of which I think he made up as he went along. Gideon was the main character. I used to beg him to tell me Gideon stories."

"Do you remember any? Who were the other characters besides Gideon?"

"Thinking about it now, it was all kind of

odd. Gideon's wife was, according to Father, an immense woman named Corpulina Porcinus (you have to say it in an Italian accent) who was, for all practical purposes, a giant. She had come to America on a ship called *La Cucina,* which the shipbuilders literally built around her while she waded in a canal. Then she was transported the rest of the way to Old Buckram by barge and hot-air balloon. I remember him saying that if she'd have been one inch taller, she would've been perfectly round."

"She was a giant?" said Threnody, now showing some interest. She propped herself up on an elbow but was still under the covers.

"Yes, basically. Father said she was *frightfully* strong (his words), and that she could 'easily crush even the most recalcitrant of cloves and the most wayward of red peppers.' "

"Ha."

While we sat and talked, I looked around Threnody's bedroom, except that it wasn't really hers, as she had said. The style and decorations had been preordained and she hadn't changed them. It reminded me of a condominium at the beach: stain-resistant carpet; walls of eggshell white; two matching, framed photographs of sand dunes and sea oats on adjacent walls (think Ansel Adams). The comforter on her bed was a generic beechen green, a guest linen of sorts, and not one she would have picked out. She had hung no posters on the walls, and the mirror over the dresser was missing the usual array of happy, silly photographs of friends. There was nothing to indicate to anyone that she was the current inhabitant of the room; that she was anything other than a transient, momentary occupier of the space. No overflowing bookcase; no Mylar-covered books borrowed from Father's library; no books on her night table with a bookmark showing where we'd last stopped reading.

"So that was Corpulina," I said. "And let's see — Gideon had a dog. Its name was Balzac."

"Balzac?"

"Yeah — after the French writer. But I remember there was some off-color joke behind that one. You can imagine."

Threnody allowed herself a little amusement and said, "Oh my gosh."

"And of course you had ol' Jim Rickey. That was Gideon's mule. In every story he found a way to be a little drunk, and then he'd run into things and get lost and occasionally he'd pass out."

"I'm not so sure about ol' Jim Rickey," she said. "He sounds autobiographical. Do you remember any of the stories?" And then she sat up and said, "Wait! Are you hungry? Should we go get a snack? Let's get snacks and come back and you can tell me a Gideon story!" We ran into the kitchen like a herd of elephants and began to open all the cabinets. Threnody got down three bowls and filled them with different varieties of chips and crackers. We had enough to eat for a couple of days. She got a cream soda out of the refrigerator and I got another beer out of the garage and we were ready for story time.

I said, "I remember one specific story about how Gideon's father found his wife — which presumably would be like your great-great-great-great-great I don't know how many greats grandmother."

"Sometimes I pretend I'm not related to the mountain people," she said. "I've been telling people down here that my family is from Pennsylvania."

"That's half true, but you still shouldn't do that. Mountain folks have a hell of a lot of character and ruggedness. It took a lot of determination for those people to survive and scrape out a living for all those years at five thousand feet of elevation. And you won't meet anyone from anywhere with more common decency and honesty than the folks in Old Buckram. That's all right there in your bloodline, just like it's in mine, and you should be proud of it."

"Whatever. You're on a tangent. Do you hear the tangent Klaxons? They are sounding. So what about Gideon's father's wife?"

"Okay. Apparently Gideon's father, whose name was Smoke, lived a hell of a long way from town. So he started dating one of the Houck sisters — there were two of them — and he planned to marry her, but the clerk of court printed up the marriage license with the *other* sister's name on it."

"What were their names?"

"Hattie and Alverta."

"Really?"

"I have no idea," I said. "I just made that part up."

"Was *his* name really Smoke?"

"Yes. Actually, that was a nickname. His real name was Barty, but everyone called him Smoke."

"Okay," she said.

"So anyway —" I said.

"That's a pretty cool name," she said.

"Smoke?"

"Yes. I like it."

"I have to agree. So Smoke was going to

marry Hattie, but the clerk of court printed the marriage license with Alverta's name on it, so he married Alverta instead."

"I wish he had married Hattie."

"Me, too."

"So why didn't he just get them to print a new license?"

"Well, according to the story, it was going to cost a whole dollar more to get a new license printed, but Smoke said he didn't reckon there was a dollar's difference between the two of them." This was the punch line and Threnody laughed on cue.

"Do you think that's true?"

"Probably not, but I don't know," I said.

"Remember when he used to play vampire with us?"

"Yes. I don't know about you, but that used to scare the shit out of me."

"The cape might have been a little much."

"The cape was fine. The coffin, the teeth, and the blood were a little much."

"Good point," she said.

She told me she missed him and I thought she might cry. I said, "I know, Bird. I know you do."

"Do you miss him?"

"I'll miss him when I forgive him," I said.

She considered this, and then said, "Do you want to sleep on my floor?"

"I do. I'd like that very much."

I read to her from her book until I was sure she was asleep, and then I read for a while longer to make sure the silence would not wake her up. I rolled out my sleeping bag and got a pillow off the couch for my head and stole one more of Cane's good beers out of the garage. I walked around and looked at all of Cane's books, none of which appeared to have ever been read. Lots of books about World War II. Several coffee-table treatises on art and art technique that he probably thought made him look sophisticated and well rounded. A large collection of religious books. His house was new and immaculate. I could see my reflection in his hardwood floors and appliances.

I finished the beer and stood there in the kitchen for a while, looking at pictures of smiling, clean-cut people I didn't know on the refrigerator. Pictures from Hawaii. Pictures from Paris. There's the fucking Eiffel Tower, no shit. That must be Venice. There's Cane in a seersucker looking very confident standing next to a silver Mercedes that probably cost $90,000. He must be loaded. You might say he had "done it right," somehow. Everything was neat and in its place. I'm sure his life was like that, too. It was

233

perfect in every way and completely fucking boring.

Without knowing it, I had inherited my father's nocturnal tendencies. I realized then, thinking about it, that he spent a hell of a lot of time awake when everyone else in his hemisphere was asleep. Now it was my turn. It's a lonely feeling, being awake when everyone everywhere is safely in the land of Nod. I was empty and my insomniac worms were back, eating at me from the inside. I finally surrendered and tried to sleep. In the morning I awoke before the sun and decided I'd spare everyone the agony of saying goodbye.

21

After four years of diligent study, I managed to graduate from college with a bachelor of arts in philosophy and absolutely no idea what I wanted to do with the rest of my life. I couldn't conceive of a possible career that would suit me or interest me in the slightest. In the midst of all this indecision, and being otherwise unemployable, I applied to law school. I still to this day don't know why I did it. It was a plan, I suppose, and one that would keep me away from home, wherever that happened to be.

Thinking back, I only remember one conversation with my father about what he thought I might do for a living, and it supplied no insight into my future deliberations whatsoever. It was some time after Maddy died. My grandfather, Helton, had suffered a severe stroke and was residing in a nursing home in Winston-Salem. The building where he was housed, unmistakably reminiscent of a commercial-grade chicken house in architecture, aroma, and exterior appeal, had one impossibly long hallway, the other end of which upon entry was too far away to see in the available lighting.

The windows to the facility were all bolted shut, we were told, for "security reasons." After a few visits it dawned on me that the latched windows were to prevent some senescent, diapered loon from escaping and wandering half-clothed and delirious through the streets of the city. As we'd walk down this airless corridor to my grandfather's room, I'd peer into the stagnant darkness of the few open doors and see the cadaverous patients in dying repose, their dysmorphic figures sunk and twisted obscenely under thin, comfortless blankets in heaps of inhuman mortal decay. We'd pass row upon languishing row of low, fetid beds and restless, rolling eyeballs, and mouths made permanently slack by age or wasting disease. Our visits were not joyous occasions.

My grandfather's eyesight and his memory were all but gone because of the damage to his brain and he didn't recognize us. His head seemed to sink further and further into his bed and into his pillow to the point that all you could see of him was a yawning, gaping mouth full of large yellow protuberant teeth. We'd just go stand in the room for a while, no one saying anything other than making stark observations of the surroundings. From time to time Father would try a window and remark, "You'd think the Highland Hospital fire would have taught them something" — referring to a psychiatric facility in Asheville that burned down in 1948 and took the lives of eight of its patients who were trapped inside.

Father eventually stopped visiting. Meanwhile, I was doing well in school, and playing basketball, and I was even interested in a couple of girls who, sadly, were not aware of my existence. Father knew none of this. For weeks he thought I was on the math team, and I'm not even sure where this came from because our school didn't have a math team. He never made it to a single one of my basketball games, despite Mother's promise that he'd see all of them. There were, of course, other matters that kept him occupied.

One restless Sunday in October we were all at home, Father having decided on this occasion not to make the pointless trip to Winston-Salem. We were sitting in various corners of the Great Room reading different books, which is what we did to escape the persistent, low-grade horror of the vulture house. For all of us to be together like that was unusual in those days. The phone rang and Mother answered it. It was the town sign-maker. He was calling to ask Father a question about punctuation.

While he did not begrudge the sign-maker the occasional bit of advice, suffice to say that Father did not enjoy interruptions of any kind. The sign-maker painted a handsome sign with nice, bold lettering, but his linguistic skills were not terribly advanced. There were signs hung all over Old Buckram with misspellings and other wince-inducing errors (GOAT'S FOR SALE / LUMBER ECT. & MORE). He had started calling Father a dozen times a year or more. Mother used to say, "At least he knows what he doesn't know."

Father talked briefly to him and then placed the phone down, yanked his coat off a hook, and banged out through the door to the outside. I followed him out and traced his steps through the courtyard and down the hill through the field where the horses were grazing. It was quiet as only quiet can exist in a small mountain town, but a storm was coming and I could feel it on my face. Down the hill toward town, from the direction of the Barrowfields, the ever-present crows took flight, ascended the hill watchfully, and settled in a tree near where we walked.

As we went along I noticed that the black-eyed Susans Mother had planted along the fence had all died. They were just a crowd of dead stalks with black heads. Drooping yellow dahlias spanned the courtyard wall, their heads too heavy for their stems. We walked under the two ancestral oak trees in the field where the crows watched, and the ground below them was hidden beneath a floor of half-eaten, decaying acorns. There were changing colors on the Morning Mountain, but above it the sky was pale and gray as far as I could see. Father and his isolation were bundled in his long black coat, his strides too long for mine.

We sat on the cold ground at the edge of the hill and looked down off the mountain into the rising mist. Father offered me a drink out of an ornate tin flask and then remembered my age. His mind was elsewhere. It was, as usual, not with me. I wondered how he had focused his attention long enough to tie his own shoes; to put on and fasten his pants and belt.

"No, thank you," I said, feeling a quickening urge to flee and unburden myself of the suffocating pain I had come to acquire only in his presence. At something unseen, the horses bolted into flight and tore off down the hill. In a moment they had circled and returned, throwing their heads about defiantly. "I wonder why they do that," I said. Without looking up, he said, "I don't know," but I'm not sure he had even seen them.

"This — all this —" He drew a hand across the sullen landscape. "All this reminds me somehow of Yeats. See the pond down there, and the quiet of it? In the summer, men are down there fishing and drinking beer. I can see them from my window. Boys and girls swim and splash and chase one another around, and people from town lay down blankets for picnics and put their feet in the water. But now the autumn has come and ended all that, and a stillness lays upon it." As if summoned to complete the scene just written, the wind came from deep within the woods and left us encircled in a vortex of newly fallen leaves.

"I like Yeats," I said, not wanting to disappoint this rare poignancy between us, but instantly I felt my response was inadequate and groped for more words just to find agreement with him. I tried but couldn't find more to say. His silence that followed assured me that my meager contribution was indeed meaningless to him.

And this was how our conversations usually went in the years after his mother died: dreadful quiet punctuated by the occasional brief exchange, followed by more contemplative dreadful quiet. And so we sat. Imagine us as two piles of rock sitting idle on the side of the mountain in this uneven field, the forest behind us issuing forth and calling back the chilling wind. Father brought his coat up around his neck and the crows rocked on the branches above our heads.

"I wish the sun would come out," I said. "I feel like I haven't seen it in a while."

"It's fine with me if it doesn't," said Father. "I keep thinking, involuntarily, that the sun is just a remorseless cosmic furnace that the earth is gradually falling into."

"It's up there," I said, pointing. "We can't exactly *fall* into it."

"It's a question of perspective," said Father. "I've always thought we looked down into the sun." Changing the subject, he said, "Do you — have any idea what you want to be when you grow up? I think it's a good time for us to talk about that." He forced himself awkwardly into the role of a parent and wavered there uncomfortably. I sensed this and adopted the corresponding persona of a dutiful son contemplating his future.

"I'm trying to decide," I said, but in fact I

hadn't considered it for a single moment. Life seemed hardly to have begun for me. My days could still be agonizingly slow, and it was hard to see past the next summer. There was a time when all I really wanted to do was to be like him. I wanted to be a writer; maybe a lawyer, too. I wanted to play sweetly sorrowful music by candlelight after everyone else had gone to bed. I wanted to be the solitary man reading at the edge of the Barrowfields. I wanted to be all that he was before the sadness came. But those days had passed, and passed irretrievably.

Thinking of all that had gone wrong — feeling a hateful bitterness inside me from his absence in my life, from my inability to understand him and his indifference to my inability to understand him, I bit my tongue almost through and said with perfect sarcasm, "Sometimes I think I'd like to be a writer." It was hard for me not to be angry, to be antagonistic toward him, and I meant this sentiment with a lifetime's burden of sardonic irony.

"Like me," he said grimly.

"Like you," I said. "Just like you."

"That's how I used to think of myself," he said. A black cat, not ours, walked along the top of the fence and disappeared into the howling woods. Father stood abruptly, shook out the rest of what was in his flask, and started back to the house. I called after him — "Where are you going?"

He came reluctantly back and stood over me, the toes of our feet touching. "Why would you say that to me?"

"Why would I say what to you?"

"That you want to be a writer."

"I don't know why I said it. Maybe I meant it."

He studied my face, trying to divine the intent behind my words. He leaned over me in a great long arc, his immense black coat buoyed by the wind and spread out behind him like the wings of a bird. "I've never told you this before, but I raised you to be a writer," he said. "I thought maybe one day you would be. All those books I read to you. All those stories. You don't even remember, do you? But I see now in light of — me — that's not going to happen. . . .

"You didn't mean it," he said acerbically. "I know you didn't mean it."

"I'm sorry." I realized I'd hurt him more than I had intended. He just kept shaking his head. His disappointment wouldn't leave him.

"You —" he started. "I thought —" More head shaking.

"You thought what?"

"I thought maybe you of all people would understand." He turned and walked away from me, and in a great rushing of wind the crows rove into the air above our heads and followed him across the field.

For years I only knew of one brief passage that he wrote after Maddy died. A window onto his grief:

People say "passed away" when they mean someone died. They might say "She passed away one year ago today," when they mean that minus one orbital period around the sun her exhausted heart shuddered to a stop and the molecules of her last-drawn breath dispersed soundlessly into the room. Spirit, *espirit, esperit, spiritus, spirare,* breathe. Saying "passed away" is softer than saying that someone *died.* Reassuringly, they might say "she's in a better place." Or "Lord willin', she's gone to find her family on the streets of heaven." "She's better off," they'll say, and everyone will nod solemnly and a man will pick at his teeth with a toothpick he's had in his shirt pocket for four days. To themselves, and to the dead, they say "Rest in Peace."

Isn't it true that the first time you talk

about someone whose waking time on earth has ended, out of habit you mistakenly use the present tense, because that's what you've grown accustomed to doing all someone's life. It's hard not to want to say, "She's a good mother to her children." You might do this once, but then your brain catches with a hollow jolt, and something tells you that language knows the truth and the truth is that she's *gone.* Then comes the preterit. "She is — she *was* — a good mother to her children," you might say. "She *cared* for her family." "She *loved* the church people and would talk all day long if you'd let her." I think of all those moments unphotographed and unrecorded, now lost to everyone for all of time. What record is there of her life? She's contained within me now.

We realize, though, because we must, that remembrance is finite. It crosses only so many generations before it fades to indistinction. One man remembers his father and perhaps his grandfather and the detail of the lives that were lived. But it's harder to see further back in time. I know the name of my great-grandfather, but our living time did not intersect. We did not walk the earth at the same time. Thus to me he's a photograph; a story I heard my grandfather tell. He's not a life I remember. And my children may not know him at all, unless by chance they can find him in a book. In time, he will be forgotten entirely, just as we all will with enough revolutions of the earth around the slowly expiring sun.

Each fragile heart now beating will one day stop. I look at my children, I feel their hearts within their chests, so gentle and quick. I know they will not go on forever. I cannot bear to consider it —

We are little more than one tree's growth of leaves in a hillside forest. We will enjoy our brief moment in the sun, only to fall away with all the others to make way for the next bright young generation.

So you see.

The fall after graduation I started law school in Chapel Hill. It was not home, but it brought me closer to home, and my heart ached as I returned again to the Old North State.

PART III

22

Charles Young, my father's former law partner, owned a little house on Rosemary Street in Chapel Hill close to campus and he allowed me to rent it while I was there. I had used him for a reference on my application, and when he learned that I might be going to school in Chapel Hill, he didn't renew the lease of his previous tenant and kept the house unrented for several months just in case I might need or want it. In return he asked only that I allow him and a few friends to tailgate there during football and basketball season when he was in town for a game. This worked out well because for every home game on a weekend the house and yard were full of people, every one of them wearing Carolina blue, and all were drinking good beer and cooking good food. The parties started early and lasted late. Even for night games, there was always one guy and his wife who you could count on to show up by nine in the morning to get the pig cooker going. It was always a hell of a good time and I picked up a lot of spare tickets.

I did well in my first year of law school and I discounted the possibility that it was because many of the professors knew me or knew of me through my father. Even though the subject of the law wasn't of any particular interest to me, it was challenging and demanded hours of daily reading and researching and pondering. I had heard my father talk about much of it in my years growing up, so arcane concepts such as future interests or even the deeply obscure "rule in Shelley's case" — loved by law professors and mystifying to students — were not entirely unknown to me and my limited familiarity lent itself to some amount of success.

I quickly formed a study group with two young men named J. P. and Tyler. They were both exceedingly bright and wonderfully odd in their own respective ways. J. P., who insisted on a space between J and P "for obvious logical reasons," was from Savannah and came from a family made obscenely wealthy when Gulfstream Aerospace Corp. went public in 1985. J. P.'s father was a big player in Gulfstream from its earliest beginnings, and after the company's acquisition by Chrysler it was reckoned that no one in the family for several generations to come would have to hold meaningful employment. J. P. nevertheless had received a world-class undergraduate education at Princeton and would talk Bernoulli's principle with you until you passed out from exhaustion. When I asked him why he decided to go to law school, he said, "I'm really not sure." His real life's ambition was to be a writer, which sadly I knew something about. He read mostly science fiction and prior to law school had two or three short stories published in pretty impressive sci-fi journals.

Tyler, on the other hand, grew up in Raleigh and came from slightly more modest beginnings. His father was an electrical engineer who worked for Bell South in Durham his entire career, and his mother was a high-school calculus teacher. Like J. P., he was first and foremost a bona fide nerd who loved intellectual abstraction. He was ambidextrous and could simultaneously work two sides of an equation on a blackboard with a piece of chalk in each hand, which was something I'd never seen done by anyone. I asked him the same question I'd asked J. P. — why he chose to come to law school when he was more suited to be an engineer or a physicist. After giving it some thought he replied, "I really couldn't tell you. I think I just needed a plan." I was grateful to have these friends.

We studied a hell of a lot and spent six days a week together, but much of the time we were talking about multifarious and sundry subjects unrelated to law. We prepared class study guides (known in law school as outlines) that were epic in scope and detail and after the three of us did well in our first semester, word got around and everyone wanted copies of them. For the second semester, I sold a guitar and used the money to buy a laptop for typing the outlines in real time as the study sessions progressed, and naturally the usual libidinous filth that comes from a group of bright, bored young men wound up blended into the outlines as I transcribed them contemporaneously with the bawdy utterances themselves. Once, for example, J. P. remarked that he had propped his book on a recalcitrant hard-on in our business-law class and thereby made it move up and down like the tail rudder of a biplane, and that wound up as a quote in the third paragraph of a case brief on piercing the corporate veil. Mostly, though, the spontaneous brilliance of these two men was made manifest in other ways. I can say with confidence, for example, that our real-property outline was the only one in recorded history to use the word *lemniscate* with respect to an analysis of the rule against perpetuities.

On the first day of our second year, a girl walked into class that I hadn't seen before. She stood for a moment just inside the doorway while looking for a seat. There was, I perceived, a quiet aspect to her nature — some distant sadness from wounds inflicted long before — but when she turned toward me I saw in her eyes and in her face a knowing brightness and a wondrous depth of intelligence and resolve.

She soon made friends with a nice group of girls in our law school class with whom I was marginally acquainted, but details about her seemed slow to appear. I learned only that she had transferred from a law school in the northeast and had family in Charleston. To my dismay, we were in different class sections and fate had cruelly ordained that we were to have only one class together that met just one day a week. Despite my best efforts, I never had occasion to talk to her except on those rare and exhilarating moments when we would pass each other coming in or out of the building, and these brief and monosyllabic exchanges were unfortunately of no more depth or meaning than what you might have with a stranger crossing the street. I never saw her at the library or out on the weekends. Rumor had it that she spent a lot of time traveling back and forth to Charlotte.

She was nicely tall and slight of frame, with white-blond hair that fell down just past her shoulders. She was quick to laugh, and her laugh was sweet and honest and full. Her every movement and gesture seemed to be evolutionarily and geometrically ideal. From top to toe, Darwin and Euclid could not have conspired to design a being more naturally and mathematically sound. Add to the above a swanlike posture and an athletic elegance, and the result was a beguiling, mesmerizing artistry that made my heart thrash wildly about whenever I saw her.

After study group one Saturday afternoon before exams, J. P., Tyler, and I sat on my front porch and I confided to them my fascination with the girl, who I learned had the curious name of Story. J. P. convulsed with laughter and said I didn't have a chance. "First of all, she seems *way* too normal for you. And you don't even know who she is. Despite appearances, she might be crazy. Do what I do and go for the low-hanging fruit."

"By low-hanging fruit, he means his own balls," said Tyler. "That's the only action he ever gets."

To Tyler, J. P. said, "Blow me." To me, he said, "She'll just break your heart. There's absolutely no good reason to torture yourself over something you'll never have. You should just get a dog."

"Oh, well, I don't know!" said Tyler. "I could just about see it working with the two of you. You're both kind of similar in a lot of ways that I can't exactly articulate."

"They have the same hair," said J. P.

"They do," said Tyler, "except hers is longer."

"She's almost as tall as you are," said J. P. "Y'all would have some *tall* babies."

"But," said Tyler, "listen to me right now. If you're going to do this, you need to be careful and not fuck it up. Don't act like an idiot, which we both know you're capable of doing."

That night I dreamed about her. She was standing in front of me, her eyes searching my face. Then she kissed me a single time and the full length of her body pressed into mine. I tried to take her hands, but she backed enigmatically away and moved slowly off into a chasm of darkness. I can tell you honestly that this sort of thing can drive a young man completely mad.

I didn't see her again for what seemed like an eternity. After Christmas break, when it became clear to me that our paths were never going to cross because of our differing class schedules, I tried to put her out of my mind once and for all. Heeding J. P.'s advice, I went to the local animal shelter in search of a dog and was referred to a local dog rescue that had just gotten four dozen puppies from a puppy mill in Reidsville that had been closed down by the police for practices that amounted to animal cruelty. The owners from whom the dogs were taken were well on their way to some maniacal canine eugenics program when someone reported the outfit to animal care and control. All the dogs were living in despicable conditions. The rescue, which had rented a farmhouse on New Hope Church Road, was adopting out the dogs (upon a suitable donation) to decently qualified persons, so I made a donation by check of federal student-loan money and set out into the yard to find a dog.

About twenty of the puppies had red silk ribbons tied around their necks. This signified that the dogs were spoken for. I was at once grateful for this narrowing of the field. One puppy, a little larger than the rest but still skin and bones, sat by himself in a small area enclosed by chicken wire. He had been marked by an orange ribbon. Every now and then he would whimper and cry out to the other dogs and claw at the fence. Most of the time he would just sit and watch. He already had large feet and looked like he was going to be a big dog.

"What's the deal with this little guy?" I asked.

"He's a sweetie. But he's not one we can let you have," said a kind but fatigued woman of middle age who had spent the better part of the previous two days transporting the dogs in crates from the puppy mill to the farm. "But there are lots more, as you can see."

"Is there something the matter with him? What's the orange ribbon mean?"

"We think he had a seizure," she said. "Maybe two. So we pulled him out to watch him. We can't give someone a dog that's going to be an unexpected financial burden." She explained that some large-breed dogs have seizures and that they require a lot of care and a commensurate amount of medicine and medical attention.

"Do you mind if I sit with him for a minute?" I asked.

"You can," she said, "but don't get your hopes up."

"Does he have a name?"

She leaned over the chicken-wire fence and examined the ribbon. "Yep. Right now he's number 42."

I sat down with #42 in the grass and he climbed into my lap and started chewing on my hand with teeth that were sharper than I expected. We sat there together and played for the next three hours, both of us watching with interest all the comings and goings as people arrived to pick out puppies, and as the well-meaning volunteers, almost all of them college-age girls, prepared paperwork and diligently screened applicants. By 5:00 P.M., #42 was asleep in my lap and I was rubbing his back. The kind lady came over to where we were sitting and said, "I hope you didn't get too attached."

Right.

"I've been sitting here with him for a while and he seems fine," I said. "I haven't noticed anything."

"I can't do it," she said. "I want to, but I can't."

"Who else is going to take him?"

"I was going to. I can look after him."

I said, "I bet you have half a dozen dogs

already."

She laughed. "I do. I can't say no to them. I used to have half a dozen dogs and a husband, but now I just have half a dozen dogs."

"Well, you don't need one more, especially if he's sick. Send him home with me. I'll take good care of him." She looked at me for a long time and then gave me a hug.

"Come on, pal," I said to #42. "You're going with me." We got into the car, he in the passenger seat, me in the driver's seat. Before I had pulled back out onto the highway, he had crawled over into my lap and settled down for a nap, his head resting in the crook of my arm.

We went to the pet store to get his supplies and before I could get a leash on him, he squatted down and peed on the slick tile floor. He was still filthy and I was afraid someone would think I was a bad parent. "I just got him," I said to people in the store who couldn't have cared less. "He's a rescue from a puppy mill. I know, isn't that awful? We're going home to give him a good bath."

We got home and I turned him loose in the backyard. He ran and played and chased sticks I would throw for him and he ate grass and threw it up and explored every part of the yard, finding four or five holes in the fence I hadn't noticed. I poured out some food for him and he devoured it after flipping over the bowl and spilling the food out onto the ground. He then triumphantly put both his front feet into his water bowl. After a while he joined me at the back steps and crashed down at my feet, panting.

"I already know what I'm going to call you," I told him. "You will no longer be forced to suffer the indignity of just being a number, #42. You are now officially named Buller."

He grew quickly, and over the course of a few months he went from being a roly-poly puppy to an animal more reminiscent of a lion cub. He was in fact the tawny color of a lion and he had a broad, powerful chest that became more muscular by the day. I walked him every morning before class and every afternoon when I came home and every night before bed. When I was in class he began eating my possessions, one by one, and sometimes several at a time. He considered my books a delicacy. One day I came home to find that he had utterly destroyed an entire shelf of books — Wordsworth, Yeats, Keats, Shelley, Byron, Coleridge, and *Songs of Innocence and of Experience* by William Blake. He apparently preferred the romantics. I found torn pages in every room of the house. He must have had a hell of a time. Once he ate a giant hole in my box spring. Another time he ate a hole in an open door.

He quickly picked up every command I could teach him. He would pout every day when I left for school and became suicidally melancholy if I went out for dinner or a beer after class. He would lie with his head in the corner facing away from me and would ignore me when I called him. Every time I went anywhere he wanted to go with me, and of course I took him everywhere I could. He never went anywhere without a toy in his mouth. A friend of mine from school once gave him a plush teddy bear that I was certain he would immediately shred to pieces, but instead, like a canine Sebastian Flyte, he carried it around everywhere and got to be well known on campus for his affection for the bear. When Buller could not accompany me for one reason or another, I'd say, "You have to stay here, buddy," and he would drop the toy he was carrying at my feet and head to the corner of the room to sulk.

Meanwhile, he continued to grow and grow until he was positively leonine. By the time he was a year old, he weighed in at an incredible 125 pounds and every bit of it was bone and muscle. He loved to chase tennis balls more than anything in the world, and whenever he was ready to play, which was often, he would bring me two or three and put them in my lap and bark at me to take him to the park. As long as I would throw the ball for him, he would continue to go get it and bring it back. By the end of our respective days, he and I were usually pretty well worn out. He came to bed with me every night and always slept with his head on my chest.

23

In the early spring of my last semester of law school, J. P., Tyler, one of Tyler's friends from Raleigh named Will, and I went to Crook's Corner for shrimp and grits one perfect Saturday evening. The day had been warm and everyone was out and about with the optimism that comes with the promise of returning good weather. The restaurant was packed with a line out the door. When we finally got inside, the hostess asked us if we had a smoking preference and J. P. replied, "Marlboro Lights." I said, "First available is fine," and we crowded into a small space at the corner of the bar and waited for our table. Men were in khaki pants and button-downs and women were in flowered sundresses of swirling colors. We were all enjoying the scenery and J. P. was pontificating about the evolutionary basis for the bull's eye aspect of the nipple when Story and five of her friends from school walked in. Naturally, they had had the foresight to make a reservation and were escorted straight past us to a table on the patio outside that was already thronged with people. After regaining consciousness, I asked the hostess to change our seating preference from "first available" to "patio," which she happily did.

"Huddle up." The guys looked at me like I was nuts. "Guys — huddle up."

Will said, "What's up?"

"I know what's up," said Tyler.

"I do, too," said J. P. "Story's here."

"She is indeed," I said. "Two things: First, I call that. You guys know what I've been going through, so please at least let me have the first shot at embarrassing myself. If she totally blows me off, she's fair game, but so help me god I will hate you motherfuckers forever if someone else winds up going home with her. I'm serious about that. For-*ever*. You don't know me, Will, but I will carry a grudge into the afterlife. Second, do not, under any circumstances, let me do anything stupid. If I drink too much, don't let me talk to her. Go get a restraining order. J. P.?"

"Yeah, I know a judge," said J. P. "I got that covered. I can have you temporarily confined."

"The key," said Tyler, "is not to say anything at all. Just be near her but don't talk unless you have to. Just try to sit there and look confident. You can only fuck it up if you talk."

"Thanks, bud."

"I'm looking out for you. I want this as much as you do."

"Really?"

"I'm tired of hearing you whine about it."

"Thanks."

Several lifetimes passed and the hostess finally came to take us to our table on the busy patio. "It's time!" I called out. " 'He that hath the steerage of my course, direct my sail. On, lusty gentlemen.' "

To Will, J. P. said, "He says shit like that all the time. You'll get used to it." Then to me, "Was that *Romeo and Juliet?*"

"Indeed," I said. "I don't know how you do it."

I tried to sit where I could see Story, but Tyler wouldn't let me. "You'll just stare at her the whole time like a stunned animal and she'll think you're a stalker."

"He's right," said J. P. "We'll tell you what you need to know."

"Bastards," I said.

Tyler related that Story's table was completely full.

"You think I'm going to go sit with her?" I asked.

"How else are you going to talk to her? Want to wait until she leaves and try to catch her in the parking lot?"

My torment thus continued for some time. Then Tyler noticed that a girl sitting next to Story had paid her bill and left, leaving a vacancy at the table. Oh, fate!

Tyler said, "You're up. Go get 'em, tiger."

"I can't just go sit down next to her."

"Yes, you can. Pretend like you're going to take a piss and act surprised to see her and sit down. You got this."

With a pounding heart and every line of romantic verse I'd ever heard or read ricocheting nonsensically through my brain and whipsawing the air around me, I walked to Story's table and sat down next to her in the empty chair. All conversation at the table came to a screeching halt. Story and her friends were looking at me as they might have looked at a naked man who had brought them dessert.

"Hey, guys. How is everyone?"

After a long second they all responded cheerily and went back to talking about the bar exam and jobs. Thankfully, the waiter came by and I ordered a beer. I sat there for a minute or two without saying anything, as if there were nothing out of the ordinary about me sitting at the table with a group of people with whom I'd not previously had any substantive communication. Tyler and J. P. were doing a hell of a good job not monitoring my progress. They were continuing as if nothing out of the ordinary was happening, and I admired their professionalism. My beer arrived and I took a long, grateful drink. I examined the patterned metal table with my fingers like it was of some real consequence and then pretended to study a menu with near-scientific intensity even though I had already eaten. Story crossed her legs and turned toward me. She and I were the only two people at the table and perhaps in the entire pullulating establishment not engaged in some conversation. We must have looked rather silly.

"I'm Story."

"Hi, I'm Henry. I saw you sitting here and thought I'd say hello."

"You saw me sitting here?"

"I saw you come in."

"And you wanted to say hello to me?" she asked.

"I did."

"Hmm." She appeared skeptical. My face began to burn and I became deeply and profoundly self-conscious almost to the point of personal incontinence. I had no business being there and I didn't have the first idea what to say to her. "Anyway," I said, choking on my words. I started to get up to leave. BethAnn, one of Story's law school friends, said to me, "Have you started studying at all?"

Thank you, Jesus. I sat back down. She was talking about the upcoming bar exam.

"I heard you got called on in criminal procedure the other day," she said, without waiting for me to answer the first question.

"I did."

"That's so crazy. I can't remember the last time a 3-L got called on. What were you doing?"

"I was reading a book," I said. "But not the textbook. Probably shouldn't have had my feet up, even in the back of the class." Story laughed and I felt my respiration decrescendo to a more medically acceptable level.

"What were you reading?" Another one of Story's friends — this time, Nichole, whose superfluous *h,* short skirts, and multiplicity of short-term boyfriends had done her no favors — chimed in. Turpitude aside, she was competing for top graduating honors.

"For Whom the Bell Tolls."

Story laughed again. Hell, yes.

"That's crazy," said BethAnn. "You're such a geek. What did he say to you?"

"After I said *pass,* he said — very ominously, I might add — he said, 'You can pass this time, but will you pass the exam?' "

"That's what I heard," said Nichole. "That's so funny. He obviously has no idea who you are." By this she meant that I was among her close competition.

"He's arguably unpleasant," I said.

"He's inarguably a vacuous simpleton," said Nichole. Touché, Nichole.

The rest of the table went back to its discussion. Story's sunshine hair was pulled back but curled around and obscured her exquisite throat. She had on a sleeveless black dress and I marveled at the contour of her arms and shoulders. There was something inherently resilient about her manner that projected itself through her posture and even the very way she put her arms upon the table. She talked to BethAnn with animation, apparently unaware that I was still sitting next to her. When she turned to me again, I said, "I should be going."

"Can I ask you a question?" she said.

"Of course."

"What do you want to be when you grow up?" It had gotten so loud on the patio that we almost had to shout to hear each other over the rising voices and sharp clanging of silverware on porcelain and enamel. She was leaning toward me and our faces were close.

"I have no idea. Probably not a lawyer. What about you?"

"I thought I wanted to be lawyer," she said. "Now I'm not so sure."

"Why is that?"

"Because I truly want to help people."

I mulled this over and looked at her and read the seriousness in her face. Her eyes were arresting. She seemed to become momentarily embarrassed at my obvious wonderment.

"What are you drinking?" She pointed with her beer at my glass of beer and tucked her hair behind one ear. I watched the remarkable economy of movement of her arm as it rose and fell. Surely a hundred or more people sat out on the patio and talked, and just as surely waiters and waitresses walked about carrying buckets of beer and people passed back and forth, but I was just as surely not aware of any of them.

"I really don't recall," I said. At that moment I really couldn't recall. "It's good, though, if you want to try it. What are you having?"

"I'm not sure. Someone else ordered it for me. It just appeared."

I took another drink. "Do you want me to get us two more?"

"Yes, please," she said. "That way we can figure out what we're drinking."

I summoned the waiter and ordered two more beers. Coronas with a lime. Keeping it simple.

"Who are you here with?" she asked. I pointed to my rowdy table where J. P. and Tyler were causing some kind of ruckus. BethAnn asked Story another question and I lost her attention and wasn't sure I would get it back. I told myself it would be reasonable for me to wait at the table until the beer arrived, which it did a moment later. Story and I inserted our limes and toasted.

"To our one moon and all our myriad stars," I said.

"Yes," she said, savoring it. "I like that. To our one moon and all our myriad stars. What's that from?"

"I might've read it somewhere." I asked her where she was from and she said, "A town in South Carolina you've never heard of, I'm sure." Her amused expression disappeared and was replaced with a beautifully furrowed brow. Her friends had gotten their checks and stood to leave. They asked if she was ready to go. She looked at me for a long second and I thought she just might stay.

At last, she said, "I'm ready." She stood carefully, and her black dress showed her body underneath it. "It was nice talking to you. I can't drink all this. Do you want the rest?" She handed her beer to me and I wondered if taking it home to keep in a hermetically sealed container in my refrigerator would signal to others the need for long-term confinement.

"Have a good night," I said.

"Thank you. I will. You, too. Enjoy the moon and all our myriad stars." And then she was gone.

24

As a going-away party from law school, my friends and I rented a beach house on Sullivan's Island for a long weekend following the last day of exams. Word quickly got out that we had made such an accommodation and soon several more people from our class had signed up to come and stay. We knew nothing about the house other than that it was spacious, very expensive, and had red-painted French doors that opened from three of the downstairs bedrooms onto the dunes preceding the beach. On Thursday afternoon as we were loading supplies into the car for the weekend, Story called me at the house in Chapel Hill. I hadn't talked to her since the night at the restaurant.

"Hey — it's Story — we talked the other night at Crook's Corner? . . . You remember — ? Okay, good. I heard you guys were going to the beach. Do you think you have room for one more?" My essential organs became paralyzed. When I had regained my bearings, I told her we would enjoy having her, and that there was plenty of room. BethAnn and Nichole had already been invited by someone else in our group, and Story said she was going to follow them down later in the afternoon. She was familiar with Sullivan's Island and just needed the address. "It's on Poe Avenue," I told her. "All the way at the end. We're in a large white house on the left on the water. You should see my Scout, if the old girl makes it down there. It's the one with the license plate that says VP-KAN."

Those of us who arrived early stood on the front porch of the house drinking beer and waiting for the others as the coral sky faded languorously toward nightfall. We had no fewer than three oversize coolers, and the sun-bleached boards of the house were the color of the ubiquitous white sand. Someone found an antique crystal bowl from inside and filled it with lunes of fresh lime. It sat conspicuously on the railing of the porch, aqueous emerald against all the sand-white planks. A reggae mix dropped from the windows on the third floor and gave rhythm to every step and movement.

J. P., lubricated by the alcohol, talked to me nonstop about writing fiction and his

attendant quest to become the next Ur-
sula K. Le Guin. J. P. was one of my closest
friends and I enjoyed him tremendously,
but the confidence with which he discussed
his probable future success as a writer and
his insinuations of superior knowledge
caused me to bristle and burn a little on the
inside. I hadn't told him about Father, so
he wasn't to blame, and even if I had there
would be nothing in the telling of Father's
story that would prevent J. P. from talking
about writing. Nevertheless, something
about how he made it all sound so easy and
color-by-numbers drove nails into the palms
of my consciousness. Thankfully on this occasion the effect was ameliorated by a degree because I was having trouble paying
perfect attention to what he was saying. The
fact was that I was preoccupied to the point
of severe distraction. I could think of nothing else but Story and whether she would
actually come to the beach.

"I think erotica is really the way to go.
That is, if you want to sell something. I may
try my hand at that one of these days." Momentarily tiptoed, J. P. moved his testicles
from one side to the other. Ignoring the
double entendre and looking past J. P. for
evidence of Story's arrival, I said, "Like
who? Like D. H. Lawrence? Or more some-

thing like Henry Miller?"

"See, that's what you can't do. You can't set out to write *like* anybody. You just have to *create.* Let it happen. Let your brain follow its natural patterns, which you can be sure in most cases haven't been replicated in nature before. And Henry Miller is hardly erotica. Just because the dreaded *c* word appears in a book doesn't qualify it as such. Read Henry Miller looking for something scandalous and you'll be disappointed — unless the word *cunt* just curls your toes."

He went to the cooler, came back with four beers, and handed two of them to me so that I was then holding three. He opened the first of his by wedging the cap against the porch railing and violently whacking it with his other hand, sending the cap hurtling off into the driveway like a Roman candle. Looking surprised, he scrambled down the steps to pick it up.

"You're so conscientious," I said.

"Tell that to my mother."

"But don't you have to read everything that has happened before so you'll know that you're not duplicating something that's already been done?" I asked, playing the game.

"First of all, that's impossible." J. P. was tall and thin — maybe taller than me —

with long limbs that spread out in all directions. To me, he resembled a kite made of very white, freckled fabric. He was always cultivating about two days' worth of splotchy beard growth à la Yasser Arafat. His features were handsome but his demeanor said "geek," and he much preferred to land in the latter category as a point of intellectual honesty. As far as I knew, he'd never been laid or even been on a real date. When he talked he gesticulated widely and his arms would twirl about to great effect.

"There's just too much shit out there," he said, and here he became a pterodactyl hovering in the air before me, a beer in each hand at the opposite termini of the wingspan. "You'll paralyze yourself trying to do that. How would you ever find time to write? And then — and *then*," he said, taking a drink, "you'll find someone you really do like and you'll unconsciously try to write like that. Now *that's* what you have to avoid."

"So what do you do?" I said. "You don't read. You just write?"

"Me personally? Oh, I read everything. I read every fucking thing I can get my hands on. I completely agree with you despite what I'm telling you. I'm crippled by fear that my shit is not going to be as good as what people are writing now, and nine times out of ten, that's why I don't wind up writing. I just recognize that it's not a good strategy, what you're talking about."

"Did you read Gaddis?" I said, trying to find something J. P. might not know in the world of letters.

"I couldn't read that fucking book."

"Pynchon?"

"I have the same feeling about Pynchon. You just can't help getting the impression that these guys write just to see how much they can put down on paper and to see if anyone will actually read it."

"Poe?"

"Poe was a pussy. I'm just kidding. Poe is awesome. I love Poe. I love him so much that I'd fuck him if he were alive. I'd fuck his hairy black tits off."

"Wow."

"What?"

"I wish I had a pen. Pretty sure you've just crafted a sentence that's never been uttered before."

"What sentence?"

"You'd fuck Edgar Allan Poe's hairy black tits off, whatever the hell that means. Pretty sure those words have never been said before, in that order, by anyone, ever."

"In English?"

"In English or otherwise."

"Arrgh! I'd fuck Edgar Allan Poe's hairy black tits off!"

"Blackbeard meets Edgar Allan Poe," I said.

"Aha! Hello, short story. Blackbeard meets Edgar Allan Poe. Were they contemporaries? Probably not. Doesn't matter. Ghost of Blackbeard meets Edgar Allan Poe. *Grandson* of Blackbeard, still a pirate, meets Edgar Allan Poe."

J. P. got out his moleskin notebook and made a few notes. I sensed the literary discussion coming to a close and felt a wave of unspecified relief pass through me.

"Where's your dog this weekend?"

"Soubrette's watching him for me," I said. "She's got a great backyard and Buller gets along with her dogs really well."

"She's probably going to call and tell you that he caught and killed a deer in her yard. You know that's going to happen. Because he could do it."

From inside someone called out that Story and her friends had left late but that they were on their way. An agonizing hour later, the eager night full of promise, a car came slowly up the street. It pulled into the driveway in front of the house and the girls, all in shorts and sandals, ponytails bouncing and bobbing, bounded out into the street, but Story was not among them. Three hundred lagging seconds passed and then another car made the bend and rolled into the space behind the first. I heard the car shift into park and saw the lights turn off. A second later the parking brake was engaged even though the ground was flat as a lake. Then an interior light went on, but try as I might I couldn't see into the car, and this agony lingered for some time until at last the light clicked off. I heard insects; waves; voices, faint and near; cars down the lane; the clickety song of a nonexotic bird, perhaps a naturalized European starling; a child being chased by another child, the second one heavier than the first; the *pshht* of a newly opened bottle of beer; the glassy *thunk* of an old one being discarded; tires on gravel; a sticky painted-shut window being forced open from the inside; the barking of a dog, possibly a neutered or aging Borzoi; and finally, dear god finally, the plastic-on-metal *plunk* of a driver's side door being unlocked in anticipation of a vehicular exit. I hadn't breathed, neither inhale nor ex-, for probably five minutes. At last, Story's blond head appeared from behind the car, her hair wild and windblown, and I was stricken. Hard to say I would have been more impressed if the clouds had parted and the lord god himself, the King, Elvis Aaron Presley, had appeared in her place. I stood there barely able to speak.

Story joined the other girls and they caromed about like cheerleaders and hugged in that cute way that girls do, and luggage was hauled out of trunks. Soon they paraded up onto the porch all in a line to the greetings and friendly catcalls of my friends. I was on the broad steps leading to the driveway as wooden as a canoe, holding a beer in one hand, the other hand rather foolishly stuck into my pocket. Story dropped her suitcase on the porch and slowly made her approach to where I was standing.

"I made it. How are you?" Demure as a flower. Sweetly unsure of herself, but sure enough. "Sorry it took us so long to get down here. Are you guys having fun? It looks like it." Unable to conjure a single syllable out of the space between us, I turned and walked into the house without saying a word.

25

Later that night we all decided to caravan over the bridge to Charleston for dinner even though not one among us should have been driving. In a mad scramble, we piled into three different cars, people sitting on top of other people, hot skin next to hot skin, heads pushed into car ceilings and necks bent uncomfortably this way and that. Off we went up the road with the windows down. Story went in one car; I went in another.

We ate at Magnolia's on East Bay. Our waiter knew we were drinking when we came in and was happy to accommodate our eagerness for more drinks, and that wound up being the bulk of our tab at the end of the night. Mercifully, Story sat at the next table over with her back to me. J. P. sat between us, my view of her obscured by his head and helicopting arms. Picking up our previous conversation, he said, "The most important thing that agents and publishers look for these days," he said, "is a strong narrative voice." I watched her laugh with the others at her table. I couldn't hear her through the noise, but she seemed to be having a good time.

"And word count is obviously important. For a work of literary fiction," he said, "you need at least, I'd say, eighty thousand words. Really, it probably needs to be somewhere between ninety and a hundred thousand. One hundred ten thousand is too many, but if the book is *really* good, you might get away with it."

"I can think of a hundred exceptions," I said. "What the hell does word count have to do with quality? Shouldn't the story dictate the word count?"

"I'm just telling you," he said. "You don't want to give an agent one more reason to throw your piece-of-shit manuscript in the trash."

Just to be contrary, I said, "If I were ever to write a book, it would have exactly one hundred ten thousand seven hundred eighty-three words in it — no more, no less."

Story ordered a round of drinks for her table. When our harried waiter came by, J. P. asked for shots. "What do you want for yours?" he asked me.

"Vodka," I said.

"Fancy," he said. "Not what I had in mind, but that will work. Two vodka shots. Good form, brother. Solidarity."

The waiter asked if we preferred one vodka over another. "House is fine if we're going to shoot it," I said. "Wyborowa if we're going to sip it." I knew nothing about vodka other than that for years I had poured my father drinks out of a bottle with this name on the label.

"Let's shoot it," said J. P.

"Then we don't care," I told the waiter. "House is fine."

"Right," said J. P. "No point in spending ten extra dollars on something that's only going to be in our mouths for less than a second. It won't even be in our mouths. We'll just be throwing it down our throats, like a pelican eating a fish."

"Like a cat eating a grindstone," I said.

"Like a cat eating a what?"

"Like a cat eating a grindstone. It has zero bearing, but all your fucking similes reminded me of it. It was something my grandmother always said. Something to do with determination in the face of long odds. She had a simile for everything."

"She could have had a one-a-day simile calendar," said J. P. "That would have been revolutionary."

We took our shots and J. P. ordered another one, this time for the entire table.

"I'm getting shitty," he said. "The last time I had vodka I got shitty and pissed in my mother's underwear drawer by mistake. I was at home visiting the folks."

"You can't get too shitty," I said. "I need you to keep me from doing anything objectively foolish or reckless or historically regrettable."

"Too fucking late." J. P. turned around to steal a look at Story. She caught him and smiled and he smiled a little guiltily. Turning back to face me, he said, "Yep. You're fucked. You are fucked seventeen different ways from Sunday. Damn, she looks good. Does she have hairy black tits? Tell me as soon as you find out. I'm going to want to see pictures. Drink. *Salud.*" And it was down the hatch with another one.

My table's check at dinner ended up close to nine hundred dollars. None of us were employed and we had all borrowed money with which to attend school, so this came as quite a shock. We negotiated with the restaurant management over our bill without success and then headed out into a steam bath of humidity. A troupe of bagpipers in kilts walked by and J. P. fell in line behind them, marching in step, and we followed. They moved south on East Bay for a ways and then went right through the front door of Southend Brewery and formed a wide circle near the entrance. On a four count, the bagpiping commenced. J. P. was soon in the midst of the tumult doing a credible Russian folk dance. A tall girl from the bar joined him and mimicked his dance and everyone clapped in unison. After ten minutes of dancing, they broke out of the ring to a round of applause and came over to the bar dripping with sweat. J. P. offered to buy the girl a drink, but she turned him down. He was momentarily crestfallen but then ordered the two of us sake from the bar and was right back in the game. I asked him if he was drunk yet and he said, "No — but I'm prancing up on it."

I sat next to Story for the car ride back to the beach. Her body felt good next to mine. BethAnn was the only one of us with the courage or, alternatively, the bad judgment, to drive back (the others wisely took cabs), so she was at the wheel. Tyler sat in front navigating and manning the radio. He got lucky and found one good song after another. The music was perfect and in the dark of the backseat I could see Story smiling and I have never been so alive.

Back at the beach house, someone proposed in honor of the luminous night and clear sky that we all walk out to look at the stars. The doors on the back of the house facing the ocean were open, and the rush and hum of the mighty rolling waves called in through the doors and pulled us out to the sea.

There is something extraordinary about standing on the shore at night under such circumstances. It is the closest one can come to feeling immortal — or to recognizing the euphoria of insignificance at the edge of an immortal sea. On clear nights the effect is more pronounced, for the stars burn numberless in the sky and remind us that time is beyond our understanding and that the universe is indeed indifferent to us — yet hardly benign.

We stood for several minutes in a broken line facing the ocean, all of us mute in deep contemplation of dark and impenetrable things.

It is customary and expected that someone will inevitably, on such a starry night, wonder aloud about the location of the Big Dipper and begin to wander around gazing upward looking for this most famous ursine constellation. It is also customary for someone to locate the Pleiades — Blanche

DuBois was not the first — and declare with certainty that it is either the Big Dipper or the Little Dipper, which of course it is neither. Similarly, it is not uncommon for folks to see Canis Major just below Orion and assume it's a planet — usually Venus — due to its remarkable brightness. Conversely, Jupiter, Venus, Mars, and Saturn, despite roaming confusingly across the sky in and out of other constellations, are almost never observed as planets by anyone other than astronomers.

All of this transpired amidst much uninformed and intoxicated speculation about said heavenly bodies, and going back to my childhood I set about to bring order to the wonders of the universe displayed magnificently before us. The Big Dipper is here, in the north. These two stars in the cup of the Big Dipper point toward Arcturus, in the Boötes. From there, we proceed on to Spica, a brilliant star perhaps fifteen degrees above the horizon on this night. This star here — yes, it is faint, but gladly it is always in the same location — it is the North Star, Polaris. See how the tail stars in the Big Dipper point to it. And see that star there — yes, the immense white one, hovering just above the ocean horizon — that is not a star, my friends, but rather that is the great

Jupiter, god of the night sky. I tell them that on a clear night, with no light pollution, people with perfect eyesight can see its moons, just as Galileo did with his rudimentary telescope so many years before. My friends express incredulity. How do I know this object is a planet? I make predictions about its future location with respect to the background of stars and this seems to satisfy even the most skeptical among them.

When the stargazing subsides, J. P. recites part of Byron's "Darkness," a spooky tale of a world bereft of the light of the sun, and then everyone takes a turn. Nichole hilariously summons forth a ditty from *Schoolhouse Rock* — " 'Lolly, Lolly, Lolly, get your adverbs here . . .' " Tyler impresses the group with a scholarly oration of the Gettysburg Address. All eyes then go to Beth-Ann, her little bare feet dancing in place, and she outright levels me with "The Fiddler of Dooney," a poem by William Butler Yeats.

"You're up," says J. P. He's talking to me.

"I can't think of anything," I say, deflecting the attention. "Someone else take a turn."

The imagined spotlight trails away. "The Fiddler of Dooney" — that was one of his favorite poems. Wonderful timing on that. In my weakened state of nostalgic drunkenness, I can't help but imagine him there with us holding court and I feel gut-sick and benumbed. My mind pushes back against an upwelling of long-forgotten memory and verse. In a moment's time I hear it all, as if ten million words from as many books fell at once onto my ears in a drowning yet intelligible cataract. I hear my father's voice and his incantations. A flood of prose, remembered, unremembered, leftover like hellish debris from a writer's son's childhood. Every word he'd ever said to me. Every poem. Every paragraph he'd written and said aloud. *Put that away,* I tell myself. *Put that away.* The revulsion leaves me at last and I watch removed as the silver star-spotted waves clamor at the beach and roar at my unfeeling heart.

J. P. resumes with Housman's "With Rue My Heart Is Laden," and this brings a pall of melancholy to our group. We all toast grimly to "rose-lipt maidens," and it looks like J. P. may now be weeping. We stand in a circle in the dark, faces in shadowed contemplation. Story is standing opposite me. Her hair is down; her arms are crossed in front of her as if she is cold. She is looking at me.

26

The morning came early for everyone, and squinting into the horizontal light of day, we all made for a beachside tiki bar just north of our house for hangover drinks and food. The girls all had on bikini tops and shorts over bikini bottoms. The guys, evincing no present intent to wind up in the water or do anything much beyond sitting at the tiki bar drinking beer and watching sports on the television suspended from the ceiling, donned shorts and polos. A whitewashed picket fence crossed the dunes between us and the water. The day was blindingly bright and hot. Before long, most of our crowd was at the bar talking and laughing with that animation often seen among those imbibing significant quantities of alcohol early in the day. J. P. made it to the bar late and sat down on the empty stool next to me.

"Did I *eat* a pack of cigarettes last night,

or just smoke them?"

"You smoked them," I said.

"Why do I smoke when I drink? I don't even know where I got the damn things."

"You bought six of them from that guy on the street. I think he might have been homeless —"

"Oh, yeah yeah yeah," said J. P. "Fucking hell."

"If you're gonna be dumb, you gotta be tough."

"Deep," said J. P. "Yet shocking in its simplistic accuracy."

"You look like shit," I said. He still had a diagonal pillow line across the side of his face.

"Do I?"

"Tyler, how does J. P. look?"

Tyler leaned over and appraised J. P. "He looks like shit."

"Damn this democracy," said J. P. "But indeed I feel like a big crusty festering piece of shitty hell. Did someone put me in the dryer last night? My equilibrium is off."

"I don't think so."

"Thank god. Because I was going to quit drinking. What happened after I went to bed? Anything?"

"Nothing that I know of. Everyone just turned in. Want a beer?"

"What the fuck. Hair of the dog, right? Anything with Story?"

I handed him the beer I'd just ordered and ordered another one. "I admire your courage," I said. "No, nothing happened."

"There's a continuum that runs between courage and idiocy," he said. "I usually fall somewhere closer to idiocy."

Tyler leaned over and said, "J. P., I think it's time to admit you've got a drinking problem."

"Someone just handed me a free beer," said J. P. "That's not a drinking problem. That's a drinking solution."

By early afternoon Story still hadn't made it out to the bar. After a while I summoned the courage to ask as to her whereabouts and was told she had decided to spend some time on the beach rather than come to the bar. I looked around at our friends and by deduction attempted to discern who might be out there with her. It seemed everyone was at the bar except Story. Perhaps she was alone. I wanted to go to her and talk when it could just be the two of us, but it felt awkward to abandon my friends for this clandestine purpose.

I finished my Corona and ordered two more. "I'm going to the beach," I said. "Probably read a little." I held up the book

I was carrying as evidence. I took the book and my two beers and headed down the wooden causeway to the beach. After walking for two hundred yards or so, I saw a figure lying in the sun. It was Story, alone, facing the ocean. I felt on fire. I walked to her across the scorching white sand and asked for permission to sit down, which she granted with a nod. She took one of the beers and said thank you as if she had been expecting me.

We sat for a long time just looking at the water without either of us speaking. I didn't want to disturb her reverie; I gathered she was in contemplation of some troubling question. We finished our beers simultaneously and, pinging her lime about in the bottom of her bottle, Story said, "Are there any more of these?"

"Yes, at the bar," I said. "I'll go get a few more."

"Wait — you'll get stuck talking to people and I'll be out here getting scurvy. Let me run up to the house to get them."

She stepped into her shorts and walked the brief distance up to the house. Moments later she returned with a plastic bag that had ice and four beers in it and several lime wedges wrapped in aluminum foil. When I gave the foil a dubious look, she shrugged and said, "I couldn't find any Saran wrap. Oh — and here's a bottle opener." She had it tucked into her pocket.

"You're a genius," I said, pulling out a Corona for each of us. She had an extra towel and helped me spread it out next to hers, then let her shorts fall and resumed her position on the beach.

Lying back now, I felt the warmth of the heated air and the wind from the ocean. Story was on her back and I turned and looked upon the length of her body. Her hair, still wet from the ocean, was folded in curls on the blanket. On her arms, her legs, her brown and sunkissed stomach, were soft honey-blond hairs, an almost imperceptible down. Her eyes were closed behind her sunglasses and her face was quietly content. Her breasts rose and fell as she breathed.

"What are you reading these days?" I asked her, sitting up to drink from my beer. She said she was reading a book about Africa called *West with the Night* by Beryl Markham, who was one of the first freelance pilots in Africa. I said I'd heard of it. She asked if I knew Ernest Hemingway and Beryl were friends in Africa. We talked for a while about literature and the books she'd read that had moved her.

From where we lay I could count at least

fourteen people on brightly colored surf-boards, most of them waiting patiently for waves to rise up out of the dormant sea. As I watched, a lithe, dark-haired girl in a wet-suit rose on a gentle swell and raced from right to left, but in an instant her flight was over and she was back in the water. The others sat passively on their boards, silhouetted in the ocean's haze.

Just beyond the row of surfers by a distance of less than a hundred yards was a large group of pelicans — probably a hundred or more. They sat idly in the water facing the surfers and the beach. I imagined for my own amusement that they had gathered to serve as a makeshift audience for the hapless surfers. A plane passed low overhead, and then the birds were on the move, awkwardly at first, then gracefully, spreading their wings and sweeping low across the water.

At long last Story rolled over on her side to face me. "You know I'm seeing someone." Execution by pistol at close range.

"No, I didn't know that."

"I am."

"I did not know that."

"So you said." She sat up and pulled her knees into her chest.

"Do I know him?" Please god, don't let

me know him.

"No. We've been dating since my junior year of college. He lives in Charlotte."

I tried to act like I didn't care. "Well, that's good. I'm sure he's a really great guy."

"He *is* a really great guy. It seems like I've known him forever. My parents sure love him."

"What's he do?"

"He's an investment banker. He works for one of the big banks. Last year I helped him pick out a condo in Uptown. The current plan is for me to move there after the bar. We're taking a little break right now. We're both trying to sort some things out before then."

"I understand. I hope you're able to work something out."

Well, fuck. This was no good.

I could feel the sand beneath my body. The breaking waves in front of me rumbled distantly; the sound surrounded me and was nearly lost to my awareness. The sun was hot on my shoulders, but perceptive of my mood, it became fickle and clouds soon moved in and brought the whole of the beach under shadow. Thunder rolled in the distance above the hush and thrum of the crashing surf and I brooded in my misery. "We should get in before the rain," I said, standing to leave. "Are you going to stay out here awhile?"

"Please wait." She put on her shorts and I knelt down next to her. She said, "Will you just let me say this? I don't know how to say this, or even *why* I'm saying this, but — it's just not the right time for me."

"Not the right time for what?"

"I don't know the first thing about you, other than what you've told me today."

"And I know nothing about you," I said. "But you're right. It's not the right time. I don't even know what we're talking about."

"We hardly know each other," she said.

"We don't know each other at all."

"And why are we being so serious? We're acting like it's the end of the world. This is crazy."

"It is crazy."

"It *is* crazy," she said. "I don't understand it. We should be out here having fun."

"I thought we were having fun."

People up and down the beach were packing up and heading indoors as the sky darkened and lightning reached down into the water. An umbrella upended by the wind skipped down the beach, chased by a mother carrying half a dozen plastic toys.

"We should go in."

"Will you look at me for a minute?" Story

turned to me, her eyes hidden behind sun-glasses.

"Will you take those off?" I said.

"Yes. Will you take off *yours*?"

"Yes."

And there we were. Two people who had not had more than a half hour's worth of conversation, and I felt as if I were losing the love of my life. It had to be madness. We sat there until the rain began to fall, neither one of us saying a word.

27

On Sunday, she and I were the last two of our crowd to leave the beach. I'd agreed to stay and clean up to help ensure the return of our security deposit, and she had kindly stayed to help me. We bagged all the empty bottles and drove the trash on the back of a golf cart to a garbage depot down the street. I straightened the furniture that had been haphazardly relocated to make room for an impromptu dance floor while Story swept the hardwood floors and mopped the tile in the kitchen. After about an hour of assiduous cleaning, it no longer looked like Page, Plant, and Bonham had stayed there for the weekend and I felt like we might have an outside chance of avoiding legal action by the owners. The sun was hot overhead, stealing color from everything.

"Do you have any idea what we're supposed to do with the key?"

Story wiped her brow with her sleeve.

"Yes, you just drop it back at the realty office on the way out. It's on the right just before you turn left to leave the island."

"How do you know that?"

"Because I saw the drop box when we went into Charleston for dinner Friday night," she said, "and the emblem on the building matches the emblem on the key."

I wanted more than anything to stay with her all day. I wanted to preserve the moment and delay our inevitable return to our respective and disconnected realities in Chapel Hill, but I knew this was an impossibility. *It's just not the right time for me,* she had said. This stuck in my gut and burned in my throat. I reached out to shake her hand goodbye, but she smiled and gave me a friendly hug instead. I knew I had to leave this behind. I told her goodbye and in response she said, "I'm thinking about sticking around here for a while. I might get some beer and go back out on the beach. It's early and it's a gorgeous day and we missed part of yesterday because of the rain. I don't have to be back for anything that I can think of."

Was this an invitation for me to stay? She had made it clear that she had a boyfriend, so it couldn't have been. I might have asked, but I didn't. Stupidly, defiantly, still stinging from being told that it wasn't the right time when I hadn't made a single romantic overture, I only managed to say that I had to "get on back," but that she should stay and have fun on the beach. She might have waved as I pulled out of the driveway, but I didn't look. Rain caught me just outside Charleston and followed me all the way home.

A lot of us stayed in Chapel Hill for the summer to study for the bar exam, and this included Story. Her remote proximity to me became an unmitigated torture. She was in my mind every waking moment of the day and every dark minute of the night. Leaves had long since returned to the trees, but in my soul it was the dead of winter. The one time I saw her, in the atrium of the law library late one evening, it appeared she would walk right by me without saying a word. I called to her and she turned and looked at me without expression, as if we had never met. The gulf between us had returned and widened. I asked how she was doing and she said, "I'm well. Busy, though." I started to walk toward her, but she retreated with my advance. I allowed her to walk away. I could think of nothing else to say. I had my chance and I'd lost it.

That night I walked out onto my back porch with Buller and saw the full moon rising over the trees. I was sick with love. I wrote to her but never mailed the letters. I thought of calling her, but each time I went to the phone I couldn't dial the number. I wrote down every detail I could recall from our time on the beach, but it seemed a separate universe and a lost time to which I could not return. I tried to read to distract myself, but everything I picked up strangled me with pain.

I was consumed. I drank to excess. Sitting in the diminishing light of candles in my sparse living room, I felt as if I were the only inhabitant of the universe. There were hours on end when I couldn't get out of my chair. A millstone lay upon me and swung about my neck. I closed my eyes and saw her skin beneath the sun and the boundless blue sky. I saw the starlight on her pensive face.

I'd bought an old piano from the music department the previous year and I played it day and night in the grips of some absurd fantasy that she would come to my house and, stopping at the door to listen, would hear me playing and at once realize the depth of my passion. Late at night I would walk to the Chapel of the Cross and play the grand piano there to no one. Schumann's *Kind im Einschlummern.* Schubert. Liszt. Chopin's nocturnes, again and again. The *Fantasie-Impromptu*! I was lost in some abstract romantic ideal. My brain would not turn off. The mazurka in A minor. I would play the *dolce* with sadness. Occasionally people would wander into the church upon hearing the music outside and I would continue to play, hunched over the piano in delirium, unable to resurrect myself even to pass a cordial greeting through my eyes. One Saturday night a caretaker for the church found me in the dark at 1:00 A.M. with two bottles of wine beside me and had me escorted out by the police.

Walking to the law library in the cool mornings amidst the running stone walls, I saw myself as a stranger to the world. I talked to no one. I would unconsciously recite Yeats's "The Sorrow of Love," a dead man among the living.

> And then you came with those red mournful lips,
> And with you came the whole of the world's tears . . .

And so finally the day came that I saw her yet again. I had gone to He's Not Here to meet J. P. and Tyler to try to shake myself from my blackness, and I found her there sitting on top of one of the picnic tables with her friends. For a long while we didn't speak. In the interim, I took the high road and started slamming blue cups. (One He's Not Here "Blue Cup" = 32 oz. of beer.) At last, she got up to leave and, in walking by me, stopped briefly to say hello. She asked how I was doing.

"I'm fine," I said. "How are you?" I was a portrait of stoicism.

"Oh —" She seemed a little surprised by my answer.

"So I take it that you're fine as well?" I said.

"I *am* fine. Ready to get through the bar exam."

"Good. I'm glad to hear it. Me, too."

"Good," she said.

Our mutual friends talked and we stood in silence. Story noticed my stack of three blue cups and raised her eyebrows. I asked why she wasn't drinking and she said she was running in the morning. We turned our backs on each other. I heard J. P. telling one of Story's friends that he hadn't been studying all that much. Story walked around in front of me.

"How are you really?"

"I don't understand why you'd ask me that," I said.

"I don't understand why you won't answer me."

"I'll answer you," I said, biting my lip.

"Well, then answer me."

"Honestly, you don't want to know."

"Then why would I have asked?" Her eyes searched my face. "You're being ridiculous."

"Am I?" I raged inside. "To hell with all this." I turned to leave, but she grabbed the back of my shirt and pulled me back. Our friends stopped talking.

"What is wrong with you?" she whispered.

I just shook my head. I wasn't going to say it. She took my stack of blue cups, forced back a drink of lukewarm beer, and made a face.

"Gawd, how long have you had that?"

"About half an hour. I wasn't going to finish it."

"You should have warned me."

"You didn't give me a chance."

When our friends resumed their conversation, she said, "I thought about you the other night."

"Oh, yeah?"

"Yes."

"The other night?"

"Yep."

That was all she was going to tell me. I tried to leave again, but she said "Wait," so I stopped and my throat closed, and I realized at that precise moment that I was going to say something I shouldn't say and could never take back, and all I could think about was that fucker Andrew Marvell and how I'd let one opportunity go by and I wasn't going to do it again, the consequences be damned.

"Story —"

"Yes —"

"Story —"

"Yes?"

"I —"

"I'm so afraid of what you're going to say right now."

"Story, I'm miserable."

"You're miserable?"

"I'm in agony," I said. "I can't concentrate. I'm dying. I don't know what's happening to me."

"What are you talking about?"

"You obviously have no idea," I said, and turned to leave. "Ladies, gentlemen — good to see you all. Let's do this again sometime."

I stormed out to Franklin Street smoldering with agitation and strode along until I'd burned off some of the angst. As I walked farther I let myself feel the warm night air and slowly began to feel strangely elated. I'd said it — more or less. At least I'd said something. I was alive. There was a quickness to all things. I noticed everything around me — every movement, every sound. As people disappeared into clubs and doors were pushed open and closed, music escaped into the street and covered me, slowly retreating. In the bars, people danced in the hot enclosed air to heavy backbeats that you could feel in your chest. I saw bodies closely joined and moving rhythmically and sexually together. The smell of their sweat and perfume was in the street. Undergraduates moved in excited, huddling groups from place to place. A taxi stopped near me and four well-pressed guys with moussed hair piled out into the street in a fog of cologne. They appeared to have dressed from the same closet. They were nice-looking boys and I imagined they would do well out on the town. I hoped they were not headed to He's Not Here. One said, "Man, I'm fucking annihilated." Another got out of the cab holding a red Solo cup of some intoxicant. Looking around for police, the boys took turns pounding it back. In three long, indelicate drinks, the mixture had been consumed. They were headed to Players. I walked past as they produced their IDs for inspection by a thick-necked sedentary bouncer with biceps as big as my head.

Farther down the street a kid sat on the sidewalk facing the street playing guitar in earnest. His guitar case was open in front of him and someone had thrown in a couple of crumpled dollar bills. Long hair of a single length fell half over his face; he had expertly cultivated the look of a traveling bard. I paused to listen and then dropped my last five dollars into his guitar case.

"Thanks, man."

"Keep at it," I said. "Ars longa."

"Ars longa," he said.

Avoiding the lunatic ravings of a man holding a homemade sign (Leviticus 20:13) and proselytizing in front of the post office, I left Franklin Street and turned toward home. A stone wall ran along the road on one side. It was crumbled in places and failed to conceal several attempts at repair, reminding me of the stone walls of the courtyard just down the hill from the vulture house, but all that was now so far away. At a cross street I came across a girl and a boy sitting on the wall under the cover of night, talking in that sweet, solemn way that people who are falling in love talk to each other. I could hear him whispering earnestly to her, not about love, but about life and his view of it and all his dreams that he could see so vividly. He was still young enough to believe in them; this was stealing her heart. I walked by them and a swell of longing passed through me. It was the feeling of Story.

28

My house — Charlie's house, rather — was a thousand-year-old bungalow with a shaded front porch on a small lot with two live oaks crowded into the front. I had forgotten to leave a light on for Buller, and I felt terrible that the poor dog was having to wait for me there in the gloom of the empty house. After struggling with the damn lock for half a minute, I went in and found that he had destroyed the houseplants left by the previous tenant and spread the dirt and dismembered plant material over three different rooms. He sat in the mess ecstatically happy, as if he couldn't wait to show me what he had done.

"Jeez, Buller," I said. "What the hell?"

He ran to me and threw himself into my legs sideways, his favorite move, the one I always referred to as the "flying burrito," and afterward I had to check myself to make sure I hadn't torn an important ligament in my knee. We wrestled for a minute on the one area of clean floor space I could find until he had thoroughly defeated me and left me with several painful bite marks on my forearms. I wiped off his saliva and grabbed a beer and my notebook, and Buller and I went outside to sit on the front porch to savor the incomparable night.

We had been so situated for an hour when a car came haltingly down the street and stopped about fifty yards away. After a few moments, it pulled forward and stopped in front of my house. I could see faces looking out as if they were lost and assumed it was a group of drunk college kids. A door on the far side of the car opened and Story stepped out. She came around to the driver's side of the car and an intense discussion ensued. I could hear what I thought to be four or five distinct voices. After a full two minutes of debate, Story turned toward the house and the car drove away, leaving her there looking uncertainly into the yard. Buller, who never met a stranger, launched off the porch and ran to greet her in the usual way — by knocking her violently to the ground. I tried to grab his collar to restrain him, but I wasn't quick enough. She knelt down to greet him and he leaped into her arms at about thirty miles per hour, like a cheetah taking out a Thomson's gazelle. Story wound up on her bottom in the dirt and Buller stood over her, licking her excitedly. It was love at first sight.

I got her up and dusted her off and apologized profusely. She graciously accepted a beer as compensation, and we sat down on the crooked steps with Buller sitting between us relishing the attention he was getting from Story. The sounds of traffic and people had been replaced with the soft and constant trilling of cicadas and crickets. A dove imitated the sound of an owl in a tree above the porch. The humidity of the day was gone.

I, like Buller, was over the moon with Story's presence. I was having a very hard time not making a fool of myself. Meanwhile, Story looked like someone at a doctor's appointment for complex surgery. I gathered she was having second thoughts about being there in the first place.

"Thank you for coming by. Are you sure you're okay?"

"I'm fine. I could use a Band-Aid for my elbow." She found one in her purse and I helped her put it on. "I am not exactly sure why I'm here."

"Do you want something to eat? Can I get you something?"

"No, thank you. It's one o'clock in the morning. Thank you for the beer, though. I told myself I wasn't going to drink. It's really good. I've never had a Peroni."

"You're welcome. It's a great summer beer. Light and crisp."

"They should hire you to do TV spots."

Story looked around and sized up the house, and Buller turned to look where she looked as if he might see something of interest.

"I really like your house," she said. "This is cool. It's so close to everything."

"Thanks. I like it a lot. It may fall down around us any second, though. My limited research has revealed that it was built by the very first North Americans, sometime just after the ice age. It was originally a burial mound."

"Where do you get stuff like that?"

"Sorry."

"Have you been studying a lot?"

"Some, but not much. What about you?"

"Not as much as I should. I've been running a lot. Anything to keep from studying. I've been doing anywhere from seven to fifteen miles a day. This weekend I'm doing an eighteen-mile run."

"Are you training for a marathon?"

"I am." She stretched her legs out in front

of her and we both admired them. Buller tried to lick Story on the face and neck. I told him to go get his ball, and after thinking about it for a second he trotted off around the corner toward the backyard.

"What's his name? He's adorable."

"Buller Copernicus."

"Bowler?"

"No, Buller."

"Oh my god. Like the dog in *West with the Night.*"

"That's correct."

"Oh, I *love* that," she said. "I didn't know you'd read that. What kind of dog is he?"

"No idea."

"He looks like a lion."

"He does, indeed."

"Aren't you afraid he'll run away?"

"No. He does pretty darn well off the leash. He just goes where I go."

After a minute, he came back around to the front of the house carrying two tennis balls in his mouth, one of them badly decayed and filled with dirt. He spit them out on the step in front of us.

"Nice, buddy. One for each of us. You can have the good one," I said.

"He's huge," she said. "How old is he?"

"About a year and a half, I think. I'm not really sure."

"God, look at his feet." She mimicked astonishment.

"Yeah, he's enormous. I hope he doesn't grow anymore. It costs me more to feed him than it costs to feed me."

Story picked up the good ball and tossed it into the air. Buller caught it and immediately spat it back out onto the step in front of her. "He's really cute," she said. We took turns throwing the ball for him.

"Does he do tricks?" She turned to Buller and said, "Sit." He sat. She said, "Lay down." He just stood there looking at her. "Buller, lay down." No response. "Does he not know how to lay down?"

"Only when he's playing cards," I said. "Lie down, buddy." Buller went flat like he was dodging enemy fire.

"I guess I shouldn't be surprised."

"Surprised by what?"

"That a dog who belongs to you only responds when he hears the correct verb tense."

"He also knows when to use *who* and when to use *whom*."

Story took off one shoe and rubbed her foot. Then she said, "I'm not really sure what just happened back at the bar."

"I'm not either. I —"

"— I should probably be going soon."

"Do you want me to drive you home?"

"That's okay. BethAnn and Nichole are taking Kim home — she's wasted beyond belief; her boyfriend is being a jackass again — and then they're going to come back by and get me."

Forgetting about Buller's leafy genocide, I invited her in to look around and we walked right in on evidence of the massacre. Buller ran in and recommenced his frolic, picking up a plant stem and pitching it into the air. I saw Story taking it all in. In the corner were my bookcases full of my favorite books (the ones that had been fortunate enough to have survived Buller's previous assault). Two guitars leaned against the wall in the other corner of the room, one acoustic and one electric. On the desk in the next room were two letters I had written to Story but never mailed. A car pulled up out front and Story waved through the window to signal she was coming.

"I have to go."

"I know. Thank you for coming by."

I could feel her friends waiting. The late hour brought with it a sense of impatience.

"Okay. I'll see you later." She gave Buller a good scratch on the head. "I'll see you, too, buddy. You be a good boy."

As soon as the car was out of sight and I

was sure it was safely down the street, Buller and I danced around in a circle like crazy people.

"What do you think, buddy? Isn't she incredible? Isn't she amazing?"

I jumped up and down and Buller jumped around with me, nipping at my shirt and tearing a huge hole in it, bringing a temporary end to our antics. I put my hand through the hole.

"Damn, Buller. I just got this shirt."

He just sat there smiling at me.

29

The next night J. P. and I went out for drinks after an all-day study session. He had somehow gotten another short story published when he should have been preparing to be a lawyer, and our ostensible purpose this evening was to celebrate. We started at a Mexican place just off Weaver Street in Carrboro.

J. P. ordered first. *"Cuatro Coronas, por favor."*

"Nice Spanish," I said. "Are you thirsty?"

"The drink service here can be a little slow. If you just order one beer, your DTs will start before you get your next one."

The waiter came back with J. P.'s beers along with a basket of tortilla chips and a small hand-carved bowl of salsa. I took one of his beers and squeezed the lime into it, spraying juice all over the place.

"So," J. P. said, "rumor has it Story broke up with her boyfriend."

"You're shitting me. Are you lying to me? Because if you're lying to me right now, I'll stab you in the fucking neck."

"And I'd deserve it," said J. P. "But that's what I heard."

"Where did you hear that?"

"I think BethAnn, who would probably know, told Rachel, and Rachel told Keith, and Keith told Tyler, and Tyler told me when I talked to him before coming here. He's on his way. But it sounds legit. They apparently haven't seen each other in a few months."

"You know I'm going to have a heart attack."

"I have to be honest with you," he said. "I kind of want her for myself."

"Check my pulse. I'm serious."

"I could kidnap her."

"You'd never get away with it. Oh, wait — I forgot you know the D. A. of Orange County. You just might."

"Yep. He was my oldest brother's roommate in undergrad. But to tell you the truth, I was going to rely more on the Stockholm syndrome. Which, when you think about it, is actually kind of considerate."

I looked around to see if anyone might be recording our conversation.

"Anyway," said J. P., "sounds like she's

got some fucked-up family shit going on, though. I don't know if I'd want to get into that."

"Like what?"

"No idea. Maybe she's adopted and she's trying to find her real family or something? I don't know. It's something weird."

"Why do I care about that? I'm going over there."

"Hold on, Delacroix. Just try to keep things in perspective. Did I ever tell you what my father said when I told him I wanted to drive to Boston to see a girl in my old-ass Volvo when I was in college?"

"No. Pray tell."

"He told me this story about these two Navajo Indians who were in love, except they were from different tribes, and they lived on opposite sides of this great, wide lake, and they were forbidden from seeing each other because of tribal custom or some shit like that that he might have glossed over. So these two Indian kids were in love but they couldn't be together, so every night they'd stare out across the undulant lake —"

"The *undulant* lake?"

"You like that? That's good, huh? So they'd stare out across the undulant lake in the hope of maybe seeing one another, even though it sounded like from the story that the lake was really too large for that to happen. And finally one starry night the young man was so consumed with desire that he couldn't take it anymore, and he just dove into the lake and started swimming. But the lake was too wide, and he wasn't a notable swimmer, and so he didn't make it. He got halfway across and sank like a box of I don't know what. Cheap imitation arrowheads that are actually just oddly shaped rocks sold as arrowheads at those touristy stores out in Cherokee territory. That's how he sank."

"Sad."

"Yes, it's terrible. And my father said that everyone in both tribes was so impressed with his dedication and valor and how much he loved her that they decided to name the lake after him. Want to know what they named it?"

"I give up. Lake True Love?"

"No. Lake Fucking Idiot."

"Wow."

"The point is that no girl is worth all that."

"My grandfather used to tell me similar stories," I said. "He said that women were like streetcars. If you missed one, all you had to do was wait ten minutes and another one just as good would come along."

"That's a heartfelt sentiment," said J. P. "I've got to remember that. My dad would love that. It's basically the same as the Navajo story, but much more concise and it avoids ethnic sensitivities."

"I'm certain my grandfather was wrong, though. I really don't think there's more than one Story out there."

"I tend to think you're right," said J. P. This might have been the most sincere thing he ever said to me.

I drank half a dozen beers in a wild ecstasy and demanded that I be driven to Story's house at once.

He said, "Absolutely not."

"Then I'm going to walk."

"Do you even know where she lives?"

"Not exactly," I said. "I can find it."

"You'll get hit by a car, you imbecile. Wait until tomorrow. Trust me when I tell you that respectable girls don't want guys who are drunk showing up at all hours of the night. It sends the wrong message. I know. Learned that one the hard way. More than once. Maybe more than twice. Why do you think I'm single? Almost got me thrown in jail once. Actually, it did get me arrested, although I guess technically speaking I was never arraigned."

"I don't believe you."

"It's true. This was a few years ago. I went to my ex-girlfriend's house and wanted to, like, get her attention, so I found a good-looking tree in the yard and up I went —"

I started laughing and couldn't stop. "You climbed a tree? What kind of tree was it?"

"A cypress tree. I have no idea. It had limbs. It was dark. It might have been a rhododendron. Who knows. I climbed the tree or whatever and didn't have a rock, so I checked my pockets and all I had that was of sufficient weight to make a loud-enough sound on the window was a loafer I was wearing, so I took it off and tossed it at her window. But instead of hitting the window and bouncing off as I'd planned, it made this colossal explosion and went right fucking through and — here's the best part — it wasn't even her window but her sister's, and her sister thought it was a burglar —"

"What else would she think?"

"— that's right — and she went screaming through the house and actually fell down the fucking steps and nearly died, although actually maybe she just fell down the steps and broke her clavicle and her right arm and she might have had a concussion from what I remember, but obviously I wasn't privy to the emergency-room report because by that point I'd been incarcerated and was awaiting bail."

"You couldn't run away?"

"No, I couldn't run away! I only had one shoe. The other shoe was inside. So, no."

"Holy Moses. And did you have to report all that to the bar examiners?"

"Yep. Nice, huh? Although all I reported was the arrest. I hope I have the chance to explain it at some point."

"You were in love," I offered as a possible explanation.

"Yes, I was in love. Simple as that. Please let me take the bar exam — *I* was in love. I've been practicing, see. Let's get another beer."

The next morning I awoke early and went for a short run, and then Buller and I picked some daisies from the yard and walked the mile or so to Story's house under the glaring sun. She was sitting on the front porch in navy soccer shorts and a running shirt, stretching after her run. I called to her from the driveway and she acted a little surprised to see me. "Well, good morning. What are you guys doing?"

"We're just out for a walk. I got you something."

"That's really sweet. Where'd you get them?"

"Public right-of-ways."

"I can't remember the last time someone got me flowers not on Valentine's Day. Daisies are better than roses anyway. They're prettier and they're more real."

"They also have the advantage of being slightly cheaper and they sometimes grow in the wild."

She smelled them once or twice and we laughed because they didn't smell like anything.

"I want to see you tonight," I said.

"We have to talk. And now's probably not the best time." As if on cue, BethAnn came out onto the porch in a nightshirt and sweatpants carrying a cup of coffee and squinted fiercely into the light of day. No bra. Hair by electrocution. Clear indications of having gone to bed without makeup removal.

"Well, hey there. Fancy seeing you here."

"Hey, BethAnn. How are you?"

"I just woke up and took six Tylenol, and I'm going to drink my coffee and go back to bed and sleep for another three hours at least."

"Late night?"

"Uh, yeah. Little bit. Don't ever ask me to do another shot, because I won't do it. Is that your dog? He's handsome."

"Buller, say thank you." Buller looked at me for direction, but the moment passed.

"Did you guys do an outline for Wills and Trusts?" BethAnn was from somewhere in Mississippi (explains the name) and her closely guarded accent was on full display.

"We did," I said.

"Would you mind sending it to me? I sucked in that class and I heard your outline was killer."

"No problem. I'll do it today."

"Don't send it today," BethAnn said, holding her coffee cup close and pushing her breasts flat against her chest with her arms. "Wait until tomorrow so I don't feel guilty for not studying on a Saturday. See you guys later." She disappeared into the house and closed the door behind her.

"I can't see you tonight," said Story. "My delightful mother's coming into town to go shopping with her friends and she's supposed to take me to dinner at the Rat, and then I promised BethAnn I'd go to a party with her."

"Who's having a party?"

"It's not that kind of party. It's a wedding party kind of thing. More like a shower. I have to take a gift. You'd hate it."

She jogged down the porch steps to see Buller. She said, "Hey, Buller boy," and scratched him hard behind the ears and under his chin. He became briefly catatonic, and when she stopped he hopped around like his paws were being burned by the cement. He licked at her frantically and gave her a giant hug that almost forced her to the ground.

"He really likes you," I said.

"I know he does. I really like him, too."

"Come by after your party."

She looked at me with those enormous, sad eyes.

"Don't say anything," I said. "I know you're about to say something I don't want to hear."

"It's going to be late when I get out. I'll come by if I can, but I probably can't, so don't change your plans because of me. I'll call you if I can make it. But don't get your hopes up."

I spent the remainder of the day in a kind of hellish limbo. It was warm and the sun was alone in a wide blue sky, so I took advantage of it and went for a bike ride and worked in the yard and read for a while on the porch and took Buller to the park and threw the ball for him until he was exhausted. In the early afternoon my stomach began to tighten, so I opened my first beer and played guitar through two more beers, at which point I switched to the piano and once again imagined Story walking up on the porch and hearing the music coming from inside the house. In my fantasy, she would stand at the door and listen and be amazed at my outpouring of emotion. Then she would wait until I began another piece and steal quietly into the house to watch me play. For every piece I played, I was like the mad conductor of a great orchestra, and when I finished I opened my eyes with a madman's hope that she'd be in the living room with me, listening and watching. This did not happen and my gloom deepened. Buller could sense my brooding and went to lie on his bed in the other room. I called to him from the piano.

"Buller — you know one thing I bloody well hate about Chopin? It's that he puts the most extraordinary music right in the middle of pieces whose beginnings and endings are virtually impossible to play!" Buller watched a book of mazurkas and polonaises slide by him on the hardwood floor. "The worst part about this," I told him, "is that we basically have to wait all day to see if she's going to come over, and she's probably not even going to come. You and I are going to be just waiting here, tortured like rabbits on a spit, and at one o'clock in the morning in all likelihood we're going to be alone and wallowing in a slough of despond. What's that, Buller? You say that women are like streetcars? That if you miss one, another one will come along ten minutes later? Well, you may be right about that in general terms, but you're wrong in this case. Or maybe you're right. Who the hell knows. What the hell am I doing here?"

Buller sounded a high-pitched bark. "I feel the same way, buddy. This is awful."

We toiled the hours away like defendants awaiting a criminal sentencing. I may have gotten a little drunk and Buller wanted to wrestle, so we did that for a while until he swung his head around and almost put one of his Great White Shark–size canine teeth through my temple. I heard the skin puncture and my head gushed little spurts of blood. Buller brought me a kitchen towel to press against the wound, or I might've gotten the towel, I can't remember.

"If I die from this, Buller, please tell whoever comes to take my body that I want my epitaph to read *I Should Have Adopted a Smaller Dog.*"

Story called me at 11:13 P.M. and said she'd just gotten out of her party. It was late, she said, so she was just going to head home and we'd talk in the morning. She had a long run scheduled for 6:00 A.M. and needed a good night's sleep. I told her I understood and then burned inside with disappointment.

All I could muster was, "Thank you for calling me."

There was silence on her end of the line and I thought she might have hung up. I asked if she was still there and another empty silence followed. Then: "Yes, I'm here. What are you doing?"

"I was playing the piano."

"You're not in bed?"

"No, I'm not in bed."

. . .

"What are *you* doing?" I said.

"I'm sad to report that I have no self-control. I'm sitting in my car — outside your house."

30

Buller and I charged to the front door and looked out. Story was indeed sitting in her car in the driveway with the phone still to her ear. I composed myself and walked outside to meet her. Before I could open my mouth, she said, "I can't stay." She didn't even get out of the car.

She asked me what happened to my head. I had affixed a surgical bandage just beside my eye and the medical tape had been awkwardly applied. All I needed was a strip of bloody gauze around the circumference of my cranium and a piccolo to complete the image. "Buller tried to kill me," I said. "Fortunately for him I've decided not to press charges."

"Oh, well — I have to get home. I was just driving by — I thought I'd say hello. I shouldn't have just stopped by without asking. I'm really sorry. It's late."

I looked into the car. She was wearing an

old-South drawstring dress, white and pale blue, and her white-blond hair was curled up on her shoulders. There was never a girl as sweetly beautiful as Story. I was melting, and she allowed her eyes to meet mine for just a moment and sharply drew in a breath, and I lost my breath and could easily have picked up her entire automobile and twirled it above my head if she had asked.

"Okay — I'll talk to you tomorrow. Sorry to bother you. Take care of your head."

"Okay."

She moved the gearshift to R.

"Story."

"Yes?"

"Will you look at me for a second?" Back to P.

"I'm kind of afraid to."

"Why?"

"I don't know."

"This is insane," I said. "I don't know what we're doing or why I feel this way. It's like I've known you for years and one of us is moving to a different continent, but that's ridiculous because I hardly know you at all."

She wiped away a tear with the back of her hand and laughed to explain it away.

I said, "Story — wait." She turned and looked fully into my eyes. I said, "I think I'm losing my mind."

"That's not true."

"I can't stop thinking about you."

"I'm sorry."

"And you feel nothing for me."

"I don't know how I feel."

Buller barked and knocked at the door to get out, causing the shutters to swing away from the front of the house. I signaled to him to wait.

"I need to go."

"I so wish you would stay."

"I know, but I need to go."

"It's a beautiful night. Can you ever remember a more beautiful night?"

To humor me, she smiled and looked out the car window at the live oaks above us and the starry sky beyond.

"Feel how warm it is," I said. "Ten years from now we'll think back on this and wish we had taken advantage of it. You know we will."

Story said, "I'll call you tomorrow," but I could tell she was wavering. I ran up on the porch to let Buller out before he took out the door completely. He shot past me straight to Story's car and tried to jump in the driver's side window, which if he had been successful probably would have ended her life. Once he calmed down, he just stood there like a bear with his head and front feet in the car and she rubbed his head as he purred mightily. He looked at me like I should go inside and leave the two of them alone.

"He loves you," I said.

"I love him, too."

"Let's go sit on the back porch and look at the stars. I won't keep you long."

"You do know something about stars, don't you."

"You might have to get out the passenger-side door."

The three of us paraded into the house, thoroughly cleaned since her last visit. She strolled along slowly, looking at everything with great curiosity in the candlelight, examining the books I'd strewn here and there and inspecting the few family photographs on the mantel.

She picked up a framed picture of Threnody — one from years before when she was no older than five. The picture catches a braided and very serious little Bird at the height of an exemplary grand jeté with a hundred miles of improbable scenery behind her, as though she were performing on a painted landscape. I remember the day; I had taken the picture. We had stopped at an overlook on the parkway just past Raven Rocks on our way to Asheville. A pilgrimage, said Father. Threnody was bounding about gracefully as only children can in the days before they become gravitationally significant, and I was snapping pretentious long-distance views with Father's ten-pound analog Nikon. I remember Mother walking through the field next to the road calling out the names of the flowers for everyone. In my memory she is turned away from me and is carrying something burdensome in her arms.

"That's my sister," I said.

"She's adorable," said Story. "That's quite a little jump."

I walked over to look at the photograph and felt my insides cleave in two as I remembered how long it had been since I'd gone to Charlotte; how long it had been since I'd talked to the little Bird.

"Are you guys close?"

"Not as close as we should be," I said.

Story made a sad face and turned her attention to another photograph, this one of my father sitting at his desk writing, with me as a child on the floor at his feet reading a book. "That's my father," I said. "And there's me when I was about three years old."

"You were pretty cute. What's that on the wall?"

"It's a bird of some kind. I think it's a crow, but it's supposed to be a raven. He had a thing for Edgar Allan Poe."

"Your dad sounds like an interesting guy."

"He was at one time," I said, taking the photograph and setting it back on the mantel.

"Are he and your mom still together?"

"No," I said. "They separated several years ago."

"I'm sorry," said Story. "Are they both still in the mountains?"

"My mother and sister are in Charlotte these days. They moved out of Old Buckram a few years ago."

"What about your dad? Where is he now?"

I told her I had no idea where he was. I said, "I was sixteen the last time I saw him." She thought about this a long time and chewed on her lip like she wanted to say something more, but I changed the subject as I always did and started time going again. She wandered then into the next room, where she stopped at the piano and touched the books of music stacked there in disarray.

"I always wanted to play," she said. "One day I will." And then she asked, "Will you play something for me?"

The room was small and the uneven floor

held only the piano, a couch, and an old chair. The piano stood against an inside wall. I sat down to play and Story stood behind me, next to me, watching. I could hear her breathing. I opened the book of music and then closed it again. I could read it without seeing it. I played the *Fantasie-Impromptu,* Chopin's posthumous opus 66, the one I always played thinking she might happen to come by my door and hear the music and know it was for her. *Allegro agitato.* Begin: an octave in the left hand struck like a bell; a foreshadowing. Then — dark arpeggios, again in the left hand, an approaching cannonade; fiercely ascending runs in the right — intricate, delicate, unrelenting. A sense of acceleration tempered by a cascading retreat, and we begin again. Breathe. Surge. Dissipate. Surge. Pedal. Pedal. Pedal. This cut-time rhythm pushes you along. After only a minute we are brought up short by a crashing left-hand cadence — and it is here that a sweet, simple melody ensues *pianissimo* that has no parallel in modern music to my knowledge. This perfect melody was, in my bursting heart, the song of Story. With exquisite, fleeting variations, it lingers, frolics, demurely relents — and is gone. The light of a single day. At once the surging, silver cannonade returns, and the melody, now hidden and faint to the ear's remembrance, becomes almost forgotten. At the end of this magnificent tumult, when the piece is drawing to a close and fading into silence, the sweet, perfect melody appears once more — this time in the left hand alone — this time only once.

As the last of the music passed through the walls and into the night, Story touched my shoulder and then withdrew her hand as though the contact had been accidental. I turned to see her walk into the kitchen, where she found an open bottle of wine on the counter, poured herself a glass, and returned to stand in the corner of the room. She said, "I've never heard anything like that before." Something was wrong; she seemed upset.

I stood to walk toward her and reflexively her lean figure became concave as she turned away. She would have retreated farther into the corner if there had been room.

"I don't understand," I said. "What happened?"

She said, "I'm sorry. I can't. Please play me something else."

"I just want to talk," I said. "Tell me what's going on."

"I know you do — but I'm not there yet."

I sat back down on the piano bench facing her. "I wish you'd talk to me."

She said, "I know. And I will. Just not now, though. I'm sorry, it's nothing you did. I just learned a long time ago that when you share too much, people try to fix you."

I didn't know what to say. I sensed for reasons beyond articulation that there was a part of her I could never reach — that she'd never let me reach, or anyone else. She'd never let me in completely.

Brightly, she said, "Please play for me. Will you play something else?"

I retrieved the bottle of wine and she settled in under a blanket on the couch with her head on a pillow. It was enough for me that she was there. I drank my wine and played into the night until I could no longer play well and the house and the world were quiet and Story was asleep.

31

As I came to know her, I saw time and again the eloquent sadness in her eyes that arose in quiet moments when she was sure neither I nor the world was looking. I learned from a series of minute clues and then finally her exasperated confession that she regarded the circumstances of her birth and adoption as strange and highly mysterious. These unresolved questions and all the various and discomfiting implications from the night she was born until now had come to trouble her greatly. The crux was this: She had never known the identity of her biological father — she was convinced beyond reason that it had been purposely withheld from her — and had spent the last six years looking for him without success over the vehement and senseless objections of her adoptive parents. She was no closer to finding him when I met her than when she had undertaken to discover him several years before, and what had begun as a mild preoccupation had grown into something approaching an obsession.

Story was born in Charleston, South Carolina, to a young mother who, for the year or so prior to Story's birth, lived in a ramshackle house next door to a sprawling cemetery in Lot's Folly, an affluent peninsula jutting west and south into the waters of Lake Conroy, a large man-made lake fed by the Edisto River just to the west of Summerville. The house, when I saw it, was abandoned and had been for some time. The roof was a carpet of green moss and only a few windows had survived. The entire lot was overgrown with trees — southern live oaks and tall longleaf pines — the former covered with nearly impenetrable Spanish moss that concealed the house from the road. The front yard was carpeted in a soft blanket of pine needles, and Queen Anne's lace grew in sparse patches along a simple stone walkway that ran to the front door.

The title to the house was acquired by the Versirecto Methodist Church in 1889 by the bequest of a long-time donor who had given away nearly all of her land for the church cemetery in several different gifts over many years, much to the grave disappointment of her heirs. The donor — a Mrs. Willa Jean Gullege — had lived there alone and aging in forced isolation from her grown children until such time that she had given the church her entire estate save the old house.

Because of its location on the peninsula, the property she gave to the church must have been worth a fortune. In the days before her death, in a final act of defiance, she asked a local lawyer to prepare a codicil to her will in which she conveyed the house and its small wooded lot in the following manner: "To the Father, Son & Holy Ghost, c/o the Versirecto Methodist Church, so long as the above-described estate is used for purposes of the Church, then to the Town of Lot's Folly to be used as a park."

Naturally, upon her death and the reading of her will, litigation immediately ensued. Her furious heirs argued — despite their unconfided concerns that they were committing some horrible greed-born heresy for which they would be well repaid in the afterlife — that under the laws of the state of South Carolina, it was legally impossible to convey property to God, and therefore that title to the house and lot should fall directly to them. The judge who heard the case disagreed, finding with an appropriate level of judicial humor and wisdom that conveyances to the almighty creator of heaven and earth, while possibly redundant, were not otherwise invalid.

The church was pleased to get the property, and it made a practice of letting out the modest little house to a family in the community most in need of the church's benevolence. For years the old house was let to an immense black man named LeArtis Moon who the locals called Clem. Clem promised to care for the cemetery if allowed to reside in the house, and care for the cemetery he did. No one knew at the time that this giant of a man had an uncommon love of landscaping. Within two seasons the entire extent of the rambling cemetery had taken on the look of a Roman sculpture garden, and it didn't take long before everyone in the county wanted to be buried there.

Yet time passed, and Clem died, and entropy and weeds reclaimed the cemetery gardens. Meanwhile, the church continued its practice of leasing out the little house to needy families, and eventually it became occupied by Frances Louise Dudevant, a French-speaking woman who everyone seems to agree was Story's maternal grandmother. She had one daughter out of wedlock — Lelia — who, a child herself, became pregnant at fifteen.

And that is where the holes in the story begin.

32

What I eventually put together was that Story was born on a rainy September morning to Lelia and a much-older father who was either married or engaged to be married at the time of conception. Further details about Story's father were unknown and seemed to be the subject of a town-wide conspiracy of silence. His personal details had been tantalizingly redacted from her birth certificate. No one could recall his name or where he was from. It appeared that the only person who had actual knowledge of his identity was Story's biological mother, and she wasn't telling.

Story had deduced from dubious sources that perhaps her father had attended the Citadel and had spent some time in the military as a high-ranking officer. At least, that was one rumor she had heard. Another was that he was a wealthy landowner from Charleston who went broke and jumped to his death from the rusted and aging Cooper River Bridge. It was to remain a mystery.

In what appeared to be a remarkable act of human decency, a married couple who lived down the street from the cemetery and attended Versirecto Methodist Church agreed to adopt the newborn from fifteen-year-old Lelia, who handed over the child from her hospital bed and did not see her again until Story was grown and in her first year of law school in Chapel Hill. The couple who adopted Story initially had no children of their own, but a child was born to them one month prior Story's adoption. They had two more children in the years shortly thereafter, for a total of four. The three children to follow Story grew up spoiled and viewed her as an intermeddler who didn't belong.

Story's adoptive parents, a Mr. and Mrs. Glauchnor, came from money — lots of it — but had earned very little of their own. They had been gifted a prime lot on the western side of the peninsula by Mr. Glauchnor's mother, and proceeded to build a three-story white-and-gray Cape Cod with a manicured yard that rolled like a golf course five hundred feet out to the lake. They drove expensive cars, wore expensive clothes, and had a dazzling speedboat that they loved to take down the Cooper River toward Charleston Harbor and the ocean beyond.

When Story was almost sixteen, her parents told her that she needed to work so she could buy her own car, an obligation she gladly accepted and accomplished by working at a local marina fueling boats and selling fishing gear. She found what she thought was a reasonably priced car she could afford and bought it. It was a 40-series Toyota Land Cruiser with 255,000 miles on it that had been sunk in a lake but seemed to work fine except for the radio. She got it for fifteen hundred dollars, and the fastest it would go was forty-five miles per hour, to hear her tell the story.

When the sister who was closest in age to Story was old enough to drive, the Glauchnors bought her a lightly used Audi sports coupe. The next child, a boy, got a new Chevrolet Suburban for his sixteenth birthday. The youngest child, another girl, who was perhaps the most spoiled of all the children, received a new convertible BMW. When I met Story, she had retired the original Land Cruiser but was driving another one that she had bought and paid for herself without the help of her parents.

Story had wanted to know her mother as

much as she had wanted to discover the identity of her father, but this former enterprise had always been met with vehement protestation from Mr. and Mrs. Glauchnor. The whereabouts of Story's mother were known — she reportedly resided near Greenville, in upstate South Carolina — but while Story searched endlessly for her phantom father, she could never bring herself to reach out to her mother, perhaps because she was afraid of what she might find, and also because Mrs. Glauchnor would collapse in sobbing fits any time Story even spoke aloud of the subject. It was also no doubt psychologically less formidable to allow herself great and wondrous imaginings of her father, a man against whose reality she would never have to compare her self-created fictions of him, than to face the possibly unromantic reality of her mother.

It was Story's biological mother who eventually made contact. They set up a meeting: Story was to travel to Greenville for the weekend. If things went well, she would stay through Saturday and possibly Sunday. Story did not disclose the meeting to her adoptive mother to preserve the poor dear's palpitating heart. She found Lelia sick in bed, embattled by an unrelenting malignancy and a host of other complicating illnesses. Lelia said she had the strength to get up but didn't want to waste it. She just held out a pallid, skeletal hand.

"I recognize you," she said, studying Story's face. "I surely do." She nodded as if a notion she suspected had just been confirmed.

"You *recognize* me?"

"Listen, Story — that's such a pretty name. Is that your whole name? I had a different name in mind for you."

"My first name's Elizabeth. Story's a family name."

They sat in silence and Lelia ran her fingers up and down Story's arm as a mother might do to a child.

"What would you have —"

"— Named you? I was going to name you Maggie. When you were inside me, I thought you were stealin' . . . I don't know what. I thought you just seemed like a little thief. Maybe I thought you were stealin' time, or stealin' life, like a magpie. And I was going to call you Maggie because you were my magpie. In my mind, your hair was black as a raven's. I had dreams where you were a little black bird, sitting on the edge of my bed. But here now I see you are more like the sun on a field of flowers."

"Maggie."

"Yes, I was gonna call you Maggie. Maggie the magpie. In my mind, that's what I believe your name is. That's what I've called you in my mind all these years. I'd say, I wonder where my Maggie is now. And now here you are."

Lelia became lost in thought. Her hands moved to her stomach, as if to warm the child that had so long ago left her womb.

"I've just got days," she said. "And days are just made of hours, and minutes, and seconds. I try to stop it, but it just keeps goin'. I hate to even sleep 'cause I know I won't get those hours back. Every single one that runs by me, this world closes a dark curtain around me more and more. I can feel my life disappearing, even as we sit right here."

They spent the weekend talking between Lelia's restless naps. Story slept on the couch at night with a single afghan blanket for warmth. The house had only one bedroom, and there were no other linens. Lelia had never become wealthy. All she had ever owned was in that house. Story looked around her — a few ceramic trinkets on the end tables; an ornate flea-market lamp; a painting of a sunset with a majestic ship in the foreground and rays of sunlight projecting geometrically from behind the clouds.

"That there gives me hope," Lelia said, talking about the painting. "That's where I think I'm goin', if I get lucky. Look at all that water and that sun comin' up. I want to be on a ship like that on that big ocean, with the sun shinin' behind me, and then I'll have it made for certain."

Her mind carried her out over the water and then brought her back. "I've never been on the ocean, not a single time," Lelia said. "Always wanted to, though, didn't you? I always dreamed about taking a big ol' ship from Charleston to Rome and meeting some nice polite boy to run off with and get married. I said, one day I'll do that. One day never came, though. One day never does. You ever been on the ocean, sweetheart?"

"Yes — once."

"Were you on a ship?"

"Yes, it was a cruise ship."

"Oh, that just sounds wonderful. Were there handsome boys just everywhere you looked?"

"Yes," Story said, smiling, "everywhere I looked."

A plain metal box, a reliquary, sat on a table next to Lelia's bed. Inside the box were letters written to Lelia from a man named Ben. The letters were undated and did not mention Story or even a child who could eventually become Story — all presumably written during the courtship, and none after. The box also contained one black-and-white photograph of a young man in a military uniform. On the back of the picture, someone had written "Love, Benjamin" in loose, low-country cursive. No other words appeared. Story gathered from all this that her father had in fact been in the military as she had once been told.

"Is this my father?" Story held up the photograph and smiled.

Lelia looked away. She hid her gaze in the darkness of the corner of the room.

"I don't know."

"How can you not know?"

"Child, I would tell you if I knew. But I don't."

"How can you not know?"

"I never did try to figure it out."

"Could it be" — Story looked again at the back of the photograph — *"Benjamin?"*

"It could be. I don't know. I *thought* he mighta been at the time."

"Well, look at me. Do I look like Benjamin?"

Lelia turned to Story and studied her face. "I don't know, child. I don't suppose you do look much like Benjamin."

353

Lelia apologized time and again for letting Story go, and she so wished it could have been different. She was so young, she explained, and Benjamin had been older, out of college and readying for a career in the military. Had he not fled, Lelia said, "he'd of been in a real predicament." Lelia, meanwhile, had no money, and her mother beat her viciously for getting in trouble. She had no choice. Lelia cried and Story cried, and they held each other and Lelia begged for forgiveness and Story offered her forgiveness over and over again. She left that Sunday evening with the photograph of Benjamin and a promise to return the following weekend. Lelia's heart stopped beating three days later. A note she left on her nightstand said the last thing in life she wanted was to see her daughter one more time and to tell her she was sorry — then she could leave this world in peace. Only a local chaplain, Story, and Mr. Glauchnor attended the funeral.

[Untitled]

I look at my watch and see time passing as the second hand moves. When I take notice again, it's a different time, and a different day, and a different year. You think you understand time, but you don't. On the rare occasion, if you are sufficiently self-aware, time will *slow* long enough for you to take it in. You look around and think *I am here* and *It is now* and this moment is important and I will hold on to it and slow time and live. And then you give way to the night, and the next day comes, and another day of your life begins. The next time you think of it is months or a year later, and you float to the surface where time resides and look back across it and instantly know all that which you have lost, and it is naught but time, and time is life. There are days ahead. You vow to make better use of those which remain. It is a lie.

Take the date and time now. It's what year? You are how old? You remember when you were a child. You remember an early childhood Christmas. A birthday cake your mother made for you. Blowing out the candles while everyone watched. Your first trip to the ocean, wading into the cold, lapping water. You remember running bare-foot outside, being chased by other children, laughing and drinking from the garden hose. You remember when you scored the winning run. When you won the fifty-yard dash. The day you got your driver's license and the first time you drove by yourself and the freedom you felt. You could've gone anywhere. You remember the first time you held hands. You stayed up all night to see her, to see him.

And the time it has taken to bring thee from that point in space and time to your reading of this page is *no time.* Snap your fingers and that is how quickly it has passed. The next ten years will happen just as fast. Time is just a human construct. It is an accident of physics and human perception. It is a factor of entropy and the general movement of a closed physical system toward disorder. All things move toward disorder. The garden brings flowers anew each year, but the dogwood tree among the many flowers shows the inexorable passage of time and you know it passes. The house decays, as does its frail and decaying tenant. Realize the immediacy of the moment and live and write down the words and be witness as time pours through you until it has dissolved

you and your soul into the emptiness and
unending quiet that is death.
— Found in the desk of Henry L. Aster.
Date of composition unknown.

PART IV

33

In the weeks and days before I left Chapel Hill, I read Thomas Wolfe's *Look Homeward, Angel* and *You Can't Go Home Again,* and I never got over them entirely. Beyond the writing, which is extraordinary for so many reasons, the books instilled in me a profound, visceral uneasiness that I just couldn't shake. I heard something too familiar, too resonant, in the voice, in the setting, in the lives and deaths of the men and women he wrote about. It was all true, I came to realize — not in the sense that he'd necessarily written only autobiographically. That's not what I mean at all. I mean to say that Wolfe, in these books, accurately, hauntingly, perfectly, depicts life and death — mine, yours, all.

I finished the last chapter of *You Can't Go Home Again* sitting on my front porch with Story and Buller keeping me company on a Friday afternoon the day before I packed everything I'd come to own into my car and headed back up the mountain to Old Buckram. Story wasn't going with me — she was going home to Lot's Folly to mend a few fences of her own — but I'd have Buller and we could survive just fine until the stars aligned and life brought me around to Story again.

"I don't understand why you'd go home when you could come stay with us." Mother had been waging an air and ground campaign for my entire final semester of law school to have me move to Charlotte. I resisted like hell and eventually won out. It all came down to the fact that I'd made up my mind to return to Old Buckram for the summer — although I wasn't sufficiently honest with myself at the time or insightful enough to say why.

Part of it, I know, was that Story was going to Lot's Folly to finally solve the mysteries of her birth, and I needed to say I had an important purpose of my own. In this case, I invented the justification that my family owned a crumbling mansion on the side of a mountain in Old Buckram, and that it was up to me to restore it to habitable condition and ready it for sale. This, after all, was partly true. After Mother and Threnody had moved to Charlotte, the old

362

house sat empty, and Mother put it on the market but didn't find a buyer for it despite months of advertising in every major city in three states. The agent said the structure needed too much work inside and out and people were scared away by the decay and the horror stories that were whispered by the people in the town. I had first stumbled upon this manufactured excuse when talking to Mother. She had asked me "why in the world" I would want to spend the summer in Old Buckram. "For one thing," I said, casting about for plausible reasons, "someone needs to do something to the house or else it will never sell."

"And you think you're the one to do that."

"I can do it," I said. "I'm very handy. Plus, Charlie has offered me a job." Again, this was partially true. Charlie had told me several times that if I ever came back to the mountains to practice law, he'd have a place for me. He and I hadn't discussed it any further than that, but I planned to call him before I got up there. "It's the best offer I've gotten so far," I said. I doubted she'd call and ask him about it.

In later conversations on the same topic, the vanguard advanced by Mother was about Threnody. "She's having a hard time," she said over and over again. "She could use you here."

"What do you mean? Worse than normal?"

"I don't know what that means, but yes," said Mother.

"How so?" I said, feeling defensive, and for good reason. I was, when I thought about it, distantly aware that I'd abrogated my responsibilities, saved only by my own self-serving denial and an unrealistic hope that she'd grow and flourish despite the shadow of my absence. For Mother's benefit, though, I'd go right on pretending.

"I can just tell," she said. "Something's not right."

"You have to be more specific than that."

"I can't think of how to describe it. She's just — I don't know how to tell you. Okay, here's an example," began Mother. "A few weeks ago on Friday, she wanted to spend the night with one of her new friends. I let her go even though I had some misgivings about it — we didn't know the family. The girls apparently got into the liquor cabinet or maybe did something worse, I'm not sure. It might've been drugs. Maybe you could tell me; neither one of them would say. But the next morning, Threnody didn't wake up."

"Because she was hungover?" I asked.

"No, not just because she was hungover,"

said Mother scornfully. "She —"

"— Well, is she better now?"

"Yes," Mother reluctantly conceded, "she's better now — *physically.* She just had to sleep it off. But they had to call an ambulance for her," she insisted. "They thought maybe she'd had an overdose."

"How are her grades? Did you talk to her about it?"

"Her grades are good, but — you know Threnody, she's not really studying. It's easy for her —"

"If her grades are good, I wouldn't worry about it."

"You're missing my point," said Mother. "There's something wrong with her. She doesn't talk very much anymore. I don't like the people she's associating with."

I laughed and told Mother I would have been concerned if this had *not* been the case. "She's a teenager," I said. "I'm sure it's just a phase. All kids go through it. I'd worry more about her if she were perfectly well adjusted."

"Henry — listen to me," said Mother.

"I'm listening."

"Be quiet for a minute and listen to what I'm saying." There was an unfamiliar, desperate edge to her voice.

"I'm listening."

"She's not okay."

I knew this. In my heart I knew it. *I'll call her,* I thought. *As soon as Story leaves, I'll call her. I'll make it better. I'll invite her up to the house in Old Buckram for a weekend, if she wants.* But still, I was going to Old Buckram one way or the other. I sure as hell wasn't going to Charlotte. I could make it all work.

Story was in a chair next to me doing a crossword puzzle and Buller was lying on top of my feet watching the birds in the trees and occasionally issuing a low, rumbling growl at people walking up and down the street. I just sat there letting it all wash over me. Story was leaving that afternoon — we were pretending like we didn't have to say goodbye — and I could feel the tide of my life retreating and I knew I had to go where it was taking me.

When I'd traveled the roads away from Old Buckram years before, I left behind everything my life had been. My family, my dear sister, my few friends, and all my memories, good and bad. My context for understanding the world. I was making a new start and I was content to leave it all behind. Indeed, I wanted to. I boxed my trophies and all my photographs and the newspaper clippings and the yearbooks and everything else that reminded me of home and walked away from it all entirely without a single glance behind. I wanted nothing to do with it, and all the memories lay dormant inside me. Now the thought of actually going home again was opening old wounds and they hurt more the second time around, but something was driving me to go. A hidden corridor in the mind that had to be explored; a door that had to be opened.

Nightmares of the wicked mansion on the hill began to wake me time and again. In my dreams I could see it high in the shadow of the mountain beneath a sky of smoke and smoldering ash, hiding in wait behind rows of diseased black trees, their pestilential branches dividing the mist and protruding this way and that to their capillaried, palsied ends. I dreamed of finding dozens of gaping shovel-dug holes in the yard with gnarled tree roots reaching into them like grasping, ravenous hands. The earth would tilt and roll and push me toward them. I was going home again.

"What's a seven-letter word meaning to renounce or give up?" Story twiddled a pencil and bit on the eraser.

"Forsake."

"Very good. Only a few more. Author of

The Stranger. Five letters. I know this, but I can't remember it to save my life. I want to say Camel —"

"Camus."

"You're so good."

"My father made me do crossword puzzles with him when I was a kid in exchange for dry cereal and basic sustenance items. They get repetitive after a while."

"I'll let you finish this one." She tossed the paper into my lap and slid the pencil behind my ear. "Okay, darling. The time has come."

"Don't leave."

"I have to. I told my folks I'd be home for dinner. I'm going to be late as it is. I need to get home and finish packing."

Story knelt down and kissed Buller on the forehead. He seemed forlorn.

"Will you call me when you get home?"

"I will."

"I hate this time of the day," I said. "I feel it every single day."

She kissed me and held me close and I drank in the fragrance of her hair and the warmth and softness of her body. Then she was gone, and I gathered up what my life had become and set out west to the home I had left so many years before.

34

Living in a city, it's easy to forget about the night sky. The stars become like forgotten childhood friends. Only far away from city lights are the stars truly visible, where on a dark, clear night you can see that the heavens have a nearly infinite depth. It is no mere canopy above us. As a child in the mountains I was captivated by the night sky. In my pajamas, I'd roll up the green army blanket Mother kept down at the end of the hall in the linen closet and try to sneak outside to lie on the grass beneath the trees to track the mathematical revolutions of the stars around the spinning earth. Looking east from the great house on Ben Hennom, the wheeling stars and wandering planets would rise like fireflies from the timeless gray shoulders of the Morning Mountain.

As a boy, lying outside under a starlit summer sky, I viewed the firmament of distant suns with hope and warmth and optimism.

As I grew older, I frequently turned to the sky for comfort, and being reminded of my slight significance within the context of the vast and enigmatic universe, I was comforted. Driving back to Old Buckram for the first time in more than seven years, returning home again, I looked out my car window and up through the windshield at the black sky full of stars once more, and I did feel some measure of much-needed comfort — but it was a lonely comfort, nonetheless.

At a crest in the Blue Ridge, when Old Buckram is still more than ten miles distant to the north, a narrow plateau appears between the mountains, flat and wide like an antediluvian riverbed. The locals call it Chilblain's Gap, but I doubt the name has ever appeared on a map. At a crossroads there you'll find a flashing yellow light, a small gas station, and nothing more. My whole life in tow and Buller stuffed into the back of the Arthur Radley with no room to spare, I stopped to buy a six-pack of beer.

The gas station had dirty windows, and a dim light shone out onto the pavement through frosted lettering that was no longer legible. Rusted cans and other trash lay in the weeds behind the station and caught the fluorescent glow from the rusted awning over the pumps. Inside, behind the counter, was a pleasant gray-haired woman with rolls of fat hanging pendulously over her belt. A quantity of thin black hair ran over her lip and around her chin, pausing only to avoid an erumpent growth on her cheek the size and hue of a Buffalo-head nickel. She had on a gaudy trinket for a wedding ring and I thought of her poor husband, likely a much smaller man than she, and wondered if he'd ever come close to smothering in the crook of her arm. She was reading a housekeeping magazine and said "Howdy" to me when I walked in.

I went to the beer cooler and passed three men, all of them older, sitting in a booth next to the window smoking cigarettes and drinking coffee. One had an enormous inflated stomach that stuck out and threatened the edge of the table. His weight showed in his arms and in his face and in his ankles. A wooden cane carved from a tree limb, knots included, was hooked over his leg. He worked at his teeth with a toothpick and then put it back into his shirt pocket for later. Perhaps this was the clerk's husband, there to keep an eye on her lest she stray.

Beside him was a man who was almost comically small next to the first man. Imagine a starched white shirt on a metal hanger with a head balanced on top. Although he must have been sixty-eight or seventy, this second man had a childlike face and the aspect of a twelve-year-old boy, if the twelve-year-old boy had been a chicken. The third man wore snakeskin cowboy boots and tight blue jeans and had a neatly trimmed mustache that covered his lip but didn't quite reach all the way to his nose. All of them wore trucker caps of cloth and mesh, and the small man's hat looked peculiar and oversized perched so high on his little head.

You could tell they had spent many a night in this gas station, talking and socializing with anyone who came in. They became quiet when I entered and I could feel them watch me walk by. As I went back toward the counter, one of them nodded his head at me. I smiled politely and paused to exchange a brief pleasantry, as is the custom in the mountains.

"Evenin', gentlemen."

Without looking at me, the larger man said, "None of *them* 'round here." They all laughed and I laughed with them.

"Son," the larger man said, "you've got it made."

"You think?" I said.

"See that boy there," the larger man continued like I was no longer standing in front of him, "he's got it made."

"He *does* have it made," said the smaller man. "He's a good-lookin' young man. Here it is a Saturday night and he's a'taking home some cold beer to drink. Prob'ly got him a girl at home, too." They laughed again and flicked at their cigarettes and the wooden cane twirled about.

"I wish I did," I said. "Tonight, it's just me and the beer."

Quick as a flash, the larger man said, "That boy just told my whole life story!" and this precipitated another burst of friendly, raucous laughter.

"Are you Henry's boy?" said the man with the mustache, looking up at me with one eye. "He looks just like his daddy, don't he, Cetus? Son, you sure have grown up in a hurry."

"Oh, yes," said Cetus, the larger man, as if he were not quite sure what to say, just like when you ask about someone only to hear they've died. "Son, I knew your daddy pretty well, back when he was working as a lawyer in town," he said. "A *good* man. There's no doubt about it."

"Yes, sir," said the man with the mustache. "He sure helped a lot of people who needed help."

The three men got quiet for a moment as they thought back on it all and I took the opportunity to leave. "Well," I said, "I guess I'd better get on home. Come with me and have a beer."

"Naw, we best stay here," said Cetus. "Good night, son. Be safe."

"Night, gentlemen."

"Say," Cetus called to me before I could walk away.

"Sir?"

"Don't you have a little sister? Where's she now?"

"I do," I said. "She and my mother are living in Charlotte. They're doing well."

I walked back to the beer cooler and exchanged my now-warm six-pack for a colder twelve-pack of the same beer. As I went to the counter to pay, I heard Cetus say, "I know where he gets that taste for beer. Comes by it honest."

From the crossroads at Chilblain's Gap to the first traffic light in Old Buckram, the miles are dark and quiet. Other than the occasional billboard (BLEVINS LUMBER CO., 200 MAIN ST., OLD BUCKRAM), there are few objective indications that you are approaching anything resembling a center of commerce.

About a mile out of town coming in from the southwest, the road widens and begins a steady incline up a long hill with pastures on either side of the road. From the top of the hill, for the first time the few town lights can be seen shining in the broad valley below. On clear nights an observant traveler will notice that much of the sky to the east above the town is cloaked in a darkness that is deeper than the dark of the sky. This immense shadow is the Morning Mountain, whose sloping shoulders rise nearly five thousand feet on the east side of the valley to defend the town from starlight and the early-morning sun. On this night, a timid white moon rose to meet me as I crossed the top of the hill, then fell again to hide behind the mountain as I made my way down into town.

There is a fear that accompanies returning to a place that holds many of your life's memories, especially if years pass between leaving and returning. For fast-moving, progressive towns and cities, the fear is that the place will have changed in your absence; that it will have gone on without you; that it will have left you behind. This reminds us too sharply that time and life continue unabated in our absence — that our impact on any place and the people who reside there is ephemeral.

For small towns, there is an opposite fear: that the town hasn't changed. That it's just the same as you left it — that the streets and the stores and the people, and the sadness and the loneliness, are the same; that it will always be the same, with you fading slowly away, insignificant, as the town stolidly but unchangingly persists.

After my protracted absence, the faintly lit Main Street showed no evidence of change, but everything had aged. I saw nothing new; nothing that would make the town new to me. The old Chevrolet place on the corner of Catawba Road and Main Street was still there, its sign a faded blue and silver, almost unreadable now. The pastel murals of old bluegrass bands and blue mountain vistas that were added to the brick facades of some of the original town buildings as part of the town "renewal" when I was a child had become even more faded. Ace Hardware, with its wooden floors and aromatic dusty seed bins, appeared to have closed.

There were no cars in town. No stores or restaurants were open. The few traffic lights flashed yellow to no one. The sidewalks were unswept and uninviting. Many of the storefronts were empty with cheap For Rent signs hanging crookedly in the windows.

The shops that remained going concerns were small operations destined for failure, all with scant wares in shabby window displays.

I had no old friends in town, and my suspicion at the time was that I was not likely to make any new ones. When you return to a place that offers more narrow horizons than the place you left, you will forever be alien to that place. You have changed; you are no longer the same person you once were.

There was little prosperity to speak of in Old Buckram during the years of my childhood, and this was not a change from how it was before. I don't believe anyone ever moved there with the expectation of finding great success, although some tree farmers made a modest living, but nothing like you'd expect. Most people who lived there had been born there, and most were content simply living out their lives without recognizable ambition.

On Sunday morning, if you were out driving, you'd see women riding to church with their husbands, their attire dark and modest — for her, a somber dress covering the knees, heavy nylon stockings bunched at the ankles and the shoes, maybe a simple necklace of faux pearls. For him, the same suit every Sunday: a black coat and cuffed pants, frayed and threadbare around the heels; a white shirt, now yellowing; a thin black tie not quite reaching the belt buckle. Faces expressionless and impassive, appearing to live in the complete absence of curiosity and displaying no evident longing for anything beyond their day-to-day existence and exhibiting no amusement or pain of life. After church they'd return home, relatives would visit, and they'd all sit or stand in the dining room and eat green beans, country ham, and cold biscuits with overly full mouths and tall glasses of milk, nobody ever saying very much. Mostly they'd talk about being poor and those who had died, always shaking their heads in resignation, but carrying on despite losing the grim battle against life and time.

In the morning, you hear the incessant crowing of the rooster from a far valley. You walk along the lonely dirt road beside a cheap barbed-wire fence, uneven and holding knots of mane or tail, the sticky milkweed in the ditch, the Queen Anne's lace growing there in the long grass and clover, and beside the road there is a catalpa tree, and a crab apple, and a black locust that is older than you are.

In the evening, darkness sets early on the land as the sun falls behind the mountains and the beginnings of a raw wind come up out of the earth. The sound of the last passing cars fades into nothingness, and the creek behind the house is left to run like an hourglass in the cold. And when autumn is subsumed by winter and the sky is white from morning until night, and the first snow falls from the pale white sky, life and hope retreat.

There is a sadness — a colorlessness — that lives in the far northwestern mountains — in Old Buckram. There is a *stillness* that exists nowhere else in the world among the places I have been. It's always there, lurking just beyond the invented clamor and tumult of the day. Yet this stillness is not one of quiet comfort. It is not the drowsy calm that descends when the earth turns away from the sun and all living things find shelter and warmth and sleep. No, it is not this. It is a stillness of *disquiet.* It is a terrifying midday silence of nothingness and desolation.

From any place in the mountains, you will see the white mist rising and churning above the valleys; the rows upon geometrically perfect rows of Christmas trees lining the hillsides; the once-green mountains in the foreground fading to shades of blue in the magnificent distance. You will see leafless trees tremble in the invisible winter wind. You will smell the wood-smoke from so many distant fires. You will see the rutted roadways and dead grass in all the yards, and a murder of crows in search of food in a lifeless field. But all this you will see in *stillness.*

You are alone in this place. Anyone who has lived through more than one winter here knows it all too well. I don't know why I ever went back. I know now that one can never leave a place completely.

I pulled onto a backstreet out of the lights of town and opened a beer that thankfully was still fairly cold. I drove west on Avernus Road back up toward old Ben Hennom, past Lambert Holler and the Sunoco station, and past the Harless valley where the dirty pie-bald cows waded in the grassy creek and looked out stupidly with muddy faces at passing cars. I drove by the severe-looking Eusebius Baptist Church, with its flat gravel parking lot and the rusted single-wide trailer in the field just behind the church, apparently uninhabited for years. Just beyond the church the road narrowed and turned to dirt and gravel as I expected.

From there it wasn't far to the driveway I hadn't seen since leaving for college.

I pulled up to the gate at the bottom of Ben Hennom at 10:45 P.M. and looked with very real trepidation at the narrow gravel road that disappeared up the hill into the darkness. I got out of the car and examined the gate in the headlights and found it was locked with a heavy chain and padlock. There wasn't room on either side of it to drive around, so I got Buller out of the back of the car and together we began the long climb up with the help of a rather sad flashlight whose batteries were fading by the second. In the dappling moonlight I saw the vanguard of black trees behind the fence and the shadow of the brooding, diabolical house behind them, and a chill ran through me, warning me not to approach. My mind briefly entertained the preposterous fantasy that the house was alive and that it hated me with all its soul; that it would kill me were I to return home and reclaim possession of it. Up the hill we went.

35

The driveway was washed out and over-grown with weeds. The dogwoods running up either side must have been hit by some kind of blight or parasite, for there were no leaves on the trees. It had the appearance of a long-dead orchard. There were no street-lights and no house lights anywhere close. The darkness was nearly complete save for a faint halo of town light that came from behind. Here and there I saw the house hiding in the dark like a great squatting skeleton. I felt sure someone had figured out it had been sitting vacant and that I would either find someone living there or evidence of animal sacrifices, or both.

It had not occurred to me to call ahead and have the electricity turned on. Brilliant. A pane of glass in the back door had been broken, but the door remained locked and appeared secure. My old key worked just as it always had and we were inside.

As soon as Buller and I set foot inside the gray-tiled foyer, I thought about the family that had lived there before us. I'd been in the house for fifteen years before I finally learned their horrific fate. Father told the grisly tale to his law partner, Charlie, and Charlie's wife, Sarah, late one Saturday night. I was in my room with the door open when the house fell quiet. I overheard Father say: "Yes, they died right here in the house." I went to the railing to listen.

"That's awful," said Sarah. "And didn't they have children?"

"There were three girls," said Father. "Mary, Tebah, and Abigail. Biblical names."

[MOTHER: "You know their names?"]

"What happened?" asked Charlie. "I'm not sure I want to know. I'm assuming it wasn't natural."

[MOTHER: "You never told me their names."]

"The parents — they died from gunshot wounds to the head," said Father.

[FATHER TO MOTHER: "I found a picture with their names written on the back. I'll show you."]

"Were they murdered or did they commit suicide?"

"That was never determined with certainty," said Father. "It was more likely that they killed themselves, although the evidence was conflicting. A gun was found with the bodies, but it wasn't clear that either one of them pulled the trigger."

This was the first I'd heard about how they had died. My blood ran cold.

"Good god almighty," said Charlie. "How in the hell did it happen?" He got up to fix himself another drink but then sat back down to hear the story.

"It's very strange," said Father. "All I know is they were found dead and rotting in their clothes, their eyes hollowed, their jaws cracked open in a posture of howling. They were lying side by side, facing each other, as if they'd watched each other die."

"Where were they? Not in this room, I hope."

"No — there's what you might call a basement area under the rear portion of the house. You access it by going underneath the front staircase and pulling up some loose boards. The builder must have carved it out of the rock before the house was built. It feels much more like a dungeon than a basement."

"That's where they were?" asked Charlie.

"That's where they were," said Father.

[MOTHER TO HERSELF: "The oubliette."]

Sarah's hand went to her mouth. Her

other hand made the sign of the cross. She was no longer comfortable being in the house.

"Can you still get to the basement?"

"You can," said Father. "Do you want to see it?"

"Hell, no."

Sarah said, "What about the girls? I'm almost afraid to ask. How old were they?"

"They were just children. Three, seven, and eleven — when they died. Mary was the youngest. The autopsies, which I've read, concluded they had all drowned."

"I don't understand," said Charlie.

"There's a small washroom upstairs on the third level. There wasn't any water in the tub when the police got here, but there was hair and blood from all three girls in the drain. Another odd detail is that there were three nightgowns, presumably the girls' nightgowns, hanging very neatly in the washroom from a line."

"To dry," said Charlie.

"Maybe we should go," said Sarah.

"It took weeks to locate them — the girls. The investigators eventually found them in one large hole back up in the woods, laid out neatly side by side as if they'd been ritualistically buried. They each had broken bones and their skulls were fractured into pieces, like they'd been dropped from a great height. But the official cause of death was drowning. The bones were broken later."

"That makes no sense to me," said Charlie.

[MOTHER TO HERSELF: "Maybe they didn't want to carry them down all the stairs. Maybe they were in a hurry."]

"What's most troubling to me," said Father, "is how the drownings were accomplished. If it was done by the parents, presumably it would've taken both of them to do it."

"What on earth or in heaven or in hell could possibly have driven anyone to do that?"

"Oh, I don't know," said Mother. "I think the house just made them all go insane."

For years afterward, I had nightmares of the three dead girls coming up out of the ground, decayed, with their rotted teeth turned to needles, coming to drown me in the bathtub. It was with this charming remembrance that Buller and I began to explore the vulture house, built as it was on the foundation of hell.

Walking through the dull, dark, and soundless house, every dreary form and shadow looked supernatural. Starting in the rear of the first floor, I found that the curtains had all been pulled closed, making the darkness nearly perfect. There were mouse droppings all over the floor; I felt them under my shoes. In the windows without curtains, viscid cobwebs with the inedible parts of insects suspended in their threads reached improbable distances and held forests of dust. I walked through one of them and had a fat scurrying spider on my head and almost down the back of my shirt.

No one, it appeared, had ever cleaned out any of the old furniture. Bedsheets, now covered in a crawling mildew, had been thrown over the lamps and chairs. These hovered ominously over the floor like bedlam ghouls and spooked Buller whenever one was encountered. I went into the kitchen and, out of an old forgotten habit, picked up the junk mail still sitting in a bowl on the counter. Reading by flashlight, I came across my father's name on an address label and shuddered.

Shreds of paper lay here and there in a downstairs office — more evidence of rats or mice, I surmised. Mother's monogrammed hand towels were hanging in the downstairs half-bath. A bar of soap, fossilized, lay in a dish next to the sink. I had gone back in time to the moment the house was abandoned. Outside, between the house and the woods, there was no light at all.

A distant thudding noise came from upstairs. It sounded like someone had dropped a book flat on the floor. I stopped to listen and Buller cocked his head and growled in his throat. After waiting two full minutes without another sound and satisfying myself to a reasonable degree that we were indeed alone (perhaps I had suffered some auditory delusion), I continued my investigation. I was opening every door and looking in every closet and under every bed. Before I put down a sleeping bag or climbed into a bed, I just wanted to make sure the house was as I remembered it, and that the damn thing was empty.

I turned toward the front of the house and went down the outside hallway and into the so-called Painted Parlour. I'd forgotten how large a room this was, and how high the ceilings ran. It could have held a merry-go-round in the center with space to walk around. The discordant, mismatched colors, jarring to the senses in broad daylight, were now even more madhouse and bizarre. Imagine, if you will, a sanitarium designed by Max Ernst. Someone had taken stacks of books and left them haphazardly in two of the chairs; I was incensed at the carelessness of this. I wanted to know why the books were not in the library, and said this aloud to the darkness. I tried to read the titles from their spines, but the books were aged and the lettering was hard to make out.

And then from above another sound, this one less distinct than the first. *It could've been the wind,* I thought, my heart quickening. A loose shutter; an open window. Buller growled again and I pulled him next to me and clamped my hand around his muzzle so we could listen. Again we waited in the dark. All I could hear was white noise.

My mind was playing tricks on me, that's all it was. A remembrance — something familiar I couldn't place — yes: Threnody bounding out of her bedroom for breakfast — like a parent who, having lost a child, still hears the child crying in the night. I thought of all our games of hide and seek in the evil, labyrinthine house when we were children, where I'd sit in that wondrous state of half-terror in the silence of some far dark corner hoping not to be found.

I waited and heard nothing else. I counted in time with the pulsing of my own blood. Why not just leave and come back tomorrow in the daylight with a sheriff's deputy? *I am insane,* I thought. *This is insane. What am I doing here?*

Upstairs a door opened and I heard some-one moving swiftly down the hall. My adrenal glands fired and for a second I couldn't move. Unable to breathe, I turned off the flashlight and stumbled in the dark down the corridor and came out in the Great Room. My eyes made out movement at the end of the second-floor hallway and not knowing what else to do, I yelled out with blood in my voice.

I had caught five young boys in the act of some adventure. It would have been hard to determine which of us, prior to that moment, had been more scared of the other. I was sure they were a band of zombies or murderers; they must have fancied me as a demon of some kind, come back to seek revenge. When I hit them with the flashlight, they froze in horror.

"Holy god almighty! It's okay, boys. What the *hell* are y'all doing up there?"

"Who are you?" one of them cried.

"I own this house. Who are you?"

"Nobody owns this house," the kid said. "Everybody that lived here died."

"Not quite," I said.

"Who are you?"

"I told you already. I own this house."

"Are you a ghost?"

"Do I look like a ghost?" By this time Buller had come into the room and added some much-needed realism to the picture.

"Are you going to hurt us?"

"No, I am not going to hurt you."

"Are you going to tell our parents?"

"I'm sure I know your parents, but I'm not going to say anything. Did you guys do any damage up there? How long have you been coming here?"

The boys had a quick conference among themselves, and then the leader called down to me. "You better come up here and have a look."

Oddly, it was comforting having someone in the house other than me. I found the spiral staircase in the corner of the Great Room and climbed its spidery helices up to the library, where we exchanged terse introductions without handshakes. I then followed the boys back up to the third floor past an unused washroom to an alcove with an oddly canted ceiling. It was full of empty beer cans, wine bottles, and other miscellaneous garbage. Someone had drawn an immense pentagram with a goat's head on one wall. It appeared that someone had started a small fire next to the window, and the wall was blackened with smoke.

"Damn it, boys. Aren't you guys a little

young to be drinking?"

"Those beer cans aren't ours," the leader said.

"Yeah, right."

"Are you going to call the police?"

"No, I'm not going to call the police. Who's the artist?" I pointed with the flashlight at the pentagram. The boys looked back and forth at one another, not wanting to volunteer the information. Then a boy said, "We heard everybody that lived here was murdered, and that's why nobody's lived here for so long."

"That's not exactly right. A lot has happened since then. Do you guys mind coming back up here one day next week to help me clean up some of this?"

The boys agreed and we shook on it, and I walked them back down the front steps and out into the driveway. One of them said he'd bring some paint out of his father's garage so we could cover up the satanic drawing. I said that would be helpful. The boys walked and then ran down the driveway into the dark, and I knew that this would make a good story for them for a while.

36

Sleeping that night was next to impossible. Every sound we heard all night caused Buller to bark, and each one had the effect of someone throwing a firecracker into the room. In the morning I walked through the house and tried without much success to straighten things up. I opened all the curtains and torrents of dust rained down on me. With the sunlight the house was no less menacing. Seeing it again after being gone for so long was shocking to the senses and made me doubt my parents' wisdom in ever moving in. I thought only a madman would walk through these irrational halls and think once of calling it home.

To my delight, though, I found a case of wine in the bottom of the pantry and five (five!) bottles of Polish vodka in a box behind the bar. In the Great Room I removed the moldering bedsheets from the square grand and dusted off the keys. After searching for some time, I located the old stack of music books in a box in the vacant dining room. I opened a book of Chopin's nocturnes and was at once taken by a deluge of grief upon the sight of Father's pencil marks and frustrated notations.

I started taking lessons shortly after Threnody was born. Mother drove me to a neighboring town once every two weeks for lessons with a pale and bony-armed yet not entirely unattractive ample-breasted woman named Ms. Springbarn. In all the years that I knew her, I never learned her first name. She was sweet in a clinical sort of way, but she was unforgiving as hell when it came to posture and technique. "Sit up. You're slouching. Watch your hands. Sit up. Watch your hands. You are not Vladimir Horowitz. Your hands are flat. Your hands are *flat.* I'm not going to tell you again." *Whack!* with a ruler. This was my first exercise in Pavlovian conditioning. That shit works, I can tell you. To this day I can't measure a thing.

She wore low-cut shirts or plain blouses that pulled open in the front and dramatically exhibited her overflowing breasts, but her excessive formality destroyed any suggestion that she was being purposely salacious. When she played for me, it was almost always J. S. Bach. She had long been a student of the *Urvater der Harmonie* and used examples from his music for every lesson. She said he had a better understanding of tonality than any of the romantics, which I preferred (and still prefer). After some time I came to love when she'd play for me — a wispy-haired, D-cupped Glenn Gould unspooling more sequacious melodies and counterpoints than my mind could simultaneously hear and comprehend. To the best of my memory, my first spontaneous arousal occurred during her private performance for me of the Goldberg Variations. As you might imagine, the source of the stimulation was the cause of some confusion for me at the time and I still wonder about it.

I practiced more as I got older and my romance with the piano deepened. At home, my practice time sometimes overlapped with Father's writing time, and this was untenable, particularly in the timeless void before Maddy died when he wrote with such horrible intensity. Architecturally speaking, the piano was situated below Father's writing table, and given that the ceiling was open between the Great Room and the library, Father could not escape the "unflagging sonic assault" (his term) from below. He loved the music and in bright moments encouraged me with great tenderness and sincerity, but my practice time was profoundly distracting for him when he was writing. A few times late at night, particularly when he'd been drinking and had momentarily escaped the dread burden of his work and his unwinnable war with time, he came downstairs and talked to me with drunken animation about all the classical pieces he loved.

One such weekend night, after Mother and Threnody had gone to bed, he poured himself half a glass of scotch from the bar and set it on the piano next to my music. The unbuttoned sleeves of his white dress shirt were soiled with graphite. I was alarmed to note that he might have aged a thousand years since I'd seen him last, but this was visible only in his eyes. Briefly, he put his arm around me for a hug and I felt an uncertainty and a frailty in his musculature and in his bones.

"I guess it's late," I said.

"Is it?"

"Yes — it's past eleven."

"I didn't realize. It feels like I just sat down. What are you working on?"

"The slow movement from the *Hammerklavier.*"

"Oh, yes! Beethoven. I knew I recognized it."

This particular piece of music, known for its technical difficulties, has forever evaded my abilities as a pianist, then and now. Yet the extraordinary beauty of the third movement, described by Wilhelm von Lenz as "a mausoleum of the collective sorrow of the world," called to me even as a young musician. I spent hours learning and repeating the first few bars, filling our already doleful house with an unspeakable melancholy. The repetition and the gloom must have been maddening.

"Please play it again so I can listen properly," said Father.

I played and he went to a darkened corner of the room and listened with his head in his hands. Without looking up, he said, "That's one of the most beautiful things I've ever heard. It's haunting, isn't it?"

"It's how I feel," I said. "I don't know why."

"How did you become familiar with it? One of my records?"

"I read about it."

Father smiled. "That's good," he said. "It sounds like you're getting close."

"I'm nowhere close. This movement is eighteen minutes long. I can only play two minutes of it."

"I meant to say that you're getting close

on the part you're working on . . ." His voice vanished into the darkness.

I tried to play through it once more, but in his presence my fingers refused to cooperate. I sensed he was growing tired of our interaction, of my playing, so I stopped abruptly and turned to face him. He stared at me and half a minute passed before he realized I was looking at him.

He returned.

"What else are you working on?" he said. "Do you know any Liszt?"

"Not yet."

"There's one you might have heard me play. It's one of the Consolations. Your mother likes it. It reminds her of starlight."

"Oh, yes," I said. "I like that one."

"Liszt was an uncommon genius. Do you know any Schubert?" Father gestured with his glass to the oil-on-canvas replica of Klimt's *Schubert at the Piano* hanging on the wall behind the piano. This was a painting my father dearly loved.

"Not right now," I said. "I used to know one simple one, but I forgot how to play it."

"I thought I heard you playing Schubert a few weeks ago."

"Not on purpose."

" 'Death and the Maiden'? Of course that's for strings."

"Yes, that's right," I said, without knowing.

" 'Death and the Maiden' is exquisite. You should listen to that and see if there's an arrangement for the piano. Liszt might have done one. Schubert was so melodic. But you know my first real love is Chopin. The nocturnes. The mazurkas. The A-minor mazurka is a nearly perfect piece of music when played softly with the appropriate Slavic aspect. Opus 17, number 4," he added parenthetically, now accelerating. "The nocturne in B major, opus 62, likewise cannot be improved upon." He sprang from the corner, his mind now catching fire, and began walking in slow circles around the piano. "Have you learned any Chopin? I don't think I've heard any. The last piece I've tried to learn, maybe you've heard it, was the march from his second piano sonata."

He never had anyone with whom to discuss his intellectual abstractions. When given half a chance, he would animate like an electrical storm. After going through what must have been a list of every composer of classical music, living, decaying, or long-dead, he strode over to the phonograph next to the bar and put on a record.

"I've got a piece I want you to hear," he

said. It was Mozart's Requiem Mass. "Listen to this. Just come sit here and listen for a minute. This is incredible." He sat in one chair; I sat in another. I didn't know then what I know now. It was impossible to keep up.

"What are they saying?"

"Day of wrath, day of anger. It doesn't matter what they're saying. Great trembling there will be. Listen to the music."

I listened.

"This sounds like a musical re-creation of World War II."

"It's Mozart, for god's sake."

"If you say so," I said. "What language is this?"

"It doesn't matter!" He got up and began to move dramatically around the room. "Learn this for me," he said, now out of breath, still dancing and flailing his arms maniacally about like a deranged conductor.

Mother yelled down from upstairs: "Henry!"

And then his darkness returned. Without a word, he stopped the music, climbed the spiral staircase to the library, and was gone.

Mother came softly down the front stairs and walked over to where I was sitting. "You know I don't mind your playing at this hour as long as you play quietly," she said. "Sometimes it helps me sleep. It's really lovely. I'm sorry. What were you playing before?" She didn't wait for an answer and drifted away from me to ascend the stairs again a ghost like Father.

Halfheartedly now, with muted strings, I played, afraid to disturb. Father's desk light had gone out. He'd finally gone to bed. The quiet of the house fell full upon me and the piano could not sound again until morning. I walked to the lamp in the Great Room and then saw Threnody lying on the floor, looking down through the railing encircling the library, watching me, just as I used to watch Father when he played. She smiled at me and waved and I smiled back.

"Hey, little Bird."

"Hey."

"What are you doing up?"

"I couldn't sleep." She was whispering through the railing.

"Are you all right?"

"I think so."

I asked her if she wanted me to make her a snack.

"No, I'm okay. Is it too late for you to tell me a story?"

I was tired and knew it was too late, but I

said, "I think we have time for a story, don't you?"

"I think so."

We met in her bedroom and I tucked her in. In a nook in the far wall was a desk, and above the desk were three shelves set into the wall. Threnody had plundered Father's book collection and many of the stolen books were lined up alphabetically on these shelves as if they now belonged to her. These were her favorite books, and we read them over and over again. I sat on the chair next to the bed and the familiar emptiness grew inside me.

She closed her eyes and pulled the covers up around her neck and said, "I'm ready."

"Do you want me to read you a story or tell you a story?"

"*Tell* me a story." She was almost asleep.

I thought for a long time and couldn't think of a good story, so I just started talking and this is what I said:

"Once upon a time there was a great tree that stood at the top of a great hill and looked out over all the land. In years forgotten the tree had been but a tiny green seed, but over time it began to grow tall and strong, until it was the tallest and the strongest of all the trees on the great hill. The tree had a friend: a quiet little crow who

402

came to sit in the tree's branches once the tree had grown tall. And they grew older together, but the tree was much older than the crow. Together, each day, they watched as the sun rose and moved across the sky, and they watched until darkness came to the great hill, and in the darkness the crow would hide from the starlight in the branches of the great tree and close his eyes for sleep. One night when the crow was sleeping a terrible storm came, and then another. Lightning came down from the sky. All around the great hill the other trees burned and fell, leaving only the one great tree, and the quiet little crow, to sit at the top of the hill and look out over all the land and watch the sun move across the sky. One day the crow said, I hope you live forever, my dear friend. And the tree responded, My dear friend, I cannot live forever. A year passed, and still the crow sat in the branches of the great tree. Again he said, I hope you live forever, my dear friend. And the tree said, My dear friend, I will not live forever. Another year passed, and still the crow sat in the branches of the great old tree. He said again, I hope you live forever, my dear friend. And this time the great old tree did not answer. Yet the tree still stands, and the quiet little crow still sits among its branches.

The sun, it passes without notice."

I sat in silence for a moment to make sure Threnody was asleep. When she didn't stir, I turned out the light and sat for another minute in the dark listening to the wind outside.

From under the covers, a small voice said, "Henry?"

"Yes, Bird."

"I'm glad you're still here. I was just checking." She peeked out from under her blankets and, satisfied I was not an illusion, tucked herself back in again.

"I'm still here."

"What are you doing? Why are you just sitting there?"

"I didn't want to wake you up," I said.

"Henry?"

"Yes, Bird?"

"I don't want you to die." She was crying.

"I know, Bird. I'm not going to die. I'm not going anywhere."

"Do you promise?"

"I promise you that wherever I go, you'll go, too. We'll be together and we'll always have each other."

"Okay. That's good."

"Go to sleep now," I said. "It's late and I know you're tired. The morning's going to come early."

"Will you sing me a song?"
"Yes, I'll sing you a song."

On this day, two lifetimes later, there was just emptiness where before there had been so much life. There was no one upstairs, and no one at the railing looking down. The piano, somehow, was not *horribly* out of tune, a fact I chalked up to the location of it deep inside the house. By nightfall I was still at the piano, now with one empty bottle of wine, one partially consumed bottle of wine, and an open bottle of vodka. There were glasses in the house, but I chose not to use them. I hadn't eaten a thing all day. Loneliness had crept into the dark and the house felt cold. The muscles in my back burned and were numb with the alcohol. Music books spread out across the face of the piano, on top of it, and surrounded me on the floor. I'd thrown one or two at the wall; these lay on the floor like great birds fallen from the sky. I played Chopin's A-minor mazurka, the opening chords so simple and so beautiful — 1-2-3 1-2-3 1-2 — the same piece Father played when I was a child. I played the nocturne in C-sharp minor, which begins in sadness, moves to bittersweet remembrance, and then returns again to sadness.

After a time I'd consumed enough wine and vodka to make my playing stupidly inaccurate. The piano, old and disconsonant, began to jangle like a band of drunken minstrels. The keys struck and raked upon the wires and grated upon my ears. My Aeolian lute! Without thought my hands fell upon the first black chord of Chopin's *marche funèbre.* I stopped as the sound slowly died away; I could play no more.

I walked out onto the porch overlooking the courtyard and down into the well of the valley beyond. It was one thirty in the morning, and, as usual, I was the only one awake. Light from my candles inside spilled red into the night. I was in the eye of the vulture. A car made its way along the dark gravel road in the valley — a curious sight at this hour in this moribund town of no earthly consequence in the persistent autumn of its bleak existence. I hoped without reason that I was getting an unexpected visitor to assuage my loneliness, but the car passed and its faint light and sound disappeared over the next hill. The night was now quiet; noise from the piano hummed in my ears and in my brain.

I am here, and I am alone.

Looking up, I saw the stars.

37

I got up the following morning, put on a coat and tie, and headed down to see Charles Young. I made my way into town and observed not with any surprise that it looked no different in the daylight hours than it had two nights before. A cool fog lay upon the town and clothed everything in gray. The Barrowfields lay off to the left — a wasteland of nothingness as far as I could see, with naught but a single wooden bench at its perimeter, now scarcely a decoration. A visitor to the town might assume that everyone who had ever lived in Old Buckram was buried there in the Barrowfields, but the mossy tombstones were but the petrified stumps of trees that were felled by some great force nigh the time of Christ and were afraid to grow again. I reminded myself that it was still summer somewhere, and that I could drive down the mountain to find the sun again and have warmth on my face before too much longer.

The law firm was located on Main Street, directly across from the county's only funeral home, whose plain brick face stared out from behind three incongruous white Doric columns. The firm was brought into existence in 1922 by Mr. Trafton Ignatius Brown III, who had received a law degree from the University of Virginia and had begun practicing law in the mountains of North Carolina when the population hardly supported it. His first law office had one room, one desk, and an old woodstove, but it did not have plumbing and therefore did not have a bathroom. Mr. Brown had to go across the street to the funeral home for this need. In exchange, he handled the funeral home's simple legal matters when they arose.

Charlie was now the sole surviving partner, having carried on the law practice despite the comings and goings of several partners and junior associates through the years. It was hard to build a large law practice in the mountains. There just wasn't enough paying work to support it.

When I walked in, a bell affixed to the back of the door sounded. The receptionist heard the bell and looked up.

"This is my lucky day," she said, rising

from her desk. She came over to where I was standing just inside the entryway. Her name was Sylvia, and I'd known her for years, from before and during my father's tenure of practice with the firm. She gave me a long hug and I thought I saw her brush away a tear. She stepped back and looked at me sideways as if to gauge my height.

"It's so good to see you. I can't believe it. You're all grown up. I haven't seen you since you were this high!" She pointed a finger into my chest. "How are you doing?"

"I'm well," I said. "I'm glad to be here for the summer — or for however long it winds up being."

"Well, we're glad you're here, too. Charlie's on the phone, but I'll let him know you're here."

The lobby was clean and neat, but it was far from ostentatious. On one wall was a framed copy of the Declaration of Independence. On another was a painting of ubiquitous "lawyer art" that must be sold out of a catalog that all lawyers get in the mail (I can only suppose). It was titled *A Country Lawyer,* and it depicted a client consulting with his attorney in a law office that had disheveled stacks of paper here, there, and everywhere. It's pretty close to the truth, I came to find out. In the corner of the lobby was a stack of magazines that were a few years old. The thin maroon carpet showed a worn path from the front door up the steps leading to Charlie's office.

Sylvia told me that she missed my father working there.

"Thank you for saying that," I said. "I know he enjoyed working here."

"He was always very kind. His mother brought him up right, I know that. He was always polite and he treated me like I was his equal, just like Charlie does. He treated me with *respect,* and not everybody does that. When you went in to talk to him and you had a problem, he listened. He was better at dealing with people than anyone I've ever known. He had a real gift for it." Hearing things like this always surprised me. It was hard to reconcile these words with the man I had known.

Charlie came down the stairs to greet me. He shook my hand pleasantly and looked at me with genuine concern. He wasn't a tall man, but he carried himself with a quiet confidence that could be intimidating. He didn't speak often, but when he did a room would grow quiet and people would listen. He was a good lawyer, but most of all, he was a good man, and an honest man, and a kind man.

I followed him back up to his office. It was the office of a working lawyer. There were no stained-mahogany bookcases; there was no ebony wood paneling. There was no improbably clean, high-gloss desk topped by an expensive lamp. Charlie's desk was hardly visible. It was obscured by a mountain range of file folders stacked five or six deep, papers extruding in all directions. In one corner of the office there might have been a hundred rolled-up surveys, many of them faded with time. A cheap wood-and-metal easel guarded several poster-board trial exhibits from trials long since passed. A row of banker's boxes made up one wall of the office. Many of them were labeled "Sheets v. Old Buckram Electric," written neatly with a Magic Marker. On his bookcase were the brown books containing decisions by the North Carolina Supreme Court and the green books with decisions of the North Carolina Court of Appeals, along with a set of the North Carolina General Statutes from 1985. He also had *Webster's Real Estate Law in North Carolina* and a Robinson on Corporations and Douglas's Forms and a book of pattern jury instructions and a treatise on wills and several other books on all the subjects known to the general practitioner, and I can tell you these books were not just for show. They were all well read. Charlie wasn't the kind of lawyer to wing anything. There is no telling how many hours he spent alone in that office at night, bent over one or another of those books, trying to understand some arcane facet of the law.

He blew out his cheeks. "After thirty-five years of doing this, I think I'm just about finished." He spoke with a convincing "aw shucks" southern accent that he might have exaggerated from time to time just from habit. People in the mountains mistrust fast talkers, and slow, deliberate speech is seen by people as more trustworthy somehow. Over time, if you want to communicate effectively, you just start to do it. He looked up at his law-school diploma and his eyes ran down the rows of framed accolades, all in modest frames. "I'll probably retire in another few years. They say that lawyers don't retire, they just die — but this one's going to. Retire."

"You think?"

"I think so. It's hard. It's awfully damn hard. Let me tell you: When you care about what you're doing, and you worry about your cases at nights and on the weekends and on vacation, it takes its toll on you after

412

a while. Listen to this. Do you know I'd been litigating for more than thirty years when it occurred to me that I don't even like controversy?"

I laughed and he said, "I'm not kidding. Well, I don't have to tell you. I wish I could tell you something different, but if I did, I'd be lying to you. Look at me. When I started, I had a head full of hair. This ain't because I have a genetic predisposition to baldness." He might have had four hairs on the top of his head.

"Do you have any big trials coming up?"

"One or two in September and October I need to start working on. You can help me get ready."

"I'd like that."

We sat for a minute as the topic we had been avoiding wormed its way into our collective consciousness and broke into the silence.

"I know it must be strange for you to be sitting here," said Charlie. "I'm still so sorry about your dad —" he began, but I cut him off.

"Thank you, Charlie," I said. "I know."

38

For the first several days of my employment, Charlie didn't have much for me to do, so he had me organize some files here and there, which basically meant putting things in chronological order. I went to court with him once or twice for small matters and he introduced me to everyone at the courthouse, from the judge to the clerk of court, all the way down to the bailiff and the janitor. The judge called him Charlie and everyone else called him Mr. Young and he was kind and very polite to all of them in equal measure.

On Friday afternoon Charlie came into my makeshift office and sat down. He looked at me for a long time before he said anything. Then he said, "You know that a lot of people here can't pay us anything." I said I figured that was the case.

He said, "We have a whole closet downstairs *full* of food and other things that people have brought in so they can pay something toward their bill. A lot of the food people bring in is good. Very good, in fact." He put his hands on his stomach.

"I thought that was just in *To Kill a Mockingbird*."

"No, no. It's right here. I guess you know as well as anybody, but I can tell you that, notwithstanding your daddy's first good lick on that big case of his when he first started, you'll never get rich practicing law. If you work at it, you can make a decent living. But you'll never get rich. Not if you do it honestly."

We sat for a moment in silence.

"So remind me why you're here in Old Buckram when you could be anywhere else. Are you going to try to get that old house ready to sell?"

"I think so."

"You've got your work cut out for you, son. That's a big house, and it's been empty a long time. I wish I knew somebody who'd buy it."

"It's hard to imagine anyone would want it," I said.

Charlie nodded and looked out the window. After a long minute, he turned back to me and said, "How are you doing?" He had a keen way of looking at you with a discernment that was at times unsettling; he did it in a way that made you be honest with yourself.

"I'm fine," I said. "But I'll be better in a few months, I'm sure."

"Do you have any idea what you want to do this summer? As I said before, we'll pay you for your time."

"I can't accept money from you."

"Then I'm not going to let you work here. If you're working here, you're going to get paid for it. But believe me — I'm not going to pay you *much,* so you won't have to feel *too* bad about it." He laughed. "Now get your stuff because you're coming over for dinner. Sarah is cooking you something special. She can't wait to see you."

I learned a great deal that summer working with Charlie. I learned that good lawyers like Charlie quietly do more good for people and communities than probably anyone would ever realize. They try like hell to achieve justice. They take clients who cannot hope to pay the full value of the legal services they'll receive, and spend their own time and their own money helping clients who at the end of the day will not be the least bit grateful for the help. And they tell their clients the truth, even when the truth is not what the clients want to hear. Lawyers catch a lot of hell in the public's perception, and admittedly there have been a few lawyers here and there who have earned that reputation fair and square. But most of them, in my estimation, are more like Charlie. And that's a good thing.

39

In early July, Story reported from Lot's Folly that things were not going well with her parents. Following Lelia's passing, and hopelessly encouraged by details of the mysterious Benjamin, she had become even more desperate to find and identify her true father. This unfortunately was not met with equal enthusiasm by the Glauchnors, who were bitter and derisive in the face of what they deemed a quixotic and pointless endeavor. The whole thing simmered just below the boiling point, and Story was alone and disheartened. She asked if I would come visit and give her a distraction from her warring family, so I gladly loaded up and drove down the mountain for the low country.

I arrived in Lot's Folly at seven o'clock on a clear Friday night. It was eighty-six degrees and humid as hell and was wonderful in comparison with what I'd been experiencing in Old Buckram, where the weather patterns were like those found in northern Ireland and on certain comets with long periodic orbits. When I left Ben Hennom six hours before, the temperature was hovering twelve degrees above freezing, certain creatures in the *Ursidae* family had returned prematurely to hibernation, and I was wearing Scottish corduroy pants, a coat, and knee-length woolen socks (mild, but not gross, exaggeration).

The entrance to Story's driveway was nearly invisible from the road due to an overgrowth of vegetation, and I passed it twice before finally making the turn. About a third of the way down the sand and peagravel drive stood a small, nearly plumb wooden structure surrounded by a quartet of magnolias and a sprawling live oak wearing rags of Spanish moss that hung all the way to the ground. In college, Story moved out of her parents' home and into this quaint architectural remnant, an old carriage house, and this is where she stayed during her infrequent trips home from law school. I'd soon find out why. Farther down the driveway, through an open wood of longleaf pine and beyond two or three more majestic oaks from the time of Moses, I could see the shingled facade of a wandering Nantucket-style abode with two levels of porches and creeping-fig ivy climbing up the brick foundation.

I stopped at the carriage house and pulled into a parking space carved out of a wall of wild azaleas. Story was sitting on the back steps reading a book with a painted daisy in her hair. In the weeks since I'd seen her last, her hair had become more blond and her limbs had become more lean. She wore a blue sundress the color of a Carolina sky and there were tan lines on her bare feet. With an extraordinary sense of cool, she closed the book and stepped into the driveway to meet me, moving to a slow, silent waltz, radiant in her honest beauty, her dress flowing around her like a carousel. I leaped out of the car almost before it stopped and pulled her close to me as we laughed and I breathed in the smell of her skin and her wondrous hair, fragrant of a green, new summer in the South and the salt air come so far inland from the waters of the inscrutable Atlantic. She took my hand and said, "Let me show you around the place so you don't get lost."

The carriage house was so much of the old South: distressed antique wooden furniture; beadboard wainscoting in every room; a painting of a magnolia in full bloom hanging on a whitewashed wall in the living room; fresh flowers in a simple glass vase on the kitchen table; and polished and uneven wooden floors throughout the house.

The first bedroom we came to was Story's. On a shelf was a sparse row of bright and happy photographs. There was one beach picture of Story as a child playing by herself in the surf, and next to it were a few vibrant shots of her in the flat blue water behind a ski boat. In one, the first of three in a parallel frame, she was on a kneeboard, swallowed up by an orange life jacket. Her face was barely visible. Her two braided pigtails stuck up into the air like antennae. The next in the series showed her on two skis as a slightly older girl, this time noticeably taller and more confident. In the final picture, a high-school-age Story was expertly cutting through the shining water on one ski amid a tower of spray made brilliant by the sun.

"Your childhood was a lot different than mine," I said.

The second bedroom had been made into an office. In this room was a desk and a filing cabinet on top of which sat four ordered and indexed stacks of newspaper clippings and copies of pages from several college yearbooks. Seeing me looking at the papers with curiosity, Story said simply, "My dad." This was her archive of materials collected on her years-long search for her father. A journal lay open on the desk. I was able to get close enough to see Story's precise handwriting on the page. More than once I'd seen her sitting on a stone wall after class, writing in the journal with a head full of thoughts. I gathered from its proximity to the other materials that it contained her most recent compilation of evidence and hypotheses on that difficult subject. She offered no further explanation, and I didn't ask for one.

We ventured out onto the porch and into the soft yard of pine needles under the warm shadows of the magnolias. Fireflies hiding in the shade blinked on and off and hovered lazily in the air. We followed a path under the trees to a shallow gully occupied by ferns and wildflowers. On the far bank of the gully, tracing vines concealed a rusted metal fence that marked the property line. Able to go no farther, we turned west down toward the water and saw the pine forest gradually give way to the front lawn, at the bountiful end of which sat what Story called "the main house." In the retreating light of the sun, the glowing edifice might have been a modest castle.

"They've called a truce," said Story. "I told them you were coming down, and they're insisting on having us over for dinner. I hope that's okay."

"Yeah, that's great," I said. "I'd be really happy to meet them. Although I feel like I might be a bit underdressed."

"You're fine. What you've got on is fine. I feel bad, though. I should've told you. Did you bring a long-sleeve shirt with a collar? No? Not a big deal. What you've got on is great."

"I'm brimming with confidence."

"I'm glad you're going to meet them, but I feel like I should be apologizing for them already. I'm afraid of what you're going to think." Story picked up a fallen strand of Spanish moss and returned it carefully to a live oak's branch that reached almost to the ground.

"It's fine," I said. "People are who they are."

It grew dark quickly and we walked back to the carriage house to get ready for dinner. Story raised all the windows to let in the night sounds and the warm, murmuring air. I felt alive. I noticed everything. I heard every sound. I was drinking it all in. Buller noticed we were preparing to leave and went to stand by the door. I asked if we could take him to dinner with us, but Story made a wrinkly face and said, "They're all dressed up. Let's introduce him tomorrow under more casual circumstances." So I got him his teddy bear out of the back of the Scout and poured him rations of food and water into the same size bowls that elephants eat out of at the zoo.

"Buller, you have to stay here, buddy," I said. "I'll be right back." He looked wounded and a little anxious.

"Your daddy's not going to be gone long," said Story, squatting in front of him and scratching him ferociously behind the ears. "I promise I'll bring him back in a little bit." She let him lick her neck a couple of good times and that seemed to make him feel better. I put on a slightly crisper shirt and we departed for our late dinner.

"What are their names again?"

"Morgan and Piper."

"That's right! Which one's your dad?"

Story laughed and pretended to take an arrow in the sternum. "Aww. You're probably better off calling him Mr. Glauchnor. Nobody really calls him Morgan except their preacher."

I rehearsed my greeting. "Hello, Morgan," I said, shaking hands with no one. "It's nice to meet you, sir. Piper, you look quite dashing for a woman of your age."

"This is going to go well."

Drinks in hand, the Glauchnors had the appearance of lounging comfortably on their square acre of back porch when we arrived. Mr. Glauchnor rose to greet us with practiced indolence and Mrs. Glauchnor put out a cigarette on an unseen ashtray behind her so we could pretend we hadn't seen her smoking. Coming over to meet us, Mr. Glauchnor said, "Good evening, son." Seeing him in person almost took my breath away. Thinking the light was playing tricks on me, my first impression was that Story could not have resembled him more if she had been his sister. Was I the first person to have noticed this? Surely not. Was I imagining it? The trouble it stirred within me clouded my thoughts for the rest of the evening.

Mr. Glauchnor withdrew his hand from mine and gave Story a sideways hug and two quick informal pats on the back. We all turned our attention to Mrs. Glauchnor, who was sitting primly sidesaddle on the outdoor sofa. When all eyes were on her, she elevated from her wicker throne like a queen and floated there a moment to allow time for our admiration to adhere. I overcame a strong impulse to bow and avert my eyes. She was a lovely peacock of a woman who, upon closer inspection, may have had the benefit of an occasional elective surgical procedure. She had a sharp nose and a sharp chin, and her breasts sat just below her shoulders on either side and about a foot apart, partially obscured by a cord of long brown hair brought stylishly forward to the front.

"It's a pleasure to meet you," I said, and she said, "Thank you."

"It's time to eat," said Mr. Glauchnor, getting right to it. "I suggest we go on in and sit down. They're keeping it warm for us, but it won't hold all night. Piper, make me a drink while you're at it."

Mrs. Glauchnor ruffled up like an ostrich, obviously horrified that he'd brought such an unceremonious end to her carefully cultivated illusion of southern royalty so soon.

We shuffled one after the other into the house where two men were standing in a tight line waiting for instructions. Both of them wore starched double-breasted chef's coats and Byzantine-era papal hats that must have cost a fortune. The house smelled of baking bread, grilled meat, and furniture polish. I lingered there a moment taking in the splendor and the array of unimpeachable decorations before Mrs. Glauchnor shooed me out of the kitchen. I wandered into the darkened dining room, where curtains had been hung in all the corners and a sweeping cyclorama depicting the Battle of Chancellorsville covered an entire wall. Story and Mr. Glauchnor were waiting in silence, each appearing to examine something on the floor. My eyes moved back and forth between them, comparing features. *You're an idiot,* I told myself. *Drop it.*

The table had been set around a faux live-oak epergne that rose a full ten feet off the table. Tea lights sat among the branches. Matching plates of pristine white butter sat at either end and bottles of red wine had been opened and were sitting on linen doilies. Next to where Mrs. Glauchnor would eventually settle, a bottle of Viognier was chilling in a damascened champagne bucket.

Every surface appeared to have been newly painted. Silk runners in parallel extended the full length of the table and dropped well off the ends. Under the table a large brown dog lay panting. Mr. Glauchnor barked at the dog and rattled at a chair. "Jim! Move, boy!" The dog did not move, so Mr. Glauchnor kicked at it. The dog sprang to his feet and skulked quickly out of the room with his tail tucked between his legs. I bent down to pet him, but he ran right past me.

"You know why we call him Jim?" Mr. Glauchnor asked me. I didn't know and wish I hadn't learned. The explanation had its distasteful roots in an old southern prejudice, and Mr. Glauchnor supplied a racial epithet to go with it. His joke delivered, he bellowed an unsophisticated laugh that echoed uncomfortably amid the high-society decor. Mrs. Glauchnor offered a halfhearted apology with a cultured smile and a dismissive wave of her hand. *Boys will be boys.* She'd heard that one before but apparently did not find it sufficiently inappropriate to warrant a reprimand. I saw Story's ears turn red. Sotto voce, she said, "I told you."

Mr. Glauchnor was more than six feet tall and had short blondish hair that was shot through with gray. He looked like a recently retired Joe Namath, if Joe Namath had employed a reputable barber. I reckoned his weight at or near two hundred and fifty pounds. He had the build of a record-setting high-school athlete who had done nothing requiring a modicum of physical exertion since then. Without much effort, I deduced that he was a spoiled brat of a man whose human worth lay in inherited money alone.

That Mrs. Glauchnor tolerated him all those years signaled to me that money ranked higher in her world order than love.

We sat down to eat and the kitchen help started around with the plates of food. There was enough to have fed twenty people with leftovers. I noticed that Story and Mr. Glauchnor handled their forks the same way and chewed the same way, and even had a way of manipulating one eyebrow independent of the other that was the same. But of course these things could be explained as learned behaviors rather than genetic ones.

"Do y'all want to take the boat out tomorrow?" Mr. Glauchnor did not bother to swallow his food before injecting his thoughts into conversation. He was also not restrained by a fear of interrupting a conversation thread already in progress. He just erupted into speech whenever a thought wandered into his mind. "Y'all can water-ski if you want."

"That'd be fun," I said. "I think we may be headed to the beach in the morning, but maybe tomorrow afternoon would work." Story nodded in approval and I asked Mr. Glauchnor if he water-skied.

"Hell, no, I don't water-ski." He finished his drink in a gulp — two fingers of gin — and tapped his wine glass with a long fingernail. Dutifully, elegantly, Mrs. Glauchnor rose to her feet and filled his glass with a tall pour. I asked Story if she was going to drive the boat while I skied. This was met with a chortling, choking response from Mr. Glauchnor.

"No, she can't drive the boat. If y'all go out, either I'll drive or Bucko'll drive." Bucko was the nickname given to Story's younger brother, whose real name mirrored Mr. Glauchnor's, of course. I wondered why he was allowed to drive the boat when she wasn't. Bucko, I was told, couldn't make dinner because he was out riding his four-wheeler somewhere.

"I can drive the boat," said Story.

"Not *my* boat. Did you see the new car in the driveway?" he asked.

"I saw it," I said. "BMW. Very nice."

"Yep. Damn nice. I needed a toy to replace my Harley. I sold that because it just took up room in the garage and I hardly ever had it out the entire time I owned it."

The conversation took a lull and Mrs. Glauchnor passed around the tray of biscuits and a canoe of butter. She wanted to make sure nobody left hungry. There was no likelihood of that.

The wine was expensive but terrible. I tried the red wine first, then the white wine.

After my second glass of the white, I asked for a beer and was given a white-napkin-clothed Bud Light in a can by one of the master chefs. Fancy.

Out of nowhere, Mr. Glauchnor shouted, "Did Story tell you she used to date a black boy?"

Story's silverware hit her plate.

"She did tell me," I said. "In fact, I've met him. He's a great guy. I have a lot of admiration for him." I had not, in fact, met him, although it was true that I had a lot of admiration for him. I felt like anyone who Story cared about was undoubtedly a good person and someone worth admiring. This produced a confused, snarled expression from Mr. Glauchnor, as if I'd committed an incomprehensible breach of etiquette.

"Well, all right." He said this to Mrs. Glauchnor as if to say, We now know where the boy stands on this issue. Better leave that subject alone in his company. I knew I had lost standing, in his estimation.

Mrs. Glauchnor dabbed at the corners of her mouth and readied herself for conversation. "Have you been down to our part of the state before?" She had wonderful manners.

"Yes, ma'am. I've spent a lot of time in Charleston over the years, but I hadn't knowingly been to this part of the state until Story and I came down a few weeks ago just for the day." I noticed a short, quick turn of Story's head in my direction and deduced that our trip had not been disclosed to her parents.

Mr. Glauchnor intervened. "When was that, exactly?" He appeared positively affronted. "When were y'all down here last month? What were y'all doin'? Oh, let me guess. Why didn't you come by here? Don't answer that. I know why you didn't come by here."

Story's hands placated the air in front of her. "We came down because I wanted to check on something at the courthouse — we didn't have a lot of time —"

"Of course that's what it was. Well, God damn it." A thicket of veins came out of Mr. Glauchnor's neck and forehead. He held his utensils — a fork in one hand, a knife in the other — like weaponry at the ready. "I guess you're never goin' to let that go, are you? I was hopin' that after your" — here he withstood the temptation to add a pejorative — "mother died, you'd a put all that nonsense to rest."

Story said no words to her father, but her eyes said *You are an unmitigated son of a bitch.* She stood and excused herself from the table. Mrs. Glauchnor apologized, half curtsied, and glided noiselessly out of the room, pursuing the daughter she didn't have.

40

Mr. Glauchnor and I sat in silence for some time as he knotted his fat hands and drank more wine and I identified all possible points of exit.

"How're your folks?"

"Not too well, to be honest."

"Where are you from again?"

"I grew up in the mountains of North Carolina," I said. "Old Buckram."

"Oh, hell yes. I've been through there a thousand times. Piper and I like to go up to Blowing Rock to buy furniture and knick-knacks and shit for her store. We always take a trailer with us so we can bring stuff back if she finds anything. This table might even be from up there." He bent over to examine the underside, as if he might find a bill of sale still affixed. "Piper has a booth at an antique shop. That's how she makes money." This remark was punctuated by his gurgling laugh. "Last year it made us, I don't know, *negative* twenty-five thousand dollars. It probably saved my life, though — so anyway, we go up there and buy antiques and ride around on the parkway looking for wild turkey and deer, but I never have a gun with me when I need it. One time I saw a black bear and her cubs running right across the road — she was probably about three-fifty, four hundred pounds — and I would have given anything to have had my hunting rifle. I'd have shot her from the car. I've got a modified Ruger with a Mauser extractor that'll absolutely blow the head and antlers off a deer. I've never had occasion to shoot a bear, though, although I hope one day I get lucky."

I wanted to say "What the fuck is wrong with you," but I kept my mouth shut. He downed another glass of red wine and unskillfully poured another. When he began to speak again, I noticed a gobbet of food — maybe a piece of shrimp — flat on the surface of his upper-right lateral incisor that really began to bother me.

"A few times," he said, "we've taken the parkway from Blowing Rock and we get off at Chilblain's Gap and go into Old Buckram to look around. Piper likes that one homestyle restaurant there. What's that place called?"

It was offensive to me to hear him talk about the parkway and the area around my hometown in such familiar and grotesque terms. Come to think of it, it was just offensive for me to hear him talk.

"The Hopedale Inn," I said.

"That's it. I took my Harley up there one time and I had a hell of a fun time driving up 321 on all those roads, back and forth, but it rained for two solid days and I couldn't get back because I didn't have any rain gear."

I nodded but could think of nothing relevant to say in response.

He said, "Do you want another beer? I'll get you one."

I said, "What the hell."

"Piper! Bring this boy another beer." The kitchen was empty; Mrs. Glauchnor must have sent the chefs home for the evening, or to their quarters, or wherever they stayed when they weren't cooking for Mr. and Mrs. G. I began to feel terrible for Story.

"Jumping back to what y'all were doing down here before — is she trying to get you in the middle of all that?" He stirred an imaginary pot with his finger. "You wouldn't be the first."

I didn't know what the hell that meant, so I ignored it and said, "She's not getting me in the middle of it. She really hasn't said too much to me about it, and she hasn't asked for my help. I get the impression that she's going to do what she's going to do whether I'm involved or not. I don't think I have any power of influence over her in that regard. Perhaps you don't either."

This pissed him off, and I thought he was going to come across the table at me. Getting himself under control, he said, "Well, I can tell you right now, y'all are wasting your damn time."

I began to wonder why he was so openly hostile in regard to Story's quest to find her biological father. After my few glasses of wine, and notwithstanding the paltry half-ounce of alcohol contributed by the Anheuser-Busch product, this played right into my unsettling and increasingly paranoid conspiracy theory in which Mr. Glauchnor was somehow Story's real father. *He doesn't want her to find out precisely because he is her real father,* I thought — and then just as quickly I pushed this out of my mind as pure lunacy. Why the hell wouldn't he tell her if he was her real father? It doesn't even make sense. I remembered my father saying it was better to remain silent and be thought a fool than to speak up and confirm it. This seemed like good advice. I thought about it critically and surmised that Mr. Glauchnor must have known something unsavory about the whole affair that he didn't want Story to know. Maybe he was just trying to protect her. Maybe her real father was in federal prison on racketeering and bribery charges. Maybe he was in state prison for murder or some other more heinous crime. That the Glauchnors were simply protecting Story from something unseemly was the simplest explanation, I decided.

Story and Mrs. Glauchnor reentered the room, a negotiated peace having been won, and sat down at the table. Story was still mildly furious and Mrs. Glauchnor was fawningly obsequious, as I'd come to expect her to be. She offered up a stream of refined and therefore meaningless apologies until Mr. Glauchnor interrupted her with an impatient wave of his hand.

"Piper — did you get him a beer?"

"I sure didn't. I'm so sorry." She sprang silently into action and, from what I could tell by listening, retrieved another Bud Light from the crisper in the bottom of the refrigerator, this one sans the delightful little napkin.

"Thank you."

"You are very welcome. I didn't open it

for you because my nails —"

"That's fine," I said. "I can get it."

After dinner, Story and I escaped and walked down to the water, where we sat with our feet hanging off the end of the dock. Next to the dock was a two-story boathouse, where a crimson and beige Mastercraft and two glinting Jet Skis were fastidiously secured and suspended by steel cables above the water. A sunburst kayak lay face-down at the end of the pier, tethered with nautical rope. Across a broad expanse of the lake looking west, a row of lonely houses marked the horizon. The warm light from the many broad windows lay restless upon the water as it flowed and retreated and flowed again into the pungent marshes.

"I could live here," I said. "It's stunning."

"Is it? I don't think I can see it anymore. I may be spoiled beyond redemption."

"No," I said, "I understand. It's the same way with me in Old Buckram. I know the mountains are beautiful. Sometimes when I walk outside in the morning, there's an ocean of mist down in the valley. And I'm up there on the hill above it, looking down like some kind of deity. And then the sun comes over the Morning Mountain and it reflects off all that infinite white and suddenly the whole sky is too bright to look at. I know it's glorious beyond compare, but because of . . . things I associate with my childhood . . . it's hard for me to see the true beauty of it anymore. Does that make sense?"

Story looked around to see things with a fresh perspective and cogitated on what she saw. "I want to see it. Maybe in a couple of weeks I'll drive up?"

"I'd really like that."

She leaned over to look down into the black water and I rubbed the small of her back.

"What did she say to you when you walked out of the dining room?"

"She said 'Elizabeth, honey, let's not make a bad first impression.' "

"Nice."

"She's lovely."

"I'm sorry about what happened in there," I said. "I didn't think about it. I should have realized not to say anything —"

"It's not your fault. They've fought me tooth and nail on this for as long as I can remember. I think it just stems from them wanting me to accept them as my parents, which if I'm honest with myself I haven't been willing to do, partly because I feel like we're just so completely different in every material respect. But I know they feel a sense of rejection when I talk about my biological parents, like they're somehow not enough for me. Like I'm going to find my real dad and leave here and never come back. They always say, 'Are we not enough? Are we not enough?' "

We walked back to the carriage house through a sculpture garden that Mrs. Glauchnor had set up on the east side of the house. The "exhibits," which she insisted they be called, consisted of mostly yard-sale junk set absurdly on short marble podiums. We first encountered a rusted ship anchor, and then a weathered bust of Triton with strands of facsimile seaweed draped dramatically around its shoulders. Then there was another anchor, this one smaller, looking curiously like at one time it belonged to a pontoon boat. The next piece was a concrete statue of a grazing deer (this one got two podiums — one for each set of legs) and so on. The exhibits were connected by a stone pathway that ran through a maze of ragged boxwoods, all obliquely lit by small lights placed at the foot of each showpiece. Story and I walked through holding hands and admired the art as seriously as we could.

"I'm surprised your dad hasn't shot that

deer already."

"Please don't say that to anyone."

After letting Buller out to run around, we opened more beer and lit candles and sat on the floor like children in a hideout and talked about Story's search for her father and all that had happened since she first learned of her adoption. She talked about going to see Lelia, and how Lelia had called her Maggie and likened her to a magpie, and how she'd found the picture of Benjamin, and how Mr. Glauchnor had gone with her to Lelia's funeral, which seemed like the one decent thing he'd done. She said, "The days are bright, but the nights are empty," and I thought of Threnody and wished she were there with us. I knew Story would make her feel at home.

With the candles still burning, Story took me into the bedroom with all her notebooks and newspapers and walked me through her earliest research to the present, starting with the original birth certificate that was issued by the health department preceding her adoption by the Glauchnors. This document she kept inside a laminate cover in a box of important things. It appeared to be the original. On the lines above the section titled "If family Bible is used as proof," the certificate listed Lelia's name as the mother

— in Lelia's own hand — but very clearly the father's name had been obliterated. It had first been marked out with what appeared to be a ballpoint pen and then covered with a thick black marker. Story said it also used to have white correction fluid on it as a third layer, but she scratched that off only to find the more permanent attempt to remove the father's name underneath. I asked how she got the original and she said she'd stolen it. I held it up to the light but could make out nothing. Story said she'd done everything but x-ray it, with similar results.

With me at her desk, she paced the room and interjected disconnected thoughts into the narrative as I went through page after page of the meticulously collected notes. After two hours of reading and squinting at photographs old and new, I just ached in my soul for Story, but I saw nothing even remotely compelling that seemed to warrant further investigation. Story was right; it was all a dead end. There were no answers to be had.

The last notebook I came to was the first one Story had started when she began looking for her father. It contained excerpts from dozens of interviews she had conducted with people on the peninsula who went to Versirecto Methodist Church and knew Lelia and had some reason to know about the circumstances surrounding Story's conception. Story told me of its contents and suggested my time would be better spent elsewhere, but I read through it anyway looking for a clue she might have missed. Again, she was right. Everyone she had talked to, probably twenty-five different people, mostly women, could recount with remarkable clarity that Lelia lived in the little white house on the church property and that her mother was an alcoholic and didn't treat her particularly well, and that when Lelia was just a girl of fourteen or fifteen she became pregnant — this was quite a scandal on the peninsula, I gathered — and that the Glauchnors, having been recently married, were kind enough to adopt Lelia's little girl. Yet bewilderingly it seemed they were unable to provide any details at all about who the mysterious father was.

By the time I finished, Story had gotten dressed for bed and she and Buller had fallen asleep together on the couch. She was at one end and he was at the other with his enormous head resting on her feet. I sat down in a chair next to her and stared at the ceiling. Sitting there and going through it all in my mind, I decided that the people on the peninsula knew. They had to know. They just weren't telling. Two ladies Story talked to remembered the names of Lelia's mother's cats, for god's sake. One lady recalled that when Lelia went to the hospital to have the baby, she came outside wearing "a little blue dress covered in white flowers with the sweetest little rickrack around the arms." Another lady, who took the family meals on behalf of the church, was able to recount the contents of Lelia's bedroom with astonishing, heartbreaking clarity ("a white dresser with pink drawer pulls in the shape of a bow," "one empty picture frame that looked like it'd been given as a gift but never filled," "a wooden jewelry box with nothing in it," "a Raggedy Ann on the bed"). It was impossible for me to believe that these ladies, all of them regular Miss Marples in their own right, had no true idea of the identity of the father. I then realized with a jolt what was even more impossible to believe: That they refused to even *speculate* about who the father might have been. This, I knew, was in complete defiance of the laws of human nature. People love to gossip. They can't help it. People will offer conjecture all day long about things they don't have the first idea about. But not one person Story had talked to cared to venture a guess about a putative father. This could only mean one thing: They *knew* who the father was.

So who was it? Why wouldn't they tell? Was it a political figure? The president? The governor of South Carolina? Castro? I had two thoughts. The first was that if the people on the peninsula knew who Story's father was, Story's parents also knew, because they'd know before anyone else did. There was no way that they would have gone through the whole adoption process without making an inquiry and satisfying themselves as to the father of the child. If they'd done this and were not able to discover his identity, surely they would have told this to Story already. It would've been an easy defense. They could've been quite honest with her and told her they didn't know and would likely never know given the time that had passed. But this is not what they said.

The second was that there must have been something extraordinary that had occurred to close all those mouths in such solemn and unyielding secrecy.

Story sensed me sitting next to her and reached out to take my hand.

"Aren't my new pj's soft?"

"They sure are."

"I feel bad that you've spent your entire

time here reading all that stuff. Am I just crazy? Would you tell me?"

With purposeful delicacy, I attempted to articulate what I'd deduced, but it came out all in a shambles. Story grew increasingly agitated as I talked. First she sat up. Then she stood, blew out the candles, and turned on the overhead light.

"You really think my parents know?"

"Yes, I think they must."

"Then why wouldn't they have told me?!"

"Have you asked them?"

"Of course I have!" She went into the bedroom and half a minute later came out dressed. She pulled her tennis shoes on without untying them.

"What are you going to do?"

"I'm just going to see if my dad's still up."

"It's one o'clock in the morning." I felt like I was in water over my head; like a critical mass had been achieved and could no longer be impeded. I suggested it would be better to wait until the next morning, but she was already out the door. The haste with which she departed prompted me to follow after her. Halfway to the main house she began to jog, and then in a few steps the jog became a run. I ran through the yard behind her. When I got there and ascended the steps of the porch, Story had already gone inside. I went in and waited in the darkened foyer, figuring I'd give it a minute just in case Mr. Glauchnor was asleep and Story came right back down.

For a long while I heard nothing and thought I should walk back to the carriage house and wait for Story there. The first sign of movement was poor Jim thumping down the stairs. After growling and then barking at me, he realized we'd met before and this caused him great, happy excitement. He jumped and trotted a little unevenly on his old hips over to where I was sitting to say hello, his tail thwacking all the furniture between the two of us and wagging his entire body. He and I sat there talking about how I was going to introduce him to Buller, which he seemed amenable to, while upstairs all was quiet and I began to feel like an ass for inciting such foolishness. I said good night to Jim and stood to leave and then heard a dull, unnerving, repeating sound coming through the floor. Cracking, splitting, god knows what, it grew louder and sounded every bit like a bloody murder when an explosion of noise came from overhead and broken glass rained down from above. I jumped entirely out of my skin and Jim tucked tail to run out of the room, presumably to flee the Armageddon underway

above us, but he made right for the mine-
field of glass that now covered the floor and
I had to collar him and carry him fighting
like a caught marlin into Mr. Glauchnor's
office to keep him from ruining his old
brown paws.

As I was closing the door behind me, Mr.
Glauchnor stomped irritably, deliberately
down the stairs (no doubt thinking *These
are my fucking stairs, by god, that was my
fucking crystal vase*), crushing fragments underfoot and grinding glass into the wood
with every step. Close on his heels was Mrs.
Glauchnor, who more or less tiptoed
through the debris, proudly trembling like a
reed. He moved by me like a locomotive in
the dark and went straight to the bar in the
corner of the living room to pour himself
another drink. Mrs. Glauchnor caught my
astonished eye and said, "It's awful, isn't
it?" All pretense was gone.

A moment later Story walked calmly down
the steps as if nothing unusual had happened. She paused once to inspect the ceiling and then ran her finger along the top of
a portrait to test for dust. Here and there
she knelt down to pick up and inspect the
larger shards of glass as if they were sea-
shells washed up on the beach. To me, she
said, "Will you help me, please," and not

knowing what else to do, I began collecting the multiplying fragments as well as I could in the dimly lit room. When we had barely a handful between us, a fraction of what would be found in the hidden corners of that house for years to come, Story said, "I think that's enough," and took mine into her cupped hands. She then went to where Mr. Glauchnor was standing and deposited the contents delicately onto the bar.

She said, "I'm going to leave now. Here's a keepsake for you to remember me by. You can think of it as a metaphor for my life, and my mother's life, and I'm happy to say all those days are gone now. Still — keep it. You can think of me every time you break something in anger."

Story walked away and I know she had every intention of leaving, never to return. Meanwhile, behind her a volcanic rage was rising in Mr. Glauchnor. He swept his hand savagely across the counter, spraying the gift of broken glass impotently into the room. He drew back his hand at once and examined with confusion the spurs and splinters embedded deep within the tissue of his palm. Then he said, "Fuck it," and let the blood drip onto his pants and onto the floor. As a parting shot to Story, he said, "Good luck."

She said, "Thanks."

He said, "Come back when you know who your parents are."

My ears began to ring in the horrible silence that followed. I had never heard anyone utter a single syllable as cruel as this; a sentence so designed to hurt another human being.

She turned to face him. "I do know one thing," she said.

"What's that?"

"I know that no matter who my father turns out to be, it's certainly not going to be you."

She caught my hand on the way out. Mr. Glauchnor charged after us, yelling incoherently. As Story pulled open the door to leave, Mr. Glauchnor slammed it shut. She pulled it open again against the weight of his hand. To her back, he spewed, "So you're leaving? Fine! Fucking leave. What you've obviously forgotten is that I'm the one who took care of you, you ungrateful little shit. I was the one who fed you. I was the one who changed your shitty little diapers. Who do you think did all that? That was *me*! I fed you and washed you —"

Something in the tone of his fracturing voice caused Story's head to swing around. "What do you mean?" she said, closing in on him. "Where was *she*? What do you mean you were the one?"

He backpedaled and she followed him into the next room, looking at him out of the corner of her eye.

"Tell me what you meant by that."

"Leave me alone."

"Tell me. Where was she? Did you mean to say that *she* didn't help you raise me?"

Had he issued a general denial, she might have written it off as a simple misunderstanding of linguistic nuance. Instead, he cowered and retreated. The time came that Story had had enough. She screamed, "Will somebody tell me what the fuck is going on?!"

Piper said, "God damn it, Morgan. Just tell her. Tell her and get it over with. She's going to find out."

"Shut up, Piper."

"Tell me what?"

"Morgan, you have to —"

"I don't have to do anything."

To her father, Story said, "It's time. Don't you think it's time?"

"No," he said in a voice without anger, a voice quite matter-of-fact. "I don't think it's time. We've had this same conversation nine million times. You know how we feel. Please, for God's sake, just let this be." He was pleading with her now. His face was sallow; his head was hanging between his shoulders like a beaten dog's. He had the waning look of a man on the ropes — a look that said, "Please don't make me do this."

"Tell me," said Story. "Tell me whatever it is —"

Mrs. Glauchnor stumbled forward and reached for Story. She was drunk and Story took her mother into her arms and held her like a child. "Tell me," she said again to her father. "Do you want to make me find out on my own? Because you know I will. One day I'll figure it out, with or without your help. I won't leave. I just want to know. It's part of who I am."

Mr. Glauchnor paced his corner of the room, clenching and unclenching his teeth. Thick undulations ran along his jawline up to his temple and spread across his purpling forehead. He winced painfully, then howled at the ceiling. "What do you want from me? What do you want from us?"

Story discarded her mother and crossed the room toward him. "Tell me who my father is."

"*I'm* your —"

"I'm talking about my *biological* father! The one whose genes I carry. The one whose eyesight I inherited. The one whose potential for congenital diseases I may pass on to my children. The one —"

"You want to know?"

"Yes, I want to know. I deserve to know."

"But you *don't* want to know."

I thought, *Oh my god — this is it. He's going to tell her something that she's never going to recover from as long as she lives.* I think this occurred to her, too. For the first time, I saw a flicker of uncertainty in her eyes. Then —

"I want to know. Tell me."

Mr. Glauchnor looked long and hard at Mrs. Glauchnor, who buried her face in her hands. I thought, *Oh dear god.* He paced; he scowled. He set his drink down and then picked it up again. He started half a dozen sentences, but nothing came out. Hiding behind his drink with a sneer like a caged animal, he said: "Your father —"

"Tell me," whispered Story. "Just say it."

"I'll tell you who your father was," said Mr. Glauchnor, losing all composure. "He was nobody! He was just some lowlife, some nobody — a dreg who lived out at the end of the peninsula. He was just some piece-of-shit human being who took advantage of your mother —"

"Morgan!" pleaded Mrs. Glauchnor. "Do not do that —"

"It's true. He took advantage of her. He raped her, and he left town."

"That's impossible," said Story, holding her stomach. "I don't believe a word of it. You're making it up." Her words were empty. Half whispered. Without conviction.

"I'm not making it up!" screamed Mr. Glauchnor in a wild panic. "He did! He took advantage of her. He raped her! That's what everybody knew happened. And the minute he found out she was pregnant, well — he didn't wait around for five fucking minutes. He's lucky he wasn't prosecuted . . ."

Story was utterly dumbstruck. I could see her thinking about it, assimilating this new information. Could it be true? Is this what she had been waiting to hear? Is this why no one would tell her? At last, she said, "I don't believe it. I don't. Why wouldn't she have told me?"

"You don't have to believe me," said Mr. Glauchnor.

My heart ached for all of them, but especially for Story. I couldn't believe this had happened. I ran back through everything in my mind: the birth certificate and all the effort that had gone into redacting the father's name. The vehement and unwavering way Mr. and Mrs. Glauchnor condemned Story's efforts to unravel the mystery. Mr. Glauchnor attending the funeral. Benjamin. The Citadel. The photographs. The remarkable fact that no one in the whole community, as insular and close-knit as it was, had any idea who the father was. Every word that was said and every word that had been written pointed only to one thing. And all at once it hit me.

I said, "What was his name?"

A horrible stillness fell on the room and the ringing returned to my ears.

"What was his name?" I asked again. "You must know his name."

Mr. Glauchnor's mouth moved, but no words came out. He looked to Mrs. Glauchnor, but she turned away. Story stared at me in disbelief and then looked at her father. The silence went on and on until I felt the house might fall in around us.

It wasn't that he couldn't think of the young man's name. If there had been such a man, he would have known the name. He would have known it and never forgotten it. The fact was that there was no such man.

41

Mr. Glauchnor began to mutter and curse. He spat on the floor and then spat again in disgust, or loathing, or hatred. He roared and came at me in a wild rage and the two of us went over backward onto the floor. Story screamed and pulled at his neck as he tried his dead-level best to beat me to death. "God damn you, God damn you, GOD DAMN YOU!" He outweighed me by a good seventy pounds and by the cords of muscle in his arms I deduced that he had not been entirely inactive in his maturity. I thought then that I was likely to die and all my thoughts ran to the past year's events and how I came to be there and whether I would have done anything differently if given the chance. I had just concluded that I wouldn't have when Mrs. Glauchnor fell down on the floor and tried drunkenly to insert herself between us.

"Morgan — you son of a bitch — you get

off him this very minute." Blood was coursing out of my nose into my mouth and running down the sides of my face. Mr. Glauchnor slowly rose and pulled me to my feet like he and I had just been two boys horsing around together. My nose had been badly repositioned.

Story looked back and forth between her parents: her father — stooped, red-knuckled, and disheveled; her mother — sitting on the floor in her nightgown, unable to right herself. No one said a single word. Mr. Glauchnor searched for words but there were none. Story hit him hard across the face, and then hit him again. He caught her arm, but she pulled free and pounded him on the chest.

"Story, stop it," said Mrs. Glauchnor, trying to stand. "I can explain."

"No," said Story. "There can't possibly be an explanation I would accept. I can't believe this is happening." To me, she said, "I'm so sorry." Then to her parents: "I never want to see either one of you again." She walked out of the house and slammed the hell out of the door. This time no one followed.

"Damn it," said Mr. Glauchnor. "God fucking damn it." My nose was still dripping blood and I caught it with my shirt.

"Piper, call the police."

"Why do we need to call the police?" I said.

"I should be charged with assault for beating the shit out of you."

"Forget that," I said. "I probably deserved it. How about just telling me how to get to the hospital."

"I'll take you," said Mr. Glauchnor. "It's looks like your nose may be broken."

"No shit. How can you tell? Because it's touching my ear?" I got dizzy and had to sit down. Mrs. Glauchnor went to retrieve medical supplies. Mr. Glauchnor had me lean my head back while he shoved a quarter-mile of gauze into my nose. The bleeding finally stopped and Mrs. Glauchnor brought forth an array of prescription narcotics and offered me a cocktail of painkillers that I refused. "I'll be back in a few minutes," I said. "I'm going to go check on Story."

With strips of gauze trailing behind my head like an unraveling turban, I walked back unsteadily to the carriage house beneath a deafening chorus of chirping tree frogs. Story was packing and crying into her suitcase and Buller was sitting on the bed like a Sphinx, watching her every move and looking very worried. Story ran to me and put her hands on my face.

"I can't believe this is happening." She backed away from me and stood turning in dizzying circles, trying to get a handle on what had just occurred. She had taken down some of the pictures. They were in a pile on the bed, as though she had thought at first to pack them and then decided not to. "So . . . *he's* my father? After all this, *he's* my father? Oh my god, that's not right. That can't be right. So he took care of me because my mother resented him? Resented me? They *all* resented me. They *all* knew, and they all resented me!"

"Story —"

"I can't stay here," she said. "I can't. I can't. I don't understand . . . I can't believe . . . I mean, what in the world . . ."

"Story, talk to me. Where are you going?"

"I don't know. I really don't know. I'm just — I'm leaving here and I'm not coming back. I'm so sorry this has happened. I don't know what to say. And you . . . I *cannot* believe you were just attacked by my insane father. Look at you. Your nose looks like it's broken really bad. Your shirt is ruined."

"It's just swollen," I said. "It's fine. I just need an ice pack."

"No, it's not. It's seriously broken really

badly. You need to go to the hospital. Please go. Do you understand that I have to leave? Are you going to be okay?"

"Let me come with you. You can't drive like this. I'll take you —"

"No. I just need to drive for a while . . . Please help me close this." I pushed down on her suitcase while she zipped it. She went into each room of the carriage house, looking for things she didn't want to forget, but left almost everything.

"Please don't leave," I said. "Let's talk about this."

"I can't believe this is happening. Am I dreaming?"

She heaved her suitcase off the bed and banged through the screen door out onto the porch.

"Let me come with you."

"I'll call you. Are you going to be okay?" I didn't answer and she drove away into the night.

It didn't take long for Buller and me to load up because we hadn't been there long enough to unpack. I sat in my car for a while to regain sobriety and perspective, and then drove down to the main house to say something appropriate, perhaps goodbye, which I hoped would come to me when the time came. Mr. Glauchnor was brooding in the dark on the back porch overlooking the water.

"Story's gone," I said. "I don't know where she's going. I don't feel like I should stay, so I'm going to head out. Thanks for the dinner. I'm sorry for all the trouble."

He asked me to sit and tried to hand me his tumbler of scotch. I waved it off, but he said, "Go ahead. I've got plenty. I'm drowning in it." I sat down and took a drink and my usual horizontal perspective on the world swam and went sideways and I thought I was going to fall out of the chair. He took me by the elbow and straightened me up and I surrendered the drink.

"I don't know how it ever got this far," he said. "There was a point at which we were going to tell her, but we didn't, and then we felt like we'd waited too long and it just went on like that and I should've known she'd figure it out eventually. I'm frankly amazed that her mother — not Piper, but her birth mother — didn't tell her when she went to see her two years ago." He got out a pack of Marlboro Lights from the drawer of an end table. "I don't smoke," he said.

"Fair enough."

"I don't."

"I believe you."

462

He lit a cigarette and offered me one.

"I don't smoke either," I said.

A minute later, a muted bang issued from upstairs, followed by another one. I stood in alarm, but Mr. Glauchnor said, "She's just slamming doors. She'll be here tomorrow. Sit down before you fall down."

I was happy to sit. Standing made my head throb and my eyes wouldn't stop watering. I could feel fabric down in the back of my throat.

"You're Story's real father."

"Yes, Sherlock, you figured it out. I'm Story's real dad. Her biological father, as she says. You've solved the big mystery. Congratulations. For more than twenty years no one has known that except for me, Piper, my mother — who, I will tell you, was sent to an early grave by all this — and Story's birth mother. Our kids don't even know. For years *nobody* knew and it was right under Story's nose and she never suspected a thing. It didn't have to be that she looked just like me. That was just God being cruel. And no one had any idea, and then here you come along."

I started to say "More people know than you think." I wanted to tell him that I thought the whole peninsula knew, but I dropped it because I didn't want to explain

463

my thinking, which at that time was a bit foggy to say the least. So instead I asked him about Benjamin.

"How in the hell do you know about that?"

"Lelia had a picture of him."

"Well, God damn. I guess you know more'n I think. Benjamin was Lelia's boyfriend at the time."

"I don't understand."

"Well, son, it ain't a pretty story."

I tried to fit all the pieces together, but it didn't make sense. He finished the rest of the scotch we had shared and poured another and finished that one in one swallow, and then poured another. "I've never told anyone this story, and I have no idea why I'm about to tell you. But I swear to God if you tell anybody what I'm about to tell you — I don't care if it's Story, Piper, anybody — I will fucking kill you with my own two hands. Do you hear me?"

Believing him without reservation, I nodded in assent.

"My mother, God rest her soul, had something like a plantation down here, except it wasn't a plantation. It just looked like one. Her daddy's family owned most of this county at one time. They had about twenty-five thousand acres — this was *years* ago, which, if you do the math, is about forty square miles of land — and over time they sold it off and made a shitload of money and my mother got some of that when her daddy died, so she had her a big ol' white plantation house with columns and gardenias and the whole bit. And she had about — I'd say ten or twelve or maybe fifteen people working there all the time, basically slaves, who cooked and cleaned and took care of the garden and wiped people's asses and whatnot. And she had these parties that everyone would come to, and one night in the summer she had a party to celebrate my one-year anniversary of being married to Piper. At that time I thought I was king of the God damn world. I was handsome and I had a big dick and I had every single thing I could ask for, and I had a gorgeous wife, and honestly I could have had any girl I wanted, and I'd been the quarterback on the football team, so really it just couldn't have been any better. And Ben, who was a friend of mine — we went to high school together — he showed up at the party with some new girl who was *a lot* younger. She was like fourteen or fifteen and not from a good family, so he wasn't exactly proud of bringing her into the house 'cause that would've been frowned upon, but God al-

465

mighty she was a beautiful girl and he was in love with her."

"That was Story's real mom?"

"Yes, Lelia was Story's birth mother." He looked around to make sure we were alone. "And let me tell you, she was like a God damn painting, I swear to Jesus. She was really something. I don't think I've ever seen a prettier girl to this day. She had big, soft tits out to here and an ass like a ten-year-old boy. Your dick got hard just looking at her. So everybody was outside walking around drinking and it was dark and I'd had too much 'cause that's what I do and Ben did, too, and he was off somewhere and I took Leely on a walk down to the lake."

Mr. Glauchnor sat for some time thinking while his cigarette burned itself out in the ashtray. I think he was going back through it in his mind; making sure his memory of it matched the reality he knew to exist.

"And you know what happened next," he said.

"I don't."

"She claimed — *she* claimed — I took advantage of her." He didn't look at me when he said this. It was hardly the protestation of an innocent man. He knew the lie all too well but no longer believed it.

"Did she go to the police?"

"I guess she might have, but my mother intervened and money changed hands just to keep the whole thing quiet. Ben left town — he was pissed as shit at me. I mean, he was furious. He should have just come to me and kicked my ass. Instead, he went by our house and told Piper."

"Holy hell."

"I hated him for that. I still hate him for it."

"So Lelia — what were you calling her? Leely?"

Mr. Glauchnor nodded.

"Leely was pregnant and you were — holy shit, you were married. Then what? You and Piper agreed to adopt the baby? Was Leely not going to keep the baby?"

"Nobody wanted the baby. The thing in my life I'm the least proud of — and there's been plenty not to be proud of — but the one thing I've done in my life I'm the *least* proud of is that one night real late I went to see Leely. This is probably two months after she got pregnant, and she snuck outside and we talked about what she was going to do and what I was going to do and — dear god — she wanted me to hit her in the stomach so she'd lose the baby."

"And you did it."

"Yes, I did it. Over and over again until

she cried. But she wanted me to."

"But obviously she had the baby."

"Obviously."

"What happened to Ben?"

"As I said, he left town. Some people were saying that the baby might've been his and who knows, maybe it could've been, but he didn't want anything to do with it. So he joined the army and two months into training he was in the barracks and shot himself in the face with a rifle. Accidentally, I'm sure."

"Jesus Christ."

"So to make a long story short, the baby was coming and we had the choice of having my whole family living in the same God damn town — in our town, the town we basically *owned* at one time — we could all live in the same town as my bastard child and watch it be raised by that poor white-trash girl, or we could adopt it, so to speak, and put a lid on the whole damn thing, which is exactly what we did."

42

After Buller and I returned to Old Buckram, Story called me to say she was staying with BethAnn in Chapel Hill for a few days and that everything was fine. I tried talking to her about what had happened, but she changed the subject. She was distant and cut our conversation short and hung up without saying goodbye. The last thing she said to me was, "I'll call you soon, I promise." I took this to mean that she needed space, and I tried to give it to her. On Wednesday afternoon she called and said, "I have something I have to tell you," which, depending on the context, are words almost no one wants to hear. After leaving Lot's Folly, she had gone to Charlotte to see her ex-boyfriend. He had lived through so much of the turmoil with her parents and she felt like he was the one person in the world who would truly understand. She had stayed there with him on Friday night and then gone on to Chapel Hill the next morning. I felt the floor give way under my feet. She told me it meant nothing at all, but that she wanted to be honest with me.

"I need to think about this," I said. "Maybe I'll call you sometime this weekend."

"Listen to me — Nothing happened, I swear to you. I slept on the couch. Being there felt all wrong and I thought about you the whole time."

The point, of course, was not whether she slept on the couch — although that made me feel a little bit better — but that she had gone there at all. She wasn't over him and it was way too early for her to be getting serious with me.

"I need to think about it," I said, still reeling from her revelation.

"What's your address?"

"You're not coming here," I said.

"I know. In case I need to send you a letter."

"Please don't send me anything."

"Just give me your address."

"I'll call you later," I said, and hung up the phone. I'd been sweeping the kitchen floor and I took the broom handle and smashed it into pieces over a wooden column, destroying the column in the process.

I yelled and cursed and slammed around until I felt like I might kick a hole in the piano and then I knew it was time to stop. As a lesser violence, I took the few pictures I had of Story and pitched them in the trash, only to retrieve them a few minutes later. I became wretched with grief to find that one of them had been ruined by my childish tantrum.

I wanted to talk to Threnody. When I called her, Mother answered the phone, so I hung up like a damn adolescent. I called back a few minutes later and they both answered, so I didn't say anything. Threnody said, "I've got it," and Mother hung up, and I said, "Hey, Bird."

She said, "I thought it might be you."

"Bird," I said, "I'm having kind of a hard time here."

"What's wrong?" This was said without detectable sympathy.

I told her an abridged version of the Story saga, but she didn't seem to care. We got off the phone in awkward silence and I proceeded to get wasted on wine and vodka and passed out on the floor next to Buller. I woke up with a nosebleed, a pounding headache, an out-of-whack TMJ, and a rug mark on my face that wouldn't go away. I'd forgotten to let Buller outside, and he had peed in the corner of the room and was so afraid I was going to be mad at him about it, which obviously I wasn't. I hadn't been to work all week because I was afraid to show Charlie my two black eyes, but he had given me a research project on equitable subrogation the previous week and needed it for court, so on Thursday morning I dragged myself off the floor and drove to the office. I made it through one entire court of appeals opinion before throwing up. I avoided Charlie all day so he wouldn't see me in my deplorable state, but he got word through Sylvia and caught up with me after lunch. The sight of me made him laugh out loud.

"What in the world happened to you? Did you step on a rake?"

I told him it was a silly accident. He said, "What's her name?"

When I got home from work that evening and opened the door, the phone was ringing, but I didn't answer it. A few minutes later it rang again. The third time it rang, I answered. It was Story.

"Are you there?"

I said nothing in response. It took restraint not to slam the phone down or smash it repeatedly against the wall. I held the receiver in my lap and considered the implications of just hanging up, then put it back up to my ear.

"Look," she said, "please talk to me. It doesn't matter what you say."

"I don't think you'd want to hear it."

I heard her sigh. She let a long silence pass before saying, "Are you going to be there for a few hours?"

"Why?"

"Because I'm on my way up."

"On your way up to where?" I said.

"To Old Buckram."

"Listen — seriously. I don't want you to come."

"Well, I'm coming. I'm on the way. I'm at some sketchy convenience store on 421 and there's a man with T.-rex arms and no teeth who tried to pump my gas, but he doesn't work here. Now can I have your address? If not, I'll just drive around until I see your car."

She arrived late and couldn't conceal her mortification at the vulture house. I had turned on every working interior and exterior light to make it look as inviting as possible, but Story nevertheless experienced a certain psychic trauma from the ghastly decay of the old mansion. I'd warned her all I could, but it did nothing to blunt the effect.

She came in through the medieval front door and marveled at the vast spaces and tiled hallways disappearing into the meandering depths of the house. I gave her a tour to bring light to the shadows and show her that no monsters were hiding inside. We climbed the spiral staircase to the library and then went up again to the third floor, where we looked out over the courtyard to the town beyond. There was no moon and the stars were visible over the Morning Mountain in the gloom. A silver cobweb decorated the old bronze telescope — an heirloom tiller on a long-abandoned ship.

"What do you think?" I said. "Faintly macabre, yes?"

She said, "It's haunted."

I showed her to the alcove with the oddly canted ceiling, formerly the neighborhood destination for animal sacrifices. The goat's head and pentagram had since received a single coat of paint, but the images were still visible, as if they had been burned into the wall with a torch. I said, "Here's where you'll be sleeping."

She said, "Like hell I am."

"Well, then I don't know what to tell you."

"How about I just sleep on the floor in your room? No offense, but this house scares me to death. I can't believe you're staying here all by yourself."

"I grew up here, so most of the demons have vanished for me."

"Still." An involuntary spasm passed through her body.

That night I held her and she cried, and when she finished crying, we talked until morning about her family, and how her father's treatment of her all those years seemed wantonly cruel in light of her new-found knowledge. She was still putting the pieces together, one by one, year by year.

"Your brother and sisters don't know," I said.

"They have to know. Why do you think they don't?"

"Your father told me."

Somehow I got to work the next day and Story studied for the bar exam at the library in town. I'd been home for thirty minutes when she arrived back at the house. I'd had a knot in my stomach all day thinking about her staying with the old boyfriend after the disaster in Lot's Folly. Despite the time we'd spent together, she and I had not yet been fully intimate in the physical sense (a deficiency I'd longingly hoped to cure in Lot's Folly), and in my boiling mind I imagined her on that exhausted night falling helplessly into his familiar arms, being greedily caressed and soothed and comforted, and allowing him that divine closeness I'd thus far only imagined.

We went outside to throw the ball for Buller. We walked down to the decaying courtyard on the side of the hill and took turns throwing as we went through the motions: "How was your day?" "Fine, how was yours?" "Did you get a lot of studying in?" "I did. Did you finish your research project?" And so on.

Story was beautiful as always. She was wearing a simple white dress that was perfect; it flowed just behind her as she moved. The dress and all the green around us on the mountain caused the baleful house to fade momentarily from view and brought to my mind a happy, nostalgic vision of Scott and Zelda playing on the terrace of the Grove Park Inn, Scott in his plus fours and Zelda resplendent in her clothes picked out special for the summer hotel. A belt of linen ran high around Story's waist, and I watched mesmerized as she untied it and refastened it just below her breasts. I longed deeply for her and thinking again that she had just been with her old boyfriend caused my anger and jealousy to return and flash hot across my face. I looked away and tried to make myself not care.

Sensing my irritation, she asked me what I was thinking about.

"You don't want to know what I'm thinking about," I said.

"It was a nice day today, wasn't it?"

"It was," I said, "and it still is." And it was, certainly, but this was bitter comfort. Buller charged back up the hill with his ball and engaged in a game of keep-away with Story as she tried to pry it from his mouth. She bent at the waist and I made myself look away again lest I transform on that very spot from human flesh into flame.

Trying to be as self-protectively distant as possible, I said, "You know how Buller seems to enjoy nothing more than to chase a tennis ball no matter how many times you throw it for him?"

Story pulled her blond hair out of her face. "Yes?"

"And have you noticed that no matter how tired he gets, he will always keep going, on and on, ad nauseam, ad infinitum, and keep chasing tennis balls, as long as someone is willing to throw for him?"

"Yes, I suppose so."

"So my question is this: Does Buller *want* to retrieve tennis balls, or does he *have* to? Does he have a choice? We're talking basic determinism here."

Having extracted the tennis ball, Story whipped it back across the courtyard into a hedge. Buller bolted fiercely after it like he'd never have a chance to chase another one.

"You know," said Story, wiping her hands on the grass, "as shitty as this is right now, I honestly feel like this is where I belong. I don't want to be anywhere else. You're half acting like you hate me, and I don't even know where in the hell I am, geographically speaking, and I'm probably crazy, but something inside me tells me it's where I'm supposed to be."

"You think this is shitty?"

"It *is* shitty. We're acting like we don't know each other. We're behaving like strangers who just met — you're talking nonsensically about canine determinism, for example — and I'm at *your* house in the hinterlands, away from everything I find comforting and comfortable, and you're barely speaking to me and I feel terrible about what's happened, but somehow in some inexplicable way I can't think of anywhere else in the world I'd rather be. I feel like I'm supposed to be here."

Softening now, I said, "I think I know what you mean."

"Do you, or are you just saying that?"

"No, I really do. I felt just that way when your dad was pummeling me on the floor of your parents' living room."

She came around in front of me and took my hands. "Listen to me. Are you listening? Yes, I went to see him, but I don't love him anymore. I know that's what's bothering you. I know that's why you're not talking to me like you used to. I don't love him. I'm not with him now for a reason. I'm here. That should tell you something. I'm here with you."

"It sounds to me like you're not sure what you want."

"I promise you. If I wanted to be with him, I would be, but I'm not. I've seen him once in I don't know how long."

"You left me at your parents' house with a bone fracture and spent the night with him."

"It wasn't like that," she said. "I was just driving. I didn't know where I was going. I was in the car for hours. I was on autopilot. It just happened."

"I'm encouraged to know that your autopilot takes you to the couch in his living room," I said.

"Stop. I was in shock. You have to understand that. My whole world had been turned on its head. I just needed a reality check. I needed to talk to someone who I knew would understand and who'd been through some of that with me and who might tell me I wasn't crazy —"

"I get that," I said. "And I'm sure there'll be other things like that. Which is okay with me. It's totally acceptable with me if you want to still see him and talk to him or do whatever. I just can't be falling madly in love with you when some part of your heart is still tied up with him. I couldn't take it."

Story almost smiled.

"What?"

"I think you just told me you're falling in love with me."

"No, I didn't."

She was holding me now around the waist, her face just below my chin, looking up at me with her eyes adorably crossed by the minutest fraction.

"I'm pretty sure you did."

What I wanted to say to her was that I was indeed entirely and unequivocally in love with her and that I had been for so, so long. I hadn't told her this, but I had felt it so many times. Part of me had hoped my foolish storybook love (and the accompanying crushing desire) would fade to something more grounded in realism once we truly came to know each other and I discovered all her repellent flaws, but my feelings had only grown with time and familiarity and I had come to desire her to the point of delirium.

"Damn it, Story," I said. "Why are you doing this to me?"

"I promise you nothing happened," she said. "I promise. If nothing else, it reminded me why he and I aren't together anymore."

All I could do was shake my head. I believed her — I wanted to believe her more than anything — but it still hurt like hell and the fact that I wanted her so much made the sting, still pricked deep into my heart, so much worse.

"Story," I said desperately, foolishly, "do you love me?"

She searched her mind for an answer but didn't find one.

"Don't," I said, pulling away. "I don't want to know."

She caught me again and folded herself into me. "Babe," she said, "I do love you. I do. I promise I do. I love you, but it's just that I'm . . . I'm *afraid.*"

"Why are you afraid?" I said. "What are you afraid of?"

"I'm afraid to love anyone."

At length Buller wore himself out chasing the tennis ball and we went inside so I could change out of my work clothes. We were both feeling better now that we had talked, and I was awash in a complex overlay of aching desire and childlike excitement about the coming evening. We had planned to get dinner out somewhere and then head back up into the mountains to explore and look at the stars. On our way into the house Story went to the bar in the Great Room and said, "I'll make us a drink!" She was getting a little more used to the house, or making a good show of it.

Light was coming in from the deepening blue of the sky and I went to the front of the house and propped open all the immense windows and the elaborately mechanical shutters to let in the cool summer air. "Your choices are vodka and red wine," I said. "There might be something else behind the bar, but I only know of the vodka and the wine."

"Do we have any tonic?" called Story.

"We do have tonic," I yelled back. "Waiter, vodka tonics all around!"

"Coming right up!"

We sat at the bar together dangling our legs as all the sweet and fragrant sounds of summer washed inside. As the light faded, a sadness began to gather overhead and in the corners of the room. "What this scene needs," said Story, "is some music."

I was lost in her. I was enraptured by every line and every curve. The subtle shadows nesting in the hollows behind her collarbones. The wondrous lines of her long, exquisite neck. One sweet meandering spiral of blond hair from her forehead down over her cheek. My eyes traced a constellation of freckles on her brown shoulder; watched half-moons rising in her unpainted fingernails. She looked at me with such mournful sadness.

I wiped away a cobweb from the phonograph set back into the wall and pulled out a few boxes of records that hadn't been played in years. We started with the Ink Spots and listened to "If I Didn't Care" three times in a row. Story then found a collection of waltzes, from Strauss to Shostakovich, and we were up dancing and the Great Room became a magnificent hall as I turned Story about and we promenaded, at times comically, from one end of the gilded space to the other. After two dances we grew weary of our improvisations and stopped to make another drink. While I searched for more music, Story toured the room as if it were a museum, moving with balletic delicacy from antiquity to antiquity. I played the larghetto from Mozart's B-flat piano concerto and we danced again, slowly. Story's radiant head was on my shoulder.

When the larghetto reached its quiet conclusion, I replaced it with an album of Chopin's nocturnes and let it fill the house. Holding hands, we made our way up to my room to change for dinner. My old bedroom had an austere drawing room adjoining it that sat partially underneath a climbing, shadowed staircase to the third floor. It had wide-slatted wooden floors and wooden walls that were adorned with nothing. At one end of the small drawing room was a wide cushioned bench with a seat of red fabric. Our bags of clothes were there on the floor. Despite the length of my stay, I had yet to unpack. The room had no windows; I lit candles to keep us company.

Story kissed me and said, "I'll go get ready." She watched me for a moment and then walked into the other room to change. I was left there with my tumescent longing and didn't think I could survive the night. I shook my head and pulled off my work clothes, and then sat down on the bench to look through my bag for a pair of shorts. Story reappeared in the doorway.

After a moment's hesitation, she came to where I was sitting and sat down on my lap, facing me, her dress falling around us like a flower. Chopin drifted up from below and the sound moved through us as if the man himself were sitting at the piano. Because of the music perhaps; perhaps because of the hushed dark under the stairs, our voices were no louder than a whisper.

"I need this right now," she said. "I need this so much." I could feel her pressing herself slowly, rhythmically, against me. Her lips touched my face as she talked. Pushing harder now. Straining against me. I could feel a growing warmth and a growing wetness. My heart began to work like a bellows.

She reached down, pulled aside the fabric that separated us, and brought me into her. She pressed herself hard against me. Her breath caught in her throat and her lips touched mine. My fingers found the back of her neck and pulled her toward me. I reached for her breasts, but she caught my hands and set them onto her trembling legs. I sought the warm bare skin of her legs under her dress, but again she caught my hands. "No," she whispered. "Just this, please . . ."

43

Later that evening, once we were dressed again, our hunger overtook us and we decided to find a place to eat in town. It was another beautiful moonless night, so I packed a cooler full of beer and loaded it into the backseat of the car along with the telescope from the observatory and a wooden stand.

"What's Buller going to do?"

"He's coming with us. He'll ride in the wayback."

"What does he do while we eat?"

"He'll just hang out in the car. As you know, he pretty much goes where I go. He won't have it any other way."

We ate at one of the two restaurants in Old Buckram that remained open at that hour. Story ordered a beer and was surprised to learn that the county was dry so restaurants didn't serve beer, wine, or liquor of any kind.

"That's why I've got the cooler in the car," I said.

"Can we bring it into the restaurant?"

"I don't think so."

"Too bad."

Our meal was interrupted half a dozen times by kind people from Old Buckram — people from my adolescence — who walked by and recognized me and stopped to say hello. I remembered very few of their names, but recalled them all as friendly souls who you could count on if you needed a hand. I tried to introduce Story to everyone as well as I could, and they were very pleased to meet her. Almost all of them said, "Story?" and needed the name repeated to be sure they'd heard it correctly.

After dinner we headed out into the desolation of the county to a place where we could hide from the lights of the town and see the planets and the stars. I hadn't done this in years and had forgotten that there are so many places you can go in the mountains where you don't really go anywhere. All the roads leading north and west from town wind up into nothing, which means that you can spend a hell of a lot of time exploring if you have the inclination.

Our ambitious plan was to try to find the place where the three states — Virginia, Ten-

nessee, and North Carolina — came together. To my knowledge, despite that the
area was once surveyed by Peter Jefferson,
Thomas Jefferson's father, there was no
landmark or monument there to mark this
geographical intersection. It is doubtful that
anyone really knows where the point is.
Many of the boundaries of the mountain
counties are uncertain and the property is
not sufficiently valuable to make a survey-
ing project worthwhile.

After driving away from civilization and
climbing steadily in elevation for more than
fifty minutes and intermittently pulling over
to look at a North Carolina map that was of
almost no use, we turned left at the top of a
ridge onto an unnamed gravel road. When
people talk about being in the middle of
nowhere, this is what they mean. Trees
would have overtaken the road if it weren't
for the fact that the occasional car on the
road still moved much faster than the trees
could move. Story was driving and I was
navigating but not very well.

"You really don't know where we are or
where we're going?"

"I honestly don't have a clue," I said. "I've
never been on this road. We might wind up
in Vermont as far as I know."

Buller yipped from the back of the car.

"Does that particular bark mean something?" she asked.

"It means he's hot. I'll roll his window down a little more."

I reached into the cooler on the floorboard and produced a Peroni. "Oh, yes," said Story. "Light and crisp!" She proceeded to drive through the night at about five miles per hour and sat way up in her seat like she was caught in a rainstorm. Woods lined the single-lane dirt road on both sides as we climbed up and up. Occasionally she slowed to a near stop so we could pass over significant ruts in the road made by heavy rains. "Hold on, buddy!" she'd call to Buller, and the car would toss around.

We saw a few opossums rambling furtively here and there and several deer standing alert in fields. There were very few houses in this part of the county. The ones we did pass were pictures of absolute poverty, with broken-down cars off to the side that were nearly hidden by unmowed grass. Many of the houses had so much junk on the front porch that it looked like they were preparing for a yard sale. Several of the houses displayed a large satellite dish in the front yard, many of which were not presently operational as evidenced by hanging wires and broken supports.

We came to an intersection of sorts where the road we were on seemed to dwindle to nothing in front of us, while a more substantial road broke off to our right and continued to ascend. There were no road signs and hadn't been any for some time. The headlights illuminated all the dust that, having caught us after following in the subtle vacuum behind the car, drifted slowly by and settled down again, indifferent to its forced relocation.

Story asked me to hand her a beer. "You're driving," I said. "You better not. If you got caught, you'd have to report it to the state bar."

"I think I can have *one* beer. Come on — give me one. Don't make me stop and get it myself, because I will."

"There are police everywhere up here."

"I bet the police don't even come up here."

"I bet you're right."

We eventually gave up trying to find the intersection of the three states and just pulled over into the grass on the side of the meager dirt road. A steep-cut bank ran up the hill to our right. On our left across the road was a wide pasture that in the starlit distance rose to a treeless knoll. We got out and I pulled apart the barbed-wire fence for

Story to climb through and handed her the cooler and the telescope. Buller found his own place to cross under the fence before I could get him through. I caught the back of my shirt on the barbed wire and had to be unhooked before I could move.

The grass was short as it is sometimes when there are cows or horses grazing in the field, but I didn't see evidence of any animals. In the mountains it's not uncommon to find livestock in a field like that. I warned Story to look out for cow excrement, which can be the least-pleasant animal excrement to step in, depending on its date of origin. I remembered then that Buller enjoyed rolling in smelly things, so I sat him down and said, "Buller Copernicus, if you roll in anything, so help me god you'll ride home on top of the car." Fortunately, he took this to heart and steered clear of whatever dung there might have been, at least on the way in.

Walking through a far mountain field on a clear, moonless night can be disorienting. You will see stars like you have never seen before, spanning from horizon to horizon. You will see the great Milky Way running through Cygnus and across the sky like a trail of summer clouds. The landmarks you usually employ for purposes of personal orientation no longer exist, because even the ground under your feet is lost in the dark, and suddenly you are there, viewing the splendor of the illuminated universe from the dark earth as it existed before electric light burned through the pitch and rendered all civilized humans blind to the night sky. If the night is sufficiently dark, you will see planets and thousands of stars and distant galaxies whose light left them millions of years ago.

After ten minutes of walking, we arrived at what appeared to be the highest point in the field. Moving by feel, I found a reasonably level spot on which to set up the telescope. From the knoll the terrain sloped gently away and rolled in shadow over silent hills and valleys for mile upon mile to a ridge of mountains that marked the visible horizon. Below us and in the distance lonely houses tucked into cold blue folds of hill and mountain were like stars in the fabric of the earth set to rival those in the fabric of the sky. I set up the telescope and first turned it toward Jupiter, which blazed just above a distant range of weathered mountains.

"How do you know that's Jupiter?"

"I took a few astronomy classes," I said. "It's about where I imagine the ecliptic plane to be, and it's about the color and brightness of Jupiter, and it's not sparkling like a star would be. And of course I don't know of any star that would be right there in that spot in the sky and be that bright at this time of night and this time of the year. If we do this right, you should be able to see a few of its moons, too. This is more or less what Galileo did in 1610."

I positioned the planet at the corner of the viewing field of the telescope, anticipating that it would move quickly out of view as the earth rotated toward it, and stepped out of the way for Story to take her turn at the eyepiece.

"Don't hold the telescope with your hands when you look through the eyepiece," I said.

"Why not?"

"Because if you touch it, you will shake the telescope and the image will become blurry."

"Wow. That's incredible."

"You can see it?"

"I can't believe I'm looking at something so far away."

"You can see a few of its moons, too," I said.

"I think I see them. They're all in a line. Where'd it go?"

Looking through the eyepiece, I brought

it back into view for her and showed her how to control the telescope so as to track the planet as it crossed the sky diagonally along the ecliptic plane and inversely to the direction you would expect due to the nature of the optics in the telescope. I then found Scorpius and extrapolated the approximate location of the Butterfly Cluster. Through the telescope, this was not an impressive visual sight, but it was nevertheless an extraordinary thing to look at something seventy trillion miles away.

"How'd you get into this sort of thing?" Story sat on the cooler drinking a beer and petting Buller.

"My father used to bring me to places like this when I was a kid," I said. "He taught me all the constellations. He always pointed to celestial objects and made me guess what they were. When there was an eclipse or a meteor shower, we'd head out into the country and put down a blanket and just watch the sky."

"Your childhood was a lot different than mine," she said.

"It was far stranger than you could ever imagine."

"Was it just you and your dad who would go look at the stars?"

"My mother often came, too. When

Threnody got old enough to appreciate it, Father would bring her along. She's an extraordinary child."

"How old is she now?"

I thought about it, but the number didn't come to me and I felt my face flush with embarrassment. "I think she's probably . . . fifteen . . ."

"I hope I get to meet her soon," Story said, saving me further humiliation. "I'm sure she really looks up to you."

I said, "We used to be close."

Story said, "You've never been here before?"

"I don't think so."

"So you don't know who owns this land?"

"No, I have no idea."

She laughed. "So we're trespassing."

"Pretty much. No one's going to care. If anyone comes out here, we'll just tell them what we're doing and it will be fine."

"We're not going to get shot?"

"I can't promise you that. Just don't try to rustle any steers."

We left the telescope and walked to an open area where a patch of tall grass lolled about in erratic waves in the graying darkness. As the night cooled, a mist came down out of the woods from across the road and concealed us from the world. I put down a blanket and we lay on our backs to face the orbiting heavens and pulled close to each other to stay warm. The sky was deeply blue and uncountable revolving suns blazed distantly in the indifferent swath of the universe above us. I thought of how terrifying the darkness would be if it were not for the illumination of star, sun, and moon, and the comfort of our mother earth always beneath us.

And lying there on the surface of this cold planet I thought about Story and her father and the pain she had suffered because of him; the pain she'd suffered from not knowing the truth, from her feeling for so many years like such an *essential* part of her life was missing. I thought about her going to bed night after night with that unresolved emptiness — and then involuntarily my mind transposed all this to poor Threnody and I was at once impaled upon my grief. What must it have been like *for her* after our father left us? What had it done to her? And it came to me again how little time we all had, and how much time I'd let pass since I'd seen her. I thought of our respective times on this earth and how she and I were tied together by so many things, and that she should've been there with me. That something inside me was torn apart, and that this act of tearing was my continued separation from her.

Story grabbed my arm. "What *the hell* is that?" We scrambled to our feet as the ground shook beneath us.

"Where's Buller?"

"I don't see him."

"Shit. Let's get out of here."

"Where are we going? What's happening?!"

We could see nothing in the dark, but I knew the thunderous noise to be horses, many of them, galloping toward us through the field. Something had spooked them and judging by the sound they were moving together in a great circle just below us on the hill.

"They're running from something," I said. "I hope to god it's not Buller."

"I hope to god they can see better than we can!"

We stumbled blindly around with our hands out hoping to run into the telescope and half expecting to be trampled underfoot. At last I found it and after collecting the cooler we moved cautiously down the face of the hill over the uneven ground. With gallows wit, Story asked me if I ever knew of someone getting killed by a horse. Blindsided, I swallowed hard and lost my words.

"We're not going to get killed," I said finally. "We just need to make sure they see us and we'll be fine. We've got to find Buller."

Almost as soon as it began, the hellish charge dissipated, but the horses, visible now but only as passing apparitions in the still-moonless night, remained watchful and strutted fiercely back and forth in the brume with ears laid back and frantic eyes rolling wildly in their heads. I counted eleven in all, including two foals, but it could have been more or less. They were beautiful, as all horses are, but neglect showed in their ribs and mud-caked flanks. I called out for Buller and at last he appeared, covered in manure and panting happily. Story lunged for him and grabbed him by the collar. He and I then walked a few feet away and I quietly lectured him man to man about how great freedoms come with great responsibility, which he accepted with maturity. With a disappointed shake of the head, I knelt down and affixed his leash. When I looked up, the horses had vanished from our sight as if they had never existed. Again we were alone, and had there not been Story to witness it, I might have wondered whether the previous scene had been imagined.

"There *were* horses here a minute ago, weren't there?"

"I thought so," said Story.

A ghostly calm and a ghostly quiet settled on the hill. In the fray I'd lost the direction of the car and a hushed debate was carried on for some time as to our proper course. After turning this way and that and recalling the relative position of the stars upon our arrival, we selected west, and as the terrain gave way in our descent I reckoned we had reckoned correctly. As we walked down the hill through the darkness, I realized then with a tingle of my spine that all sound had been stolen from the world. There were no birds singing or calling. No crickets chirring. There was no babbling brook, and no hum and drone from a distant car reached our ears. I began to long for even the sound of my own breathing, but I was loath to break the inviolable silence.

We could see next to nothing. Story stepped on a loose stone and twisted her ankle but assured me it wasn't bad. A fear was rising in my throat, a faint panic that we had become lost. Buller, his leash tied to Story's belt, followed behind us, his nose to the ground. Thus we trudged along, three intrepid explorers, feeling our way down in the foreboding dark.

"Are we going the right way?"

"Yes, I think so," I said.

"It's colder out than I thought it would be."

"Yes, it is."

"I don't think we're going the right way. We should have been there by now."

We stopped and reviewed our position. A blanket of mist lay in every direction and had now shaded even the stars overhead.

"If we keep walking, we'll eventually run into a fence," I said.

"And then what do we do?"

"We follow the fence until we find the road."

"How do we know what direction to go in once we get to the fence?"

"We'll be able to tell," I said.

"Will we?"

"Yes, of course." I was hardly so sure. But then a halo of light slowly rising from behind the mountain told me the moon was near and my hope returned. I believed us to be heading west, but the moon lay behind us and to the right, meaning we were moving north instead. I said to Story that we needed to head back left, but she didn't respond.

"Story?"

Still, she said nothing.

I came around to her, and in the dark I discerned an unmistakable look of horror on her face.

She whispered, "There's someone there."

"What are you talking about?"

"There — *directly* in front of us. There's someone *there.*" She pointed but would not take another step. At last I began to resolve a shape almost out of the corner of my eye. A lone horse, white with a white mane and rutilant eyes, skeletal and specterlike, was revealed inch by subtle inch from the parting gloom. It stood alone before us, lambent in the waking light of the nascent hornèd moon. Had I been a superstitious lad, I could have believed she was death come to take us. I called to her, but she stood eerily unmoved. I talked to her as I neared, but she remained as still as a statue. I extended my uncertain hand to stroke her forehead almost in disbelief as to the reality of the vision, but all at once she came alive and bolted away, as vortices of fog and mist curled from her bloodless mane and tail.

Behind me, Story cried out — "Buller!" Frenzied by the witch-horse, he had begun to squirm and fight to pull away. Story fell on her knees as he backed out of his collar. He had lost his mind and could not be contained. I yelled for him to stop, but he ignored me and tried to run down the white mare, biting viciously at her fetlocks on a dead run. The mare stumbled and then bucked and almost kicked him in the head. This left him dazed and the witch-horse escaped into the night. I ran madly through the dark after him calling his name and came within a dozen feet of him when the horses, led by the white mare, came surging out of the darkness, their wild, rolling eyes aglow in the moonlight like embers in a pit of fire. With the sound of a hundred locomotives, they thundered across the leveling field toward us — veritable chariots loosed from the gates of hell. Buller, the poor boy, just sat down and probably closed his eyes. I reached him, screaming, before the horses did and flattened him to the ground. I remember the astonished look on his face and his initial terror until he realized it was me. I held him underneath me until they had passed and circled and calmed again. I called for Story and she called back that she was okay.

In the new light of the moon we found the fence and trailed along beside it on hard-packed dirt back across the way. Up and down we went, along stretches of more barbed wire, until we found a right angle in the fence as it turned parallel with a dirt road resembling the one we'd been on. I said, "Thank you, Jesus." Story said, "Praise be," and we began to breathe a little easier. Story was the first to see the car. Then and there we made a spit-in-the-palm pact that all future nocturnal adventures would involve a flashlight and a compass. "Just to be safe," said Story. "Just to be safe."

44

I put Buller in the back of the car and took a towel to him as well as I could while he patiently listened to the remainder of the castigation he had coming to him. With the aid of the interior light, Story found ticks crawling all over her socks and shoes and got undressed down to her underwear on the side of the road to make sure she didn't have any anywhere else. I did the same. In half an hour, we were relatively tick-free and dressed again and ready to head back down toward Old Buckram. Story said, "We could've died," and I said, "Nature red in tooth and claw," and she said she'd want to throw together an estate plan before crossing through another barbed-wire fence in the mountains.

She drove and I banged my shoes together out the window to knock off the dirt and we kept the windows down so we could breathe. We listened to Doc Watson for a while because it seemed to fit, and then I put in a Dan Bern CD at maximum volume (faded to the front to avoid ear-canal injury to the faithful canine in the back) and sang every word of "Estelle" and then started it over and sang it again and Story picked up what might be called the chorus ("Why baby, why baby, why baby, why / Have you turned your back on love . . .") and sang that part along with me until we were hoarse. Then we listened to more Dan off the same album and I elaborated for a while about why Marilyn Monroe should, in point of fact, have married Henry Miller, as Dan so eloquently suggests, and eventually we found our way back to state-maintained roads again. As we went along, something about the night and its pervading emptiness edged us into silence. I turned off the music and we watched the double yellow lines disappear under the car until we were hypnotized by the headlights. We were the only car on the roads we traveled. We were the only inhabitants of the earth, and if not for us there would have been no reason for time to exist at all.

"I would love, love, love to see the sun come up in the morning. Do you think we can?" We made it back to the house and it was just turning 2:00 A.M. Story wanted to see her first sunrise over the Blue Ridge Mountains.

"It's going to be hard to wake up after getting only three hours of sleep," I said.

"Should we just stay up?"

"I will if you will."

"I'll fall asleep. Maybe," she said, "we could sleep outside — on the porch!"

"We could do that."

"Can I fall asleep in your arms, and will you wake me up when the sun comes up?"

I said, "I would like more than anything for you to fall asleep in my arms."

"But will you wake me up when the sun comes up?"

"I'll certainly try." I wanted to see her with the first light of the morning on her face.

We took a pillow and my sleeping bag out onto the second-story porch with a few blankets and put the blankets down as a mattress with the sleeping bag on top. After stepping out of our clothes like two kids going skinny-dipping, we dove into the sleeping bag and pulled it up to our necks. Buller found his spot on a blanket next to us. The night was dark, save a distant glow of light from town. Story's head was on my chest.

"I'm very happy that you're here," I said.

"I'm very happy to be here."

"I'm going to miss you when you leave."

"But I just got here."

"I know," I said, "but I can tell already."

Story kissed me on the forehead and tucked her head back under my chin.

"I'm proud of you," I said.

"Why are you proud of me?"

"Because you're incredibly courageous."

"Why do you say that?"

"In your life, what you have done has been courageous. All of it. You've done what you thought was good and right, even when people told you that you shouldn't. You followed your heart in the face of adversity. In the face of people discouraging you at every step. You never gave up, and I respect and admire you for that. My mother told me a long time ago that the true test of a person is not how he conducts himself when everything's going well, but how he handles life when everything is coming crashing down around him. I'd say you've had your fair share of that — but you're better for it, and you're stronger for it, and I'm proud to say that you're my friend."

Story kissed me and said, "Thank you for saying that."

As my eyes adjusted to the dark, more stars became visible above the mountains until the sky was nearly full, and the insect

507

calls from the woods behind the house rose and fell like the waves of the ocean.

Without looking at me, Story said, "Sometimes you hold me as if you think I'm going to fall." She kissed me again and pulled herself into my arms and the night was all around us.

At 5:25 A.M., a full forty-five minutes ahead of the sun, the birds began excitedly warming up for their morning symphony. I opened my eyes to find Story curled into me and still asleep. I touched her face and pushed her hair behind her ear. When the eastern sky began to lighten, I whispered to her and she awoke. We watched as the earth turned slowly toward the sun.

I made us what little breakfast there was to be had while Story looked through the books left in Father's library. With the whole of the house fully visible in the light of day, she could see it for what it was. She asked me if my father actually read the books in his library or if he just collected them.

"I don't think he read them all," I said, "but he read most of them."

"Impossible."

"It would seem so," I said, remembering a time when Father was challenged on this very point. It came one winter night when the aptly named Dick, one of Mother's über-academic siblings, was visiting from the northeast. After twelve years of postgraduate studies, he had become first a proud professor of English and then the dean of the English department at a small fancy college for rich girls, and as you might imagine, there was occasionally a prickly palpable tension between him and anyone else who had an opinion on the arts.

It seemed to me that Father usually avoided any such discussions with Dick and politely demurred on most points of contention, but on this cold night the fates had set them on a course for a mighty collision that could not and, in the end, would not be avoided.

We had all been driven indoors by the wind and the snow and found ourselves sitting in the opposite corner of the library from Father's writing room as firelight painted the walls and Uncle Dick expounded pedantically upon English verse while Father's thoughts lingered elsewhere. The men, as usual, were well into their cups and all the cheeks were rosy. I sat next to Father and might as well have been invisible. Mother, having had a cocktail or two of her own — a rarity — was happy and giddy for conversation, but was also roundly ignored by the boys.

Dick, wearing a one-color tie and laden almost to the point of suffocation with a scarf that could easily have been ten feet long, sat with his feet in his chair and admired all of Father's books from behind his horned spectacles. I could tell just occupying the same space as Father rubbed him the wrong way. He'd pontificate about one obscure literary point or another and say to Father, "Don't you think so?", assuming Father couldn't possibly be acquainted with that bit of specific knowledge.

"One thing I'm finding more and more, and I'm sure you are, too, is the importance of the hemistich to early Germanic alliterative meter. Don't you think so? The hemistich?"

Father never took the bait. He'd merely say, "I'm not too familiar with that," or "That sounds interesting," or "I'm afraid you lost me there." Mother wanted Father to be more engaging and chewed the side of her cup like she was watching her favorite prizefighter take kidney punches on the ropes.

After half an hour of this unilateral banter, Dick sensed a weakness, or so I imagined. He sat for some time staring holes through Father, who, looking straight up at the ceiling like he was watching for an eclipse, was happily oblivious. Dick hatched a plan. He slid out of his chair to take a turn about the library. After making two full sock-footed laps, he said, "Henry, you've got one *hell* of a lot of books here."

"There are quite a few," said Father, smiling, still on eclipse-watch.

"A *lot* of books," said Dick.

"Yes," said Father. "There are. Some of them were here when we moved in."

"Oh, well that explains a lot."

"How so?" said Father.

"You might have more books than even I do," said Dick, as if this would be difficult for anyone to imagine.

"You don't have this many books," said Mother.

"You haven't seen the books in my office!" said Dick. "You've only seen what I have in my house. Add the ones in my office to what I've got in my house and I've got *a lot* of books. I just don't keep them all in the same place. They're too valuable."

"I'm sure you do, honey," said Mother. "I'm sure you just have stacks and stacks."

"Where do you get your books?" said Dick.

"I've just picked them up over a period of

years," said Father. "From bookstores all over the country and the occasional estate sale. I order some from dealers. A few of them have been gifts, but not many." Father's face was red in the cheeks. He was uncomfortable talking about himself.

"I like to collect books, too," said Dick, "but I also like to *read* them."

I thought, *Oh, shit.* The gauntlet had been pitched and there was no avoiding it.

Mother stood up and suggested we play cards, but this diversionary tactic fell short. No one responded. She sat back down.

Dick's implication was not lost on Father, who left his eclipse and returned his attention to the room. I could tell he was ruffled. He thought carefully for a moment, and then said, "Dick, I don't buy these to look nice on the shelves."

Dick scoffed. "So you've read all these?"

"No, I haven't read them *all,* of course. There're one or two over there I haven't read" — pointing to the section where the books on foreign languages were kept — "and that stack there contains a few I haven't gotten to yet. There's one on relativity that looks oddly incomprehensible. But otherwise, yes — mostly."

My pulse began to quicken and I feared a great embarrassment for my dear father. He was setting himself up for certain failure. I knew that's precisely what Dick had in mind, once and for all.

With one finger, Dick tipped a book out of a nonfiction section, catching it by the spine in midflight and opening it deftly in one movement. "How about this one?" It was volume II of H. G. Wells's *The Outline of History.*

Father, wearing the uneasy look of a man standing before a firing squad, perhaps now sensing what he was in for, squinted to see it and then said, "Yes, I read that one — and its companion. Quite good, if not a little stilted for my tastes."

Dick tossed the book down on a table and Father winced a little. Dick found another one. "How 'bout this one?"

"That one, too," said Father. "But you're in nonfiction. That's not so much my territory. Try me in fiction."

"Fiction it is," said Dick, dickishly. He cantered around to the other side of the library.

And so the games began. With Mother protesting the whole affair ("This is silly!"), Dick announced, "Here's what we'll do. I'll call out a passage. Something fairly notable or not too obscure, of course. You tell me what book it's from. All the passages will be from books in *your* library, presumably ones you've read. This'll be fun."

"Okay," said Father. "Fire away."

"As you could guess, knowing me," Dick said with two quick taps to his temple, "I've got a few things stored away here and there." By this he meant he had some things memorized. "This'll be an interesting . . . *test.*"

"Do your worst," said Father.

Dick did a little dance, squeezed his chin as if it were an udder, and studied the towering rows of books. He was pleased as punch. To himself, he said, "I don't want to make this too difficult. Let's see . . . Oh! I've got one. This will be good. You'll probably know this one." Then, apparently summoning from memory, he called out professorially in his orator's voice, " 'And there steals over the tongue the first flat dead taste of winter —' "

"Got it," interjected Father. "*Confessions of Nat Turner* by William Styron."

Long seconds passed. Dick looked a bit perplexed.

We awaited the verdict. Father took a drink.

Neither Mother nor I dared to breathe.

Overcoming his initial surprise at the quick response, Dick said, "No. Want to guess again?"

"Guess again?" said Father.

"You were close," said Dick. "It *is* William Styron, but the book is *Lie Down in Darkness* — not *Nat Turner!*"

The air went out of the room, as they say. I felt bad for Father. I felt humiliated for him and for our family. Dick smiled in self-congratulation and said, "I'll think of another one." I didn't want to watch.

Father took a drink and said to me, "Hand me *Nat Turner.* It's the orange one right there next to where your uncle's standing. There's a sword-wielding angel at the top of the spine."

I did as I was told. Before Father opened the book, he closed his eyes and recited the entire passage from his chair.

"Then you know it," said Dick.

"I do," said Father. "But it's not *Lie Down in Darkness.* It's in *Nat Turner.* You've got the wrong book."

"No, I don't."

"I'm afraid you do," said Father.

"I would not make that kind of careless mistake," came the pithy, plosively punctuated reply.

"This is not a debate."

"That's right," said Dick. "It's readily ascertainable!" Both men had their hackles

515

up now. Dick opened Father's copy of *Lie Down in Darkness* with an exasperated sigh usually reserved for tedious children who are asking foolish questions. After a minute of flipping pages, his head resurfaced with a look of disillusionment and I felt a glimmer of hope. He said, "It's not where I thought it was. In my mind I can see right where it is."

Father handed me *Nat Turner* opened to a page and said, "Deliver this to your eidetic uncle."

Dick read the lines in disbelief. He surveyed the room a little blearily as if he half expected to see some bizarre dreamscape encircling all of us. I waited for him to pinch himself.

"*Nat Turner* it is," he said. "How very strange. I could have sworn . . ."

It was an extraordinary moment. Father 1, Dick 0.

Recovered now, his blood flowing again, his pace quickened, Dick said, "Let's change the rules a bit." He slid Father's chair around to face the wall so that Father was turned away from the shelves of fiction.

"Do I need a blindfold?" said Father.

"This will do," said Dick, orienting the chair just so.

"What's the game this time?"

516

"I'm going to select a book and read you a passage from it," said Dick. "Same basic idea. I've turned you around so you can't see the book I'm reading from. Simple as that."

He returned to the bookshelf and walked up and down, occasionally shooting a furtive glance toward Father to make sure he wasn't peeking, presumably. He was humming the "Battle Hymn of the Republic." Rising to the tips of his toes, he plucked a book from high off the shelf, opened it to the middle, and carefully chose the passage he would read.

"Here's a good one. Are you ready?"

"Quite," said Father.

And Dick began again in his orator's voice, but this time with a little less certainty: " 'So did the great ship come to port —.' "

Father cut in. "Too easy. Too easy! Thomas Wolfe, *The Web and the Rock.* Published in 1939 and sold for three dollars. I'll do Thomas Wolfe with you all day long. Ask me another one."

Dick snapped the book shut and dust flew into the air. "Good guess. A very good guess. I'll give you that one. Of course you'd know a North Carolina writer."

Father took a drink. He had his game face

on, as they say, and it was fearsome to behold.

Dick cleared his throat, twirled off his scarf like a lariat to get down to business, and chose another book, this one a nondescript, small, yellowish hardcover from a shelf close to the floor. With a self-moistened thumb, which had he seen it would have sent Father into a rage, Dick turned audibly back and forth through the pages.

"Ready?"

"Indeed."

"Here we go. 'A thousand times he mentally asked forgiveness of his pure chaste dove —' "

" 'And a thousand times over he kissed the cross she had given him,' " said Father, finishing the sentence as if he were reading over Dick's shoulder. "I love that one. *Torrents of Spring.* Turgenev. Garnett translation, of course. You'll find my notes in the front. I read it not too long ago."

I looked at Mother in amazement. She was smiling sweetly like she knew something we didn't.

"Yes, I see," said Dick, as he shelved the Turgenev horizontally in the wrong place and picked another book at random. To himself he said, "You seriously can't be that lucky."

Dick cleared his throat again, and then: " ' "I come from hell," said Morten —' "

"I come from hell," Father repeated to himself. "I come from hell."

"Take your time," said Dick. "Shall I read more?"

"No," said Father. "Please give me a moment."

" 'I come from hell,' " Dick said again, as if that meager clue would be sufficient for anyone. " 'I *come* from *hell.*' Really, take your time."

"Another moment," said Father. He was sitting up in his chair now, waving his glasses in the air in front of him, summoning. He was whispering "Morten, Morten, Morten —"

"Time's up!" spouted Dick triumphantly.

"It's from *Seven Gothic Tales,*" said Father. "Isak Dinesen. Introduction by Dorothy Canfield, I believe. That particular version you're holding was printed in 1934. Your excerpt is from . . . 'The Supper at Elsinore,' unless I'm mistaken."

Dick stomped one foot. "Jesus Christ!"

"As a point of curiosity," continued Father, "note the three different printings of that book — see them all there together — and how the weight of paper used for each creates a slightly different width for each."

Dick was amazed. He had witnessed a bona fide miracle, or at least you'd think he had by the look on his face. I wanted to jump out of my chair and dance around the room very inappropriately.

Father now seemed to be truly enjoying himself. He said to Dick, "Do you want to trade places? I'll ask you a few?"

Dick, oddly, was not interested. Being out in the snow earlier had suddenly made him tired. When he had said his good nights, Mother got up and kissed Father on the forehead, as one might kiss a child. "Please be nice to him tomorrow," she said, almost as if Father had done something wrong. She left the two of us there in the dark. Father just stared at the wall.

"Just trust me," I said to Story. "He read them."

The chairs and table in the dining room were still covered with dust, so we took our breakfast out to the courtyard, which was now wild and overgrown. I hadn't noticed the extent to which it had deteriorated in so short a time. Story had overcome her initial horror and now talked romantically about what it would be like to live in the great house on the hill. The simple beauty in her heart saw the romanticism of the idea, just as my parents had many years before.

She said, "Maybe one day you'll marry someone special, and the two of you will come back here and take over the property and make it beautiful again." I knew, though, that once I left this time, I'd never come back, even if I were given a million lifetimes of the universe. I recalled telling Threnody that one day she and I would have our own little house at the beach, just the two of us. She might have believed me at the time, but whether it had been real or not didn't matter. All we needed was to allow ourselves to imagine that it could be true — that one day it might be true — even though we both knew we would never get there. I regretted the broken promise all the same.

After our foreshortened night of sleep, Story lay down for a nap in the early afternoon in a bright room with the summer wind blowing in through the curtains. I wasn't tired, so I found myself outside walking around the hill and reminiscing about days of old. I toured the fence line around the house and remembered the horses galloping in the pasture. Time and weather had warped the boards and several had fallen and lay rotting on the ground. The fence was a Theseus's ship of mountain architecture, having managed to survive for twenty or more winters, albeit solely on the foundation of resolve assiduously maintained by my mother. She had been the caretaker and warden of Ben Hennom: with rare exceptions, nascent life grew and flourished in her care against the odds; old life persevered for her out of simple respect. Such was the life of this old fence. Now, in her absence, its spirit had fled.

In my childhood my mother worked countless hours outside in the courtyard, on the overgrown esplanade, planting flowers and trees, putting up bird feeders, trying to bring the hedges back into some kind of shape, and clearing the hillside pastureland for the horses. She trimmed and cultivated the rows of shrubs that ran through the grassy courtyard below the house. She rebuilt the failing stone walls and walkways from stone she unearthed and carried in her old rusted wheelbarrow out of the woods. In stark contrast to the wicked house and in defiance of its wickedness, she kept her own Garden of Eden on the hill. On a resplendent Sunday morning in the summer, if she caught you outside, she would say, "Let me show you what I've planted!" And excitedly she would take you on a walking tour of her new lilacs, daisies, and irises that surrounded the hill among the many dogwoods and ancient green trees. In spite of the unforgiving weather, she also managed to have something coming up no matter what the season. The Lenten rose would be the first to appear as winter came to a close, sometimes blooming when hard-packed snow still sat in the shadows of the hills and trees. She would pick a small vase of these for the dining-room table, and it became a symbol to everyone of the coming spring. Next were the daffodils and crocuses and violet phlox planted in the field on the south side of the hill. Facing south and therefore protected in some measure by the house, these would arrive in early spring after being awakened by the warming sun in February and March. Mother loved to walk through the field and identify every new shoot and flower as the days grew gradually longer.

She hung birdhouses all over the hill and constantly monitored them for activity, becoming as ecstatic as a child when a family of birds would move in. She loved the cardinals and the Carolina wrens, and the little gray tufted titmouses, and the goldfinches, and of course the hummingbirds. I often thought that Mother had the soul of a little songbird that loved nothing more than to dart happily through the forest, singing all the while. On some mornings she would wake before sunrise and start the coffee and take Father from his desk and they would go out to see the Milky Way tumbling perpendicular to the horizon, with the last of the planets falling into the fading dark of the west. "You would be amazed at how many extraordinary things you can see in the sky before the sun comes up." I heard her say this time and again.

I walked down to the old barn and found to my surprise some of her equestrian implements hanging just inside the door as they had always been. Her curry combs that were used to brush the horses; a hoof pick; the knife we used to cut the baling twine from the bales of hay. She had sold or given away the saddles and bridles, but almost everything else remained. I found her old clipboard hanging from a wall above the feed bin. On it were notes reflecting a simple chronology of the births she oversaw there on the hill, the medicines given to the foals, and so on, all in my mother's handwriting. This was an unbearable sadness. I hurt so much for my mother that she had reached a point in her life that she had no choice but to leave behind all that she loved so dearly.

I looked for and found the old path behind the barn leading into the Gnarled Forest. I knew I was going to the top of the hill, but I would not acknowledge to myself that I would wind up there. I was deceiving myself, telling myself that I'd turn around after a short distance and come down in time to see Story awaken from her nap. Yet I walked on. The path was now hidden in places by leaves and fallen trees, but I knew the way. The rock outcroppings, the laurels, the rhododendrons I used to sit inside for hours reading books. Onward and upward I climbed. I was hurrying now — racing to get to the top. Sweat ran down my face and into my eyes and mouth. My breath was short. I was running up and up and up.

I came upon the clearing and slowed to a walk in the heather to catch my breath and clear my eyes. I came to the perimeter of the bluff and saw what it was that I'd come to see. After all this time — after all these years — it remained steadfast there at the edge of the world, watching over the valley below. We had not changed it. It had found a way to persist.

When I returned to the house, Story was awake and sitting on the front porch reading one of Father's books.

"There you are!" She got up and came to

meet me in the driveway. "I looked for you."

"I'm sorry," I said. "I went for a walk."

"You're soaking wet. You look like you ran a marathon. Did you walk to town and back?"

I said nothing in reply.

"Will you come with me for a second?" she asked, taking my hand. "I found something I want to ask you about."

I followed her into the house. She walked quickly up the ensanguined staircase to the hallway leading to the library, and then down another hallway, and finally into an open doorway. The room was for a child, with rows upon rows of plastic horses lining the walls. A pair of child's glasses lay upon an otherwise empty dresser. The walls were painted white and pink, and wooden letters on the walls spelled MADDY — after her grandmother.

45

Mise-en-scène: Night in the vulture house. The apsis at the end of the library under starlight. An enclave of gathered furniture within it: the clergyman's bookshelf; Father's chair in which he scanned the heavens for an eclipse the night of the literary duel. On a table next to me, a pricket, a candle, a flame. With ghosts for company and the sound of rotting wood, I kept watch all the night as gales of wind poured through the open windows below and searched the house, finding nothing. Story, in my bed, slept. I emptied two bottles of wine and spent the guttering hours in grave contemplation of all that had come before. In my brain, his words, his voice, on repeat: Each fragile heart now beating will one day stop — (mine, yours, all).

When morning came, despairing of what had been lost and still half drunk and half delirious from a lack of sleep, I put cold water on my neck and called my sister.

"Bird, it's me. Can you talk?" A searing pain followed from her silence. "Bird, listen — I've been thinking. I've got some things I want to say." With no good place to start, I began all at once: "I know I haven't been around much in the last few years. I left because I had to. You know that. Some part of me really thought I was going off to get an education so I could come back and get you and we'd go do all the things we always talked about doing. But then I got there and the pain from home was too great and I couldn't make myself come back and I couldn't make myself even think about it. But I'm getting better. I'm feeling much better and it's going to be different now —"

"I don't want to talk about it," she said. "Not now. And anyway, I don't believe you. I stopped believing you a long time ago."

"What are you doing today? Let me come get you."

"You wouldn't."

"I would," I said. "I promise. I'll come right down."

"You've made promises to me before." I knew better than to ask for examples. I was only too well aware of what I'd done and not done. Outside, a misshapen red sun bled slowly over the mountains in the east.

Through a window I watched it climb into the sky as minutes passed without a sound from Threnody.

"I remember one specifically," she said. "You said you'd come back. You said I'd still see you all the time. And then — you left. You left me there in that house and didn't take me with you and you never came home and you never called and never read to me and the books were not the same without you there to read them, but they reminded me of you and just said to me that you were gone, and the cold silence of that whole horrible house said you were gone and wherever you were, you weren't thinking about me —"

"I went to college," I said. "I just went to college. That's all. I had to go. That was expected of me." I didn't know what to say. Threnody's voice had become choked with tears and pain, and the tears came for me as all that pain came pouring out.

"I would've gone with you," she said. "Did you know that? I wanted to. I would've gone. I would have. Part of me really thought you were going to take me. Isn't that stupid now? And when you left the first time for the first few months, in my mind I thought you'd be coming right back and that you'd come back to get me. I even packed."

"You packed?"

"I had a suitcase in my closet, and every Friday I'd get it out and organize it and put it back so I'd be ready." I felt like I could no longer breathe. "But you never came back," she said. "Not once, ever. You just went away and you never came back. Little Maddy went away, and then Father went away, and then you went away."

"Threnody, my god — I wish all that had been different," I said. "But there's nothing we can do about it now. It's over. We can't go back."

She set the phone down and I could hear her crying. I called for her to pick up the phone again. "Thren, do you want to come up here for a few days? It'd do us some good to spend some time together."

"I'm sure you're busy."

"I'm not. I'll take the whole week off. We'll do whatever you want."

"I don't want to come up there," she said. "I still hate that old house. I hated it when we were growing up in it and I still hate it. I don't know how you can stay there now and sleep under the same roof where —"

"I know. Listen — it was hard at first. And I'm not going to say that now I don't think about it a million times a day, because I do.

I think about you and I think about Father every single time I walk through the library. I'm sure that goddamn bird is still on the wall, and I'm sure Edgar is just sitting in there in the dark, waiting for me to come in. And I think about you every time I sit down at the piano and start to play. I remember you looking down at me from the railing, listening and smiling. Do you remember that? And I remember you singing with me like a little bird in your child's voice and all the songs we sang. And every time I come out of my room and see your doorway there I think about you lying on the floor, coloring in your coloring books because you were under house arrest for some mischief I got us into, and I think of all the books we read and the hours you and I spent on this hill trying to make sense of everything.

"And yes, I think about little Maddy, too. I think about her all the time. I think about her when I walk down her hall and go by the room she lived in for three years, and I think about how much she loved the horses, and I remember when she got those big glasses because she couldn't see and how sad that made us. I think about standing with you at her funeral and trying to explain to you what was going to happen to her now that she was gone, and I think about how the flowers everyone had sent were so pretty, and how for the first time in a month it had stopped raining and the sky was so blue and it ran on forever and there was no horizon, and how *every single bit* of life's promise had been destroyed for all of us — and I couldn't imagine that time would even carry us to the next day. I think of all those things. That's what's in my brain every time I come up this driveway and walk through the front door. But it's all a part of this house and a part of our lives. We can't go back and change what happened."

Threnody said nothing. Then she said, "Do you really think you can come get me?"

"Yes, sweetheart, I'll come get you. I'll pick you up as soon as I can get down there."

She hung up. I continued to hold the phone to my ear until the pulsating blast of white noise shocked me back to reality. The sky had become gray with the shadow of a thousand birds moving unsteadily over the eroding ground. Fleeting.

Story came to me with sleep in her eyes and took my fallen head into her arms. When I could speak again, I told her I was going to Charlotte to get Threnody.

■ ■ ■ ■

I vomited in the shower. I stood there holding the rail, feeling as if I'd been slammed in the stomach; feeling as if all my insides had been pulverized into a bloody and sickening dust. I knew that I couldn't run from it anymore. I had tried for nine years. People always talked about the past and all the memories they had and I didn't have any. I only looked one way. The arrow of time for me moved in only one direction and that was forward.

46

For his birthday the year he left, I bought my father a marginally rare edition of Camus's *The Stranger.* I got a good deal on it because it had been price-clipped to hell and had a tear on the front of the dust jacket and might have gotten wet at some point, but it was a copy of the first American printing and I knew he didn't already own a copy of his own because there wasn't one in the library. As we sat there together he opened it and began to read but never made it beyond the first page. Many years would pass before I would discover why. He was stopped cold by the first line of the book.

That day, Father's birthday, had brought no cake and ice cream; there had been no colored candles to blow out. Threnody had painted him a darling picture of a crow in a little green tree with a few sprigs of grass growing at its trunk, and this he had folded and put in his desk. There were to be no other gifts, and no celebration was had. When night came, Father and I sat in our places — he in his desk chair, me on the floor with my back against the bookshelf next to his desk. A searching wind rattled at the window and stirred the candles that lit Father's writing room. The walls ran high into the darkness away from the light, as though the room were open to the cold black sky above. Were it not for this illusion, this enclosed space would have felt more like a tomb.

Father said, "Please pour me another glass of wine." There was an open bottle in a box next to where I sat. Then he said, "Shall we put on some music? You and I always used to listen to music. I have so many fond memories of that."

This warmed me, and I said, "I'd like that."

"Softly, though. Don't wake up your mother. What should we listen to? Schubert's *Winterreise*? No, not Schubert. You know what I've been listening to are the late-period quartets."

"Whose?"

"Beethoven's. The A minor, third movement is my favorite. Do you see it? It's right there." I started the music and in the first quiet swell of the strings he held out his glass to me with a trembling hand but looked away so as not to acknowledge the weakness. In his face was sadness; in his eyes lay resignation and defeat. He savored the wine as if it were the last glass he'd ever have.

"I love Spanish wine, I'll tell you. I've loved it my whole life. It's the fool's nostrum — take my word for it. It might've been the death of me."

"You're almost out," I said. "Perhaps you'll live."

"No danger of that. I have another case in the pantry."

"I worry about how much you drink."

Ignoring my concern, he put his nose into his glass and drew back his lips to show his vampiric canines. Then he said, "If you ever think 'I have enough time to do that — I'll just pass the time today and make my art tomorrow,' then you have already lost. Time has fooled you into thinking it exists."

I told him, as I always did, that I did not understand.

"That's to be expected," he said. "There are some ideas that cannot be communicated; they can only be experienced. These are not things I have always known, or that I knew when I was your age, for I surely

536

didn't. These are things I have learned."

On this night I was content just to sit there with him; to be in his presence and to have his momentary attention, even as it wandered. He rarely made sense to me anymore and I resented the distance that had grown between us, but in spite of all my anger and perplexed rage I still loved him dearly — although much of the child's love I had once felt had been replaced, I think, by a souring and pathetic sympathy for the wasted existence my father had come to represent. Yet I knew he had a good heart, and a kind heart, and on this night it was comforting to simply be near him.

"I've been meaning to tell you for such a long time," he said, "you're a very bright, very compassionate young man. I see so much of your mother in you, and that is something for which you should be very proud. She is an extraordinary woman. She is much stronger than I have ever been. Somehow she has tolerated me and all my eccentricities — yes, I know — all these years, and her love for me has never waned, even though I've given her plenty of reasons. And I see some of myself in you — which emboldens and yet terrifies me at the same time."

"Why does it terrify you?"

"Look at me. Is this what you want to become?"

I would have lied to him, but he didn't give me a chance.

"You've been so good to your sister. It's wonderful to see how close you two have become. You've been more like a father to her. The way you read to her every night. The way you sing to her sweet songs until she falls asleep. You've been the parent to her that I should have been. I trust that you'll continue to do that."

"Of course I will," I said. "Always."

"I need you to help me look after her."

"I promise I will. Of course." Outside, the wind gathered itself noisily in the valley and came to overtake the house. Yellowed papers moved from Father's desk to the floor and remained there. He thought for a moment, then said, "Please start the music over. Did you hear it? Just listen for a minute." And we listened for a time as the strings in their immortal sorrow made the dark more dark, and the wine more red, and the candles more lonely.

"There is no music that has ever been created that is more beautiful than that," he said. "I wanted the words in my book to be that beautiful. To be that exquisite. To be that perfectly sorrowful. It was something I could never hope to achieve. This I realized. . . .

"Do you want some wine? I suppose you're nearly old enough. Or you will be soon. Have some. This will be a moment you'll remember. The time we shared wine together." Fumbling, he reached for an empty glass at the corner of his desk, filled it, and handed it to me. "Come sit here."

He had just that day taken all the pages of his book and put them into a box with the title page facing up. In simple type, it read:

THE BURNING OF SERVETUS

A NOVEL
BY
H. L. ASTER

I sat upon the box, feeling then as if I were guilty of some sacrilege; as if I were sitting on a gravestone of a dear friend. Thinking of his empty life's project, I stole a look at Poe and the perched black bird and sensed for the first time the absurdity of it all and instantly felt a well of pain for my sweet dear father. Until that moment there was a hidden part of me that had wanted to believe in him without reservation. Now the careful facade dissolved before my eyes and it hurt me deeply, for I saw in his dimming face a knowing sadness that comes when those who believe in you can no longer believe —

His toast: "May time pass more slowly for you."

We drank together and the wine burned my throat and tongue like wine from the church's communion.

"I know," he said, "you'll have better things to do with your life. But in the event you have idle time on your hands, if such a thing exists, perhaps you'll write a book of your own. Maybe you can pick up where I left off. You can add your time to my time and maybe that will be enough."

"You still have time."

"Time is only enough when you have the will to do something with it. And I do not. Damn this life and this house," he said. "I once wished to visit Valldemossa, but it came to me instead."

I said nothing. I could think of nothing to say. His fatalism was only words to me. All I knew was that he was my father and the only thing I wanted to do then was to protect him. I wanted to keep him forever. I would keep him and care for him as he carried the remnants of his broken dreams. In that way we would survive, or so I thought.

"All this," he said, "will be over in the blink of an eye. Hasn't it passed just that quickly so far? It won't change for you. It will run its course and carry you away. Time," he said, "is nothing, after all, but man's explication of hell. In truth, neither time nor hell exist, but time will steal your soul in a way that hell never could."

Nine days had passed since we had buried little Maddy. The next day Father would kiss Threnody goodbye.

47

She was sitting outside when I arrived at Hurricane's house in Charlotte. She climbed into the car before I could get out to give her a hug. After orienting the vents to her liking and adjusting her seat backward, she allowed herself a look at me. Her look said, "And here we are again."

She had grown taller but still seemed uncomfortable with her new height and the span of her limbs. I noticed a manufactured delicacy to her movements — an unnatural attempt at gracefulness — that I hadn't seen before and which troubled me. Her big brown eyes were sad and her face was sallow, and a bitter pain contracted her around an invisible point. She was curled in upon herself like a frozen leaf.

All she had with her was a pair of sunglasses and a hardcover book. As a rule, no one in our family ever went anywhere without a book. I put my arm around her and said, "Hey, Bird." She diminished within my embrace.

"I'm sorry it took me so long to get here."

"That's fine. I've just been outside for like two hours. I think I got sunburned pretty bad on my arms, but I finished my book. I should have brought another one. Maybe we can stop at a bookstore."

"Are you coming back to the mountains with me? Where's your bag?"

"I haven't decided yet. I just have to get out of here for a while."

"Is Mother here?"

"No."

"Did you tell her I was coming down?"

"No."

"Did you leave her a note?"

"No, but I'll call her later."

We drove around for a while looking for a place to eat, and after hitting every manhole on Park Road going and coming, we went through Uptown and wound up on Central Avenue near Chantilly and just beyond Plaza-Midwood, where we found a Mexican restaurant with outdoor seating that looked festive enough for our purposes. A dozen wooden tables sat on a stone patio shaded by an awning which bore the resilient but now-faded colors of the Spanish flag. It undulated lazily in the rising heat of the day.

Alternating red and yellow circus umbrellas provided redundant cover from the sun, and sun-bleached spiraled streamers ran along the corner trellises and fell down here and there and then ascended again in improbable Lissajous curves that compressed and decompressed with the atmospheric perturbations of passing cars. We arrived before noon, so the restaurant was nearly empty and two waitresses in white blouses and close-fitting black pants sat in the shade waiting for customers to arrive.

Threnody ordered a cream soda, which they didn't have, so she settled for a Coke, and I declined a margarita and instead ordered a Bloody Mary, which was made to order. The patio stones, laid by a drunk man or a blind man unskilled in masonry or possibly both, made it damn difficult to get one's chair not to rock back and forth, but the table, we discovered, had been bolted to the ground, and although ours appeared to be at somewhat of a slant, it had the dubious advantage of relative stability.

"It's a nice day," I said.

"Is it?" said Threnody. "I'm cold for some reason." She rubbed her hands together and shivered visibly even though it was growing hot outside. Our drinks arrived and I asked Threnody if she was hungry. She said no

544

and pushed the menu to the other side of the table.

"Do you want an appetizer?" As a kid she loved appetizers.

"No, I'm really not hungry."

"Can we have a minute to look at the menu?" I asked the waitress.

"*Sí,* of course."

"*Gracias.*"

"*De nada. Tómese su tiempo.*" We were taking our time.

Two men in undershirts and paint-spattered cargo pants sat to our left in the corner of the patio near the street. They were un-showered and unshaven, and I counted six empty Pacíficos on their table. The ashtray they shared was full of ruthlessly extinguished cigarettes. One of the men had started dropping his spent cigarettes into a nearly empty beer bottle where they smoldered and smoked up the glass with nauseating effect. Both men leaned into the middle of the table as though they were hatching a conspiracy, but the discourse that reached my ears comprised only job complaints and petty politics.

My Bloody Mary came to the table with a phallic javelin of compressed meat protruding from the top of the glass. At first I couldn't figure out what it was or whether it was intended to be edible. I extracted it carefully and laid it on my napkin.

Threnody said, "What is that?"

"I wish I knew. Beef jerky, maybe?"

"What's usually in a Bloody Mary?" she asked.

"Blood, of course. That's the first ingredient. Then intestines taken from cadavers. A few bile ducts. Patellar tendons. Celery. A bit of vodka."

"Lovely. Can I try it?"

"Why the hell not," I said. "Father gave me wine once before I was old enough to drink. You won't like it, though."

Threnody put her straw in my drink and made an awful face. "And look how you turned out," she said.

"I guess that could go either way."

"I'm just kidding."

We sat for a while making small talk about the book she'd just finished and what I'd been reading, and how she didn't fit in at school or in life — a pleasure we shared — and she told me that Mother was having a hard time with Hurricane. We talked all around the gaping hole right in the middle of both of us. I ordered another Bloody Mary, this time without the meat pole, and gave Threnody the celery and the olives. Now I was shivering with an imagined cold of my own, and with an unimagined emptiness that one day would have to be filled, if we could ever figure out how to fill it.

A drab little wren, a beggar, pranced around under our table scavenging for crumbs. Threnody slowly slid her foot over to him, hoping he would hop onto her shoe, but each time she got close he would jump and flap his dusty wings and then come back again a little farther away. She wanted to order some bread to feed him, but before our waitress returned he shot away and took up residence above a doorway across the street. The sun was overhead now and burned through the awning and the red and yellow of our table's umbrella, and everything was the filtered color of red Spanish clay.

"There's something I've been meaning to ask you," said Threnody. "It's really important."

"Ask me," I said.

"Why did we all get these stupid fucking names?"

We laughed together and she smiled.

"You have a beautiful name. There's no one in the world with your name."

"I wish I knew what it meant," she said. "I mean, I know what it means, which is depressing enough in its own right. I just don't know why it's my name."

"It's from a poem Father wrote before you were born."

She was surprised. "A poem? No one ever told me that. Do you have it?"

"I don't, but I'm sure it's somewhere."

She was sad again. "Our father, the writer," said Threnody.

"Yes," I said, "our father, the writer."

"Do you know what he said to me?" she asked.

"Father?"

"Yes."

I could feel the wound inside me involuntarily starting to open. I didn't want to talk about this. I didn't want to talk about Father or any of it. We'd all done such a good job of pretending. At least I had. Of not facing what had happened. Of not ever facing it.

"Before he left," said Threnody.

"Before he left?" I said. "The day he left?"

"Yes," she said, growing impatient.

"No. I don't know what he said. How could I know that?"

I wasn't sure I wanted to know. No, I was sure I didn't want to know.

"He told me you'd take care of me," she said.

"He said *I'd* take care of you?"

"Yes, that's what he said."

"What about Mother?"

"You're missing the point."

"What *is* the point? Bird — of course I'll take care of you."

"You don't understand," she said, her voice breaking; her voice anguished. She choked on the words. "Listen! He said *you* would take care of me. You."

Threnody brought her eyes to mine and waited for me to understand. I noticed her hands gathering and twisting and shredding her paper napkin in her lap. Slowly a light grew in my mind and I allowed myself to realize —

"*That* day he said that?" I repeated stupidly. So he'd left it to me.

"The day. Before you almost ran over me —"

"No, Bird, I didn't know. I don't know what to say. I didn't know —"

"I guess there's nothing *to* say. You *could* say you're sorry. That's one thing you could say. Because obviously you haven't, and I've been in one place and you've been off traveling all over, going on trips without me, apparently without a single thought for what I was doing —"

"It wasn't like that. It wasn't. And I *am* sorry," I said. "I'm so sorry. But, Bird —

that's what I'm trying to do now."

"No, you're not," she said. "No, you're not. You're probably going to spend three hours with me to make yourself feel better and then you're going to drop me off with Mother again and I won't see you for three more months, and then you'll probably head back to the beach with Story and you guys'll get married and get a house and have kids and *then where the fuck will I be.*" She was shouting and the world was spinning and my stomach dropped with an acute sense of forgotten responsibility, as though on a walk I'd turned my head for a moment's distraction and lost my only child, directionless, in a multiplying field of wheat, never to find her again.

"Why do you think I went to the beach with Story?"

"Don't you remember calling me drunk that night? After you went down there and her father tried to kill you and she went to her boyfriend's house and you were alone?"

I had, in fact, forgotten that I'd called her, and now the agony of the whole event — of Story's horrible discovery, of the singular, oppressive loneliness I'd felt when she'd left me there in Lot's Folly with people I didn't know and didn't care to know; of the long starless, moonless, planetless nighttime drive back to Old Buckram beneath an empty close sky that stayed empty mile after mile and grew more lonely each time I looked up hopelessly for stars that weren't there and culminated with me standing hungry and exhausted and bloodcaked in the driveway of the vulture house with a broken nose as an invisible sunrise died behind a wall of fog and smoke and gloom; add to this the numbing, red bleeding depth of hell's own sorrow that would come with knowing she'd gone to see him in her time of greatest need and the thought that I might have lost her and lost her again — all of this came instantly back to me magnified, and I closed my eyes with the pain. Threnody, I know, saw my eyes close and knew the pain wasn't for her. I was making her point.

She said, "Will you take me home now?"

"I asked you to come to the mountains to stay for a while. Will you at least do that?"

"You think I want to go back to Old Buckram? Why would I ever in a million years want to do that?" She was scornful and hurt.

"No," I said, "I'm sure you don't. But we can go anywhere. I'll take you anywhere you want. Just tell me. You and me. Where do you want to go?"

She thought about it and said, "I've never

really known."

She sat back and crossed her arms and stared out into the street. Minutes passed and she looked at everything that could be seen except for me. The two beer-drinking painters were gone, but I hadn't seen them leave.

"Bird —"

She didn't respond.

"Bird, look at me."

She began to cry. I'd broken her heart. Life had broken her heart. All of it had. Maddy — Father — me. It wasn't fair.

"It's over now, Bird. I'm here now. We don't have to go back."

"I knew something bad was going to happen," she said, still crying and covering her face with her hands, talking through them.

"Stop it. It's okay —"

"I didn't know where you were, or where Mother was. We were upstairs and I was reading and he was working in his office and I went in and asked what he was doing and watched him write something I didn't understand on a piece of paper and then he sat down and kissed me, and he cried and held my face and said he was sorry and that you would take care of me — I didn't understand any of it."

"I'm so sorry."

I held her hand while she cried and her whole body shook and I felt again that I'd failed her. The waitress came by and asked if we wanted to order but then went back inside. I moved to the chair next to Threnody and put my arm around her.

"I hate him for leaving," she said. "I hate him for leaving *me.* He didn't have to do that. And I hate him for the fact that I have no idea who he was for my entire childhood. I didn't know him at all. He left me with nothing except for ten thousand books and a thousand questions and nightmare memories of him floating around the house like some kind of ghost."

"He didn't want to leave us."

"Yes, he did. He must have. That's what happened."

"That's in effect what happened, but that's not what he intended by it."

"I don't know how else to explain it."

She dried her eyes with her napkin and tried to turn off all the emotion, to seal off that part of her that would never heal, but I knew more tears would fall as soon as she was alone again.

"He was hurting, too," I said. "He hurt worse than any of us."

I involuntarily recalled the Latin words

I'd forgotten and had tried so hard to forget. To myself, I said, *"Consummatum est."*

"What?"

"That's what he wrote on his book that you and I couldn't understand. He wrote *Consummatum est."*

"I don't know what that means. What does that even mean?"

"It means 'It is finished.' I came across it one day when I was studying for a Latin test at Wesleyan. I still remember that. I felt like I'd fallen into a well."

"The book was finished? Is that what he meant? He finished it?"

"I don't know," I said. "Those were the last words of Jesus on the cross before he died, at least in the Latin translation. He said *'Consummatum est.'* It is finished. *Et inclinato capite tradidit spiritum.* And he bowed his head and gave up his spirit."

Threnody thought about this for a long time. She whispered the words "He gave up his spirit" as if to test how they would sound in her mouth. I took her hand and held it in my hands. We began to share in our pain.

After he'd said goodbye to Threnody, I would never in my life see him again — except once on the hill at the top of old Ben Hennom where the lonely tree stood. As

Threnody sat in the rain-darkened house and waited for him to return, he was hiking up the mountain to be alone. After searching for him on the Barrowfields and screaming until I'd lost my voice, I went up the mountain the next morning when there was light enough to see and found him hanging from the lonely old tree, its branches full of crows.

48

I returned to Old Buckram following my time with Threnody, and Story and I spent the better part of a month trying to get the house back into some kind of shape, albeit with little visible success. I realized walking through the house one late-summer afternoon and feeling a lingering sense of something undone that, apart from the murderous oubliette, there remained one room I hadn't entered since I'd been home again: that small, almost hidden chamber at the corner of the library where Father read and wrote for all those years. Mercifully the door to this room, already half obscured by the geometry of the hallway leading to it, was closed when I arrived, and part of me was content to pretend the room was locked from the inside or simply nonexistent. Within limits, I was happy to leave well enough alone. I tried my best to forget about it and might have succeeded but for the few terrifying nights I was awakened from discomfiting dreams, dreams in which I'd walk weightlessly down that hallway and open the door just to find him sitting in there writing as he always was — except that in my dreams the enigmatic bird that had formerly roosted over Poe's expressionless visage all those years had found a new perch, inert and immobile, on Father's slumped shoulder. In those dreams I was always desperate to talk to him, but I could never move past the threshold of the room and he never turned to face me and words never passed between us.

After standing in the narrow hallway for an eternity and thinking of every possible reason not to go in, I tried the handle and the door pushed easily open into the darkened room. I felt for a switch but couldn't find one, so I waited a moment in the doorway hoping my eyes would adjust and wondering if Father's hell-ravaged ghost was going to appear and whether the bird would be with him. On the wall to the immediate right of Father's desk was, I perceived, a faint circle of light coming from a small, round window that had been shuttered in some way. Even though I'd spent a quarter of my life in this room sitting at Father's feet with a book in my hands, I don't know that I'd ever noticed it before. I crossed over to it in the cavernous dark and with my hands found a subtle latch that opened a wooden cover. The cover fell open from its hinge to reveal a little rose window with delicate tracery and alternating panes of clear and colored glass. Standing on my toes, I looked out the window over the slate tiles. Far below I could see Story walking among the cone flowers and spiraling lady tresses with a bouquet of flowers in her hand. Along the courtyard's crumbling walls, yellow dahlias bobbed their gentle heads as she passed by. Farther out, immense black crows sat in the distant field and watched. They had come back. He, of course, had not. I thought, *They are waiting for him.*

I saw the room in the new light and made my inventory. The desk, I discovered, was the same as he left it. The raven or whatever it was on the wall. Wolfe. Poe. Chopin. A first-edition copy of *The Stranger,* price-clipped, chipped, and cocked. A signed first edition of *Look Homeward, Angel* that he prized more than any other book. A first edition of *Tales of Mystery and Imagination* signed by Harry Clarke in blood-red ink. A Bible, King James, black leather cover. Three candles; copious spent wax. A bottle of Hill's Absinth, empty. Two bottles of vodka, empty. A bottle of Spanish wine, also empty. A book of matches. A lamp, no bulb. Fifty-one journals, handwritten. The title page of an unpublished novel. *Consummatum est*. Nine years of collected dust and a handful of pictures that must have meant something to him.

I opened *The Stranger* to read the inscription in my own hand. I turned the page and saw the first line of the book: "Mother died today." I was beginning to understand.

Story and I went back to Charleston on a warm Friday afternoon in September and rented a room with a large second-floor balcony overlooking the Battery and Charleston Harbor. We sat outside in wooden rocking chairs as the warm air lifted her hair off her shoulders and twisted it back and forth and around. In the twilight, we watched the couples move up and down the street as the sound of the harbor waves softened and muted their voices. There was a small table between us on which we had situated a small bowl of strawberries.

I asked Story for a beer, and she reached into the cooler and fished one out that had been soaking in the ice water so long that the label had begun to disintegrate and peel off. She took a long drink before handing it to me. I stared at her in disbelief, as I always did in such circumstances, feigning amazement that she dared to presume I would share something so precious. Without looking at me, she reached over and took my hand. The streetlights had begun to come on, and we heard the sound of horseshoes on the cobblestone street below — a carriage tour of the city.

Just then a beaming Threnody came out onto the porch with a map of the city spread in front of her like a sail and began enumerating all the places she wanted to explore that weekend. First on the list, not surprisingly, was Sullivan's Island, to see where "The Gold Bug" was written. It was in our blood, I suppose.

I said, "I'm happy you're here, Bird."

She said, "I'm happy I'm here, too."

Sitting there, I tried to bring the moment into reality. I wanted to remember this, but I wanted something more. I wanted to know that I was alive right now. I desperately held on to the moment, moved by the realization that life and this experience were as ephemeral as breath. Perhaps this frozen time was more for them — for Father, for Maddy — than for me.

I looked over at Story as, with amusement,

she watched the people go by below us. I followed the path of her gaze down to the street where a young couple walked arm in arm. The young man, full of the moment, looked up at the sky as he walked, trying to make out the first faint stars of the evening.

And then time rolled on.

49

I worked up the courage one bright October day to visit his grave for the first time since we lowered him into the ground. His headstone was as he wrote it:

HENRY LARVATIS ASTER

A Stranger to This World,
Time Took No Notice.
Non Omnis Moriar

I thought of him there beneath the dying grass, silenced as he was by unrelenting time before he was able to give voice to all that surged and roared chaotically inside him. I imagined briefly that I could be his living eyes and ears; that I could see and hear in his stead on that cool autumn afternoon; to breathe in the wood-smoke from the first fires of the evening; to feel the lonely excitement of nightfall in our timeless town; to taste the honeyed warmth of scotch on my tongue; to know life and the ephemeral joy of all things living, just for a minute, for my father. To allow him to see and feel again, through my eyes and body, the exquisite autumn of October in Old Buckram.

He had left a letter for my mother. It said:

My love — my dear love — my Eleonore. You believed in me all these years when I gave you no reason to believe. You gave your life for me. All the hours you cared for our sweet children; all the hours you waited alone as I sat solitary in my world and wrote. All that time is gone; you gave it to me. I am so terribly sorry. No man has ever so loved a woman as I loved you.

"It broke my heart," Mother told me later. And by this she meant she had achieved this state as a permanent condition.

I don't know when he wrote this letter, or what his final day and his final hours must have been like. How hopeless he must have felt; how narrow his life must have become. Thinking that life had dealt him enough pain for a lifetime. Recognizing the absurdity of it all. Having learned all too well the futility of it. Knowing he had hurt others, and himself feeling the knife of this pain because of it. Knowing he had let us down before, and would again.

In my mind, I imagine him getting up that morning knowing what he planned to do. I can see him sitting down at his desk one final time to write this letter, just moments before he kissed Threnody and told her goodbye. Just moments before he took his life's work, his life's unremitting toil, and set it aflame.

I found it, my father's book, that night on the Barrowfields. At the industrial spool, the makeshift pyre, where Maynard had intended to burn Faulkner but almost immolated my father instead. To my eye and to my ear it appeared in the unfamiliar starlight to be blackbirds taking flight at my approach. It was not. The birds were pages from his book caught by the coming wind — burned, blackened, lost.

As I sit now, in this shaded bower, it is almost May and the dogwood petals are somehow uniformly scattered throughout the even grass of the courtyard like stars in a green and yellow sky. The birds, with their calls, compete with one another by trilling and chirping and dancing from branch to leafy branch. The wind has quietly stolen the round flowers of this poor Bradford pear, the latter being fortunate to have survived this past winter with all the snow and its sadly divided trunk. A cardinal and a Carolina wren appear to discuss briefly who is to be first into the birdbath and then both fly erratically away. Buller brings me his ball and I throw it as far as I can from a sitting position, just to have him bring it back and drop it on my papers again. He is tireless.

After returning here, I was in the backyard inspecting two tragically unhealthy dogwoods that exhibited several unattractive dead limbs. A neighbor from down the hill who, curiously, has taken to visiting from time to time, a female of substantial age and a similar quotient of opinions, tottered up the hill to see what I was up to.

"I wonder what happened to these trees," I said rhetorically. "I wonder if the roots were damaged somehow."

"No," she said, looking out over the valley. "They just got old. That's what happens to them when they get old."

Some of us, I suppose, get to live out our lives like that, slowly dying, sometimes so slowly as to be almost imperceptible to anyone but ourselves. Others are not as fortunate. They fall away into the impossible darkness that is death without the benefit of even so much as a bloom. And yet we all live our lives as if assured of tomorrow.

ACKNOWLEDGMENTS

I am grateful for the support and insight of the following extraordinary people: Chris Clemans, Sarah Bedingfield, Nathan Roberson, Rachel Rokicki, Rebecca Welbourn, Francine Toon, Anna Webber, Anna Jarota, J. Todd Bailey, J. P. Davis, Carrie Ryan, Eric Taylor, Billy and Heidi Royal, Ashley Taylor, all the wonderful folks at Horack Talley, and also my family: Lauren Lewis, Ashley Lewis, Henry Keats and William Kepler, Ray and Devan Vaughn, Lindsay Kahrs and Matthew, Shelly White, Brandi de Jager, Cheryl Lewis, my mother, and Phillip E. Lewis, my father.

buck·ram (buk′rəm)
n. A coarse cotton or linen cloth stiffened
with glue or similar substance and used,
inter alia, to make book covers.

The employees of Thorndike Press hope you have enjoyed this Large Print book. All our Thorndike, Wheeler, and Kennebec Large Print titles are designed for easy reading, and all our books are made to last. Other Thorndike Press Large Print books are available at your library, through selected bookstores, or directly from us.

For information about titles, please call:
  (800) 223-1244

or visit our website at:
  gale.com/thorndike

To share your comments, please write:
  Publisher
  Thorndike Press
  10 Water St., Suite 310
  Waterville, ME 04901

LP Lewis
Lewis, Phillip
The Barrowfields /

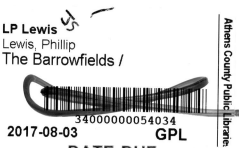

34000000054034
2017-08-03   **GPL**

Athens County Public Libraries

DATE DUE

SEP 0 5 2017		
SEP 1 9 2017		
NOV 1 6 2017		
MAY 1 0 2018		
		PRINTED IN U.S.A.